Pieces of the Past

Pieces of the Past

By Joe Broadmeadow

Copyright

Print ISBN 979-8-9927210-6-5

ePub ISBN 979-8-9927210-7-2

Dedication

I dedicate this book to my lifelong friend, Ralph Ezovski. They say things happen for a reason; I have my doubts. But things that happen in life become a permanent part of you.

Ralph and I shared a bond that transcended the ordinary. From our first meeting in John Needham's Latin Class in the eighth grade in Cumberland, Rhode Island, all those years ago, to our twenty years together at the East Providence Police Department, to our retirement years, our friendship was a force that even death could not sever.

As you will figure out, Ralph is Detective Evoski in the book. The name is not a poorly designed pseudonym. And the character in the book doesn't reflect even one iota of Ralph's career, but I had to include him.

The name has a story behind it. Another outstanding cop we worked with, Gordon 'Ray' Remond, always massacred Ralph's name. He couldn't say Ezovski.

Ralph said, "Come on, Ray, it's E Z." Later, he just learned to accept it.

Those of us who wore the badge and stood firm when everyone else retreated will forever embrace the deep bond of the thin blue line. I hope officers today have the same quality people next to them as I did.

Serving with such outstanding cops alongside such a friend was an honor, and I will remember it all my life. Cops like Ray and Ralph and a host of others made the job better.

Ralph made it infinitely so.

Since Ralph played a big part is shaping my experiences on the job, I wanted to memorialize him here. Farewell, pal.

~ ~

Table of Contents

~ ~

~ ~

~ ~

~ ~

~ ~

1 Before There Was Light

When her screaming stopped, so did his joy. The silence of their surrender, a pathetic hope for relief by death, offered no bliss, only despair of the devil's evil in this world. Soon, he would need to hunt the next one.

Closing his eyes, inhaling one last cleansing breath of the coppery essence, Gideon commanded his followers to dismember the demon's shell. Destroying the human shell was necessary to prevent the demon from rising again, at least as this one.

It was a difficult but solemn task.

They'd saved the woman's soul, though she never thanked them. A wretched creature, fallen by sin. Pale, thin, a shadow of her former self. The sunken eyes, pallor, and missing teeth all testament to her enslavement to drugs.

She threw her God-given beauty away by selling her body to feed the devil's grip on her soul. Drugs were the devil's favorite temptation, and she'd fallen for them hard.

But they'd given her a new purpose in God's plan, even if she couldn't see it.

Now, they would use her as a warning to others.

And there would be others, like the ones before her. The devil never stopped stealing souls, but neither would Gideon stop saving them. God called him to this mission, and he would fulfill it.

It was time to pray for the strength to continue.

After wiping his hands on the towel offered by the acolyte, another of the devil's victims who couldn't meet his eyes out of shame for his fall into sin, he dropped it onto the sticky puddles on the floor. Pushing aside the plastic sheets surrounding the altar, he walked away surrounded by the others with bowed heads.

He'd leave them to the final tasks while he sought divine guidance to seek the next soul-stealing devil.

Waiting in his room as the sanctification continued, Gideon closed his eyes, reliving the joy of the devil's demise. He'd saved a soul and returned her to the Lord.

In this, he found some solace.

Blocking out the sounds of those engaged in the disposal process—these useful idiots in the Lord's service—he gave thanks for God's gift of purpose.

The devils often fought back; they made it fun. God wanted him to enjoy his work. That's why he chose Gideon. This latest one, this pathetic sinner did bring him joy with her pathetic and false claims of embracing the Lord, but Gideon knew it was a mask for the truth. She'd invited the demon in through her transgressions, then cried when she realized the wages of her sins.

This one thought to use a demon's trickery to escape.

She begged.

She pleaded.

She cried.

She offered herself in the vilest way. But Gideon, as God's sword on earth, would have none of it. He never fell to the trickery of the devil and false pleasure of sinful flesh.

That's how the devil takes your soul.

You cannot accept their offer. It is forceful, focused, and false. One must take from the devil what *he* will not willingly give, not receive anything offered.

Accepting anything from the devil is to surrender your soul and abandon the Lord.

Once the devil knew you were incorruptible, the screaming started. That's when their punishment began. Gideon reveled in the moment. Through the Lord's power, Gideon stripped them of their will. Sometimes, it took hours, sometimes days, but eventually, the demon would become weak and vulnerable.

This is when they were the most dangerous; to believe anything else was to risk the corruption of the soul. There was one solution.

Pain. Unimaginable pain would free these pathetic souls from the devil's power.

Searing, endless, piercing agony penetrated the hollow human shell hiding the demon devouring their soul.

The pain was necessary. It was a tool, a device to drive the devil mad within the sinner and bring them to the surface. Reveal themselves in the presence of God's sword on Earth. Only then could the innocent ones be saved.

Gideon exulted in his skill at inflicting pain. Pain confuses the devil, weakens his hold of the soul. The more pain, the weaker the grip.

What remained behind would soon return to the dust of creation, reductus in pulverem. Angels took the redeemed soul to heaven, and Gideon's crusaders would begin the hunt for the next demon.

"Where do I send this one, Gideon?" Max asked, hands jammed in the pockets of his stained jeans, his shocking red hair a rat's nest of tangled confusion. Taller than Gideon, he stooped his shoulders, demurring to the power of this man he worshipped.

"Use Israel. Tell 'em to take the bag to the shopping center near the bowling alley. You'll find many devils lurking there. This will put the fear of the Lord in them."

"Israel? Are you sure we can trust him?" Max asked. "He seemed hesitant when we found this one."

"He'll come around. Learning to follow the lord's commandments is hard. The fog of his drug addiction still haunts him. But I have seen light in his soul. He has the spirit within. Now go, we have more souls to save."

Max bowed his head, turning to leave.

"But Max," Gideon said.

"Yeah?" Max said, turning back.

"If he fails us, it is a sign the demon has reentered his soul...you know what to do."

Max nodded once, then left.

Gideon watched his devoted assistant leave the room. His loyalty was unquestioned, but with the others, he had his doubts. Perhaps the devil had found a way inside his little group?

This could not stand.

It was time to send them to their reward and replace them with others. Their sacrifice would be unpleasant yet necessary. This was a war for humanity's soul, requiring martyrdom.

There was no higher calling than to die for God's kingdom on earth. It was time for some to fulfill their destiny.

"Tatiana, come here, child. I need to speak with you..."

II **Puzzle Pieces**

East Providence Police Department HQ
March 21, 2010
750 Waterman Ave
East Providence, RI

Detective Frank Lachance had a secret. He needed to tell his lieutenant, but interrupting his boss while he was reading the newspaper was fraught with risk. No one dared. But, hey, what's the worst that could happen?

"Hey Lt., come look at this," Detective Frank Lachance said. "Tell me what you think."

Detective Lieutenant Joe Ford looked over the top of the Providence Journal, twisting his feet apart on the desk to get a view of the young detective.

"Frank, does it look like I give a shit about your latest discovery? Let me remind you, it is Sunday morning. And what do I do every Sunday morning before anything, and I mean anything else?"

"Read the paper," Lachance answered. "You must be the last person in the world who still does that."

"And therein lies the problem in this country. A bunch of illiterate morons glued to their digital devices lacking even the basic ability to discern news from nonsense. Now, if you know what is good for you and don't want to spend the next few months cleaning out the evidence room, you'll shut up until I *finish* my paper."

Lachance sat in nervous silence, fidgeting, staring at the front page of the paper while Ford read the mid-section. The young detective's impatient tapping of his feet removed any hope of peaceful concentration. After a few moments, Ford gave up. It was like trying to ignore a new puppy. You weren't sure if he wanted to play or was about to shit all over the rug.

"Fine," Ford said, dropping the paper on his desk. "What is this monumental revelation you've achieved?"

"Joe, it's about the body parts. I talked to a friend of mine from the state police, and we think they're connected."

"Were connected," Ford said, "that's why they're body *parts* now instead of a whole body. But I'm glad you and Trooper Dudley Do-Right figured out that elusive element."

Lachance picked up his laptop and came back to Ford's desk. Plopping the computer down on the newspaper, tearing the front page, he offered a meek "oops."

Ford glared, fists clenched, muscles straining. It took all his self-restraint not to throttle him.

"Do you want to die? Give me a minute, my goddamn gun is around here somewhere."

"Come on, Lieutenant, give me five minutes. I'll get coffee *and* your favorite pastries plus grab another Journal and the Boston Globe if you like."

Ford slid the paper from under the laptop, ready to roll it up and whack him on the nose. "Frosted Apple turnovers?"

"As you wish."

The kid's enthusiasm reminded Ford of himself a century ago when he was an ambitious first-year detective. It was not contagious. Ford was immune to any passion like this after thirty years of rolling in shit with the dregs of the world. He'd had his fill of putting up with wannabe hero political cops who got all their ideas from TV but ran and hid when shit hit the fan. It saps the life out of you.

But this kid was smart, good at his job, and showed potential. He paid attention and would learn. Ford decided to humor him for five minutes. Plus, for a frosted apple turnover, he thought, I'd remarry all my ex-wives.

"Okay, Columbo, whaddya have?"

The look in his eye said it all, 'who?'

"Ah jeez, never mind, show me what's worth risking my wrath over."

The kid spun the laptop so Ford could see. A spreadsheet with highlighted cells filled the screen.

"This is an Excel spreadsheet. A spreadsheet..."

"Stop there, kid. Yeah, I understand what a spreadsheet is. I know my way around computers. I'm old, not dead. Tell me what this piece of work shows, save the technology lecture."

The kid smiled. "Cool, okay. You know about the various body parts turning up in the city?"

"Hmm, body parts in the city?" Ford reached out and smacked the backside of his head, putting the rolled newspaper to good use.

"Stop talking to me like you're the school resource officer in a kindergarten class. Everybody in the whole fucking state has heard the body parts story. Jeez..."

"Sorry, Jerry Paulson from the state police and I think there's a pattern to them. A message the killer is trying to give us."

Ford leaned back in his chair. "Know what I think? I think sending you two knuckleheads to that FBI Serial Killer Profiling seminar was a fucking mistake. I told the Detective Captain, but he wouldn't listen.

"He has his head so far up the Attorney General's ass trying to land the head investigator position and retire, he jumps at any idea the AG throws out, and the homicide task force was the latest. I knew you and that trooper would start salivating for your very own Ocean State serial killer. You'd invent one if you had to."

"Listen to me, Lieutenant. Look at the spreadsheet. I put the date of recovery in one column and the recovered body part in another. The first was seven months ago. They are found on the same day, the last Saturday of each month. And if you sort by date of recovery from oldest to newest, it looks like he's sending us a human jigsaw puzzle."

Lachance slid the mouse around and sorted the date. "The first discovery, 8/29/2009 was a left foot followed by 9/26/2009 right foot, 10/31/2009 left leg, 11/28/2009 right leg, 12/26/2010 left arm, 1/30/2010 right arm, 2/27/2010 torso."

The one missing part, the head, was all they needed to complete the puzzle.

Ford looked at the screen. No doubt the kid was onto something.

"I also added in location. At first, it didn't help. Didn't seem to be a pattern. But when I plotted them on a map, I could see it. One by one. It moves, south to north, left to right."

"No shit, Frank. No shit," Ford played with the columns. This kid might be the one he'd been looking for. Someone to mentor before he pulled the pin.

"What do you think, Lieutenant?"

Ford hesitated for a moment. If word got out they are looking at this as a serial killer, the media frenzy would drive us crazy. Strictly speaking, it wasn't a serial killer. We had one body, or at least pieces of what we hoped was one body. But no one was convinced this was one victim.

The DNA results were skewered because the bad guys soaked the body parts in oxygenated bleach, which wreaked havoc with the tissue and blood. The crime lab was still working on extracting usable samples.

Thus, the lack of progress identifying the victim or victims.

Much worse for me, Ford thought, if the AG finds out, he'll turn it into a fucking circus. This had to be handled with caution. Temper the kid's enthusiasm with rationality.

"This is smart work, kid. But we gotta keep control over it. Limit who knows. If any of the suck-ups around here find out, they'll tell the world. Some of these assholes are so close to the politicians they could wear their ass for a hat.

"The only thing keeping this off the lead story every night is that state senator getting caught in his car with his pants down, playing hide the sausage with a fifteen-year-old girl.

"Once they tire from flogging that guy, they'll come charging back to this some assembly-required nightmare. At least until some other politician steps on his own dick."

Ford tapped his finger on the desk, looking at the kid who looked like a five-year-old being held back from seeing what was under the Christmas tree.

"Tell you what. We work this off the books for now. No reports in the system. Back to paper notes, and we'll lock them in my office at night.

"I'll call Captain Murray at state police headquarters. He owes me a big one. He'll keep this between us. I'll have him send your Trooper Knucklehead counterpart down here like you're chasing burglars or some such excuse."

Lachance bounced around like a nine-year-old told he was going to Disney. "Great, I have a few ideas on some things we might do with new technology the FBI uses. I'll see what I can come up with."

"Frank," Ford said, in his most stern lieutenant boss-type voice. "Work it, but quietly. Understood?"

"Yes, sir. Ah, there is one more thing, Lieutenant."

"What's that?" Ford said, dropping the paper onto his lap one more time.

"It's, ah, this Saturday is the last Saturday of the month."

"That is true. I'll put a gold star on your calendar lesson."

"Lieutenant, if the pattern holds, we will find another body part this Saturday—the head. Let's run a stakeout. Maybe get lucky."

"Hmm, how should I find enough cops to run this stakeout and keep it quiet? Not to mention getting El Hefe to pay for it?"

The kid smiled. "That's why you're the Lieutenant."

"I got a better idea, kid." Ford's brain was always searching for a solution to make everything someone else's problem.

"How about I have you assigned to the SIU with Lieutenant Williams? He loves this shit as much as you do. It can be his headache. I'll take care of that; your job is to pick up my apple slices and be sure you pick the ones with thick frosting. Now move."

Ford watched the kid fly out the door. Almost missed that joy for the job, he thought. Almost.

Whatever possessed me to let him talk me into this? One year left, one more year, and I'd run out the door. Thirty years done, with a pension to cover my bar bill. This last year was supposed to be uneventful, not some reality TV series.

But no worries. he had a solution.

Reaching for his cell, Ford hit the speed dial for Lieutenant Josh Williams.

"Special Investigations Unit."

"Hey, Josh. Joe Ford."

"Lieutenant Ford, what can I do for you this fine morning?"

"Josh, I'm getting El Hefe to give you that extra body you've been whining about. Det. Lachance will be transferring into your unit tomorrow. And he comes with a bonus."

"And what might that be?"

"He has his own trooper. I believe they are both housebroken. Two for the price of one," Ford chuckled. "No need to thank me."

"Why do I have the distinct feeling I am getting screwed here?"

"To borrow a line I just heard, that's why you're a Lieutenant." Ending the call, he resumed reading the paper. All was right with the world.

III   The Big Picture

At 8:30 a.m. the following day, the knock on the door seemed hesitant, almost reluctant. A muffled "Lt. Williams?" followed the knock. Silence for a minute, then it repeated. Josh Williams glanced over his computer at Det. Tommy Moore.

"Tommy, you gonna sit there or are you planning on opening the door?"

Moore shook his head, putting his index finger on his lips.

"I vote to sit here in silence," he whispered. "Let them think we're out. It sounds like that goofy Community Relations guy. Probably wants us for a dog and pony show at some elderly housing talking to old ladies about being street smart.

"Last time they were on the street they were riding horses."

"You are a piece of work. Open the goddamn door. If it is Community Relations, you volunteered."

"Fuck me," Moore mumbled, swinging his legs off his desk.

"Yes, you did," Josh said, grabbing his coffee.

Josh watched Moore maneuver around the maze of four desks. The office, designed for two detectives, now held four. There was no direct path. Stepping around file folders and assorted equipment, Moore contorted his way through the congestion.

Grabbing the handle, yanking open the door, he was surprised by Det. Frank Lachance standing there with another cop he didn't recognize.

"Frank, what's up? Lt. Ford send you to take our pastry orders?"

"Let 'em in, Tommy, they are coming to work with us," Josh said, waving Lachance in.

"Thanks, Lt. This is Det. Jerry Paulsen, Rhode Island State Police."

"State Police?" Moore said, a smile crossing his face. Snapping to attention, he offered a mock Three Stooges salute. "I'll use small words from now on."

Paulsen smiled. "From what I've heard, that's a challenge for you."

Moore laughed, putting out his hand. "Pleasure to meet you, Detective Paulsen."

"Jerry will do. Seems we're gonna be spending a lot of time together."

"Tommy," Moore answered. "We're at a premium on desk space, but that one is free for now. You guys can use that and the conference table in back."

Once everyone settled in, Josh told Lachance to lay out the story.

"Sounds like you're onto something with the pattern, and I think you're right about next Saturday, but even narrowing it to the north of the city covers a lot of ground.

"Was there anything about how the body parts were placed that might help? "

"Let me show you something," Lachance said, unfolding a map of East Providence. Marked on the map were the locations and details about each body part they'd found.

"See it?" Lachance asked.

"See what?" Moore asked, peering over Lachance's shoulder.

Josh came over, and they studied the map. Moore broke the silence.

"Holy shit! It's a body laid out over the city."

"Yup," Lachance said. "As soon as I put the info on the map, it jumped out at me."

"Is there anything else?" Josh asked. "Near highways, the bike path, anything consistent about where the parts are placed?"

Lachance looked to Paulsen for ideas.

"There was one thing," Paulsen said. "When we got the call for the right leg, a neighbor reported what he thought was a loud motorcycle revving its engine. But we checked doorbell videos of the area and didn't see any bikes.

"Of course, it wasn't full coverage, so it may have been outside the video."

'How about off-road trails?" Tommy asked, "Someone unfamiliar with motorcycles might not recognize the difference between a street bike and a dirt bike."

Paulsen chuckled.

"What's so funny?"

"At the scene, I mentioned that to the Lieutenant in charge. He told me he wasn't sending any other troopers into wet, muddy woods, but I was welcome to go myself.

"I went in with a couple of your uniform guys, and there was a mess of tracks but nothing we could trace back to the location."

"Well, that at least gives us something to go on." Josh picked up the phone, putting his hand up to silence the group as he put the phone on speaker.

"East Providence Fire Department, Captain Anderson speaking."

"Captain Anderson, how are you?" Josh said. "How's things at the fire department? Any new recipes yet?'

"Oh, you're a scream Williams. Never heard you or that fat ass Moore complain when we fed you, though, did we?"

"Hey," Moore yelled, leaning over Josh's shoulder. "Who are you calling a fat ass? They had to transfer you off the ladder truck because they were afraid you would bend it if you even managed to waddle higher than three steps."

"Yeah, yeah. What can I do for you, Josh? You need me to send rescue and tranquilize Moore?'

"Not today, but I will keep it in mind. I need to borrow your two ATVs for an operation next Saturday. Can you arrange that?"

"Ah, this doesn't involve one of your infamous Foliage Tours, does it?"

"No, no. Police business. Can we use them?"

"Sure, why not? I'll have them dropped off wherever you say."

"I'll let you know. Thanks, Andy."

Josh hung up, then called the Chief's office.

"Good morning, El Hefe. Might you have a moment to speak with me? Okay. Be right there." Ending the call, he looked at Moore. "You take these two and go scope along the riverfront from the old railroad bridge up as far as you can go. Call Pawtucket PD to give them a heads up you'll be poking around on their turf.

"Check for any trails with access from the river. Anywhere somebody might make it out onto a roadway and leave something where it will be found."

Moore smiled. "Can I take the 4X4? The seizure was settled last week, and it is ours to use."

"Okay, but if you dent it or break anything you're paying for it, capisce?"

"Got it, boss. Let's go boys. This is gonna be a sweet ride."

As they started for the door, Jerry Paulsen said, "Hey, Tommy, what's a foliage tour?"

Moore chuckled. "It's a special tour we hold each year. Rent a bus and go bar hopping."

Paulsen scrunched his face in confusion. 'What's the foliage part?"

"A cleverly disguised cover. We call it a Fall Foliage Tour because it sounds harmless to girlfriends and wives. And we go in August to beat the rush."

"And that works?" Paulsen asked.

"The rush part, yeah. The clever disguise, ah, no, but most of them are happy to have us out of the hair for a day anyway."

Paulsen shook his head and followed them out the door. "Some of the older guys in headquarters warned me about you EPPD guys, said you are a unique bunch."

"And proud of it," Moore said, leading the way.

As the trio left the office, Det. Dan Lynch and his partner, Det. John Harris, wandered back in. "Where are they headed off to?" Lynch asked.

"Long story. Cancel any plans for next Saturday night, we have some business to attend to. I gotta go let the Chief decide if he wants to know anything. Depending on his answer, I'll either be right back or there for a bit. Just sit tight."

The two nodded as Josh headed toward the detective's reception area. Passing by the secretary's desk, he leaned over to her. "Helen, if anyone is looking for me, tell them I am gone for the day. Okay?"

She shrugged. "Why would today be different from any other day? Most people stopped asking me a long time ago. They got tired of the same answer."

"That's why you are my favorite." Josh smiled, heading toward the Chief's office.

He was back in the office in five minutes.

"I take it the boss preferred to remain in the dark?" Lynch said.

Josh nodded. "He did indeed. Did I ever tell you about how we started SIU?"

Both detectives shook their heads.

"When Chris Hamlin came up with the idea, her, the Chief, and I went and met with the Chief of Pawtucket PD about their Special Squad. So, after talking about how successful it was, the Pawtucket chief asked if there were any questions.

"Our chief said, 'So how do you keep track of what they're doing?' And the Pawtucket chief said, 'Oh, that's easy. You don't want to know what they're doing,' and burst out laughing."

Harris almost spit out his coffee. Lynch shook his head.

"And thus," Josh continued, "came about our own version of don't ask, don't tell. The chief, and this is why he has been the chief for so long, prefers plausible deniability."

"Works for me," Lynch said, leafing through the reports from the body parts puzzle case.

IV   Needle in a Haystack

Josh and Detective Paulsen leaned against Paulsen's car in the parking lot on the East Providence/Pawtucket line.

They watched groups of kids and their parents shuffling into the USA Skating Rink. The parents had that look of continuous exhaustion from shuttling to all the activities. The kids running on pure adrenaline.

All oblivious to the dark reason for the detectives' presence.

After a few minutes, the fire department arrived with two ATVs on transport. The fire lieutenant climbed out of the truck and walked over to Josh.

"I'm supposed to leave these things with you. Before I do I need to know who is gonna operate them and where they'll be used."

Josh winked at Paulsen, pushing himself away from the car.

"No, Lieutenant, you aren't entitled to that information. Captain Anderson authorized this. I'm certain a captain outranks a lieutenant even in the fire department. Kind of like he's the head chef and you are the salad guy."

Josh looked at the two firefighters trying to hide their smiles. He didn't know this lieutenant, but he knew the type. They considered anything under their control as personal property and did everything they could to avoid letting anyone touch it, no matter what the circumstances.

"Listen, Williams, I don't give a..."

Josh stepped forward, putting himself inches from the man's face.

"First, that's Lieutenant Williams to you. Second, I don't have time for this fucking nonsense. So, tell your guys to take those ATVs off the truck, or I will get them off. But make no mistake, they are coming off that truck."

Flustered, the man backpedaled and nodded at the firefighters. Moving back toward the truck, away from Josh, the distance gave him a measure of courage.

"Anything happens to this equipment, it will be on you," he said, trying to sound forceful. "You'll have to explain it to the city."

Josh smiled. "Oh, don't worry. They'll come back in perfect condition."

"They'd better," the man said, reaching to close the door. Before he could, Josh grabbed it. The speed of Josh's move forced the man back his seat, eyes wide with fear.

"Unless," Josh said, a smirk on his face, "during this operation, they are destroyed or shot up by the bad guys. But you'll have the memories." He slammed the door and walked away.

As the truck pulled out of the lot, the driver put his left hand out the window and gave Josh a thumbs up.

"It would seem," Paulsen said, "even the fire department has its share of idiots with rank."

Josh chuckled. "Bet he won the best baker contest."

Moments later, the rest of the squad showed up in the new 4X4.

"Tommy," Josh said, talking like a concerned father, "this is not your permanent ride."

"Yeah, yeah. I figured it might be handy on some of the dirt roads along the river. Besides, I want to ride one of those," he said, jumping on the first ATV.

"I know I will regret this," Josh said, "but okay, you can take that one with Lachance. John, you and Dan ride the other. I'll take the 4X4, and Jerry will use his car. I'll stay south, and Jerry will head up to Pawtucket.

"Let's play smart here. I know how much you like chasing things, but if we're lucky, and they show up, I want to grab the guy with a minimum of Wild West stuff.

"Keep us in the loop, and don't try to be a fucking hero. My guess is it is futile, but still worth trying."

Moore fired up the ATV and ran it around the lot, pulling the front wheels off the ground and spinning on the back tires.

Paulsen laughed. "You should video that and send it to that anal fire lieutenant. It would put him off his feed for a month."

"Don't give anybody any ideas, okay? Let's hope we get lucky."

After making sure all the portables were working— although no one would be shocked if they failed at the critical moment—the group headed off. Josh watched Moore and Lachance disappear into the woods toward the river southbound. Harris and Lynch headed north toward St. Mary's Cemetery.

"Okay, see ya," Paulsen said, climbing into his car and heading up Prospect Street. Josh walked to the 4X4, reaching for the door. I hope I'm not wasting everybody's time chasing ghosts.

Eight hours later, he had his answer.

"705 to 701" Tommy radioed.

Josh keyed his mic. "Go, Tommy."

"Ah, you think we need to keep this going?"

"Gimme a minute." Josh parked the car and stepped out into the cool spring night. This had always been a long shot, and now it looked like a complete waste of time. He should have known it would never be this easy.

"701 to all 700 units, let's bag it for the night. Meet me back at USA Skates, and I'll arrange for the ATVs to be picked up."

Thirty minutes later, with the ATVs back with the fire department, although the Lieutenant who was so worried about their welfare didn't trouble himself to come back for them, the troops headed back to the barn.

As they pulled into the lot, the radio came to life.

305-308, respond to Newport at Pawtucket Ave for a suspicious package. Reporting party will meet you there. Caller says there's a large amount of blood in the vicinity.

"Oh, what the fuck," Josh said, wheeling the car around and heading to the call.

"701,"

"Go ahead, Lieutenant," the dispatcher answered.

"Have those units secure the scene and wait for me to arrive."

"10-4, Lieutenant."

"305, I got it. Show 308 and I out at the scene."

A small group had gathered near the leaking cardboard box. The officers pushed them back and blocked off the road, sending cars into the other lane. Officer Ken Smith, who'd done several tours in Iraq, knew the unmistakable coppery smell of blood.

"308 to 701."

"Go, Kenny," Josh answered.

"You might want to start BCI up here. This is definitely a crime scene."

Josh banged his hand on the steering wheel. "Son-of-a-bitch," he muttered. Keying the mic again he said, "701, Notify BCI and the Detective Commander."

"10-4, Lieutenant, I'll take care of it."

Within a few moments of arriving, Josh knew this was not some coincidence but another body part. The box was too small for a body or even a head as they suspected might be left. But it was no doubt human blood and a lot of it.

Witnesses reported a male on a motorcycle dropping the package before speeding off with the lights out. No one got a plate and could only describe the man as dressed in dark clothing. Left little to go on.

Once BCI had documented the scene, they gingerly opened the top of the box. Inside were several towels soaked in blood. Once they were pulled back, the full horror inside revealed itself.

A plastic bag drenched with human blood, likely broken when the box was dropped—perhaps on purpose to add to the horror—lay on top of two eyes, two ears, and a tongue stapled to a piece of cardboard in their relative positions on a human.

"What do you think, Lt.? They changing their pattern?" Frank Lachance asked.

Josh shook his head. "Nah, they're adding to the terror. They *wanted* civilians to find this," Josh glanced around. "Frank, does your phone have a video camera?"

Frank gave him a quizzical look. "There are phones without cameras?"

"Never mind, go to the corner, video the cars driving by and anybody you see paying too much attention here. My guess is they'll want to enjoy the benefits of their labor."

Frank grabbed his phone and started working.

"Tommy, come here," Josh said.

"What's up?"

"Go walk through the crowd. Anybody the least bit hinky, call me."

Tommy's eyes lit up. "You got it, boss."

"Take Jerry with you."

Tommy hustled off to hunt in the crowd.

Josh's cell rang, and he recognized the number, Chief Brennan.

"Chief," Josh said.

"So, we missed 'em, eh?"

"Seems so. We had the area right, and I don't think they spotted us, but I can't be sure."

"Now what?" the Chief asked.

"If we can ID this victim, maybe that will give us something to work with. I'll call Dr. Foster at the crime lab and try to get him to expedite the DNA profile."

"Okay, keep me in the loop. We'll have to release something for the press, but we can hold off until Monday."

The call ended, and so did the effort to catch the bad guys for the moment. Tommy and Jerry, despite their best efforts, saw no one worth rattling their cage. They'd review the video from Frank's phone, but they had little hope.

V A Brief Shining Glimpse of Evidence

The line rang several times before it was answered.

"Dr. Foster, Josh Williams, East Providence PD."

"Josh, how are you?"

"Doing well, doctor, doing well. I wonder if I could ask you for a favor?"

"You can ask. If I can help, I will. If I can't, I won't make excuses."

"Fair enough. Two of my detectives are on the way with some critical evidence. Are you familiar with the body parts being found in the city?"

"Of course, I am, Josh. One would have to be a hermit not to."

"True," Josh answered. "Anyway, the evidence they're bringing in, we believe, relates to this case. We had a stakeout in place because of the pattern related to the placement of the parts.

"If you can speed up the DNA analysis, it might help us ID these guys and save some future victims. They're still active and it's escalating."

"Hmm. Okay, I told you I wouldn't mislead you," Foster said. "We have a backlog of sexual assault cases with detectives all over the state making the same plea. It all boils down to prioritizing resources.

"I won't promise anything, but I'll try to have a preliminary sample analyzed in a few days. Running it through the state database will be no issue. As to the FBI database, that's out of our control."

"That would be appreciated, Doctor. I may be able to cash in some favors with the Feebs. One roadblock at a time. Thank you."

"I'd like to say anytime, but I'd be lying. Take care, Lieutenant."

Josh ended the call, looking at the faces staring at him.

"So?" Tommy asked.

"He's gonna expedite the state analysis. As to the FBI database, we are on our own."

"Maybe we'll get lucky," Tommy said.

"There's always hope. Anyway, until we have something else, we go back to doing it the old way. Tommy, you and I will canvas the neighborhood. Maybe someone noticed the bike; give us something more useful about the guy.

"Frank, you and Jerry run down any missing person reports. The ears had piercings. I realize that may not matter anymore, but I am betting they're female. I'll have the shift commanders put out something at rollcall about the motorcycle."

Josh glanced at his watch. "Let's meet back here in three hours."

VI Just a Feeling

Officer Ken Smith pulled up in his cruiser as Josh and Tommy headed out the door into the rear lot.

"Hey, Lt., can I talk to you for a minute?"

"Sure, Ken, what's up?"

"I was thinking about the incident the other night and I remembered a motorcycle I spotted a few days earlier. A guy flew by me on Newport Ave, speeding, weaving in and out of traffic. I started after him, but we got a call for an accident with injuries, so I had to back off."

"You think it was the same guy?" Tommy asked.

Ken shrugged. "Dunno, but here's the thing. There was a woman on the back of the bike and when they passed me, she looked over at me. Now, I'm not sure about this, and it happened pretty fast, but I could have sworn she was crying. She had, I dunno, a strange look about her. Like she was sad and terrified at the same moment. It was that look that caught my eye.

"After we cleared the accident, I tried looking for the bike but couldn't find it."

"Get a plate?" Josh asked.

"Partial," handing Josh a slip of paper. "I had dispatch try running various combinations, but things got busy, and it slipped my mind."

VII   Hunting Where the Game Trail Leads

Standing in the chief's office, Josh waited for the argument against running the stakeout again.

"You sure you want to try this again in the same area?" Chief Brennan said.

"I do, I think they're escalating things. The media, from the box we found last month, created a tidal wave of news. If they're looking for publicity, they'll want to show they can do things right under our noses. I think Lachance is right about the pattern—they're placing a body over the city so the head of this last victim will be up north.

"But wouldn't the pattern point elsewhere next month?" the chief asked.

Josh shook his head. "I spoke to a friend who's a shrink with a background in sociopaths. He says the placement of the last package is a change in the pattern. He thinks they're looking for more notoriety. With all the shopping centers and traffic in Rumford, they'll draw more attention. Something's changed and they're escalating.

"I'll have some units rotating toward Riverside just in case, but I think Rumford is our best bet."

"Okay, you gonna shake down the FD for their ATVs again? That fire lieutenant threw a hissy fit about how dirty they were last time."

"That was the best part, Chief." Josh smiled.

* * * * *

Two days later, it was déjà vu all over again. Dispersing the team from the parking lot, Josh decided to sit for a while with the truck off, sipping his coffee.

The sudden noise of the motorcycle caught him by surprise. Cops always hope a stakeout pays off, but they also doubt they'll get that lucky. Crime is more shit luck than organized.

Across the street, the bike appeared from the old Fram Corporation property, lights out, idling as the rider looked up and down the street.

Are you fucking kidding me, Josh thought, reaching for the radio.

"701, 701 to 700 units. I got a bike just coming out of the woods onto Pawtucket Ave from the old Fram Corp building. The driver is wearing a backpack. His lights are out. Stand by for additional."

Josh debated about trying to head out of the lot to intercept the bike or remain where he was until the biker chose. Either way he was at a disadvantage. There was no way he'd be able to follow if the bike went back into the woods.

A moment later, the bike decided for him, pulling across the street and onto New Rd., headed toward Newport Ave.

He's looking for a more public place like the last one, Josh thought, if it even is the guy.

"701, he's on New Rd., hang back, don't spook him. The plate is bent a bit, but the first few numbers match the plate

Ken gave us. Keep the ATVs out of sight, they will catch his eye. Jerry, you back in the area?"

"Right behind you, Lieutenant," Paulsen answered.

"Okay, let's see where this takes us. Tommy, switch to Channel 1 and tell them we may need some marked units. But have them stay away from the shopping center for now."

"10-4, Lt. I'm over on Lester St. right outside your old Monster Mansion place."

"Monster Mansion?" Paulsen asked.

"Long story," Josh answered. "Ok, everybody sit tight, keep him in sight but don't spook him."

Hanging back several car lengths, Josh watched the bike catch the light at Newport Ave. He'd put his lights on, obviously didn't want to attract cops, and appeared like any other bike out for a night ride.

The light turned green, and the bike headed north on Newport, then turned into the shopping center lot.

"Okay, he's in the shopping center. Tommy, head up toward Narragansett Park Drive in case he makes a run for the woods or the reservoir. Danny, you and John make your way to Taylor Drive. I want to box him in.

"Jerry, you come from the back and stay over near Burlington Coats. Hang on, he's pulling up to a car; there's an older woman trying to load groceries into her car. Hold back a bit. What the hell?"

Josh watched as the rider climbed off the bike and helped the woman load her groceries into the car.

"He's helping the woman load her car."

"He's what?" Tommy said. "This can't be our guy. He's a freaking Boy Scout."

"Give it a minute. I want to at least ID him."

The biker climbed back on the bike and headed toward the bowling alley.

"Everybody got eyes on him?" Josh asked. "Let's watch for a minute."

As the units maneuvered into position, Josh moved closer to the bike now parked near the side of the bowling alley. Hidden in the shadows, Josh couldn't quite make out what the driver was up to.

"701, I'm getting out on foot. He's parked west of the front door to the bowling alley, sitting in the shadows. Let's not wait, this is probably a waste of time. Give me a minute to close on him then shut down any way out. Jerry, you come in behind him."

Josh waited a few seconds before sliding out of the truck. They had disabled the interior light, so the biker paid no attention to him when Josh opened the door.

On a night like tonight, there'd be leagues bowling and the place would be busy. If this was the guy, he'd blend into the crowd. Few would pay attention. A perfect cover. And if not, they'd wasted the night watching the rare exhibit of politeness with the old lady.

Trying to keep a row of cars between him and the biker, Josh made his way closer. As he appeared from between the cars, the biker looked at him.

He appeared to be in his thirties, average height, thin, telltale signs of a junkie. It was difficult to see much of his face because of the baseball hat pulled low over his eyes. But Josh knew he was watching him.

Josh continued at an angle toward the door, which brought him closer to the man. The backpack he'd been wearing was hanging on the handlebars as he leaned against the bike.

Out of the corner of his eye, Josh saw Paulsen driving up the row of cars along the building. He'd put on his bright headlights, blinding the biker, enough to distract him from Josh.

Before the biker could turn around, Josh was on him.

"What the fuck? Get off me, man." the guy yelled, trying to struggle away. Paulsen was there in a second and the fight went out of the guy.

"Calm down, pal. We're cops." Josh said. "Relax." He reached into his pocket and produced an ID and badge.

"I ain't done nothin'," the guy argued, leaning on the bike and avoiding looking at the backpack. His hands were jammed inside a ratty old military field jacket pocket.

"701 to 700 units. All set, we have him under control. Front of the bowling alley," his eyes never leaving the suspect.

"Take your hands out of your pockets, slowly."

"Why?" the guy said, his voice shaky.

"Cuz, he said so," Paulsen said, towering over the guy.

As the other units arrived, Josh asked, "You got a license?"

"Yeah, but I wasn't riding this. It belongs to a friend. He's inside."

"Ah, I see. Okay. Well, show me your license anyway," Josh said, smiling. He loved it when they started the conversation by lying.

"What's in the backpack?"

The guy never even glanced at it. "Dunno, it's not mine."

"Ah, so you're just watching it for your friend? Where's your license?"

The man shrugged. "Dunno, must have left it at home."

"Okay, what's your name?" Josh said, stepping into the man's personal space, forcing him to lean back against the wall.

"Why?"

"Because he fucking asked for it," Moore growled in the man's face.

"I don't have to give you anything. I haven't done anything. If I am not under arrest, I'm leaving," rising from the bike.

"I'd rethink that if I were you," Josh said, pushing him back on the seat sidesaddle. "Now, let's cut the bullshit. I saw you riding the bike. I have every right to make sure you have a license. And if you don't have a license, we'll charge you with operating without a license and impound the fucking bike. Understand now?"

For the first time, the man couldn't help but glance at the bag. It spoke volumes.

"If you can't produce a license, we will take you into custody until we can establish who the fuck you are and who this bike belongs to, understand that?"

"Do what you gotta do. I ain't saying nothin' else."

"Hey, Lt.," Lachance said, "the bike has an expired registration listed to Israel David Jenkins out of Riverside. Washington Street, in the maze. His DOB is 7/25/1981. And, lo and behold, his license is non-existent. None anywhere dispatch can find."

Josh smiled. "And are you Israel David Jenkins?"

"Which part of fuck you don't you understand? I ain't saying nothin' until I talk to my lawyer."

"Cuff him," Josh said, "We're done playing here."

Tommy grabbed Jenkin's arm, spinning him to the wall. Jenkin's tried to push himself off. Tommy leaned in, kicking Jenkin's legs apart, putting him off-balance.

"You don't want to do that," Moore snarled. "As much as I would enjoy pounding you into the ground, we don't have time for this nonsense. Do yourself a favor and avoid acting like an asshole."

Jenkin's relented, and his body went limp. Resignation took over. Whatever resistance he once considered disappeared. He knew it was over for him.

Tommy patted the guy down, felt something, then reached into the right front pocket of the field jacket.

"And what do we have here?" he said, handing a woman's wallet to Josh.

"Well, well. What's this?" Josh said, examining the wallet, credit cards, cash, and driver's license. And here I thought you were a Boy Scout. Unless your real name is Majorie Vartanian. I'd say you're an odd-looking seventy-six-year-old woman."

"I found that. I was gonna call you guys."

"Yeah, right," Josh said.

As the cuffs went on, Josh examined the outside of the backpack. "This is yours too, right? Or did you find this with the wallet as well?" waving the bag in his face.

"What are you, dense? I don't know nothin' about nothin'."

"That's the most intelligent thing you've said all night. Although it is a double negative implying you know something."

The confusion on Jenkins's face said it all.

"Call a marked unit to transport." Josh spun Jenkins around and pushed him toward Tommy. "Tommy, you and Danny follow him in. Put him on ice, away from anybody else until we figure out what we have here. And no calls until I get there, understand?"

"You got it, Lt.," Moore said, reaching for his portable and dragging the guy away from the bike.

Once the guy was in the car and gone, Josh turned back to the group of detectives.

"So, what do you think? We open the bag as part of the inventory search and tow the bike, or do we maybe try to write a search warrant?"

"Man, I miss the old days," Det. Harris said. "We'd have already opened the bag and been done with it."

"I know, John," Josh said, "But if this turns out to be the guy, we have to tread gingerly. I mean, it's probably some coke or meth, but I still don't want to give some smart lawyer an opening to suppress this shit."

Josh thought for a moment. "Let's put the bike in the back of the 4X4 and transport it to the station. I'll take custody of the bag and will give the on-duty AG a call."

VIII   An Abundance of Caution

Josh clicked off his cell."Well, that was a colossal waste of time."

"What'd he say?" Tommy asked, sitting on the edge of the desk.

"He said, and I quote, 'Both are legitimate approaches to the matter. Use your best judgment' end quote."

"I told you that guy was a putz. Let's take a peek and decide."

"I don't know, Tommy. We fuck this up, and we'll all be back in the bag writing speeding tickets."

Moore grinned. "Well, that's all the state police do, so let Paulsen do it."

Paulsen grinned back at him. "You're a real comedian, aren't you? I say we have the time. Let's write the warrant. Remember the Von Bulow case a million years ago? Nobody thought they'd needed a warrant, but the court tossed the evidence, and the son-of-a-bitch walked."

"Wow. That case was a bit before your time, no?" Josh asked.

"Yup, but my dad and his partner worked on it. He told me all about it. Nobody even considered getting a search warrant since the family brought the bag with the insulin to headquarters. But the court decided otherwise.

"I say write the warrant. We still have time with the guy. Anything back on the prints yet?"

"Good question," Josh said, reaching for the phone.

"BCI, Detective Skeffington."

"Hey, Lars, anything on our friend yet?"

"Not on the prints. I got possible hits on the name and an alias on a warrant out of Mass for probation violation. Need to dig some more."

Josh hung up the phone. "Okay, there's a possible active warrant for a parole violation out of Mass. When I have the info from BCI, I'll write the warrant affidavit.

"John, can you fill in the details about the bag on the warrant pages? I'll attach the affidavit as a separate document.

"Tommy," Josh said, turning to face him as he looked at his watch, "Call Bovi's, tell Judge Marciano we will be there in an hour or so. Have Barbara give him another scotch on me."

"You sure he'll be there?" Moore asked.

Josh laughed. "It's seven o'clock on a Saturday on a long weekend. He's there. And if, by some strange coincidence, he's not, the only possibility being that he is dead, there'll be a couple of other judges there as well.

"The problem is they might read the warrant, not just sign it." Josh reached for the keyboard. "I guess I'll have to make this a legitimate one."

* * * * *

An hour later, the detectives stood around the bag, ready to open it. As expected, Judge Marciano glanced at the warrant, signed it, then tipped the glass of scotch at the bemused Josh and Tommy.

"There's only one thing I care about in these things," the judge said, "the address. I'm okay with it as long as it's not mine or the Bishop's.

"Happy hunting, boys. I'll be here for a while if you need anything else," returning to his drink and the fifty-something barfly he was regaling with judicial wisdom and an open bar tab.

On the way back to the station, Tommy was chuckling.

"What's so funny?"

"Marciano. He's a piece of work. All he cares about is the address."

"That's nothing. One time, he told Chris Hamlin and me that he never reads the affidavit because he might have to suppress the evidence someday."

"Are you kidding me?" Tommy said.

"Nope, that's the Judicial selection process for the State of Rhode Island, your honor."

* * * * *

"So, open it," Tommy said. "And we can go have a couple of drinks ourselves."

Josh put on a pair of gloves, then slid the top zipper. Pulling the bag open, the circle of detectives all looked in.

Depending on who told the story, the next few moments would be described as a gruesome horror movie, raucous comedic mayhem, or a combination of both. Who could ever predict how they'd react to seeing a human head in a bag?

"Holy shit!"

"Jesus Christ!"

"Hey, you puked on my shoes, Lachance!"

"You might want to quit while you're a...head."

Cops use callous humor not out of disrespect for the dead but as a defense against the horrors of the job overwhelming them. This qualified as one of the more troubling ones.

Josh collapsed in the chair, staring at the head without its eyes, ears, and lips.

"It looks like we aren't going anywhere," he said. "Tommy, call BCI. We need this processed ASAP. I'll call the Chief. John, call the AG's office. Not that nitwit on call; I have the Deputy's number in my contacts. Tell him what we have.

"And one other thing," Josh added, looking everyone in the eye. "We keep this in-house as long as we can. We don't need the media crawling all over the place."

Paulsen took another peek. "I'm gonna have to call headquarters. No pun intended,"

"Yeah, of course, Jerry," Josh said. "After you do, you and Tommy take a ride, get a description of this guy's house, and sit on it 'till we get there. We're gonna write a warrant for that place as well."

Josh looked at Lachance. "You okay now?"

"Yeah, sorry, Lt."

"No worries, I almost tossed my cookies as well. You are now the evidence custodian for this."

Lachance's eyes grew wide.

"Don't worry, you don't have to touch anything. BCI handles that. You stay with BCI as they process and document things. Take lots of notes and write a statement once they secure everything in the evidence room. Work with the BCI guys so there are no inconsistencies."

"Got it, Lt. Sorry again."

"Listen, Frank. This was because you took the initiative. Wherever this goes, you deserve a pat on the back. Nice job. Both you and Jerry hit it on the head with this one. Sorry, didn't mean it to come out that way."

"Yeah," Tommy said, "don't let success go to your head."

Twenty minutes later, the East Providence police chief realized his plans for the long weekend were doomed. The AG called his press guy and told him to start on the press release.

And the circus came to town.

While Josh knew this would happen, he worried that politics might overwhelm what was probably the biggest case in this city ever.

IX Missing Pieces

Josh leaned over, whispering into the SRT commander's ear. "Ready?"

"On your word, my liege Lord," Captain Bill St. George said.

"Okay, hit it. Once secure, we want BCI to take over and process this. I hope there aren't more body parts, but who knows? Tell your guys to be as judicious as they can. I know how much they like breaking things."

"Only what's necessary in the pursuit of justice," the team commander smiled. He keyed the mic on his headset. " Go! Go! Go! Hit it."

Their intense training paid off despite the chief's constant complaints about the cost. The team was inside, the building swept for other occupants, and secured for the long, tedious processing search within ten minutes.

"All yours, Josh," the commander radioed. "We'll hang around in case this leads us somewhere else."

The team immediately found more body parts, locating several legs, arms, and hands in a large freezer.

As Josh stared into the freezer, Tommy touched him on the arm.

"Lt., there are two more like this downstairs."

"Jesus Christ," Josh mumbled, stepping back as one BCI detective took pictures while another videoed the evidence documentation process. Torn pages from the Bible, highlighting various quotes and hand-scrawled versions of others, covered the walls.

Tommy and several other detectives came over to stare, each reading the lines while trying to understand the horror inside this otherwise normal house.

Mark 16:17 These Signs will accompany those who have believed: in MY name they will cast out demons, they will speak with new tongues.

Acts 19:15 And the evil spirit answered and said to them, "I recognize Jesus, and I know Paul, but who are you?"

Revelation 16:14...for they are spirits of demons, performing signs, which go out to kings of the whole world, to gather them together for the war of the great day of God, the Almighty

1 Timothy 4:1 But the spirit explicitly says that in later times

some will fall away from the faith,
paying attention to deceitful spirit
and doctrines of demons.

Scrawled along the top of one wall, in what appeared to be blood, were words that chilled Josh's thoughts.

Every time you overcome a
demon; you grow stronger. To kill
a demon is to grow closer to the
Lord. Take solace in the death of
one possessed for you have
saved their soul.

Beneath the words, a cross in smeared blood, blackened by time, added to the horrors.

The silence lasted for just moments but felt like hours. Josh was the first to break it.

"What... the... fuck... is... this?"

"I'm not sure, Lt.," Frank said, "but I have seen nothing like this, not even in a movie. This is a Stephen King story come to life."

"All right, we'll figure this out later," Josh said. "For now, let's take this step by step and document everything. I better go call the Chief. He'll want to see this for himself."

* * * * *

Twenty minutes later, Chief Brennan arrived at the scene. Josh came out to brief him.

"You sure you want to share this nightmare?" Josh asked as Brennan started toward the door.

Brennan stopped for a moment, looking at the house. "Every time I have stood outside a crime scene, the contradiction of the outwardly normal nature of a place concealing the horrors humans can inflict on each other makes me question the idea we are an evolved species.

"How many times have I driven by a place like this without knowing the terrors it contained?"

"Getting philosophical in your old age, are we?" Josh said, trying to soften with humor what no one could understand.

"You will, too, someday. It will hit you that we exist as disposable sponges absorbing all this shit, so most people don't have to," he sighed.

"Okay, let's get this over with, then I can go home and not sleep for a few days."

* * * * *

After several hours, the evidence list looked like a compilation of traumatic battlefield amputations.

Five arms, seven hands, four legs, two torsos—one male, one female—three feet, and an entire jar of eyes made the list. In the basement was a makeshift morgue complete with an autopsy table and instrumentation.

This wasn't *a* horror movie it was *the* horror movie with enough material to create an entire library of nightmares. The most difficult part to deal with was the incongruity of the scene and the appearance of the person they had in custody.

Israel David Jenkins was not the image of a monster. Scrawny, thin as a meth addict but without bad teeth, he was anything but frightening. Pathetic, yes, frightening, never. Not the least bit intimidating despite his momentary bravado when they'd caught him.

He also wasn't someone who'd attract people. Combining that with his less than intimidating physicality made it even more confusing. He looked like someone who had never been in a fight or, if he had, would've lost badly.

Trying to meld the head in the bag and the scene in the house with the guy was counterintuitive. Josh recalled a seminar he'd attended about serial killers. Despite their portrayal on TV and in the movies, they were not the least bit scary at first sight.

They tended to be cordial, outgoing, friendly, and charismatic, and that was how they succeeded. They had a natural ability to make people relax in their presence. Part of their deception was the ability to physically overwhelm someone before they alarmed them to the danger.

They were lions silently creeping through the grass, impossible to see, then pouncing when the prey was most vulnerable.

None of this fit Jenkins. Which led to one horrifying conclusion. He didn't work alone.

Monsters don't attract people. The ones who hide the monster within are the most dangerous. A necessary and deadly skill for those inclined to hunt humans. Falling under the spell of personality was a mistake. It was dangerous, always. It could be fatal for their victims. That is what these predators did, hunt their victims for psychosexual, sadistic reasons.

Why they did it might play a part in a trial—a defense attorney might convince a jury this person could not control these urges—Josh and his team had to deal with the more practical part. Who were these victims, and how did they come to be members of this macabre dismemberment society?

And, more importantly, where were the real monsters masquerading as humans who did this to them?

X Always Best to Start at the Beginning

Tommy broke the silence. "Maybe we can create a jigsaw puzzle to figure out where the pieces go," he said. The remark was met by a roomful of incredulous stares.

"How the hell did you pass the psychological for the job?" Chief Brennan asked. "Whatever the hell is wrong with you is no little thing."

"Pass it? I was supposed to pass it?" Tommy answered.

The chief shook his head, massaging his forehead. "Okay, much as I am not inclined to do this, I think we need some more help with this one. What do you think, Major?"

Major Jasper Sutcliff, Detective Commander from the Rhode Island State Police nodded. "I agree. We need the Feebs on this one. Just the forensics alone will overwhelm both our agencies. Hell, it will overwhelm every agency in the state."

"Yeah," Josh whispered to Jerry Paulsen, "and give you someone else to blame."

Paulsen had to turn away to hide the smirk.

"Okay, Josh, you call the FBI office. Who was that agent you worked with last year on that gang shooting?"

"Freddy Robertson, Fred the Hammer. Great guy."

"Yeah, him. I liked him. And I don't usually say that about the Feebs."

"They can be a handful," Josh said, reaching for his cell phone.

"Handful?" Tommy said. "They use the seagull management approach. They come in, shit all over everything, then fly away, leaving us to clean up the mess."

Chief Brennan stared at Tommy. "You have a colorful way of saying things, Detective. You should have been a comedian. On second thought, you are a comedian; you just work at the wrong place."

"Thanks, Chief. I'll take that as a compliment."

"Of course you will," the chief said, then left the room with Major Sutcliff, saddling the troops with the job of managing the mess.

"Okay, we need things to move quickly," Josh said. "They won't be able to contain the story long; someone will tip the media." He turned his attention to the phone. "Hey, Fred, Josh Williams, give me a call ASAP. We have a good one on our hands and need some help." Josh tossed the phone on the desk.

"Tommy, you and Frank tear this guy's life apart. I want everything about him since birth. Dan, you and John go interview the neighbors. See if they can shed light on the guy.

"I figure we have about two hours before there's a herd of reporters flooding the neighborhood and everybody fighting for their fifteen minutes of fame. And I don't want..." He was interrupted by his cell buzzing.

Glancing at the screen, he furrowed his brow at the unrecognized number. "Josh Williams," he answered, and his face went red. "No, I won't be doing that. Not gonna happen. Go right ahead, call the Chief's office, I don't give a fuck. He'll tell you the same thing." Clicking off the call.

"Who was that?" Tommy asked.

"The fuckin' AG's public relations guy. Wants me to come to a press conference."

"You should go," Tommy said, a smirk crossing his face. "Hold the head up and ask if anyone recognizes them."

Even Josh couldn't help laughing at the image. Then, his phone rang again.

"Josh Williams. Hey, Fred, can you come over to the PD? We got a major headache on our hands and want to share the joy."

XI I'm From the Government...

The intercom system blared as the detectives huddled around the desk watching the news blizzard.

"Lt. Williams, call the receptionist,"

"Hey, Mary, what's up? Okay, be right there."

Josh entered the records division, stopping at the receptionist's cubicle.

"That's him," the receptionist said. "He showed me a badge, but I didn't want to let him in just in case he's some sleazy reporter."

Josh laughed. "Oh, he's even worse than that, Mary. He's the scum of the earth. Whale shit, which is on the bottom of the ocean. A real sleazeball."

"Oh, a friend of yours, then," Mary smiled.

"Yup, Fred Robertson, FBI."

"Oh my," Mary said, "I didn't realize."

Josh laughed. "No worries," He winked at the embarrassed woman. "He's used to it."

* * * * *

"So, what's with the high security?" Fred asked. "Last time, they just buzzed me in."

"Mary thought, and I agree, you looked suspicious."

"I get that a lot. So, what's the mystery? I noticed the media horde salivating in the front lot."

"We found a body."

"Just one? Must be someone unique to garner this attention."

"Some assembly required. It's body parts, lots of 'em. And I know you like puzzles."

Fred stopped in his tracks. "Lots of parts? I read about you guys finding some. What do you mean by lots?"

"Let's say enough to build several complete humans. And, I thought, who better to share the pleasure of fitting the pieces all together than my friend Fred the Fed?"

Fred took out his phone, searching through his contacts.

"What are you doing? Don't you want the details before you call the Grand High Poohbah at the Justice Department?"

"I'm not calling anybody; I'm blocking your number."

"Smart ass," Josh said, shaking his head. "Come on, we are all eager to be wowed by your wisdom, oh magnificent one."

XII   The Nightmare is Just Beginning

Josh, Tommy, Jerry Paulsen, and Fred Robertson stared at the list of body parts recovered from the house. If they hadn't seen it for themselves, they'd never believe it was real.

"I have to stop taking your calls, Josh." Fred said. "This is the stuff of nightmares."

"I have to learn to stop letting my guys talk me into these things," Josh added. "But here we are. So now what?"

"Well, I'll call DC and request a forensics team up here. No insult to your guys, Josh, but we have equipment worth more than the city budget. The DNA analysis will be a bear, but I think, under the circumstances, we'll have a priority push on it.

"I'll ask the US Attorney to put in a word with Justice. Good job on keeping the media in the dark so far. How'd you manage that?"

Josh chuckled. "I told the AG's press guy the only way I'd agree to a press conference now was if I could bring the head there for identification. It was Tommy's idea, although he was serious about it. I knew they'd choose to defer for the moment.

"Maybe you can have the US Attorney reach out and tell them any public release of info about the case had to come from the US Attorney herself. It might delay the inevitable leaks."

The internal landline rang, and Tommy grabbed it. "Yeah, uh huh, okay, got it." He slammed the phone down.

"Too late, there's a herd of reporters in the lobby and a couple of satellite trucks setting up in the front lot. They don't have the location yet, but that's only a matter of time."

The phone rang again. "Yeah, yeah, we know...oh sorry, Chief, didn't know it was you. Your office?" he pointed at Josh. "He's on the way."

While Josh and Fred went to the Chief's office, Tommy and Jerry went to peek at the media frenzy.

"Yikes, those aren't local guys, there's a couple of network ghouls leading the pack."

Jerry shook his head. "This is gonna turn into a cluster fuck."

Tommy smiled. "Watch this." He opened the side door, and the crowd charged toward him. Soon as they got close, he slammed it shut. "I love fucking with them. Stay here and watch."

Jerry watched the lobby as the crowd jockeyed to move closest to the door. Then, Tommy opened the door on the other side, and the crowd charged that way.

Once again, he slammed the door as the stampede approached,

Making his way back to Jerry, the smile on his face was huge.

"You keep doing that, and the whole station is gonna tip over."

"Just can't help myself," Tommy said. "Let's go get coffee. I have a feeling the next few hours will be damage control here. Then we'll head back to the house, after we grab coffee of course, and make sure we have it secured to keep the media crowd away."

XIII **Information Blackout**

Gathered in the conference room, the detectives considered their next move.

"You think the Chief's statement will keep them at bay?" Josh asked.

"It won't hold them for long, but at least it will buy us time for the forensic team to get here," Fred said. "The US Attorney got them sent right away. Guess it pays to be on the President's reelection committee.

"I had a text from the team commander. They are loaded up and should be in the air soon."

"Let's hope we can keep the scene for them," Josh said. "Damn area isn't called the maze for nothing."

As they sat in the office, Det. Harris and Lachance came back in.

"Anything?" Josh asked.

"The usual," Lachance said. "Nice guy, quiet, always waved, never seemed to be anything but a working guy. Couple reported seeing a couple of different vans at the house but didn't think anything of it.

"He's been there a while, but nobody really knew much about him."

"So, nothing, right?"

"Yup, nothing."

Okay," Josh said. "One of the uniform guys who works the area said he thought the guy came from Pawtucket. Give Pawtucket PD a call and see if they ever had any contact."

"John, see if you can find the guy on social media. We recovered two cell phones at the house and the one he had on him. Let's get warrants to search them. Do financial backgrounds as well and check the property listing. Could be something there."

"You got it, Lt.," Harris said, and fired up his computer.

"Anything else you can think of Fred?" Josh asked.

"Nope, you got it covered. I'll head to the airport and wait for the forensics team then take them to the scene. Once that happens, of course, the real circus will start. Let's make sure we have enough bodies to secure the perimeter."

"I can help with that," Jerry said. "Nothing the Colonel likes better than his uniform troopers on TV. I'm sure he'll send all we need."

Josh chuckled. "That'll keep my boss happy. Nothing he hates more than paying overtime for cops to stand around drinking coffee and flirting with reporters. Makes him nervous they'll start telling war stories about him."

Fred's cell rang. "Robertson. Yeah, no I understand. Let me make some arrangements." Ending the call.

"What was that all about?" Josh asked.

"They want me to arrange for the body parts to be sent to Quantico to expedite processing."

XIV   **Special Delivery**

Fred and Josh considered the best way to move the body parts to Quantico.

"A field trip?" Frank Lachance said. "I'll go."

Fred looked at the enthusiastic young detective. "God, I miss when I had that ambition. Okay, son, you're it. Problem is, how are we gonna pack them for transport? Gotta keep 'em frozen. There aren't that many coolers at Walmart."

Frank held up his hand. "Standby." He grabbed his cell and made a quick call.

"Thanks, Hank. I owe you one. What's that? Oh, yeah okay, I owe you a lot." Putting the phone down, he came back to the huddle. "Problem solved. Teamsters Local, of which I used to be a member before joining the PD, has a refrigerator truck available they use for training.

"They'll deliver it to us first thing in the morning. And just so happens I have a CDL license to drive such a vehicle."

"Frank," Josh said, "you are one of a kind. Who's gonna ride shotgun?"

"I guess that will be me," Fred said. "It will be easier getting the evidence submitted if an agent is with him."

* * * * *

The next morning, as promised, two Teamster trucks arrived at East Providence PD headquarters. The driver of the refrigerator truck, a giant of a man with a scar from above his right eye running all the way across his face to below his chin, battle scars from strikes in the past, jumped down and tossed the keys to Detective Lachance.

"I set it to -10º Fahrenheit, so it should stay frozen solid. What are you loading in there?"

"You really want me to tell you?" Frank asked.

The giant nodded.

"Body parts. Lots of 'em,"

The man turned away, blanching at the thought. "Sorry I asked." He climbed into the passenger seat in the other truck, and they drove away.

Frank looked at Josh. "I bet he *never* drives that truck again. I should find a mannequin arm and leave it in there when we're done."

Josh shook his head. "You're spending too much time with Moore. Stay away from him, he's a bad influence."

"Who's a bad influence?" Moore said, coming out of the front door of the station.

Josh smirked. "Like you have to ask."

* * * * *

It took the better part of the morning to document and load the ghoulish evidence into the truck. The process was deliberate and tedious, but necessary. They had no idea of knowing how many victims they were dealing with or where this case might lead.

Yet if they could identify the victims, relatives could take some comfort in the care exercised with their deceased family members.

"Ready to go, Frank?" Fred asked, glancing at his watch. "If we leave now, we'll miss the traffic on the bridge into New Jersey and be at Quantico by 7:00. The lab guys won't be happy, but shit happens."

"All set, I packed some food for the ride." A grin slowly crossed his face.

"Food? You packed food?"

"Yup, chicken fingers." Then let out a laugh.

Robertson shook his head. "What did Lt. Williams tell you about hanging around with Moore?"

"Get in the fucking truck, Frank," Josh said. "Drive carefully, you wouldn't want to explain to some troopers in New Jersey why you spread body parts all over I-95 if you have an accident."

Robertson chuckled as he climbed into the passenger seat. "You sure he's old enough to drive?" pointing his thumb at Lachance.

"He's got a learners permit, good luck," Josh said, shutting the door behind Robertson.

The engine came to life and the truck rolled slowly out of the lot. A state police cruiser led the way and would hand off the truck at the border to Connecticut state police and down the line until they reached Quantico.

Frank reached for the truck radio, but Robertson pushed his hand away. "No distracted driving for you. I pick the music." With a few clicks on the phone, he linked to the Bluetooth system.

Soon the sounds of smooth jazz filled the cab.

"You've got to be kidding me," Frank said. "We're gonna listen to that the whole way?"

"No, no. Of course, not," Roberston shook his head. "I'll change to something else at each state border. Next up will be some classical music and, of course, when we hit New Jersey, I'll play Simon and Garfunkel's *America.* You know, all come to look for America, watching the cars on the New Jersey Turnpike. Something to fit the mood of our mission."

Frank shook his head, checked the mirrors, and turned onto I-195 West. The state police had cleared the two emergency travel lanes due to the never-ending construction on the Washington Bridge, so the already aggravated public was seething as they flew past the stopped traffic.

"I hope they don't take it out on the Teamsters if they remember us driving by them," Robertson said.

"Don't worry about the Teamsters. They have a way of taking care of themselves."

Settling into the rhythm of the trip, Frank found himself enjoying the music. If he wasn't driving a truck loaded with severed limbs and torsos it might be a fun ride.

XV   Hidden in Plain Sight

Detectives Lynch and Harris walked in the office, both carrying file folders. Josh and Fred were going over the inventory list from the Quantico lab, making sure they matched the original list.

The trip to DC had been uneventful considering the contents of the truck and Frank had acquired a new affection for jazz music.

"Wha'cha find out, John? Any progress on the property records?" Josh asked.

"Oh yeah, got it right here," John said, dropping the folders and shuffling papers on the desk. "Yeah, here it is. The house was bought back in 1977 by Rose McGuire for $85,000. Taxes are up to date. No building permits or alterations made. And it was an all-cash deal, no mortgage was ever listed.

"McGuire used the address for voting records and her driver's license. The license expired in 1979, and she hasn't ever voted in the city or state from what I can find. No other vehicles registered there except the motorcycle.

"The housing authority cited her for failing to maintain the property due to overgrown trees and yard waste. The charge was dismissed when she put the property in compliance."

"Anything else? How old is she?"

Harris shrugged. "According to her last driver's license, she'd be fifty-four. But I can't find any records after the 1979 license expired. No other property in the city, no marriage certificates, death certificates, nothing.

"She just vanished."

"Okay. How about you, Frank? What've you got for us? Your little vacation is over you know."

Frank couldn't stop glancing at Fred, then went back to shuffling the papers on his desk. "Ah, a few things. Nothing startling but I, ah, I had..."

Fred stood up and stretched. "I think I'll take a walk outside." He walked over to Frank. "I'll be gone for exactly fifteen minutes. Use the time wisely."

Robertson walked out the door, pausing a moment to wink at Josh.

"He knows?" Frank said.

"Of course, he knows you got something using shall we say unorthodox methods. This way he can truthfully say he didn't hear anything."

Frank blushed for a moment, then took a deep breath. "Okay, ah, my brother works for the IRS, right? Criminal Investigator. He looked into some things and found some unusual banking transactions using the Washington Street address.

"He suspects money laundering. It's all older stuff, 80s and 90s, but was pretty substantial. Says we need a court order from a federal grand jury to, ah, see the records."

Tommy Moore laughed. "Wow, there's hope for you yet. And here I thought you were another Boy Scout acting all on my honor and stuff."

Frank blushed again. "You can't let anyone find out I talked to my brother. He'd lose his job."

Josh put his hand on Frank's shoulder. "Listen, you did good; lives are at stake here. Bending the rules isn't exactly the crime of the century. Fred will gin up an affidavit with a conveniently created, and quite ephemeral, confidential informant and provide the US Attorney enough probable cause for a grand jury subpoena for the information. Good work."

Josh went back to his desk, put his feet up, and tilted his chair back. "Okay, we know they used the place to launder money for a while then something triggered this descent into madness. What was it?"

XVI   Information Overload

Josh stared at the files piled on the table.

"I was worried this would happen," Josh said. "I was hoping we'd find something about the guy, but this is overload. We need to be a bit more methodical than our usual stampede approach."

Police departments all over the Rhode Island and Massachusetts had run-ins with him, most treated him as if he was a harmless nutcase.

He'd been field interviewed late at night wandering around neighborhoods, but there was never anything to connect him to anything criminal. Most agencies considered him one of those night people who wander around every city and town in America doing nothing but creeping people out.

The closest he'd come to getting arrested was when he ran on a cop in Scituate down near the reservoir. They caught up to him at the Johnston line, and held onto him until the morning to see if any reports of break-ins came in. When nothing happened, they dumped him back at the line and told him to stay out of Dodge.

Not entirely legal, but often effective. At least for the agency who warned him off.

And he had that inexplicable criminal luck. There was an error in the entry into NCIC for the warrant out of Massachusetts. Whoever entered the warrant transposed the date of birth. The EPPD dispatcher caught the error and verified the dob with the arresting agency when they ran him. Otherwise, if Josh and his team relied on the arrest warrant to take him into custody, things might have taken a different course.

A sharp lawyer could have filed a motion to suppress the search, and the head in the bag might have been inadmissible.

Tommy Moore and Dan Lynch looked at the stack of documents on the desk.

There was a missing person file from almost every department in the state, many with multiple files. Some cases were recent, most were years, if not decades, old. The preliminary results from Quantico put the date range of the body parts from one to ten years, but it wasn't precise. Some were older but the effect of freezing made identifying the age of the remains challenging.

All of the victims were adults, which somehow made it easier to deal with, but not much.

They needed to find relatives to gather DNA samples. That alone would take an army of detectives. East Providence didn't have an army, they had a squad. This would not be a quick case.

Then there were the guys in the AG's cold case unit. A new development on the political spectrum, they were salivating at the prospect of handling their first case.

They wanted a piece of the pie and were driving Josh crazy with requests.

And there were the public inquiries and tips. It ran the gamut from genuinely sad cases of parents seeking information on kids who'd run away to the psychic nutcases claiming they had visions of the faces linked to the bodies or that the body parts were used by aliens in experiments.

Josh let Moore deal with the lunatic fringe. "Takes one, Tommy, they are your people," he told the grumbling Moore.

The one thing that jumped out at everyone was the lack of any East Providence missing person reports in the last year. Everywhere else was their hunting ground; this was their home. As Tommy ineloquently put it, "You don't shit in your own backyard."

Sifting through all the reports, something kept nagging at Moore.

"Holy shit!" Tommy said, shuffling back and forth through a stack of papers. "Holy fucking shit!"

"What'd ya got, Tommy?" Josh asked.

"I couldn't figure it out at first," Tommys said, more to himself than Josh. "I couldn't see it because of the way I was looking at things."

Josh stood up and walked over. "See what, Tommy? You gonna share or what?"

"Look," Tommy said, pulling all the reports together. "I couldn't figure out why Jenkins was all over the place. On the dates he had contact with local cops, nothing happened. At first, I just thought he was a wandering nut, and it had nothing to do with our case.

"But then I looked at anything happening in the days after the contact. And lo and behold I saw it."

"Saw what?" Josh said, now standing right at Tommy's desk.

"Jenkins was a scout. He'd spot locations where they could snatch someone. There are three missing person reports, all females, reported within two or three days of the local cops rousting Jenkins.

"No one connected him to the case because, well, you know these missing person reports involving adults almost always turn out to be bullshit. With the cases that turned out to be a real missing person, no one ever connected their contact with Jenkins and the actual disappearances.

"I bet there are some matching cases in Massachusetts as well."

"Good work, Tommy," Josh said. " Ties the little rat fuck in a nice little knot."

XVII   Organizing Horrors

To keep things organized, they created a spreadsheet with a tab for each "individual." Josh rejected naming the parts—Moore had suggested Peg for one of the legs—but even without the macabre humor the results were equally ghoulish.

Unknown Person One, Left leg. Unknown Person Two, Right leg with foot, etc. Until they had the results from the DNA profiling, they treated each limb as a separate individual.

The media, always quick with catchy phrases, had dubbed the case the Frankenstein Murders which compounded the number of calls from the lunatic fringe.

Once the furor died down, most reporters sought other means of scooping their competition. One reporter went so far as to hack into the local power company to check the electric bills.

When that failed, she took to interviewing meteorologists about the severity of thunderstorms including images of the rusted and bent TV antenna attached to the house casting shades of mad scientist laboratory.

All that was missing was a crowd of angry citizens with torches and pitchforks. Never doubt the creativity of bored reporters on slow news days.

Time worked its inevitable magic, driving the press to focus on other things, but they knew there was more coming. They kept the story alive with the occasional updates and interviews with long retired cops and FBI agents trying to recapture the glories of their past careers.

Ignoring the distraction, Josh and his SIU team, along with the state police and FBI, continued to interview witnesses and potential family members, and track down the suspect's life history.

It took almost a month for the lab at Quantico to complete the analysis of the body parts.

The results were staggering. They'd positively identified nine individuals, tentatively ID'd three, and could not ID five more. They had seventeen victims from the body parts alone, with evidence of others in blood and DNA recovered in the processing of the scene.

The wall in the SIU looked like a macabre puzzle collection with body part images bearing names, partial IDs, or FNU LNU designations.

What they needed was for Israel David Jenkins to agree to an interview, but the public defender had other ideas, at least until they could work out a plea deal.

For the moment, the team would keep plugging away.

XVIII Something Wicked This Way Comes

Ten weeks from the day they discovered the house of horror, Josh was sitting sipping coffee in his office. Fred Robertson sat at another desk reviewing the latest reports from the field.

Tommy Moore came bopping in. "Hey Lt., what's with the black SUVs out front?"

Josh looked over his coffee cup. "What SUVs, Tommy?"

"Out front, two of 'em. And a whole host of guys that look like Fred the Fed here, only nicer suits. You know, not off the rack."

Robertson never looked up, just flipped Tommy the bird.

Josh put the cup down and started for the door when his desk phone rang. At the same moment, Robertson's cell chimed in.

"This can't be good," Tommy said, staring at his own phone, "for you guys. I'm not invited."

"Yeah, Chief," Josh said. "Yup, Fred's here with me. Okay, be right there."

Josh hung up the phone and then looked at Robertson. His eyes gave it away, this was trouble.

"What's wrong with you?" Josh asked.

"Ah, nothing, nothing. Just that was the Deputy Director of the FBI. I don't get many calls from those guys."

"They want us in the Chief's conference room."

"Yeah, Josh, I know."

Josh studied Robertson's expression. He knows something he's not telling me. I bet they're gonna take the case away from us, and he doesn't want to be part of it.

"Come on, Fred, Let's go listen to why we're incapable of handling this and need to give it up."

Robertson didn't move or reply.

"Earth to Fred, earth to Fred. Come in, Fred. You in there?" Josh said, tapping him on the head.

"What, yeah, let's go," Fred said and made a beeline for the door.

XIX An Inquisition of Sorts

As Josh and Fred walked into the conference room, the conversation stopped.

"Now I'm sure this is bad news," Josh said, trying to smile and lighten the mood. "Okay, I'll save us all time. You're moving the case out of our hands because it's beyond our resources. I understand why you might think that, but let me ..."

The Chief held up his hand. "That's not it, Josh. Please sit down and listen."

Josh glanced at Robertson, who'd moved to the back of the room, whispering to an agent Josh had never met. Josh took a seat and waited.

"Josh," the Chief said, "this is Deputy Director Wilfred Jones. He runs the Forensics, Digital Analysis, and Behavioral Analysis Unit sections of the bureau."

Josh nodded.

The Chief waved his hand around the room. "The rest of these agents all work for the Deputy. We will be adding them to the overall investigation, supporting us from Quantico."

Josh hesitated a moment before he spoke; he knew there was something more to this. There was no way they'd fly all these agents up here to introduce themselves.

"And?" Josh said.

The Chief cleared his throat. "And, ah, I'm gonna let Deputy Director Jones explain the rest.

Josh turned in his seat to face Jones. "Director," he said, nodding at the bespectacled man who looked more like a mad scientist than an FBI agent.

"Josh, are you familiar with mitochondrial DNA?"

"I am, kind of. You inherit it from your mother, correct?"

"That's correct. We use it to link offspring to parents. It can be useful, particularly in cases like this where there are multiple mitochondrial exemplars.

"And in this case, we were able to use it for many of the samples for identification."

Josh nodded. "I understand all that. But you didn't need to come here to explain that. A phone call would do just as well." Josh leaned forward, folding his hands on the table. "With all due respect, Director, get to your point."

Jones glanced around the room. A female agent spoke up from the crowd, the one Fred was speaking with in back. Jones looked at her and nodded.

"Josh, my name is Jennifer Holmes. I run the FBI cold crime database at Quantico."

Josh nodded.

"The director brought me into the case to run the DNA evidence recovered at your crime scene."

My crime scene, Josh thought, they're not taking it away from us, they've found something bigger.

Holmes walked to stand near Josh, then continued. "My background is DNA forensic analysis. We ran all the unidentified samples against our database, and we got a hit on a cold case from 1976. It was a kidnapping and murder. Fourteen-month-old twins, a boy and a girl, taken from an apartment. The female infant's body was recovered a few days later. The boy was never found.

"I was surprised the DNA was in the file, cases back then didn't have access to DNA testing. Some enterprising investigator must have followed up at a later date and submitted the old evidence.

"The State of Rhode Island charged the parents, Rose and Richard Martins with murder and sexual assault on the female child and kidnapping and murder of the male child.

"The father was found not guilty after trial, the case against the mother was dismissed. It is an unsolved case."

"So, you're saying our guy is the missing boy?" Josh asked.

The stress indicators on the agent's face gave him the answer.

"No, he is not the missing boy, but he does have a genetic link to other DNA recovered at the scene." The agent took a deep breath, then looked Josh directly in the eye.

"We also ran the samples against a broad range database. This includes criminal, military, and security clearance DNA profiles and got a mitochondrial match from the military data."

Josh leaned a little more in, resting his elbows on the table, hands folded in front of his face. "So, you have a suspect for us? Someone who might be involved?"

The agent glanced at her file. "We have identified an individual who shares the mitochondrial DNA markers with the murdered infant from 1976.

"While we can't be certain, we believe that individual to be the missing brother of the murdered infant."

Josh glanced around the room. He knew from experience that everyone in that room knew something he didn't, waiting to gauge his reaction when they told him.

"Okay, so who is it, and where can we find him?"

Holmes spun the sheet in front of her around and slowly slid it to Josh. He grabbed the sheet and quickly read through the standard evidence report identifiers in the first few lines.

Finding the results section, his brain went into overdrive. He felt his heart rate spike and the rest of the room seemed to darken. He was alone with the words on the page.

"DNA profile matches with 99.998% certainty with the sample taken from USAF recruit Joshua Williams, United States Air Force, Lackland AFB, 21-January-1991.

"The DNA match is the likely fraternal twin of Rose Martins."

The rest of the paper was a blur. Josh fell back into the chair, staring at the ceiling.

XX   Everything I Believed True Was a Lie

The chief looked around the table."Let us have the room," the Chief said.

Director Jones started to object.

Chief Brennan, a giant of a man, rose from the seat. Standing 6'8" tall, he was not easily intimated or ignored.

"Let me remind you, you are here as my guests. I will have a word in private with the lieutenant here, and you will extend the courtesy of accommodating me. Please wait outside the conference room."

The director stood, and the crowd started for the door.

"Agent Robertson, stay please," the Chief said. Fred looked at the Deputy Director who nodded.

Once the room was emptied, the Chief took his seat.

"Josh, I apologize for the ambush. They told me they had significant information to share. I should have known the feds would try to fuck with you on this. They see ghosts in the architecture." He turned to Robertson, "Present company excepted."

Fred nodded and then took a seat next to Josh.

"Josh," Fred said, putting his hand on his shoulder, "You okay?"

Josh shook his head and shrugged. "I don't know. It's a bit much to take in. I mean, I knew I was adopted. My parents told me as soon as I was old enough. They said someone found me wandering alone when I was about two and the state placed me in foster care.

"I never had any desire to find out what happened to my biological parents. I mean, what kind of parent loses a two-year-old and doesn't go looking for them?"

Chief Brennan stared into space, pacing the room. "The feds are gonna want you off this. But..."

Josh's anger rose to the surface but calmed down when Brennan put up his hand.

"But, that ain't gonna happen," Brennan glanced at Robertson, then turned back to Josh.

"I'm gonna let you in on a little secret. I'm leaving this year. I've had enough. I had planned to leave two months ago but then this shit happened so I couldn't.

"I turn sixty-five at the end of the year and they're gonna make me pull the pin, but I wanted to go on my schedule. But I will tell you this. We are gonna bring them back in here and I will make it very clear you stay on this case if that's what *you* want."

"Damn straight, Chief. This may be personal but it's still the biggest case we've ever had. There is no way I'm leaving it." He tilted his head toward the door. "They might not agree."

"Fuck 'em if they want otherwise. Our city, our case. If they don't like it, they can pull their troops out. But I have a feeling they won't want to miss out on the good press. Lord knows they need it.

"Fred, what do you think?"

Josh and the Chief both locked eyes on him. "They'll put up a bit of a show, rant and rave about compromising prosecutions, but in the end, it is your case. Bottom line is, at this point, we don't have jurisdiction anyway. That can change, but for now we are here by invitation. I think you can persuade them to agree to leave things as is."

"Go get 'em, let's set 'em straight on this and move on."

XXI The Way of the World

Brennan watched the parade fill the room, Director Jones leading the way.

"Okay, I want to make one thing straight before we continue. I've talked to Josh about this situation, and I believe it is in the best interest of the case he remains involved."

Jones started to object, but Brennan put up a hand.

"If you would, Director, hear me out."

Jones nodded for Brennan to continue.

"I've known Josh since his first days out of the academy. Since then, he's had an exemplary career. While these are unique circumstances, I want everyone in this room to understand me. My decision is not negotiable. While we appreciate the help from the bureau, this matter is an East Providence case and will remain as such.

"If the bureau does not wish to continue assisting in this matter, we will accept that and carry on. If they choose to stay involved, we welcome it and will carry on. But in either case, Josh is the senior officer in charge. That's the way of the world here at EPPD."

Brennan paused to gauge the reaction. Most heads were nodding, there were a few silent but obvious dissenters, and Director Jones seemed lost in thought.

"So, what's it gonna be?"

Jones cleared his throat. "Chief, while I will not hide my reservations over Lieutenant Williams's continued involvement in this case, and I want to be clear this is my professional opinion not rising out of any personal issue, the bureau will respect your decision. Lieutenant Williams will continue to have our full support and cooperation.

"There is one more thing. I would like to assign Special Agent Jennifer Holmes here to the case full-time. Since DNA forensics are going to be a critical part of any prosecutions arising from the case, her forensic background will be invaluable."

"Fine," Brennan said, "We appreciate the help." Brennan glanced at his watch. "Okay, we spent enough time on the peripherals, let's go back to work and see who else might have had a hand in this case."

As the crowd filed out, Brennan held Josh back.

"Listen, Josh, I understand this has been a bit of a shock. If you want to take the rest of the day to digest it, go for it. The feds will be priming their spy, Agent Holmes, to keep them in the loop. I bet they think Roberston has gone native on them."

Josh chuckled "He may need a new job before this is over. You hit it on the head. Holmes is a good agent but young and ambitious. She'll be their eyes and ears here. We need to keep that in mind if there's going to be any coloring outside the lines. I trust Fred, but there's no need to create complications."

It was Brennan's turn to chuckle. "I can see why you trust him. He's not the typical fed, is he?"

"He'd take that as a compliment," Josh said, then his eyes went blank as he looked to the floor.

"What is it, son?"

"Something that came up in the property search. Harris found the name Rose Maguire linked to the property. He couldn't find anything else about her.

"But Rose...hmm. I wonder if she might be a.k.a. Rose Martins, my sainted birth mother? Too many coincidences for me."

"Jesus, this is getting weirder by the minute," Brennan said.

"Chief," Josh said. "I think I will take you up on that offer. I want to go talk to my wife about this before she hears it from anyone else."

"Go, I'll see you in the morning. Fred can cover you with the troops, right?"

"Yeah. Fred can handle that. Thanks, Chief."

"No thanks necessary, Lieutenant. You keep in mind that what happened all those years ago doesn't change what you are today, okay?"

Josh nodded, reaching for the door.

"And one more thing," Brennan said, a smile breaking out on his face. "If you're gonna fuck this up, wait until I am retired, okay?"

"Thanks for the vote of confidence, Chief."

"You're welcome."

XXII   Blood is Thicker

Keira Williams leaned against the kitchen cabinet looking out the window as Josh pulled into the driveway. Hmm, she thought, sneaking home for a little afternoon romp are we, Mr. Williams?

Josh came up the stairs from the garage and put his briefcase on the floor. Walking over to his wife, he wrapped his arms around her.

"Playing hooky from school, are we?"

"Sort of," Josh said. As he nuzzled her shoulder, his muffled voice told her something else was going on.

She pushed him away. "What's wrong?"

"Nothing's wrong, well, I mean, it's something I want you to hear from me."

"I'm not liking the sound of this. You remember I am an amazingly effective divorce lawyer, right?" She smiled, trying to lighten the mood.

"Nothing like that," he answered. "Besides, I know you. You'd bury me, not divorce me."

"True. Gun, shovel, and alibi on standby. So, what is it? Tell me. Whatever, we'll find a way through it."

Josh took her by the hand and led her to the couch near the fireplace. He took a deep breath, and the story came pouring out.

Keira put her arms around him. "Oh, Josh, I'm so sorry. But it makes no difference to me, to us. I'd love you no matter what happened in the past. You were a baby, what happened then was out of your control."

Reaching for both hands, she pulled him up from the couch, dragging him toward the stairs.

"Where are we going?" Josh asked.

"Do you really have to ask?"

* * * * *

Later that afternoon, they'd come down from the bedroom, taking their dog, Tripod, for a walk in the woods. Tripod sniffed every blade of grass, wrestled with sticks twice his size and weight, and chased squirrels and rabbits.

Something difficult to do for a three-legged dog.

Two months ago, Josh spotted the dog in a kennel at the East Providence Animal Control facility. Found abandoned beside the road, the staff had little hope anyone would adopt a dog missing his left front leg.

Having lost their lab, Cassidy, to cancer, Josh had sworn no more dogs. Then, he made the mistake of looking at the dog's eyes. The rest was history. Even Kiera fell in love at first sight with the goofy dog.

They walked in silence, holding hands and enjoying the warm, afternoon sun. A bountiful spring made the woods a vibrant leafy green.

"Are you gonna tell your mother?" Keira asked, breaking the silence.

"I probably should. She and my dad were always open about the past. They said it was up to me if I wanted to find out more, but I never did." He stopped in his tracks, eyes closed, absorbing the sun through a gap in the canopy of the forest.

"Now, I am gonna have to find out a lot more than I ever wanted to."

"Together, Josh. We'll do this together."

Josh hugged her, then whistled for Tripod. "Come on, gimpy. Hurry up." The dog bounced over in his ungainly yet surprisingly quick gait. "No treats here. Back at the house."

At the sound of the word, house, Tripod was halfway there before they came out from the woods.

XXIII Living in the Past

At the office before 8:00 a.m., Josh was eager to see where this would take him. As he sat at his desk, the door to the office opened, and Chief Brennan walked in.

Josh rose.

Brennan waved his hand, "No need, Lieutenant. You know you're the only one in the entire department who does that, right?"

"Old habits, Chief. Old habits."

Brennan collapsed into one of the chairs and spun it around to face Josh. "So, how are things?"

"Fine. I told Keira everything. She's ready for whatever comes from this."

"Are you?" Brennan asked, eyes locked on Josh, rolling the chair to the edge of Josh's desk.

"Chief, I learned a long time ago that it's a mistake to live in the past. All it does is create turmoil. Nothing changes. My sister was murdered, my biological parents were charged with the murder, and one was found not guilty. The case is an unsolved homicide. These are the cases cops live for.

"As far as I'm concerned, I have a responsibility to try and find out what really happened. More importantly, we have new victims from the more recent past, with relatives who have a right to know what happened to their loved ones. That's what I am going to focus on.

"I'm okay with it. I always knew someday I might find out more about my past. This is that time. I just didn't expect it to play out quite this way."

"Who would?" Brennan said, stood, and then looked at Josh. "And what if you find out your parents *were* responsible for what happened to your sister and you?"

Josh closed his eyes for a moment, gathering his thoughts. "Then I guess I won't be bragging about my biological parents to anyone, will I? Besides, I had a mom and dad. That's all that matters."

Brennan nodded. "Good for you, son. You keep reminding yourself about that."

They heard a key clicking into place and muffled voices outside the door, Tommy Moore's easily recognized non-stop chatter. Brennan moved with remarkable speed to block the door from opening.

Moore struggled against the resistance, and Brennan held him back.

"Open the fucking door, moron!" Moore yelled. "Or I will kick your ass all over the parking lot."

Brennan waited until Moore put his back into it, then stepped aside. The detective came flying in, tumbled to the ground, and started yelling all manner of threats.

As he jumped to his feet, he ran into all six foot eight of Chief Brennan.

"Ah, good morning, Chief. I, ah, I'll call maintenance to fix that door. Somebody might get hurt."

Brennan smiled, then strode out the door. Josh shook his head.

"Tommy, it is always an adventure with you."

"How was I supposed to know El Hefe was in here?" he said, rubbing his head where he hit it on the wall. "Next time, text me."

"Nah, I enjoyed the morning entertainment."

* * * * *

Over the next few minutes, the rest of the team sauntered in. Josh dragged them all into the Chief's conference room to give them more space. He and Fred Robertson laid out the plan.

"Okay, first, we need somebody to head over to Pawtucket PD for copies of the original case file," Josh said. "Frank, you and John handle that. Tommy, you head over to the AG's office and get their files."

Josh shuffled some of his notes.

"Once we have those files, we'll need to go through them for anything that might link them to our suspect. Fred, where are we with ID'ing the other victims?"

"Okay, we have a total so far of seventeen vics. Nine identified, four tentative ID's, and four unknowns. Quantico is running all DNA samples and the prints we lifted through all the databases. It will take some time for it all to percolate back to us.

"In addition to the ones we've identified, the forensics team recovered blood and DNA evidence not related to the body parts, including the one involving Josh here.

"That case, the murdered infant, may be the key to understanding what we're dealing with here."

Robertson looked at Josh. "I have a suggestion here to keep the DC crowd off our back."

"What's that?"

"Let me deal with anything related to the historical case from Pawtucket; you run the body parts aspect. It will provide an aura of separation that will keep them less likely to pull the case as we make progress.

"Bottom line is we have no idea where this is gonna take us." He turned his attention to SA Jennifer Holmes. "Jennifer, what do you think?"

"I think that's smart, Fred. Whoever the AUSA is they assign to the case, assuming we take the case federal, will be getting all sorts of pressure from DC. The less we give them to use, the better it will be for us to control the case. And there is one more thing we need to consider and be prepared to handle."

"What's that?" Fred said.

"The media storm when they find out about Josh being related to the murdered infant. There's no way this is gonna stay out of their hands."

Josh rubbed his forehead, resting his elbow on the desk.

"Josh?" Fred asked.

He hesitated for a moment, then leaned back in his chair. "So, we hold a press conference and release the information."

"I'm not sure that's a good idea," Fred said.

"Fred, if one of the news stations gets the story, they'll play it up for all its worth. Then, the rest of them will play catch-up, trying to out-story the story.

"If we bring 'em all in together, put it out there in our own way, we get to contain the free-for-all."

"You up for all that?" Jennifer asked. "It would have to come from you to make it work."

"Well, I didn't join the PD to be a press spokesperson," Josh said. "But if that's what it takes, that's what it takes. When do we do this?"

Jennifer looked at Fred. "You're gonna have to convince the powers that be in the US Attorney's and the AG's offices. She's gonna catch shit from DC. The AG will worry about the effect on his campaign."

"No worries, we catch shit from DC all the time, and she'll handle it. Josh, you and I will talk to her today. A call to the AG will suffice. He seems good with plausible deniability. Then, we can plan the news conference for tomorrow."

"No, Friday," Moore interjected, causing everybody to look at him.

"Friday, why Friday?" Josh asked.

"Everybody knows you release bad news on Friday, so by Monday, it's all faded away."

"Boy has a point," Fred added. "Friday it is."

XXIV The Art of Information Control

The door to the inner offices opened and a young woman walked out. "The US Attorney will see you now," the aide said.

"Thank you," Fred replied, leading Josh down the corridor to the conference room.

As they entered the room, they were greeted by Crisha Michelson, the US Attorney for the District of Rhode Island, and Assistant US Attorney Charles "Chap" Nyland.

"Good morning, Fred. Good morning, Josh," Crisha said, extending her hand. Her grip always surprised people. Before joining the US Attorney's Office as an AUSA and later rising to become the US Attorney, Crisha spent ten years with the Rhode Island State Police.

She kept herself in excellent physical condition, and her appearance masked her physical strength. Yet it was her brilliant mind that set her apart from most. While most US Attorneys were smart, she was in a class of her own.

Many saw her as a possible candidate for the Senate when the venerable senior United States Senator for Rhode Island, Antonio Vincent Delgado, decided to step down.

"Is it safe to assume this has something to do with that nightmare of a case you're dealing with?"

Fred nodded. "Crisha, I'm gonna let Josh explain."

"Well, have at it, Josh. We haven't spoken since that disaster of a case with your friend Hawk Bennett blew up my world. There seems to be a pattern with you."

"That was a fun one, wasn't it?" Josh said. "I'm glad I avoided most of that. Anyway, you're right. This is about the body parts case. Are you aware of my connection to the case?"

"Indirectly. The visiting dignitaries from DC did not see fit to illuminate this office on the results of their meeting. But I have my own sources telling me there is a twist."

Josh smiled. "I'm sure you do, and twist doesn't even come close. Back in the mid-seventies, there was a case out of Pawtucket involving kidnapped fourteen-month-old twins, a boy and a girl. The girl's body was found a few days later. The boy was never found.

"They charged the parents and tried the father first. He was acquitted, so they decided not to pursue the case against the mother."

'And what, you found evidence regarding the missing boy at this house in East Providence?"

Josh took a deep breath. "Sort of."

"Sort of? What does that mean?"

Josh folded his arms across his chest. "I *am* that missing boy."

* * * * *

"Well, that went about as well as expected," Fred said as they made their way out to the car. "At least she agreed to let us hold the press conference."

"Yeah, I suppose that's true. But she wants it here."

"And she's doing us a favor. We get ahead of the media storm, and she takes the heat from DC from anybody with their panties in a bunch because we stole their thunder. It's a win-win for us, Josh. Now we can focus on what we have to do."

XXV You Can't Pick Your Relatives

A fiftyish woman with unnaturally blonde hair piled on top of her head sat a desk eating an éclair. Crumbs littering the desk clearly established this was not her first pastry of the day.

The other hint being her chair was invisible beneath her giant ass.

"Who wants the file?" the records clerk mumbled, crumbs escaping from her maw adding to the growing pile, not even bothering to look up.

"I'm Detective Frank Lachance and this is Detective John Harris. We're from East Providence Police, and we have evidence relating to this case."

"So, contact the detective handling it," she said, glancing at the two detectives.

"We can't."

Putting her coffee mug to the side, she stared at the two men. "Why not?"

Frank started to answer when John broke in. "Because he's fucking dead. Everybody who worked on that case is probably dead. How about you move your fat, lazy ass out of that chair and go find me the case file or, if you're incapable of that, the officer in charge of this joke of a records division.

"How about you try doing your job?"

"I will not be spoken to like that," she huffed, her jowls bright red..

"I just did," Harris answered. "Now waddle over there and find me someone with a brain."

The woman's jaw slowly opened, but no words came out. She stood up, slammed a file on the desk, and disappeared into the back office.

A few moments later, the stereotypical cop with thirty years on the job, as shown by the row of hash marks extending to his elbow on his uniform sleeve, came shuffling out of the back office.

From his appearance, this was the most exercise he'd had in decades. One of his Lieutenant's bars hung crooked on his collar, the other was missing.

A clip-on tie hung from a handcuff-shaped tie clip, something last seen in a fifties cop show. The white shirt, or at least originally white, had stains covering stains all along the front.

The man was a testament to someone incapable of doing anything remotely connected to actual police work. Burying guys like him in records was an act of mercy. His ass wouldn't fit in a police car.

"Oh boy, I know this guy," Frank mumbled under his breath. "I needed a file from here once before. If you thought she was stupid, he'll make her seem like the President of Mensa."

"Mensa? What's Mensa?" John said.

Frank glanced at him sideways. "Never mind," turning back to smile at the red-faced, mouth-breathing, agitated records division commander.

"Lieutenant McElroy, how are you, sir."

"Never you mind how I am. Who do you think you are coming here and talking to my people that way?"

"Just a misunderstanding, Lieutenant, a bad attempt at humor by my associate here. Did your clerk explain the reason for our visit?"

"She did. That file is in the archives."

The statement ended there. No further explanation seemed forthcoming.

"Well, how can we get it from the archives?" Lachance asked.

"Get it? Why do you need it again?"

"Did you read about the case we have with all the body parts?"

"No, I don't do any police work outside of this office."

Harris turned away and whispered, "He hasn't done any police work since he weighed under three hundred pounds."

Lachance kicked him in the leg. "Well, Lt., it is a very important case that may, and I emphasize *may*, have something to do with the case file we're asking about. It's important we get it."

The resignation on the man's face said he now knew there was no way to avoid his getting the file. He sighed, then leaned against the counter winded from his half marathon walk from his office.

"Well, the archives are in the basement, three floors down, and the elevator doesn't go there. I'll have to go get it myself. Come back later," and started to waddle away.

"When later, Lt.?" Frank asked.

"Later, after I have a chance to locate the file. I have other duties. Use your best judgment on coming back."

Completing the marathon, the lieutenant disappeared back into his office.

"Well?" Frank said. "When should we come back?"

"Three floors, no elevator. My best judgment is to wait until we see the rescue pull up to the front of the station. The fat bastard hasn't walked up and down three flights of stairs since the Civil War."

Frank let out a laugh.

"Frank," a voice called out. "What the fuck are you doing here?"

"Hey, George, how are you?"

"Great. What's up?

"John, this is George Montgomery. We went to the academy together. George, meet John Harris. We work together in SIU."

After the pleasantries, Frank explained their dilemma.

"Hah, Lieutenant Jabba the Hut hasn't been in the archives in centuries. He'll try to ignore you, and then, if that fails, he'll complain to the front office about how busy he is and needs more help.

"You'll have the file sometime next year if you wait for him. Hang here for a moment."

Ten minutes later, Montgomery returned.

"Come on," George said, shaking a set of keys in the air. "I know where he hides 'em in his office. Well, he doesn't really hide them. He leaves them hoping someone will do what I am about to do. I'll find the file for you."

* * * * *

Back in the car, Frank thumbed through the file, blanching at the crime scene images of the dead infant. "She almost looks like she's asleep." He muttered to himself.

"What?" John asked.

"Nothing, I don't like seeing dead kids."

"Really, you might want to consider a career change, it sort of goes with the territory."

"Yeah, I know. I had a call once when I was in uniform. I walk into the house, and a woman hands me a dead baby. SIDS death. She was screaming at me to save her.

"The baby was long dead, cold...nothing I could do," he turned away, looking out the window, wiping at his eyes.

"That happened the day after I found out my wife was pregnant with our first."

"Wow, that sucks man. Sorry."

"Like you said, goes with the territory. But, weird this whole thing about the Lieutenant, eh?"

"It's a strange world, partner."

"Yeah, I mean, how do you deal with the possibility that your parents killed your twin sister and tossed you away?"

"You can't pick your relatives. Besides, Josh is a smart and resourceful guy. He'll see his way through this and, when this case is over, we'll all have a war story to beat all war stories."

XXVI **The Stuff of Nightmares**

Josh looked up from the file on his desk. "Hey Frank, can you call the AG's office and see if they have contact information for a former Assistant AG named Charles Goforth?

"He was the original prosecutor. Far as I can tell he's still alive, but the Bar Association shows his license as inactive."

"Sure, boss, I'm on it," reaching for the phone.

"Can I ask you something, Fred?"

"Ask away."

"One thing bothers me. Did you see that report from the two cops who went into the apartment the night before? I looked at the list of documents in the discovery filing and the one the PD kept for their files.

"The statement isn't listed in the discovery list."

"No, I didn't see that. Maybe an oversight?"

"Could be, sometimes these major cases overwhelm people. Just thought it was odd."

"Wouldn't the defense pick up on the discrepancy? Focus on that kind of inconsistency to create doubt?"

"Perhaps. Or maybe the PD never gave them the internal document. That or the statement came *after* the initial reports were put together."

"You are the suspicious sort, aren't you, Lieutenant?"

"Key to my success." Josh closed the file and handed it back.

"Thanks for letting me read through it. Not trying to overstep our arrangement, but if the prosecutor is still breathing, he might have some other information that didn't make it into the file."

Fred nodded, put the file into a box on his desk, then put it on top of four other boxes stacked on the floor. "Believe it or not, we have some more files coming in from DC by courier today. They've identified two more victims and recovered other DNA from some more unknown ones.

"And are you ready for the best part?"

"Sure," Josh said, leaning back in his chair.

"The eyes were pickled."

"Oh, what the fuck," Tommy groaned, "I love pickles. Now I can never have pickles again."

"Pickled? This maniac was *eating* this stuff?" Josh said.

"It would appear so. This is becoming a thing of nightmares. But no need for us to starve. What say we grab lunch before they get here? It's gonna be a long night. And," looking around the office, "I think we need more space."

"I have an idea," Tommy said.

"I am almost afraid to hear this," Fred said.

Tommy flipped him off. "Let's use the exercise room downstairs."

"Isn't that where the cops work out?"

Tommy shook his head. "Nah, why would they go there when the local gym has more pleasant scenery? The only cops who go there use it as a cheap alternative to a hotel room when they get the heave-ho from the wife.

"I'll admit I spent a few days there during my second marriage."

"Why not the first one?" Fred asked.

"I was in the Marine Corps then. When she divorced me, I already had the squad bay."

"And is there another Mrs. Moore? Post-second wife?"

"Oh yeah," Moore smiled. "But I'm a changed man. I've seen the error of my ways."

Fred glanced sideways at Moore, eyes narrowed.

"This one's rich," Josh explained. "Daddy owns thirty or so restaurants and bars all over the world."

"Ah, I understand why you've reformed."

Moore smiled and pointed at the Rolex on his wrist. "Lunch time. We can go to Greggs; I love their pickles," then let out a laugh. "When we get back, I'll have maintenance change the lock, evict any cops in exile down there, and set the hall surveillance camera to monitor the door."

Fred shook his head. "When this is over, I'm gonna have the Behavioral Analysis Unit do a study of you. You're not from this planet."

XXVII **This is Why I Quit College**

Tommy walked over to Jennifer's desk."So how exactly do you get DNA out of the tissue?" Moore asked.

SA Jennifer Holmes looked over her glasses at the detective. "You really want to know, Tommy?"

"I do. It might help me understand the process."

"Okay, it is fairly straightforward. The process of extracting DNA from frozen tissue begins with thawing the tissue in a lysis buffer. This buffer contains detergents, enzymes, and salts that break down the cell membranes and proteins, allowing the DNA to be released into the solution.

"The lysate is then centrifuged to separate the cellular debris from the DNA-containing supernatant. The supernatant is then treated with agents to remove proteins, lipids, and other impurities while preserving the DNA. The purified DNA is then precipitated and centrifuged, and the pellet of DNA is resuspended in a buffer. Finally, the DNA is ready to be used for downstream applications.

"The extracted DNA is then mapped and compared to known samples or for submission to databases for searches."

Josh, seeing the blank stare on Tommy's face, chuckled. "Jennifer, you lost him right after 'fairly straightforward.'"

It was Jennifer's turn to laugh. "How about this? We squeeze the DNA juice out and create the profile from that."

"Got it," Tommy said. "That other stuff is what made me quit college." Happy with his newfound DNA knowledge, he went back to reading through the file from the AG's office.

"Josh," Jennifer said, "can I ask you something? Feel free to tell me no."

"Go ahead, ask away."

"Why didn't you ever try to find your biological parents?"

"Hmm, well, I suppose it was a couple of things. While my parents never told me not to, I had a feeling they'd be disappointed somehow. And to be honest, I really didn't want to know. As it turned out, these things have a way of coming out no matter what we do.

"What is the Buddhist saying? Three things cannot long be hidden, the sun, the moon, and the truth."

"Wow, a philosopher cop. I'm impressed."

"We're not all as dumb as Tommy over there. Some of us can actually read."

"I heard that," Tommy said, without looking up.

Josh chuckled. "Seriously, Jennifer. How do you think the DNA from my, ah, my sister—seems so weird to be saying that— got there? I mean, the body was found twelve miles from there thirty-two years ago. From what I recall in reading the, ah, the ah, the news stories in the Providence Journal archives there were no obvious physical injuries on the body. The cause of death was asphyxiation."

Josh shrugged, opening his hands in a gesture of confusion. "How *did* her DNA end up there?"

Jennifer tapped her fingers on the desk, composing her thoughts. She took a deep breath, then slowly released. "In my experience dealing with young victims, absent any blood, the most common way DNA is deposited at a scene is one of two ways: sexual contact or tears.

"Tommy, was there evidence of sexual penetration of the infant? I haven't read the file."

"The ME said no penetration but there was some evidence of vaginal abrasion. The father claimed he masturbated while holding the child," Tommy said. "He gave a statement to the state police when they asked him about semen stains on the blanket they found wrapped around the body. Fucking perv."

Jennifer nodded. "Well then, it is likely that was not a one-off incident. If the father brought the infant to the house, and there was some other sexual contact, that could explain the DNA. And it is likely there would be tears as well." She paused again.

"An infant would experience discomfort in any sexual exploitation, even absent full penetration, and tears are likely. I would consider those the most likely scenarios."

Josh let that sink in for a moment. "Thanks."

"Sorry, nothing in this case is going to be pleasant."

There was a sharp knock on the door, then it opened. Chief Brennan walked in, followed by a man pushing a hand truck loaded with more file boxes.

"I come bearing gifts," the Chief said, "or at least I come with someone else bearing gifts." He pointed to the one open area in the office. "Put them over there."

The courier dropped the boxes, punched a few keys on his iPad, then turned to face the group. "I need a signature for the delivery."

"I got it," Josh said, running his finger over the screen. "Thanks."

Once the courier left, the Chief looked at Josh. "I assume the bill I signed for changing the locks in the exercise room is related to your space problem?"

"Yes, sir," Josh said. "It was Tommy's idea."

"Hmm," Brennan said as a smile crossed his face. "A space shot solved a space problem." Sending the group into peals of laughter.

"Wow, you've been practicing your comedy routine for the nursing home, eh, Chief?" Tommy said, laughing along.

"I think I will miss you the least," the Chief replied, heading back out the door.

"Guy loves me," Tommy said, digging into the reports. "When I finish this file, I'll move everything down to our new storage area."

XXVIII A Roll Call of Horror

Two hours later, with the office free of all the file boxes, the group settled in for a reality check.

Fred nodded at Jennifer, and she stood to face the group. Behind her was a large posterboard covered with FBI investigative reports separated into sections. One for each identified victim.

"Good morning. Today, unfortunately, I have the onerous task of laying out the information on the victims identified through the recovered body parts.

"Once I run through the names and the most current information, Lieutenant Williams will be assigning teams to each victim for further investigation. Some of these victims date back to the 1980s and 90s; others are more recent.

"For our purposes, we will investigate each victim, but our initial efforts will focus on the most recent. This offers the best opportunity to uncover any criminal associates, crime scene locations, or additional evidence related to the unknown victims and identify the UnSubs.

"Any questions before we start?"

"I have one," Frank Lachance said, raising his hand.

"Go ahead, detective."

"This whole thing got started when Jerry Paulsen and I started looking at the body parts left around the city," cocking his head toward the posterboard. "I don't see any mention of them on that board. Why?"

Jennifer smiled. "Very observant. We think it best if we segregate these cases. It's obvious the suspect in custody is too young to have been involved in the older cases. His involvement started much later.

"At this point, it is not clear how he became involved. While it is certainly a safe bet he transported some of the body parts from these cases, it is not absolute. What is certain is someone else is, or was, involved.

"For the purpose of eliminating the possibility of a defense attorney raising the issue of an unidentified perpetrator as an alternative theory at trial, we want to keep the cases separate.

"If we uncover clear evidence of the suspect's involvement in other body part incidents, which I think likely, we can adjust this approach. Does that answer your question?"

Frank nodded. "I would like to be involved in the other case when we decide to focus on it."

"You will, detective. You will." She looked around the room. "If there are no other questions, I'll begin."

The only reaction was chairs shuffling, notebooks and laptops opening, and a few deep breaths to prepare for a rollcall of horror.

"Okay," Jennifer reached for the first file.

"Victim number one. Vanessa Ramos, age 23 at the time of her disappearance, 3/14/2012. Cause of death undetermined. Method of identification DNA Military database, US Army. The body part associated is her right arm.

Limb was severed with medical precision. Two tattoos, "US Army Infantry" and "Vanessa, 2-3-11" According to State of Rhode Island Vital Statistics, subject gave birth to a female child on 2-3-11. Military records show General Discharge, Disciplinary Issues.

"Subject has arrest record for drug use and prostitution. Active court warrant for Failure to Appear/Sentencing. Last known contact was date of disappearance. Subject spoke with her attorney about the pending court date. No other contact with relatives. Child, who is now four years old, in custody of paternal grandmother and aunt, sister of victim."

"Follow-up interviews with attorney, grandmother, and sister. Also check with Army Central Personnel Office for any known associates and more info on discharge conditions."

Jennifer returned the file to the board and grabbed the second one.

"Victim number two. Paula Criado, age 24 at time of disappearance, 2/19/12. Cause of death undetermined. Method of identification DNA Military database, US Marine Corps. Body part associated is left arm. No tattoos, ME said there were signs of needle injections and possible suicide scars."

"I say mark it as a suicide," Tommy interjected. "One less case to investigate." Bringing the room to laughter.

Jennifer glared. "How many suicides have you seen where they managed to sever their own limbs?"

"Ah, one. This one."

The agent shook her head. "What have I gotten myself into?"

"Ignore him, Jennifer," Josh said. "You'll be better off for it. It's how we tolerate him."

"Fine, let's get through this, okay? Where was I?" scanning the file. "Oh yeah, possible signs of suicide attempts," she glanced at Tommy, who held up his hands deferring to the gravity of the moment.

"Limb also severed with medical precision. Her last known contact was by telephone with her parents, saying she was on her way home from USMC Base at Quantico for annual leave before deployment to Japan. Military records show her AWOL. Parents filed a missing person report with local police, ah, Coventry PD.

"We'll need to follow up with parents and Marine Corps Personnel records and request a copy of the missing person report from Coventry PD. Although, I'm sure they wrote it off to someone deciding the Marine Corps wasn't for them and taking off."

The remaining files told a similar story. Several commonalities were at once clear. Almost to a person, they were enlisted military. All had disciplinary issues; drug use, insubordination. Two of the victims had prior arrests for prostitution. One had an outstanding robbery warrant related to an escort service.

However, one victim stood out from all the rest, Tatiana Vaca. Identified from DNA extracted from her head, she had never been in the military, never arrested, and had no contact with the police.

A college student at PC, she was pre-med. This made everyone sit up and take notice. She went missing before her finals in the first semester of her senior year. Her absence sent up warning signs as in her entire time at the school, she had never missed one class.

The problem is she was an only child, and both parents died in a car accident when she was sixteen. She lived with a distant cousin until graduation from high school and earned a full scholarship to PC.

The only reason her DNA was on file was through a genealogical service where she tried to locate other relatives. She did not belong to this group. Not that the others did, but she was the one oddity among similarities.

"That can't be a coincidence," Josh said. "All this evidence of medical-level separation of limbs, and we have a pre-med student in the mix who doesn't fit the profile of any of the other victims?

"There has to be some connection with Providence College. Some people or group she met there. In my short-lived career there—I was pre-med myself for a brief shining moment—I met quite a few alumni who were doctors and nurses. That has to be the link. That's where we start."

"I agree," Jennifer said. "That is our best lead so far." She glanced at her watch. "Okay, how about we take a short break, then Lieutenant Williams will assign the teams."

XXIX A Lottery Nobody Wanted to Win

Josh looked around the room, waiting for everyone to settle in.

"Okay," Josh said, "if everybody is now satiated, it's time to see whose lives you will tear apart." As the words came out of his mouth, he looked at Tommy.

"Don't even think it, smart ass."

"I wasn't gonna say a thing," Tommy answered, but his grin said otherwise.

"Yeah, right. Okay, we've broken things up into four teams. Team 1, Fred and John. Team 2, Jen and Dan. Team 3, Frank and Jerry. Team 4, Me and Tommy.

"Team 1 will handle anything related to the Pawtucket case. When we finish here, you guys reach out to the Chief's office in Pawtucket. He's putting together a team there to work with you.

"You guys also have the victim identified through DNA and without recovered body parts, Rose Cardosa."

Josh handed off the file to Fred.

"Team 2 will take victims number one through four, Vanessa Ramos, Paula Criado, Aurora Braz, and Alessandra Lopes.

"You also will handle the unidentified victims for now since Jen will be the contact for the FBI lab in Quantico. As we identify them, we may redistribute them to the appropriate teams." Josh handed the file to Fred. "Here, pass this to Jen."

"Team 3, you have victims, Solange Daniel, Isabel Rodrigues, Dafne Toste, and Sofia Monteiro. Little bit of background on Dafne. When I was in uniform, we arrested her on a robbery charge. She punched out some old guy in Bovi's and grabbed his wallet. She was a fighter. Put up a good struggle when we caught her. Whoever took her out had their hands full. There might be something to that, drugging the vics maybe? Just an FYI." He passed the file along. "And in her defense the old guy was a perv, put his hand on her ass so it wasn't exactly the crime of the century.

"Team 4. Tommy and I will handle the background on the suspect, Israel David Jenkins, as well as victims Tatiana Vaca, Finian Cary, and the latest ID'd victim, Donovan Truell. These are the outliers among the victims. We can also serve as backup should anyone need additional help.

"Any questions?"

"So, this is it?" Frank asked. "We're not getting any more help from anyone?"

Josh shook his head. "We decided to go with what we have for now. The background investigations should be straightforward. Once we delve into them, if anything requires search warrants or surveillance, we'll reach out for more bodies.

"I think we have enough bodies," Tommy said. "Or at least enough parts."

Even Josh couldn't help laughing. "That may be, Tommy. But I have a feeling this is gonna turn even more bizarre before it's over. Okay, go to it. We'll meet each morning to discuss any progress or problems.

"If anyone needs something from Quantico, coordinate with Jen. Anything from the AG's office, I'll be the point of contact. For the US Attorney, use Fred. Okay?"

Josh looked around the room as the teams moved off to huddle and plan. How did I ever win this lottery, he thought.

XXX   More Than Just a Name

rank looked at Jerry Paulsen. "I don't care what the Feebs think. There's no way this guy isn't responsible for the dumping of those body parts,"

"No shit, but what she said makes sense. I read the case file from the incident in Pawtucket. When they tried that piece of shit father for the murder..."

Frank's eyes grew wide as he looked past Paulsen, stopping the detective's words mid-sentence.

"What?" Paulsen asked, turning to see Josh standing behind him. "Oh, ah, sorry Lt."

Josh shook his head. "No need, the father *was* a piece of shit. If it turns out he was my father, I had nothing to do with it. Go on and finish your thought."

Paulsen turned back to face Frank and gave him a wide-eyed oops expression.

"Well, during the trial, the defense attorney constantly argued about the ladder being evidence someone else took the kids. Why would the father use a ladder?

"Then the statement from the cops about climbing the ladder the night before the disappearance didn't help. What the fuck were those guys thinking?"

"Wait a minute," Josh interrupted. "The defense *knew* about the statements? The cops climbing in the apartment? I read the file, and the statements weren't listed in discovery. I wondered if the defense knew about it."

"Oh yeah, they found out," Paulsen said. "And get this, the sergeant took the ladder down after they climbed it. Unbelievable. You'd have thought they'd at least try to contact the occupants and make sure there was nothing to it."

Josh shook his head,

"I looked through the ProJo archives. One of the reporters had a hook into Pawtucket PD and they let him read over the file. Probably trying to generate some positive pre-trial publicity.

"The reporter found the statements and asked the defense lawyer about them. Major fuckup. Defense moved to dismiss based on incomplete discovery. There was a hearing before the judge, but he let the prosecutor file an amended discovery.

"If we can find the trial transcripts there might be more."

"I assume it was a big part of the defense's case," Josh said,

"Oh yeah. The prosecutor tried to argue it was all part of a plan by the parents to cover up the crime—and the cops were following normal procedure when they found the ladder and didn't know about the missing kids—but, well, we know the result. Juries don't want to believe such evil exists in the world. Especially involving parents."

"You have a point," Josh said. "I agree it is the best course, for now. Let's focus on the victims we know. They are more than just names from the past, right?"

"You got it, Lt.," Frank said. "Come on, Jerry. We've got to head down to Galilee and meet the parents of one of our vics."

Josh watched the detectives leave the office. Alone with his thoughts, the idea that his father, or more correctly sperm donor, was a cold-blooded murderer of one child and had thrown away another one, despite the jury's verdict, weighed on him.

Then add in the possibility his own mother was involved.

Maybe, he thought, deep down inside, it's why I never wanted kids. Maybe there is something greater at work here stopping me from having them?

"Lieutenant?" Jennifer's voice took him back to reality, he hadn't even heard her come in.

"Yeah, sorry. Daydreaming."

"Have you had a chance to read the Pawtucket case file?"

Josh hesitated. Not sure how to answer the question.

"Listen, I understand the Deputy's insistence you stay out of that matter, but you're a good cop. There is no way you *wouldn't* read that file. I would."

Josh smiled. "Yeah, I read it."

"Did you read the mother's statement?"

"Ah, no. I kinda focused on the father first. I planned to read it at some point."

"Well, I don't know if this will make a difference to you, but the mother claimed the twins were from an affair she had with another man. She didn't name him, but I thought..."

"Better adulterers than murderers for a mom and dad?"

"Yeah, kind of."

Just the Two of Us

"Thanks, that actually does help."

XXXI   Connecting the Dots

Driving along the winding side streets in Galilee, Rhode Island, Frank said, "I'd love to buy a house down here."

"Not on a cop's salary," Jerry said.

Once just foot paths to the water from South County trail, they lacked any semblance of organization or planning. First encampments of the natives, then houses of the settlers carved the landscape. Whatever was the easiest path for man or beast became the layout.

Galilee was one of the tiny villages throughout Rhode Island. The tiniest state in the Union was home to over four hundred village subdivisions within thirty-nine cities and towns.

Quonochontaug, Arkwright, Nooseneck are among the more colorful names. Galilee, on Point Judith, is part of the town of Narragansett. One inevitably encounters the historical reminders of the once dominant Native American tribes—Narragansett, Wampanoag, Pequot, Nipmuc, Niantic—that lived in the area until the arrival of Europeans.

Galilee, named by a Canadian fisherman from Nova Scotia who thought the area's rise along the sea mimicked the biblical town of the same name, became home to a growing port of fishing boats.

Across the channel leading into the port of Galilee, legend has it that during a chance encounter, a lost fisherman, pointed and asked a local what that area was called. He was told it was Jerusalem, in keeping with the biblical theme.

Thus, one can visit Galilee and Jerusalem without leaving Rhode Island.

Once home exclusively to fishermen working the oar and sail-driven fishing boats, time had changed the boats and the residents. The boats, now all diesel, still fished the waters off the coast, but few fishermen could afford to live here.

Oceanfront property in the Ocean State was expensive and even tiny houses with ocean views, or walking proximity to the water, commanded astronomical prices.

Driving along the ocean and oceanfront properties, they arrived at 321 Meshanticut Avene, the current home of the parents of Solange Daniel, victim number five on the list.

"So how do you want to handle this?" Frank asked.

"Delicately, my friend, delicately. They already know she's dead. I'm not sure what else they've been told but having somebody tell you they've found your missing daughter's leg cannot be a pleasant experience.

"Let's see what their reaction is to us being here."

As they got out of the unmarked cruiser, the door to the house opened. An older gentleman, gray-haired with a salt and pepper beard and rugged build wearing a URI sweatshirt came out and walked to meet them.

"You guys here about my daughter?" he asked. "My name is John, John Daniel." An awkward smile crossed his face. "And yeah, my friends call me Jack." He put out his hand to Frank.

Frank shook his hand. "I'm Detective Frank Lachance from East Providence Police. This is Detective Jerry Paulsen, Rhode Island State Police."

Jerry shook his hand. "Nice to meet you, sir. Sorry for the circumstances."

"Thank you," the man nodded. "We always knew this day would come." He glanced back at the house. "My wife is ill. She has cancer and dementia. She's not usually aware of what's going on. We can go inside if you like, but she'll keep asking when you're gonna bring Sol home.

"It might be better if we stay out here. Besides, I'm not sure there is much more I can tell you. We never understood why she disappeared or how she ended up..." his voice broke, and he turned away.

"Sorry, all a bit much to take in."

"No need to apologize," Jerry said. "We were hoping you might know any names of people she hung around with or who might know something about her."

The man shook his head. "She was a good girl growing up, a bit wild in high school, but what kid isn't? When she told us she was joining the Army, we were nervous and pleased at the same time. I was in the Navy. I thought the disciplined environment might be good for her."

"Was she close to anyone in the service? Anybody she was friendly with or talked about?" Frank asked.

The man thought for a moment. "There was this one girl. They came home together when we lived in East Providence."

At the mention of East Providence, Jerry and Frank exchanged glances.

"They were on ten-day leave before going to AIT, ah, Advanced Infantry Training. I don't remember her name, but I may have a picture. If you don't mind waiting here. I'll go grab the photo album we kept."

"No, of course not," Jerry said.

A few minutes went by, and the door opened again. Solange's father walked over to the car and opened the album on the hood. Thumbing through the pages, he stopped at a picture of two young women in Army fatigues standing in the front yard of a small but well-kept house.

"This was on Jefferson Ave in Riverside. If I'm not mistaken, the girl's name might have been Vanessa. But I'm not sure."

"May I?" Jerry asked, reaching for the album.

The man nodded.

Sliding the picture out of the sleeve, Jerry took his cell phone and snapped a picture. Using his fingers to blow the image up, he showed the phone to Frank.

The image was fuzzy, but the last name on the uniform was readable, Ramos.

"Thanks, Jack. You've been very helpful. Our condolences on losing your daughter."

"Thank you," he said, then took a deep breath. "Can I ask you something?"

"Of course."

"Will you tell us if you find out what happened to her?" A tear fell from the man's eye.

"Jack," Jerry said, putting his hand on the man's shoulder. "I will come here myself and tell you whatever we find out. You have my word on it."

* * * * *

On the other side of the bay, Jen and Dan were trying to find a company called Braz Construction. The company address came up on a driver's license for Aurora Braz's brother, Teofilio Braz, the only next of kin in her military records. Parents were listed as deceased before enlistment.

Driving through the alleys of the business center development, they tried to spot the suite numbers.

"Not very well marked, are they?" Dan said.

"Not at all," Jen answered, then pointed. "Wait there's 21, we're looking for 23. My guess is that door. There's a name on it, but it's too faded to read from here."

Jen parked the car, and the two investigators got out. As they made their way to the door, the name became clearer, 'Braz Construction.'

"Not exactly a Fortune 500 company, eh?" Dan said.

"Not by a longshot." Jen banged on the door. Then banged harder. Nothing.

Just as they turned to leave, they were both startled when the door was wrenched open. A man stood leaning against the door frame, wearing boxer shorts and a wife-beater t-shirt, rubbing sleep from his eyes. Hair disheveled, eyes bloodshot and rheumy, his gravelly voice completed the hangover picture.

"What, ah, what do you want?" the man said.

"Are you Teofilio Braz?"

"Who the fuck's asking?"

Jen held out her ID.

The man squinted to read it, then stood straighter. "FBI, what did that bitch say I did now? Talk to the local cops, they know she's nuts."

With no other clues, the two investigators now had a clear picture. The guy was living in the office, tossed out by a wife or girlfriend, or both, most likely.

"That's not why we're here," Jen said. "Do you have a sister named Aurora Braz?"

This brought the man's full attention. "You found her?"

"In a manner of speaking," Dan said. "Sorry to tell you this, but she is dead."

"Hmm, figures."

"You're not surprised?" Jen asked.

"Nah," the man shook his head. "I knew she was never coming back. Never should have given her that hundred bucks. She didn't leave it for me, did she? Or anything else of value? You know, as next of kin?"

"Nope," Jen said. "Can we come inside to talk?"

The guy glanced over his shoulder. "Ah, the place is a mess and..." He was interrupted by an angry and clearly intoxicated female voice.

"Teo, what the fuck are you doing. Come back to bed; you owe me one."

"I gotta go, there's nothing else I can tell you. I haven't seen or heard from her. Go ask her Army buddies. They might have something."

"When did you last see her?"

Braz rubbed his head and shrugged. "I don't know, a year ago, maybe more. Wait, it was last July because I was working on building a deck on Block Island. She wanted to come out there and stay with me. I told her no."

"You got any names we can use?" Dan asked. "Or pictures?"

"We weren't exactly the picture-taking family type, so no, no pictures. But I remember one chick; she was a friendly one. A big set of tits on the bitch." No sign of embarrassment in his description.

He snapped his fingers twice. "Name was Lessie, I think. They called her Lessie the Lizard, but I don't think she was a rug muncher." A smile crossed his face, and he glanced over his shoulder.

"As a matter of fact," reaching down and rubbing his crotch, "I *know* she wasn't."

Jen looked at the man, boring her eyes into him.

"What?" the man said.

"Nothing. I thought Neanderthals were extinct."

"I'm not Nander talls, I'm Portuguese."

"No shit," she said, walking away. "Come on, Dan. This guy can't help himself, let alone us."

Back in the car, Dan thumbed through the reports. "Here," he pointed, turning the page toward Jen. She glanced for a moment then went back to driving.

"One of the vics is named Alessandra, Alessandra Lopes. Also, US Army. Can't be a coincidence, could it?"

"Probably not, but we have to verify."

Jen's phone rang, and she put it on hands free.

"Holmes,"

"Jen, it's Frank and Jerry. Listen, we visited the parents of Solange Daniel. Her father had a picture of her home on leave with another soldier. We were able to see the name Ramo on her uniform name tag. Has to be your vic, no?"

Jen looked at Dan.

"Probably," Jen replied.

"Frank, it's Dan. Our witness wasn't so helpful, but he did give us a nickname for one of our victim's friends. It was Lessie. Wanna bet this links our vic to one of the other ones on your list, Alessandra Lopes? They were all Army. Maybe enlisted together or met in basic."

"Holy shit. Okay, we have one more stop, then we'll be back in the barn. Talk to you then."

* * * * *

Josh and Tommy came back to the office at 5:30. They were surprised to see everyone still there.

"Was Happy Hour canceled?"

"Nope, Lt.," Dan said, "But we have some news we wanted to share and *then* go to Happy Hour."

Josh listened as they laid out what they had found.

"So let me get this straight. We are pretty sure we can connect at least four victims, Ramo, Braz, Daniel, and Lopes, through the Army. And, we can put Daniel as living on Jefferson Ave, which practically overlooks the crime scene location. And we have a picture of Ramos at the Jefferson Ave house at some point with Daniel.

"That about right?"

"You got it, Josh," Jen said. "Not a bad day's work, eh?"

Josh nodded. "Not bad, not bad at all. First round is on me."

XXXII Clearing the Mists of Time

Fred Robertson pulled up to the front of Pawtucket PD headquarters on Armistice Boulevard.

"I'll be right back," John said, then sprinted toward the door. A few moments later, he emerged with two Pawtucket PD detectives in tow.

"Fred Roberston, FBI" put out his hand as they climbed into the back seat.

"I'm Kenney Johnston and this is Michael Pratt. We work Special Squad. We thought you guys might want to go check the crime scene area and then stop at the Judicial Records center for the file in the archives, if they can find it."

"Sounds good," Fred said. "They close to each other?"

The two Pawtucket detectives exchanged glances.

"Very," Kenney Johnson said, "they are the same place."

"What?" Both heads in the front seat turned to stare at Johnson.

"Yup, the original garage was bought by the state and turned into the Judicial Records Center Archive. The inside is obviously changed, but the exterior and area where they found the body is pretty much as it was."

"Wow, that certainly makes it convenient," Fred said. Okay, which way?"

Following the directions, they rode in silence for a few minutes. Then John interrupted the quiet.

"Can I ask you guys something?"

"Sure," Johnson answered.

"Did you guys hear anything about the cops who climbed the ladder into the building the night before the incident?"

The exchange of glances said more than intended. Something both Fred and John caught onto.

"Only that most guys were surprised the fat ass sergeant made it up the ladder without bending it."

John laughed. "Seriously, anything ever percolate up about why they would do that?"

John knew he had to tread carefully here. Disturbing things a police department prefers to keep undisturbed can be tricky.

"I know this," Detective Pratt said. "The report wasn't filed until *after* the body was found. That's three days later, not the next day as the report date shows."

"And how do you know that?"

"One night in the FOP hall the officer who was there came in. He was retired by this point and already half in the bag. You know how cops love to tell war stories? Drunk retired cops live for them.

"He started in on one story and another and eventually got to the Martins case. He claimed he wanted to file the report the night before the incident, but the sergeant told him not to bother.

"He said he thought about it, then filed it when they found the body. Said a Detective Commander ordered him to change the date to the morning of the incident. Said it would make the department look bad.

"You know what I think?"

"What's that?" John asked.

"I think he was right. It would make us look like idiots. And some of those guys back then *were* idiots. Political hacks hired for their political connections, not their police work.

"But I will tell you this, because that's what you're really after, no one ever thought the cops had anything to do with the murder or disappearance. They only wanted to hide their stupidity. That answer your question?"

John nodded, then turned back to the front. "Yup, it sure does. We have our own fair share of brown-nosing ass-lickers on the job as bosses."

"Every agency does," Fred added. "Believe me when I tell you."

"Right here, Fred," Kenney said. "The building on the right. Where the entrance is now was where the garage door used to be. Park the car, and we'll go for a walk."

As the four detectives stood eyeing the building, a man in a suit emerged. He stared at the four, then walked over. The lanyard with the ID card, rumpled suit, and the slightly annoyed scowl had civil servant written all over it.

"Something I can help you with, gentlemen?"

John smiled. "Did you have anything to do with the kidnapping and murder that happened here back in the '70s?"

The question caught him off-guard. "Ah, no. Of course not."

"Then you can't help us."

"Who are you?" the man demanded, "what media outlet?"

"We're not the media," Fred said. "I'm with the FBI."

"And we're real cops," John added with a grin.

"Yeah, real smart asses, you mean," Fred added, then turned back to face the man. "Why did you think we were media?"

"I had two of them snooping around here. They said they needed to see the original trial files on the Martin case."

The man's words caused Fred and John to exchange looks.

"I told them since the guy was found not guilty, the files were all destroyed."

"And have they been?" John asked.

The man looked around and then leaned in. "Well, the trial transcripts were, but I came across an old filing cabinet with all the pre-trial motions for both defendants. That I have. Why do you want them? I'm not sure I should let you have access."

"We are reexamining the case," John said, stepping toward the man. "We'd like to take those files with us."

The man shook his head. "Nope, nothing leaves this office. Those are official files, and they are not..."

John stepped toward the man, invading his space. "Listen, this is a major case. This has nothing to do with the records center itself, but those files may be important to identify a whole bunch of dead people.

"Now, unless you want a public relations shitshow over your keeping those documents and impeding our investigation, I suggest you hand them over. But just so you understand, we are taking those records one way or the other. Either you hand them over or get pummeled as I walk right through you and take them. Got it?

"Now, unless you have something else to contribute, lead us back to your office, hand over those files, and we will be on our way."

"What agency are you with?" The man's anger was boiling over but tempered by uncertainty.

"The Rhode Island State Police. Call headquarters and ask for Colonel Paulsen."

"I might do that." The man spun on his heels, storming back inside with John right on his heels. He appeared a few moments later, bearing a smile and two large three-ring binders. Handing them over without a word, he charged back into the building.

"State Police?" Fred said. "Colonel Paulsen? You're gonna get that young trooper in some shit."

"Nah, they'll think the guy is a nut. Besides, we'll be long gone before he even gets somebody on the phone to talk to him."

They spent a few more minutes walking around the scene, then headed back to Pawtucket PD HQ.

When they got to the station, a uniformed sergeant waited for them.

"Okay, which one of you smartasses decided it would be a good idea to jerk the records center director's chain?"

The others all looked at John.

"So, wiseass. Because of you I just had my ear chewed off by some pissed off Lieutenant at state police headquarters *and* the records center director. I suppose you think that's funny?"

"Sorry, Sarge, the guy was being a dick. I just messed with him a bit."

"Yeah, well, I'm off at four. Don't mess with anyone else until after that. Got it?"

"Got it," John answered.

The sergeant walked back inside, leaving the four standing on the steps.

"See," John said. "I told you Paulsen wouldn't be in the shit."

"What is it about you EPPD guys?" Fred asked. "Is being a smartass a job requirement?"

"Nope," John said. "But it is worth bonus points."

The two Pawtucket cops laughed

"Come on," Kenney said, "Besides this stuff from the records center, we have some more files we found for you guys."

Two hours later, with another box full of information, Fred and John headed back to EPPD headquarters.

"Fred, do you have the feeling we're not being told everything?"

"Yeah, I'm not sure if it's a CYA situation or something worse. They both went out of their way to mention no one thought anything sinister about it. Methinks they doth protest too much.

"But it would seem to me they're just messengers carrying out specific instructions. We need to talk to Josh about it."

XXXIII Divining the Past

Putting several boxes of donuts on the table, Josh waited for the feeding frenzy to begin.

"Okay, everybody, help yourselves to the donuts, courtesy of the chief of police," Josh said. "Then we'll start the status update."

"I don't recall buying donuts this morning," Chief Brennan said, standing in the doorway of the conference room, blocking most of the incoming light and causing Josh to spin around in surprise.

"Oh, ah, good morning, Chief. I read your mind and knew you'd want to extend your welcome and thanks to our compatriots from the FBI and state police. I took the liberty of ordering on your behalf."

"I see. And did that include the boxes I noticed in the OIC's office, dispatch, and detectives?"

"Of course, have to take care of the troops, right?" Josh smiled.

"Fine, but if one of those nosey-ass council members starts whining about those expenses, I'll have you explain them. Better yet, I'll have the city deduct it from your paycheck."

"Of course, ah, we're getting ready to go over the current case status. You're welcome to sit in, ah, sir."

"Well, that's very ecumenical of you, inviting me to my own conference room. Can I have a donut as well?"

"Sure, all you want. Just not the ones with bacon bits."

The Chief pulled his hand back from the box.

"That's Tommy's favorite; it's the only way we can keep him under control."

The chief glanced at Tommy—frosting on the detective's lips and pieces of bacon bits covering the space in front of him—and just shook his head. A sheepish grin crossed the detective's face.

"Now I am *certain* I will not miss you at all," the Chief said, grabbing a glazed donut and retreating to the back of the room.

"Okay, now that the dietary differences are resolved, we'll start with Team One; Fred, you have the floor."

* * * * *

The meeting lasted over an hour. They'd made progress with linking some of the victims from their military connections but hadn't found the common denominator linking any of them to the crime scene or Israel David Jenkins.

Jenkins himself had proved an enigma. It was as if he had appeared in Rhode Island from nowhere. There were no prior arrests except a disorderly conduct charge from 2000 handled by a summons to the Municipal Court in Pawtucket. Thus, there were no prints or DNA on file for the guy. The case was filed.

They'd only found the record through a newspaper archive search listing a story on Municipal Court cases reported in the Pawtucket Times.

They found no school records, birth certificates, voter registrations, nothing to gain insight into where he was from or how and when he arrived.

The FBI ran his image against their facial recognition system but found nothing. His prints came back negative as well.

DNA was another thing.

While there were no DNA matches in the national criminal or military databases, there were matches with two of the victims, Paula Criado and Dafne Toste. They all shared DNA markers showing they had related males as biological fathers, either brothers or cousins. Based on the percentages, they were probably half-sisters, and Jenkins shared the same father with one of them.

While this was interesting, it added little to the two bigger questions. Why did this guy have pieces of bodies and DNA from the victims? And why was he scattering parts around the state every month?

The FBI Behavioral Science Unit—more commonly known as profilers—promised an analysis soon. With no other information, the sheer number of victims seemed to offer the best hope for figuring out the story.

"Okay, if nobody has anything else," Josh said, "let's get back to it."

Most of the detectives slowly filtered out, some grabbing a last donut before leaving. Josh and Fred stood talking in the back of the room. John Harris hung back from the others.

"Something you need, John?" Josh asked.

"Ah, yeah, Lt., Fred and I went to Pawtucket PD the other day and we wanted to give you a heads up on something."

Josh glanced at Fred, then back to John.

"Go for it."

"I'm, ah, we're pretty sure the guys from Pawtucket aren't giving us the whole story about the cops climbing the ladder into the apartment."

Josh blinked a few times, lost in troubling thoughts. "You don't think...come on, what's this, one of those phony cop novels where there's a conspiracy behind every door?"

John shrugged.

"Fred?"

"Let's say if I were a betting man the odds are good there's something more to this. Maybe they hoped this would never see the light of day again, but I got a bad feeling from their reaction when John asked about it."

Rubbing his hand over his mouth, then over his crew cut hair, Josh let it sink in. "Okay, since it is ancient history it's probably not very important but good to keep in mind. Let's keep this among ourselves for now.

"I'll talk to Brennan. He worked a lot with Pawtucket's Special Squad when he was in narcotics. Maybe he has someone he can talk to."

"Thanks, Lt.," John said, leaving the room.

"Any other bad news, Fred?"

"Nope, good news actually. I tracked down the prosecutor from the original case. He's down in Kiawah Island, South Carolina, near Charleston."

"Wow, he's still alive?" Josh replied.

"Yeah, he was a rising star back then. Youngest lead on a murder case. He's in his eighties now, but when I talked to him on the phone, he knew all about our case and wanted to talk with us."

Josh was lost in thought for a moment.

"No," Fred said. "I know what you're thinking, but no."

Josh stared for a moment. "Come on, there's no way anyone from that case is ever gonna be prosecuted. Both the father and mother are dead. What difference will it make if I go with you?

"I understand why your bosses wanted me out of it, but that's just them covering their asses. We need to find the link between Jenkins and that case. Someone else was involved with all these murders. Finding them, if they're still alive, is more important. You and I can gain something from this working together."

Fred rubbed his forehead, then let out a sigh. "Okay, you can come with me, but we can't pay your expenses. If Justice sees an expense charge for you, they'll blow a gasket."

"No worries, Brennan will pay for it."

"Brennan will pay for what?" Chief Brennan asked. His penchant for silently appearing at the most inconvenient times had vexed officers and politicians for years.

"How does someone your size manage to appear out of nowhere?"

"Years of practice babysitting wayward cops." Brennan smiled. "Especially cops like you."

Josh chuckled. "Fair enough. Do you trust me, Chief?"

"Trust has significant consequences, but I suppose I do. Why?"

"Then I need to purchase a plane ticket to Charleston, South Carolina, to go with Fred here and interview a witness."

The chief nodded his head, and Josh could see the man's mind working.

"Do I want to know who this witness is?"

Josh smiled.

"Well, then, I guess I trust you. Send my secretary the details. I'll expense it out of office supplies; the city comptroller never pays much attention to that." He stepped towards Josh.

"Josh, I realize you have questions about the past. Just keep in mind it changes nothing about who you are. As a cop and as a person. Got it?"

"Got it, Chief, Thanks."

Once Brennan left the room, Fred said, "He's a good guy, isn't he?"

"The best. We're gonna miss him."

"Maybe they'll make you Chief."

"Hah," Josh laughed. "The politicians in this city have been waiting to crown the mighty midget for years. They can't wait for Brennan to go. Come hell or high water, they'll find a way."

"The mighty midget?"

"A long, or rather short, story. Records Lieutenant. Uses lifts in his shoes to make himself taller. He'll be a disaster as chief, but that's the price of politics."

"Don't I know it. Ever met the Director of the FBI?"

"Can't say that I have."

"Let's just say he had to study to figure out how to spell FBI."

"Really? Wow, I guess it is universal. Anyway, let me go ask Brennan about contacts with the Special Squad. How about you book us some flights to South Carolina?"

"Think we should call the guy first? Give him a heads up?"

Josh smiled. "I prefer to surprise him a bit. Gauge the reaction. I've heard some of the older guys mention him. He's supposed to be a good guy, but who knows what skeletons might be lurking?"

It was Fred's turn to smile. "I like the way you think, Josh." then headed out of the conference room.

Twenty minutes later, Josh walked into the office.

"Flights are booked," Fred said. "0630, Tuesday."

"What nothing earlier?"

"There is actually, want me to rebook?"

"No, that's fine, thanks," Josh said, dropping into his chair.

"What did Brennan say?" Fred asked.

"He's gonna call the captain who ran the unit back then. Says if there was anything screwy about the case he'll know."

.

XXXIV The History of Incompetence

Charlie Goforth walked to his bar.

"No shit?" he said, pouring a second round of gin and tonics. The sun had dipped below the horizon. Clouds from a disintegrating afternoon thunderstorm refracted the rays into a rainbow of color.

Sunset over the ocean is always good for the best light show on earth, and Charlie's small but charming cottage had an unobstructed view.

Josh took two drinks, handing one to Fred.

"Yup, I am the missing twin."

"No shit? Must have come as a bit of a shock."

"You could say that." He pointed to a pod of Atlantic bottlenose dolphins stirring the water as they fed on a school of spot tail bass.

"You ever fish the beach?" Josh asked.

Charlie shook his head. When I was younger, I could handle the cold and surf. Now, I stick to the lagoons. The spots breed there, and you can catch big fish. Only problem is landing the fish before the 'gators get 'em."

"Bet that makes it exciting," Fred said.

"It's like a game. I usually catch and release, but every once in a while, I keep one for dinner."

"Charlie, did the name Jenkins ever come up in the case?"

"Jenkins, Jenkins, hmm, not that I recall. I did go over my notes on the case." His eyes narrowed on Josh. "A friend told me somebody was asking about me, and I knew this had to be the case. Thought you'd catch me off-guard a bit?"

Josh shrugged. "Force of habit."

"Don't blame you. I'd have done the same thing. But I haven't had time to review the whole file."

Both Josh and Fred leaned forward.

"Wait, you have the whole file?" Josh asked.

Chalie smiled. "Yeah. Let me give you a little background. When we were investigating the case, it became apparent from the beginning the parents were involved. But we wanted to be cautious," he looked at Josh. "We assumed the boy was dead, and it would only be a matter of time before we found the body.

"We wanted to make sure we'd explored all options before we made an arrest. Our plan was to put the case before a grand jury. This would buy us time and might push one of the parents to flip.

"Then, that idiot Deputy AG at the time, Wolfson, issued warrants and sent the state police and Pawtucket Police officers assigned to the Fugitive Task force to arrest the parents. He didn't even bother telling the detectives working the case.

"I lost my shit on the asshole. He didn't realize the implications of what they'd done, all for the sake of a five-minute story headline."

"It started the clock on bringing them to trial, right?" Josh said.

"Exactly; instead of using the grand jury to build the case, now we had six months to bring the case to trial. Even with discovery and motion delays, it created a major headache for us.

"While speedy trial motions by a defendant are rare, they do happen. The whole publicity stunt just created an unnecessary complication in an already messy case.

"And, of course, they now had representation. We knew any lawyer worth their salt would never let us talk to them. They may not have been the most loving bride and groom, but their attorney would tell them we couldn't force them to testify against each other if they were married."

"Ain't love grand," Josh said, looking out at the ocean and sipping his drink.

"Can I ask you something, Josh? Not to be insensitive."

"Sure," turning back to face the man.

"The DNA match, is it for both parents or just one?"

"It's a match for the mitochondrial DNA, the mother."

Goforth nodded. "Not that you care what I think but I always believed the mother's involvement was compelled by domestic violence. We had information that Martins was not the father and was physically and psychologically abusive.

"I think she and, sorry to say this, the kids, were the victims of abuse. She was terrified of her husband. One of the reasons we decided to try the father first was we hoped a conviction might force her to open up about the murder. While she'd still face jail time, we could justify mitigating the sentence under the circumstances."

Josh nodded; he appreciated the gesture, but it didn't change reality.

"Charlie," Fred said, "you mentioned a case file?"

"Yeah, before we dismissed the case against the mother, I had a complete copy of the entire file made. I've kept it all these years. Why? I have no idea. Let me go get it."

A few moments later, Charlie returned with a banker's box, struggling to lift it onto the table.

"Wow, you did keep the whole file, didn't you?" Josh said, lifting the cover off the box.

"That's just box number one. I have three more."

Josh looked at Fred. "We can't go through these here, we need to ship them back," turning to Charlie. "If that's okay with you?"

Charlie nodded. "Of course. I was never sure why I even bothered to keep the files all these years. Drove my wife crazy when I packed them in the car to drive here.

"Maybe I knew someday, something would happen, and they'd be useful. Take 'em all. My wife will be thrilled to have them out of here."

"Thanks, Charlie."

Charlie stared out at the beach for a moment, took a long sip from his drink, then turned back to face them. "I'm gonna tell you something I've never told anyone before."

Josh and Fred exchanged glances.

"Many years after the case, I was at a retirement party for a prosecutor I worked with. There was a guy there who looked familiar. After a bit he came over and introduced himself. He'd retired from Pawtucket PD and worked as an investigator with the AGs office."

Taking another drink, he continued.

"He was the patrolman at the scene of the incident the night before. It was obvious he'd had a few drinks, but he said he wanted to tell me something about the case. Then launched into the story without waiting to see if I even wanted to hear it. What he told me sent shivers up my spine."

Charlie paused for a moment.

"Let me do this. How about I tell you the whole story from my perspective, all I learned living with the case for months, and what this retired cop told me about the night before the kids went missing. Then, we can decide on dinner. Sound good?"

Josh and Fred settled into their seats, and it soon became apparent Charlie was a gifted storyteller. They found themselves transported back to 1976, listening to a remarkable, if tragic, story of the realities of justice.

XXXV **Stairway to Hell**

Morin's Garage, Pawtucket, RI
Date: November 20, 1976
Time: 0200hrs

The quiet night was interrupted by the radio call.

"C-21 to S1."

"S1. Go ahead."

"Can you meet me on Hill Street near Morin's Garage?"

"10-4. Give me ten minutes."

Pawtucket Police Officer Tim Sullivan leaned against the hood of his patrol car parked alongside a dark, dingy, two-story brick building. The faint odor of gasoline, oil, and antifreeze permeated the air. The metal framed screens covering the two ground-floor windows were wrapped in weeds as tall as the officer. Some weeds were long dead, while others still struggled to survive. The bitter Rhode Island winter would soon settle the matter.

Emerging from the cloud cover, the intermittent light from the full moon created a grayish dismal pallor to the area, drained of color like a black-and-white photo. The light shimmered off the shards of smashed beer bottles, now one with the gray-brown pebble-strewn dirt. An alley, camouflaged by old tires and more weeds, obscured by the darkness, made its way to the back of the building.

The cool November air helped the tired officer stay awake on his fourth consecutive sixteen-hour shift, as did the coffee from Dunkin Donuts a few blocks away. Not open twenty-four hours to the public back then, the baker left a pot on and the back door unlocked for officers to help themselves. While it yielded no profit in the cash register, the constant visits by the cops kept anyone considering breaking in at bay. Free coffee and a couple of donuts were cheap insurance.

Sergeant Mike McGoughlin arrived on the scene, pulling up to Sullivan, who was leaning on the hood of the cruiser.

"Hey, Sarge."

"So, what's up?"

"A ladder," Sullivan said, motioning with his coffee cup toward the alley.

McGoughlin tried to turn in his seat but couldn't quite manage. "You're gonna make me get out of this car? This better be something good."

McGoughlin, struggling to reach the zipper of his coat but unable to see it due to his beer-grown gut, got out. Sullivan walked to the head of the alleyway. McGoughlin came up next to him and then saw the ladder. It led to a second-story window. They couldn't tell if the window was open from where they stood.

"So, did you see anything? Besides the ladder?"

"Nope, but this place has a complete collection of car thieves and drug dealers hanging around when it's open. Maybe one of the more ambitious ratfucks decided to make an after-hours visit. Nobody should be here now."

"Yeah, I know this place. The guy who runs it is a piece of shit. Drug dealer, car thief. Probably a fuckin' perv as well. Into little kids from what I've heard. Never enough to charge him, of course, but worth bearing in mind."

"So, what do we do?"

"Up we go. We get a free peek inside. Might get lucky and find something the Special Squad guys can use to get a search warrant and get rid of the fuckin' rat. You first, in case the ladder breaks. I'm more valuable to the department," McGoughlin said with a smile.

Making his way to the top, Sullivan found the window slightly ajar. It lifted easily, and he could see what looked like a footprint in the dust on the sill. The print pointed in. He turned to see McGoughlin right behind him. "Sarge," he whispered, pointing at the print on the windowsill, "should I go in?"

"Yeah, move your fat ass out of my face and be quiet. I don't want anybody pushing the ladder back like we're invading the castle. Get in there," reaching up to push the officer to move.

"But there's a print here," Sullivan said, trying to avoid the sill.

"Just go, but be careful," McGoughlin said, glancing back down the ladder, wishing he'd passed on the last several dozen donuts.

Sullivan half slid, half fell in. As he did, his pant leg smudged the print, erasing it completely. He turned back and pulled McGoughlin in. McGoughlin looked at the sill. "Uh, Oh, there goes your career in the Crime Scene Unit."

"What? You pushed me."

"Should have been more careful," McGoughlin said, shoving past the incredulous officer.

They looked around, realizing it was a furnished apartment. A small TV sat against a wall on a dresser. Two faded gray, saggy, spot-stained, and worn easy chairs faced the dresser, and two bouncy chairs for infants sat facing the window.

"I thought you said this was a garage?" McGoughlin whispered. "Somebody is living here."

As the words left his mouth, they heard the distinctive sounds of someone snoring.

"Jesus, Sullivan. Let's get out of here before they wake up and think we're breaking in."

Making their way back down the ladder, they returned to the patrol units.

"Should I do a report?" Sullivan asked.

"About what?" He spread his arms wide. "How you talked your sergeant into breaking into someone's house? Besides, nobody got in there. Whoever put the ladder up was probably working on the building. If nothing comes in tomorrow, just forget about it. Now go hide like everybody else is doing; it's 2:15 in the morning. Nothing else is gonna happen tonight."

"Okay, Sarge, thanks."

"And Sully?"

"Yeah, Sarge?"

"Find another place to sleep besides buildings with ladders going up to windows."

Sullivan chuckled, then jumped in his car, pulling away into the night.

McGoughlin looked back at the ladder, considered pulling it down, then decided against it. With my luck, he thought, I'd drop the goddamn thing and have to explain to that idiot Lieutenant of ours how I broke my foot.

He lumbered back to the car, not so gently sliding in. The car rocked from side to side with the added weight, then settled out. These curious kids got to learn to stop being so goddamn nosey. He dropped the shift into drive and started to pull away when something caught his eye.

What the...he thought, then put the car back in park. One part of his brain told him to just drive away, but another voice from deep inside told him not to. A memory from the past when he was a young cop.

The years take their toll on police officers. What was once clear and straightforward became opaque and complex. Nothing is ever black and white; it's always a million shades of gray. Now McGoughlin faced one of those moments where there were no good options, just less evil ones.

A baby's shoe lay on the ground, hidden by weeds against the wall below the window they'd climbed in. Blocked by the ladder, they'd missed it the first time.

Now what do I do? McGoughlin thought.

Indecision can be paralyzing. What were the chances this was nothing more than just a piece of trash that fell out of a trash can, or a bag being dragged to the dump? Was there anything here other than coincidence and overactive imagination?

Why would this mean anything?

McGoughlin stared at the shoe for a moment before choosing. Reaching his hand up to the roof, he pulled himself back out of the cruiser. He walked to the ladder, reached through the bottom rung, and grabbed the shoe. Then, he pulled the ladder down and tossed it against the wall.

Spotting a closed trash bin at the building next door, he walked over, tossed the shoe inside, and then went back to his car.

There, he thought, good deed for the day. Cleaning up trash.

Unseen to the sergeant, Officer Sullivan had stopped on his way out of the lot and was walking back to speak to the sergeant. When he saw the sergeant toss the shoe in the trash, he backpedaled into the shadows, raced back to his car, and prayed he'd be able to unsee what he'd never wanted to see.

XXXVI Dead and Gone

Date: November 21, 1976
Pawtucket Police Dispatch Center
8:10 a.m.

The emergency line at Pawtucket PD lit up.

"Pawtucket Police, Dispatcher Sadler."

"My children are gone. My children are gone."

The dispatcher later recalled that the calmness of the voice didn't match the story.

"My babies are gone, my babies are gone," a woman said. In the background a male could be heard calling out and the sound of things being moved around.

"Ma'am, what is your address?"

"217 High Street, above Morin's Garage. My babies...my babies..." And the line went dead.

Ten minutes later, Sadler heard from the on-scene sergeant, "S1 to dispatch."

"Go ahead."

"Notify detectives and division commanders. We have two missing infants...twins. One female, one male. No sign of forced entry. Send me some more units to set up a perimeter."

By midnight, they'd made little progress.

Sgt. McGoughlin walked into his worst nightmare as he entered the shift commander's office.

"What's going on, Lt.?"

"Two missing kids, infants. Taken from an apartment above Morin's Garage...You okay, Mac? You look like you've seen a ghost?"

McGoughlin shook his head. "No, no, I'm fine. Tired is all. Anything I need to give out a rollcall?" He tried to calm himself, but he knew the shaky voice was giving him away.

"Is there something you need to share, Sergeant?" the Lieutenant asked.

"Ah, did you say Morin's Garage?"

"Yeah, why?"

"Ah last night, around 2:30. One of my guys spotted a ladder going up to a second-story window. We checked it out and there was nothing. We didn't even know anyone lived there. It looked to us like it had been there a while, there were weeds growing on it."

"Jesus Christ! What cop?"

"Tim Sullivan."

"Is he working tonight?"

McGoughlin looked at his rollcall list. "Yup."

"Right after rollcall, you and he take your asses over to detectives for statements. Jesus Christ, why didn't you think to at least have dispatch make a note about it?"

McGoughlin shrugged. "It seemed like nothing, Lieutenant."

"Yeah, well nothing might bite you in that fat ass of yours, Go!"

Outside of rollcall, McGoughlin pulled Sullivan aside.

"Listen, there's no reason to tell them we went into that apartment. We didn't see anything anyway. Far as we know, the kids were either already gone or still there. Either way, keeping this to ourselves won't hurt nothing."

XXXVII   No Good Deed...

The search for the missing infants would go on for several days with nothing to show for it. The once less-traveled street became the scene of a media frenzy. Every manner of lunatic jostled to be interviewed by the desperate reporters looking for anything to run on their one-minute blurb for the 6:00 p.m. newscast.

The theories about the kidnappers ranged from pedophiles to gang bangers to alien abduction, something had to fill the airwaves. All the cops would say is they had no further information.

On the fourth day of standing around hoping for a break, there was a palpable change in the level of activity. The reporters would finally have their story.

One of the officers walked through a vacant field right behind the building again. Beneath a pile of brush, visible only if one crouched down and put your head parallel to the ground, was the body of the infant girl, Rose Marie Martins. She was wrapped in the blanket her parents reported missing from her bed, her head lay resting on a neatly folded cloth towel.

If not for the location, one might think she was blissfully asleep.

But the reality of her death was all too apparent. The officer fought back his initial instinct to pull her out and hug her, but he knew better. Fighting back tears, he reached for the radio.

"C...ah C 21," his voice cracking. "Behind the building in the field, send detectives and a supervisor. I found one." Then the tears poured out, and he couldn't stop them. The vision of his own daughter, not much older than the baby in the brush pile, roiled his mind.

As the herd of officers converged, all he could manage was to point, then walked off to be alone for the moment trying to remember why he'd taken this job. They don't warn you about dead kids. Then again, how could they?

Several officers chose to focus on keeping the media back. A necessary task that might prevent them from suffering the nightmares those who would see the body would endure for years.

The one silver lining of the whole matter, if one was an optimist, was they never found her missing twin brother. Despite searching the ponds at Slater Park, sending divers into the Blackstone and Seekonk Rivers, and digging many holes all over the city and state, the body would never be found.

The pessimists among the cops, the overwhelming majority, believed giant carp in the river devoured the boy. Many refrained from ever fishing there again.

Others thought they'd buried the body beneath the foundation of a building under construction near the Martins apartment. Because a politically connected corporation owned the building, no judge would sign a search warrant to tear up the floor despite several attempts by investigators to get one.

The optimists didn't really believe he was still alive, but the sliver of hope made it easier to move past it.

So, the cops focused on what they had.

The physical evidence showed little to corroborate the parents' contention that the children were taken in the night. The inconsistent statements they gave to the police cast more doubt. In the jaundiced view of the detectives, they were outright bullshit.

James Martins, Sr., a longtime chop shop operator and drug smuggler, engendered little sympathy and eventually stopped cooperating. His wife, after first laying blame on her husband, also stopped cooperating.

But it would be something they'd both said in their statements before they stopped talking that would put them under sharp focus as suspects. The one consistency between them was horrid to hear.

A forensic analysis of the blanket wrapped around the girl found semen from James Martins. When confronted with this evidence, both husband and wife gave consistent explanations for its presence. Something even the seasoned investigators had never encountered.

James Martins claimed, and his wife corroborated the story, that whenever she refused to have sex with him, he would masturbate. And, more remarkable, they both claimed this sometimes happened while he was holding the baby.

Not one detective could ever recall anyone ever admitting to such a bizarre practice. This also drew the interest of the new FBI Behavioral Science Unit. It later played a big part in eliminating the possibility someone other than the parents caused the death of the girl and the disappearance of the boy.

Due to the nature of the case, the Attorney General's office sought help from the FBI and the Rhode Island State

Police. Nothing works to reduce—if not eliminate—inter-agency rivalry better than a dead kid, let alone a fourteen-month-old infant. The investigators worked to formulate a theory using the resources from the FBI profilers and the impressive experience of the investigative team.

The Assistant AG assigned to the case did a good job of keeping the political pressure off and focused on building the case. But politics is an insidious thing. It often clouds the judgment of the most conscientious and honest of individuals. It also plays a big part in who gets selected for important positions that come under the umbrella of those elected to office. Influential positions are often filled by those with questionable and dubious qualifications.

None more so than Deputy Attorney General positions in Rhode Island. There are some who've held these positions with integrity and competence. And then there was the current crop.

The sitting Attorney General, Henry Charles King, Jr., was a sincere but naive political phenomenon. Top of his class at Yale Law. Law Clerk for the Chief Justice of the Supreme Court. He was bookish and scholarly, yet he had a way of endearing himself to people. Charisma, with a bit of schoolboy shyness, served to mask any personality failings.

He'd shocked everyone when he returned to Rhode Island to run for office. Everyone assumed he'd take a position with the Justice Department for a few years than sign on with a top law firm. But those who made these assumptions didn't know Henry Charles King, Sr..

King Charles, as his friends called him, once held his own lofty political aspirations of his own. And, but for that unfortunate incident and photo in St. Maarten with the woman twenty-five years-old in appearance but sixteen years-old chronologically, he might have been called Senator or even President King.

But since there are no such things as secrets when more than one living person knows them, he resigned himself to being a King maker rather than wearing the crown. He'd found his calling, if not his heart's desire.

King Charles told Junior, his reluctant Crown Prince, when it was time to return to Rhode Island and he dutifully did.

Since the fuel of politics is money, the Henrys had a political war chest many presidential candidates could only dream about. The election was never in doubt, nor that it was merely a way station to the Senate and the White House.

Henry Jr. now sat in the corner office on the top floor of the AG's office building on Pine Street and listened as one of his Deputy AG's, Richard Wolfson, the son of a political ally of King Charles who wanted more than anything to be in Henry's seat, argue they should arrest the Martins couple and charge them with kidnapping and murder.

"Why the rush? What does the case AG say? Are there any downsides to an arrest now?" the AG asked, criminal law being something he'd only taken a passing interest in.

"There are none," Wolfson assured him, belying the fact he'd never tried a criminal case or represented a criminal defendant, having spent his entire law career specializing in injury cases where the attorney realizes the bulk of the settlement largesse. "A big press splash just before you announce for the Senate is worth it."

King considered things for a moment. "Okay, call the case AG up here and have him draw up the warrants."

"Are you nuts?" Wolfson said. "This is your moment, not his. He can try the case and do all the press conferences he wants. You need to do this."

King smiled. "Yeah, you're right. I'm the AG. I decide. Draw up the warrants and we'll schedule a press conference for the morning. I'll call the case AG and tell him my decision."

"No, you call him in for the press conference and he can find out then. Why give him a chance to steal your thunder? These career guys all have contacts with the Providence Journal and local TV reporters. He'll leak it to make himself the hero."

King studied Wolfson's face for a moment. "You know, not everyone is motivated by politics."

"They may not be motivated by it," Wolfson said, "but you can bet your ass they all *play* at it. Especially the career guys in this office."

"Okay, I'll have my secretary call him in the morning and schedule the press briefing at 8:30 before the courts open."

XXXVIII The Politics of Justice

Department of the Attorney General
Providence, Rhode Island
March 17, 1977, 8:15 a.m.

The door to the AG's office opened and Charles "Chuck" Goforth walked in. Behind him, several reporters could be seen filing into the conference room. Goforth glanced back, then walked over to stand in front of the desk. AG King stood looking out the window at the traffic now filling the streets of Providence. Several of the remote TV broadcast trucks made the narrow roads even more challenging. Deputy AG Wolfson sat on a leather chair to the right side of the AG's desk going over some papers.

The phone on the desk rang. The AG nodded and Wolfson picked it up. After a moment, he glanced at the AG and nodded. "Hold them until I call you back." Then he ended the call.

"So, what's up, General? What did you need to talk to me about?" Goforth asked.

King came around and leaned back on the front of his desk. The mahogany masterpiece once sat in the office of the Secretary of War during World War II. King Charles had it brought in from his house when his son won his first election.

They had to cut out a wall to bring it into the office. The joke was it was the size of a small aircraft carrier, and the Henrys had turned it back into its original purpose. This time planning attacks on political enemies rather than the Japanese and Germans.

"Chuck, we issued arrest warrants for the Martins couple. Pawtucket PD and the state police have arrested them and will arraign them this morning. This was a decision I made, and it has nothing to do with any issues with your work on the case. I hope you understand."

Goforth stared in disbelief the two men. It took all his strength not to reach over and throttle Wolfson. He took a deep breath, calming his rage. "I see. Well, did the Deputy explain how he has now lit the fuse on bringing them to trial? Did he explain that bypassing the grand jury process, for which we had flexibility, will force us to trial in six months? Did he explain that, if we fail to do that, the case may be dismissed with prejudice, and we won't be able to charge the two people most likely responsible for this crime?"

Goforth glared at Wolfson, stepping toward the man, and enjoying the brief moment of fear on his face. "With your vast trial experience do you have even the slightest inkling of the fucking nightmare you've unleashed on this case?"

"That will be enough of that," King said, trying to be firm but now doubting the advice from Wolfson with Goforth's reaction. "This was my decision, not Deputy Wolfson's. If you have an issue with it, it's with me."

Goforth spun around. "Let me guess. You'll want to parade us all in there and put on a big dog and pony show for the media on how you've saved all the little children from these monsters. Well, count me out. I now have to tell all the investigators, who, to a person, will surmise this was the dumbest decision ever made in this office and that we now have a ticking time bomb ready to blow this case apart. I just hope they can find a way to defuse it. If you want to pull me off the case, so be it. But until then...arrrggggh. Leave me out of this fucking circus."

He stormed from the office, slamming the door and startling the AGs secretary as she pretended not to hear the argument.

XXXIX Who to Try First?

AGs Office
Providence, Rhode Island
August 3, 1977, 4:30 p.m.

Chuck Goforth sat at his desk pouring over the forensics from the Martins case. While the evidence recovered from the scene and the body of the infant, Rose Marie, was shocking, would the jury believe it? Was it enough to make the leap from bad parents to killers?

That was the problem.

He reread the report identifying the semen stains on the towel found under the child's head and matching them to James, the father. He then searched for one of the statements Martins had given to the police where he admitted to masturbating while holding the child and using the towel to wipe himself off. He claimed he did this because Rose refused to have sex with him. He also claimed Rose had several affairs with other men and he was uncertain if the twins were his.

This would make the jury wince and understand this was a dysfunctional family, but would it be enough to convict? Goforth was uncertain.

There was a knock on the door, and the Attorney General came in. "Good morning, Chuck. How are you?"

"Good, General, good. What can I do for you?"

King closed the door behind him, then took a seat on the edge of Goforth's desk, folding his arms. "Have you decided which one we try first? Which is the strongest case?"

Goforth remained silent for the moment, still mulling the pros and cons in his head. It was not something that could be decided with just cold logic. Trying the parents of a murdered fourteen-month-old girl and her missing twin brother would always be an emotional, gut-instinct choice.

This case hinged on circumstantial evidence. It would require a jury, many of whom would be or have been parents themselves, to accept the fact that a mother and father, either together or with one agreeing to help the other after the fact, killed one infant and likely killed the second one, then tried to dispose of the bodies.

They would have to overcome one body having been found, which the defense would argue was a warning from the real kidnappers.

A logical question in the mind of every juror, and perhaps enough to rise to reasonable doubt, would be why leave one body where it would inevitably be found and dispose of the other one?

They would have to absorb the horrors of the forensics and the inevitable tears from the defendants and then find them guilty of killing their own children. It was a monumental task. But, in Goforth's mind, there was only one choice. Try the father first. If you can convict him, it would be easier to convince a jury to believe the mother had to know what happened. And her lack of cooperation, despite any legal warnings she did not have to provide a statement, would be lost in the trial's emotions.

But, if you can't convict the father, who presented a less sympathetic persona, a conviction against the mother was highly unlikely.

Goforth looked up at the AG. "We try the father first. It's the only thing that makes sense."

The AG nodded, stood up, then left the office. Goforth knew in a matter of minutes the media would be getting summonsed to another press conference. He reached for his phone.

"Lieutenant Morrison, Chuck Goforth."

"Hey, Chuck, what's up?"

"Gather the troops, we need to have a pre-trial meeting."

There was a pause on the line. "Now? It's 4:30 on a Friday. These guys have guns, you know."

"Not in this office, in my other office. Christopher's, 5:00 p.m. I'm buying. We just decided to try James Martins first."

"We'll be there in ten minutes."

Goforth chuckled. "It's a twenty-minute ride from the station. How you gonna manage that?"

"Watch us. Don't want to give you time to change your mind. Bring lots of money; we are thirsty." The line went dead.

XL **What is Reasonable Doubt?**

Superior Court
Providence, RI
November 21, 1977, 9:30 a.m.

All prosecutors understand one thing about juries; reasonable doubt confuses every single jury member. They try to understand. They struggle to be honest about it. But ultimately it all comes down to a gut feeling. No amount of evidence can overcome the instinctual nature of humans.

Deep down there is always some doubt. The trick is to make the jurors understand the difference between any doubt and reasonable doubt. To do this, they must deal with the complex nature of being human.

We all bank on first impressions. They are difficult to overcome despite later familiarity. Put a reasonable and honest person on a jury, and they will do their best to follow the judge's instructions. They will try to ignore statements or outbursts in a courtroom when the judge tells them to. They will listen to the evidence and try to absorb it as best they can. But, in the jury room, human nature rules. More often than not, they decide the case subconsciously even while struggling to understand the difference between reasonable and no doubt.

When a case such as the State of Rhode Island vs. James Martins, Sr. comes before a jury, the sheer horror of the matter raises a subconscious and visceral aversion within any normal human. They find it hard to believe a father capable of such acts, let alone a mother.

Prosecutors must do more than present clear evidence. They need to overwhelm human nature. It is no simple task.

When Charlie Goforth stood before the jury to make his closing remarks, he faced a monumental task. He needed to balance the horrors of the case against a normal human's reaction to such matters. A murdered and sexually assaulted fourteen-month-old infant, disposed of by the people who should have been willing to sacrifice their own life for the child, is a nightmare few want to believe possible.

He knew those on the jury would struggle to make that leap. Especially those who had ever held their own child in their arms. How could a father do this? How could a mother let this happen?

So, Charlie did what any good prosecutor would do. He went step by step over the elements he needed to prove. He avoided making too much of the horrific nature of the case and focused on eliminating any other explanations for what happened.

He looked each juror in the eye trying to see if there was any acceptance of the State's allegation or resistance to it. He kept his tone quiet and even keeled unless he mentioned the name Rose Marie. Only then did he let emotion in. A peek at the reality of a dead baby. He wanted them to become the protection she never had.

Closing statements are command performances. While not evidence, they are a way for a prosecutor to use all the skills of persuasion without the dry, often tedious, process of introducing evidence.

Goforth was a master. But he faced an overwhelming task, convincing a jury that a father murdered his own daughter and likely disposed of his son like yesterday's trash.

When he was done, he'd drained himself of emotion. Something he hoped the jury would absorb. Collapsing into the chair at the prosecution table, he studied the jury for any hint of success, or doubt.

Lt. Morrison patted him on the shoulder. "Nice job, Charlie. Nobody could do better." But Goforth had his own doubts. Not about the case, but the realities of how politics forced his hand to rush to trial.

He paid little attention to the defense counsel's final argument. He knew they would emphasize the incongruities of a father committing this act on his daughter and they would offer many smokescreens as alternate theories of the case.

In the end it would all fall to the twelve members of the jury and human nature.

* * * * *

The jury would take a day and a half to reach its verdict. The court jesters, in the guise of experts, would all pontificate that the delay boded well for the prosecution. But how or when the jury reached its verdict was unimportant.

The foreperson's voice was strained and racked by emotion, but the words reverberated in the silent courtroom.

"In the matter of State of Rhode Island vs. James Martins, Sr. on count one, Murder, we find the defendant, Not Guilty. On count two, Kidnapping, we find the defendant, Not Guilty."

Reporters rushed from the court to call in their stories. Goforth slumped in his chair, the strain of the past few months finally taking its toll.

The media would spend the next few days criticizing the AG's case. King would distance himself, claiming he relied on the case prosecutors to do their job, effectively blaming Goforth.

Once the frenzy died down, assisted by the latest scandal in the mayor's office in Providence, Goforth would move on to the next phase. Given the results of the first trial, trying the mother was considered hopeless and the case was dismissed.

King would run for Senate and lose. Goforth eventually rose to Deputy of the Criminal Division under a new AG and garner many accolades for his work in reducing the effect of politics.

But he would never forget the case, or the victim. He knew he'd done all he could to prove the case. He didn't think of it as winning or losing, that was the stuff of television shows and movies. He believed in the law and the system. More often than people want to think, knowing someone committed a crime and proving it were two very different things.

He would carry a little nagging doubt about his handling of the case for the rest of his life. But that was the life of a prosecutor.

Rose Marie Martins would be buried in a quiet, private ceremony. Her parents, now divorced, would attend but neither spoke to the media, or each other.

James Anthony Martins, Jr. would never be found. People would often comment on how strange it was that the parents never seemed to make any effort to find their missing son, but they weren't surprised by that fact either. Reasonable or not, there was no doubt in the mind of most people.

Time moved on and the case faded into history.

XLI   **Wish I Knew Then**

Kiawah Island, South Carolina
September 2010

Charlie finished the story and the last of his drink.

"Okay, history lesson over, how about I throw some steaks on the grill before I make more drinks?"

"How about you let the government take you and your wife out to dinner?" Fred said, smiling and flashing his government credit card.

"Oh, no need for that. I have plenty of..." A voice interrupted Charlie mid-sentence.

"Listen to the man, dear." Charlie's wife said, walking into the room. While she was close to Charlie in age, her pacing and demeanor gave off an aura of the young at heart.

And the red hair gave the unmistakable aura of agelessness.

"You always complain you get nothing for all the taxes we pay. Here's a chance to for a rebate without fudging your tax return."

"Gentlemen, this is my wife, Bridget. My Irish tempest."

"I think you should listen to your wife, Charlie," Josh said. "My wife, Kiera, has the fire of the Irish as well, and I've learned to do what she says."

"Listen to her? I am terrified of her," Charlie smiled, putting his arm around the woman. "I learned to do what she says a long time ago. Haven't I, dear?"

"Not without a long and difficult training period, but you came around." She looked at Josh and Fred. "We belong to the golf club here, and it's only a short walk, less than a mile along the beach."

Josh's eyes opened in surprise.

"Young man," she said, catching the reaction. "I walk that whole beach every single day. Ten miles." She smiled. "But I will take my time if you boys can't keep up."

Josh laughed, putting his hands up in surrender. "It wasn't you I was worried about. It's my partner here. He's an office dweller by nature."

"Slick recovery," Bridget said.

That gave everyone a chuckle. Closing the cover on the files, they headed out for dinner.

The hard-packed sand made for an easy stroll, and the light, still warm fall breeze, the sound of the waves breaking just offshore, and the full moon peeking over the horizon made it a pleasant walk.

"I can see why you like it here," Josh said. "My wife would love this."

Bridget reached for Josh's arm. "Well, young man, when you find the answers to what you are looking for," she leaned in and whispered, "I overheard the conversation—you and your wife should come back and visit. We have plenty of room."

"We just might do that, Bridget. Thank you."

XLII   Secrets are Immortal

As Fred settled into his seat, Josh looked out the window. The last of the passengers on the Southwest flight did a desperation search for seats other than the middle as those in rows with empty seats tried avoiding eye contact.

It was almost like natural selection, the vulnerable being selected by unconsciously broadcasting weakness. But soon enough the seat drama was over, and the plane backed away from the gate.

Fred leaned over to Josh. "You ever hear back from Brennan?"

"Oh yeah, let me show you the email. He confirmed pretty much everything Charlie said."

"No shit?"

"Frightening how some things that may seem unimportant and meaningless can create catastrophic consequences," Josh said. "Brennan's buddy said they suspected the kids were alive when the cops went into the apartment. Had they contacted the Martins, it might have spooked them and changed the way things turned out.

"No one knows for certain, of course, but it made sense with the timeline." Josh's voice drifted off for a minute.

"It would have made for a very different world for you, wouldn't it?" Fred said.

"What's that? Oh, yeah. Definitely." Josh went silent again.

Fred turned to stare out the window. Now, he thought, I can make my own choice about how much I relate of this to the US Attorney. It might spark a maelstrom of activity, none of which would be helpful.

Josh went back to reading his notes. He glanced at Fred and wondered if he should tell him he considered talking to the lead prosecutor about this revelation. But what would that accomplish, just create more drama for everyone.

A few hours later, as the pilot announced the beginning of their descent into Providence, Josh made up his mind.

"Hey, uh, Fred. I think we need to keep this little revelation to ourselves for now."

Fred smiled. "You read my mind, my friend. You read my mind."

XLIII Somebody's Gotta Do It

Tommy started to sift through the files. "Why me?" Tommy asked. "Frank is a better choice."

Josh never looked up from his reading. "First, because I said so, which should be enough, but mainly because you are good at sifting through things quickly. There may be something in those files we can use. If anyone can find it, it's you."

Tommy started to argue, then decided against it. "All right, I'll go through the files. But if anything is gonna happen on the street, I wanna be part of it."

Josh looked up. "Of course, Tommy. If there are doors to knock down, you'll be the first one in."

"Good," Tommy said, walking back to the pile of boxes.

"You have the hardest head, and we don't have a battering ram," Josh added, bringing the entire room to howls of laughter.

Tommy's right hand came from behind his back, flipping Josh the bird, but even he had to giggle at the comment.

"Can I at least have some help moving these to the conference room?" Tommy said, carrying two of the boxes and nodding at the others.

"I'll help," Frank said, "I have some time before my next interview with Isabel Rodriques's mother."

* * * * *

Two hours later, Tommy and Frank came back into the office. The quick glance from Tommy telegraphed something ominous. Frank wouldn't make eye contact with Josh.

"What?" Josh said, "How much worse can it be than what I already know?"

"Lt., this means nothing. It's just a bunch of psychobabble bullshit by some FBI eggheads down in Quantico. I should probably just..."

"Tommy, whatever it is, just hand it over." Josh put out his hand.

Tommy looked at Frank, who shrugged then pretended to find something interesting on his desk.

Tommy handed the folder to Josh. "Doesn't mean shit, Lt. Doesn't mean shit."

"How about you let me read it and decide for myself, okay?" He took the folder and laid it on the desk. He started to open it but could feel two sets of eyes staring at him.

"You two get the hell out of here. Go get coffee or something. Whatever this is, I will be fine. Now go."

The two detectives wasted no time getting out of the office, leaving Josh alone.

Once the door closed, Josh opened the folder. Inside was a cover sheet from the FBI Behavioral Sciences Unit dated 22 Jan 1979. From his time at the FBI National Academy, Josh knew this was known more generally as the profiling unit, and its official title was now Behavioral Analysis Unit.

This unit had a reputation for outstanding work profiling unknown subjects—the UNSUBS, who committed horrific crimes—with uncanny accuracy based on reviewing the evidence and circumstances of the crime scenes.

They were rarely, if ever, far off in their analysis of perpetrators. Agencies throughout the country used them extensively in cases involving serial killers, rapists, and other heinous offenders.

This report concerned the incident in Pawtucket in November 1976 and was started on a request by Pawtucket PD for investigative assistance. It began with a synopsis of the incident—the disappearance of the infant twins, subsequent discovery of the body of the female infant, and the search for the then still missing male infant—and then went into some general description of the conclusions.

Josh knew the process. The FBI wanted the crime scene evidence, photographs, timeline, and victim information. They wanted no suspect information so as not to taint the analysis.

Josh read to the bottom of the page... "the following analysis should be considered as significant information for developing and targeting any potential suspect(s). Information is included to assist investigators with interviews of suspect(s) such as interview location, timing, and personnel best suited to conduct the interview to improve the likelihood of a confession."

Pausing for a moment, Josh considered stopping there. But curiosity overwhelmed him. He knew he was about to read things about his mother no one should ever have to read, but he also had a job to do.

Whatever came next would change nothing. Whatever she was, he told himself, doesn't mean I am the same as her. He turned over the page and the words from all those years ago shattered everything he'd ever hoped was true of his past.

XLIV   Nature or Nurture

Fred walked into the office. "Hey, Josh." He got no response. "Hey, earth to Lt. Williams, are you there?"

Josh looked up from staring at the papers on his desk. "What?"

Fred walked over and looked at the heading on the page. "What's that?"

Josh handed the file folder to him. "Here, read for yourself."

Fred took the folder and flipped through the pages. When he reached the conclusion, he took a minute to read through the information.

* * * * *

"Based on the information submitted, the following is a high-level summary of the likely perpetrators based on crime scene analysis and victimology.

Analysis of Crime Scene

> The recovery circumstances of the body indicate the involvement of a perpetrator or perpetrators with a familial or caretaker relationship with the infant. The wrapping of the body with the blanket from the crib and the placement of the head on a cloth towel demonstrate a deep psychological need to comfort the child despite the circumstances.

Based on these circumstances and the overall analysis of the crime, we conclude the most likely perpetrators are the parents or caretakers of the children.

Subject One: Male, Father

The child's father, or primary male caretaker, is likely a blue-collar worker in a semi-skilled job. He will have completed high school but not attended college. He will be of below-level intelligence with little interest in things other than television.

He will own one or more dogs of one or two breeds, German Shepherd or Doberman. He will drive a large, older model pickup with areas of partial restoration clear.

He is likely to have had prior contact with the police for drug dealing or minor assaults stemming from alcohol use. He will have committed at least one offense against a child i.e., indecent exposure or contact. He may have been in prison for minor offenses, i.e., trespassing, peeping tom, petty theft.

He will come from a broken home with a domineering mother and a sibling who was the preferred child of the mother. His father, if in the picture, rejected him as unworthy of affection.

Subject will exhibit a propensity to physical violence and mental abuse of spouses, sexual partners, and children.

He will have intense sexual attraction to young children and likely used the female infant as a surrogate for sexual gratification, most often in a masturbatory manner.

As to the missing male infant, the subject would project his own feelings of rejection onto the male infant and resent any affection or protective action by the mother toward the child.

While it is possible the male infant was also killed, the child was likely taken by the mother and given to someone unfamiliar to the father for protection (see analysis of mother.)

Subject Two: Female, Mother.

The child's mother has deep-seated pathological anger toward the female child yet deeply cares for the male child, almost to the point of ignoring the female.

The mother will be a high school dropout or have a GED level of education. She will never have held steady employment, working part-time jobs such as waitress or bartender at various locations.

She will come from a household with a domineering father who likely favored male children. While there is the potential for sexual abuse, she was likely severely restricted from having any male friends and discouraged from educational pursuits.

She would have prior arrests for theft or embezzlement from employers and done some time in prison.

The mother would feel intense jealousy and rage because of the relationship between the father and female child. She will perceive the child as a sexual rival for her husband's attention yet hold conflicting maternal feelings toward the child.

Given the condition of the body and the totality of the circumstances, it is most likely the mother killed the female child. The placement of the body indicates some level of care and concern.

As to the male child, it is likely she arranged for the child to be given to someone else to protect him from the father's sexual attention after the female child was killed.

She would have planned the action over several months. Once she showed the dead infant to her husband to reclaim his affection, they would conspire together to stage the abduction and body recovery.

As an investigative recommendation for recovering the missing male infant, focus on anyone who served time with the mother who was childless but desired children.

Should more information become available, we may hone the suspect's background, recommend more effective investigative actions, and refine the information to a higher degree."

* * * * *

"Wow," Fred said. "That's quite the story."

"Yeah," Josh said, still lost in his thoughts.

"Hey, listen. This ain't you. The profilers are good at what they do but this isn't a deep analysis of your mother's psychological makeup. It's all the things she did *after* she was an adult.

"You know as well as I do, we are all a little crazy. It's how your parents raised you, the quality of your home life, that makes the difference. All this says is she did bad stuff as an adult.

"Josh, in the argument about nature and nurture, nurture is usually the key. As a matter of fact, nurture can overcome most issues arising from nature."

Josh nodded. "I know, Fred. But it is hard to read something like this about your own mother. Let alone one you didn't even know *was* your mother."

"I understand. But if you were some homicidal maniac or predator, do you really think you'd be where you are today?"

Josh shook his head. "Probably not."

"Let me tell you something about my father. While in his own way I believed he loved me and my brother, he was a distant person. The demons he carried from the war would rise whenever he drank, which was quite often, and he would lash out at us.

"This was when they kept such family matters private. They explained the bruises and black eyes as just kids being kids. My mother was so terrified as to be paralyzed. It wasn't always a happy childhood.

"But we turned out okay. And so are you. Whatever your mother's issues, they aren't yours."

"Thanks, Fred. Just gonna take some time to absorb, I guess," he paused for a moment, but it gives me a thought. Can we have the Behavioral Analysis Unit work up this case?"

"Already in the works. Soon after I heard about the multiple body parts I contacted the SAC in Quantico. I expect to have something soon."

"Cool, and thanks again, Fred. This is gonna be one fucking amazing war story."

"No worries, Josh. No worries."

XLV   Oh, What a Tangled Web

Josh posted the latest results on the board. "Okay, let's settle down," Josh said, addressing the weekly update group. "Since our last meeting, we have identified several commonalities among all of the victims, with a couple of exceptions.

"We'll spend most of the meeting discussing these links, but I want to point out the outliers. So far, we have found no link between Tatiana Vaca, Finian Cary, and Donovan Truell—the female PC student and two male vics—and the other victims or to each other.

"Our theory right now is they may be connected to the UNSUB or UNSUBS, the primary actors in the case. We'll dive into it later. For now, I want to focus on the common denominators among the nine identified victims."

"Fred, you're up."

"Thanks, Josh. Okay our vic Rose Cardosa, female, age twenty-one at the time of disappearance. We matched her DNA through US Navy records which is also the source for Dafne Toste DNA.

"She was officially discharged for discipline problems, but it turns out it was for being AWOL from her tech school. Some REMF—Rear Echelon Motherfuckers for the draft dodgers in the crowd—in personnel didn't feel like doing the full AWOL process and just initiated general discharge proceedings. From what we learned the unit commander at the time was a drunk and didn't pay much attention to details.

"While she had some disciplinary issues, they really weren't enough to warrant the discharge. She just went missing, and nobody bothered to look."

Fred shuffled the reports, then continued.

"As to the Pawtucket matter, we have the file from Pawtucket PD, for what it's worth, nothing of much use in there. Let's say that once the trial ended, nobody put much effort into continuing the investigation, and the file was treated like a dead fish. They buried it.

"Josh and I did meet with the original prosecutor." Fred saw the reaction from Jennifer and wondered if she'd be calling DC about the detour from the original agreement. "He had a complete copy of the case file, from the initial investigation through the jury verdict form.

"We are still going through it, but there may be something that points to a connection between that case and our UNSUBS."

"I just love all this FBI talk, UNSUBS is so cool," Tommy interjected, getting a laugh from the crowd. "We should have a secret handshake when we meet."

Fred shook his head. "I'm glad he stays here when this is over."

"We're not," Frank said.

Tommy smirked.

"One other thing, the Behavioral Analysis Unit is running a full review of this case. The agent in charge is coming up at some point to discuss their findings. If you aren't familiar with their work, I have no doubt you'll be impressed. They have a way of getting inside the minds of perps just by reviewing the crime scene evidence. Quite frankly, what they can do is spooky.

"I've worked a number of serial murder and rapist cases with them, and they are uncanny when it comes to describing the suspect's character and lifestyle. They are a great resource for helping identify likely suspects in these cases."

He closed the folder and started to walk away, then stopped. Turning to Tommy, a smile crossed his face. "I told them about you, Moore. They want to bring you back to DC and study you for a bit. I'm sure Chief Brennan would agree to the request. I'll go ask him after the meeting. Down at Quantico, they love having live nuts to examine."

More laughter erupted, and even Tommy had to laugh at that.

Once the noise died down, Jennifer took center stage.

"Okay, there is the same commonality with our vics. All served in the military. Ramo, Braz, and Lopes in the Army. Criado was in the Marine Corps. All identified through enlistment DNA.

"Braz has a brother, Teofilio Braz. Real piece of work. Had nothing to offer about his sister. All he was concerned with was the hundred dollars he lent her back in July 2009.

"We traced ferry records for travel by Braz to a worksite on Block Island, and he traveled there between July 14 thru July 18. No one saw Aurora Braz after that date.

"That fits with one of our other victims, Alessandra Lopes. Braz's brother remembered a friend called 'Lessie." Military records show Aurora Braz and Alessandra Lopes in basic training together in March 2008. After Advanced Infantry Training, the Army assigned them to cryptology school starting in June2008. They began missing training dates and were discharged in August 2008."

John took over the briefing. "We also found that Vanessa Ramos was in the same basic training company as Braz and Lopes. That's how they knew each other. So far, that's the only link.

"Paula Criado went to Parris Island after enlisting in the Marine Corps in February 2007. She suffered a minor injury and was recycled back to week 8 of training. This started a series of disciplinary issues.

"After she completed boot camp, the Marine Corps assigned her to cryptology school. She excelled at the school for the first several months. Then she began missing training dates. Discharge followed in June 2008."

"So, if I have this straight, Braz, Criado, Lopes, and Ramo, were all discharged around the same timeframe, right?" Josh asked.

Heads nodded in response.

Josh turned to Frank Lachance. "And your vics? Same story?"

Frank looked over his notes. "Solange Daniel is still listed as AWOL by the Army since June 2008. No explanation for the lapse in time. Isabel Rodriques was discharged from the Army, June 2008. Monteiro is still listed as AWOL July 2008. And Cardosa was discharged from the Navy, June 2008."

"Well, there it is, a commonality to these vics all leaving the military around the same time."

"True, Josh, but we still can't link them all together," Fred said. "Some knew each other. Others, as far as we know, didn't."

"As far as we know now, but I think it's worth digging deeper. We've spoken to all the living relatives, and other than a few pictures, there's nothing helpful. Instead of focusing on their background, let's concentrate on what happened after they separated from the service.

"Fred, can you or Jennifer use your contacts at DOJ to pry info from the Department of Defense? Get as much on the date, time, and location of the discharge proceedings as you can. Maybe there's something there? They had to have met the UNSUB around that time."

"I can do that," Jennifer said. "I spent time at the Pentagon before I left the Air Force. I've got some good contacts there."

"Good, anything else?" Josh looked around the room. "No? Okay. Fred, can you find out when the profiler unit might have something for us? I want to coordinate any info from them with anything we get from DOD."

"I'll call them now."

"Okay, that's it for now. Let's continue gathering more info on Jenkins and the outliers. Maybe there's something there that will point to who Jenkins was working with and how the others fit into the picture. Meet again next week. Thanks."

Everyone started to leave the room.

"Wait," Josh said, and everyone stopped. "Something just clicked. Cryptology. You guys said several of the vics were assigned to cryptology schools, right?"

"Ah, wait it's in my notes," Fred said. "Yup, I didn't make the link, but Cardosa was cryptology as were all the others except Solange Daniel and Isabel Rodriques, but we didn't focus on their military specialties."

"How much do you want to bet the connection is the crypto school? Don't they run some joint operations training across multiple units? Mixing Army and Navy personnel?

"I bet that's the link. They were all assigned to the same cryptology training section. Maybe that's where we'll find the UNSUBs as well."

"Weren't you a jarhead, Moore?" Fred tried to contain a smile. "That's part of the Department of the Navy, isn't it?"

"Yeah," Moore snarled, "the men's department."

Fred chuckled. "Calm down, wild man; I was a Marine as well."

"You were?" Tommy said. "I knew there was a reason I liked you."

"Okay," Josh said. "If the Marines here are done hugging each other, back to work. Jennifer, see if my theory holds up. Have your contacts send us copies of the class list for the crypto schools including any instructors assigned."

"Will do, Josh. Good catch." Jennifer said.

"Thanks, let's hope it's not a dead end."

XLVI   Dissecting a Life

Tommy waved a file in the air, then tossed it on his desk. "How can someone just appear out of nowhere?" Tommy said. "I mean, there is nothing on this Jenkins guy except that one minor thing in Pawtucket and the vehicle registration."

"There has to be something, Tommy." Josh said. "Did you look through all public records, vital statistics, schools, credit reports, property records?"

"Lt., with all due respect, I know how to do a background check and there is nothing on this guy. Everything we have for this guy says it's a bullshit name. It was just shit luck it matched the warrant out of Mass. And even that turned out to be wrong. There's no way this sick prick doesn't have priors somewhere."

"I'll call the public defender's office, maybe they'll agree to an interview. But we have his DNA from the arrest and there's been no match except to two of the vics." Josh reached for the phone, flipping through his contact file.

"Okay. I doubt the attorney will agree to anything at this point. Why would he?"

"She," Josh said holding the phone away from his mouth.

"What?"

"The defense attorney is a woman. The name is on the arraignment sheet. I am on the line now," focusing on the call.

"Oh, cool."

"No, no. I understand," Josh said. "Thanks"

"She said no, right?" Tommy smirked.

"What she said was no, but there's more to it. Jenkins called the public defender's office and said he doesn't want their services. Their office is arguing against it, but she said the likelihood of the judge refusing the request is minimal."

"No shit? Is someone paying for a lawyer?"

"Better than that, he is representing himself."

"And he has a fool for a client," Tommy added.

The phone on Josh's desk rang, and he hit the speaker button. Before he could say anything, a recording started to play.

"This is a call from the Adult Correctional Institution being made on a line accessed by prisoners. Will you accept the call?"

Tommy looked at Josh and mouthed, "Holy shit."

"Yes, I'll accept the call."

A moment later, a voice said, "Lieutenant Williams?"

"Speaking, who's this?"

"Lieutenant Williams, this is Israel David Jenkins. I'd like to talk to you about my case. I think I can help you."

"I'd be happy to talk with you, Israel. How about I come up there in the morning, I can arrange a private meeting through the warden's office."

"That will be fine. I look forward to meeting with you."

The line went dead.

"Holy shit," Tommy said, out loud this time. "Why do you think he wants to talk?"

"Because he's looking at life without parole and he knows his only chance at leaving prison alive someday is to give up whoever was involved with him."

The office door opened, and Fred and Jennifer walked in. Jennifer had several file folders with her.

"Here's the info from DOD, class lists, instructors, etc. Lots of names to sort through."

"Got a new development," Josh said. "You might want to sit down."

Fred and Jennifer exchanged glances and then sat.

Okay, what's up?" Fred asked.

"Just got a call from someone familiar to you guys."

"Oh yeah?" Fred said. "Who?"

"Israel David Jenkins," Josh said.

"Jenkins?" Jennifer said. "Is his attorney aware he called? It could create problems."

"Not anymore. He fired the public defender and wants to represent himself."

"No shit?" Fred said.

"That's what I said," Tommy added.

"Brilliant minds, Tommy," Fred said. "Are we gonna talk to him?"

"In the works. I gotta call the warden's office and arrange a private interview room. They have him in protective custody but there is no such thing in prison. I might want to give a heads up to the AG as well. They might want to sit in and send someone to the hearing in court about Jenkins dumping the public defender.

"I don't want to complicate things for him by having them thinking he's talking to cops. I've worked with the warden before. They have an area in the medical wing with no prisoner access."

"Can I suggest something," Fred asked.

"Sure."

"Before we talk to him, let's arrange a conference call with the guys in Behavioral Analysis. Besides divining who these bad guys are, they are whizzes at suggesting interrogation methods and staging for maximum results.

"One of the agents is an academy classmate of mine, Ralph Esposito. I'll get a hold of him and set something up ASAP."

"Works for me. The more leverage we have to challenge him, the better. Call 'em now. Whenever he can talk, I am there."

XLVII Psychobabble and Nothing More

Fred's cell rang. "She's coming here?" Fred said into his cell. "When? Okay. Yeah, we'll be there."

"What was that all about?" Josh asked.

"That was Ralph Esposito, the agent I told you about. He thinks any discussion before interviewing Jenkins should be well thought out. He suggests getting him away from the prison as well. He can't come up because he is prepping for a trial but he's sending another agent."

"Do you know him?"

"Her. Only by reputation. She was the case agent on the Chula River Strangler case. Almost got herself killed when she spotted a guy matching her profile at one of the old crime scenes.

"He saw her moving toward him and shot her twice. One round hit the vest and spun her around. The second round caught her in the leg, severing an artery. There was an agent there who'd been a Navy Corpsman in Iraq. He saved her life."

"What happened to the bad guy?"

"She still managed to fire off two shots herself while lying on the ground. Hit him center mass and dropped him on the spot."

"Wow, tough lady." Tommy said. "Women who can shoot scare me."

"And she's brilliant, too." Fred added. "She's a board-certified psychiatrist and has a law degree."

"Yikes, smart women are even scarier."

"Nah, you'll like her, Tommy. She's also quite attractive."

"Oh brother," Josh said, "Just what we need around here, a pretty FBI agent."

"Hey," Jennifer spoke up. "What am I, butt ugly?"

"Oops," Josh shrugged. "I meant no, ah, no, ah. You're a fine-looking woman."

Jennifer chuckled. "I can shoot, too, you know."

Josh put up his hands in surrender.

"Wow, Lieutenant Josh Williams speechless," Tommy said. "I thought I'd never see the day."

"Shut up. Don't you have anything to do?"

Tommy laughed. "Yup, me and the ugly FBI agent are off to city hall to trace the property records for Washington St."

"Go, smart ass. And bring back something useful."

"Sir, yes, sir," Tommy snapped a salute. "As you command, sir." And out the door they went.

Fred looked at his watch. "Thompson lands in an hour. Let's head down to the airport."

"Thompson? Is it Emily Thompson?" Josh asked.

"Yeah. Why? Do you know her?" Fred asked.

"Ah yeah, well I used to. She was a special assistant AG right out of law school. Handled a few arraignments for us. I heard she'd left but didn't know she went to med school."

"You want to go pick her up?"

"No!" Josh said, a little too much insistence in his voice. "Take Frank with you. He started this whole nightmare; I'm sure he'll enjoy listening to the psychobabble about the UNSUBS."

Frank perked up when he heard his name. "Thanks, Lt. I'd love a chance to talk with a profiler."

"I knew you would, Frank. I knew you would. Especially a pretty one."

XLVIII It's All Theater

Frank Lachance read over the report from the FBI Behavioral Analysis Unti. "And this stuff really works?" he asked. "The bad guys notice this stuff?"

"This does indeed," SA Emily Thompson said. "Truth is, they don't even realize it. Here's the thing about guys like Jenkins; he's just a pawn. From what you told me of his arrest his bravado was all an act.

"He is no more prone to violence than any other person. What he is susceptible to is fear. He fears authority and at the same time he craves having someone in authority controlling him.

"He was willing to leave body parts all over the city just to belong. He was directed to do so, and this gave him a sense of self-worth. It made him feel important. Something he had never experienced beforehand.

"The UNSUB running the show is the real psychopath. If he had a longer relationship with Jenkins, arising to the level of parental control, he could have turned him into a full-blown killer. They weaponized the guy. I bet we find others like him in various stages of adaptation to the circumstances."

"Like being assimilated by the Borg?" Frank said. The satisfaction on his face made Emily smile.

"In a manner of speaking, just like that. My guess is Jenkins was a product of an unstable single-parent home, likely a mother who worked as a prostitute, dancer, or escort. There were no steady male influences in his life. All of the men were transient.

"They likely moved around a lot and never had anything resembling a permanent home. He'd have been in and out of schools, never at the same school for more than a year or so.

"If there were any grandparents it is highly likely it was just a grandmother involved in the same business.

"My guess is he was physically abused by multiple individuals and left home when he was old enough to survive on the street. Perhaps as young as twelve."

"Twelve?" Frank said. "At twelve I could barely make my own lunch."

"You'd be surprised what desperation can drive people to do." Emily continued. "At some point he came into contact with the UNSUBs. They would have groomed him for minor crimes at first; auto theft, shoplifting, then progressing to burglary and sexual assaults.

"I'm shocked his DNA hasn't popped up at other crime scenes. I have no doubt it will eventually be recovered in several crimes in different states."

"We are running a wider search, should have that by next week," Josh said.

"Then I suggest you wait for those results. It will offer more information to use against him. Right now, he believes he is in control. The more background you have to confront him with, the more he'll panic."

"I worry he'll change his mind."

"Who's doing the analysis?"

"You guys at Quantico."

"Give me a minute," Emily said, reaching for her phone. "Yes, hello Special Agent Emily Thompson, FBI. Might I speak to the Attorney General? Yes, of course, thank you." She put her hand over the microphone and held the phone away from her mouth.

"The AG happens to be my father's best friend. It helps to have connections," she said then went back to the call. "Mr. Attorney General, how are you? Okay, Bill, how are you? Good, all is good. I have a favor to ask. I need to light a fire in Quantico, and I am not quite at the level needed. I wouldn't ask if it wasn't important," she paused a moment to listen.

"Perfect, there's a DNA analysis request pending from a case in East Providence, Rhode Island. We need those results ASAP. Thank you so much, yes, yes I will next time I am in Washington. Thanks, Bill."

"Well, aren't you the one," Fred said. "A rabbi in DC. Full of surprises, aren't you?"

Emily shrugged. "Sometimes you just gotta do what you gotta do. My bet is we'll have those results tomorrow or the next day at the latest. Then we can move ahead with getting him here."

The door opened and Josh walked in. An awkward silence ensued when he and Emily saw each other.

"Hey, Josh, Been awhile, eh?"

"Ah, yeah, yeah. How are you? You're a shrink now and an agent, impressive."

"Still the same girl from the old days, just more letters after my name. How've you been? Running the show here I see."

"Yup. Lucky, I guess. Nice to have you here."

"Thanks, glad to be back in Rhode Island. You'll have to catch me up on the latest with the AG's office,"

Josh saw the intense interest in him and Emily reminiscing, changing the subject. "So, what are you talking about."

"I asked about how staging the interview helps," Frank said, breaking the spell.

"Good question," Josh said. "How does staging the interview the way you propose help?" Then he buried himself with moving papers on the desk.

Emily paused, watching Josh try to appear distracted, a sly smile crossed her face, then refocused on the others,

"Okay, there are two things this guy wants, someone who needs him and someone to tell him what to do. He wants a strong male figure in his life. During his entire time growing up women dominated him. Thus, the apparent ability to dispose of female body parts as if they were just trash.

"By having one of the interviewers, and I suggest it be a female, act in a condescending and domineering manner, it will trigger his past resentment and rage. Once this happens, and it will be readily apparent, there will be a dramatic change in demeanor. Josh then orders the female out of the room.

"This will establish a rapport with Jenkins. Fred can then replace the female and make some negative remark to Josh about her, quietly but loud enough for Jenkins to hear; this will further cement the bond.

"Fred should act cordial but professional, impersonal. This will put a bit of fear in Jenkins. He'll want to hold onto the bond with Josh, to please him by being helpful in the investigation. Fred's part will be to keep him off-balance, so he doesn't become too comfortable. He will fear Fred and realize the only way to keep Josh in the room to protect him from Fred will be to offer information."

"It's a variation on good cop bad cop with a better understanding of the human psyche. Having windows for him to see outside will remind him he has lost his freedom. It will also remind him his co-conspirators are out there enjoying their freedom, sparking a desire to find a way out. That's why we recommend bringing him here. Even the ride will reinforce his predicament.

"Once you get going, he'll try to minimize his actions, i.e., deny knowing what was in the packages he was leaving. He will put the blame on the others. Using the women's names with the body parts will increase the stressors in his mind.

"Up until his arrest, he could deny the humanity of the victims. Having their pictures on the wall will disprove this denial. He'll then switch to another tack. He hadn't killed them. And I am certain he had no part in the killing. In his mind, leaving the body parts around the city was an act of contrition. He was reuniting the victims with their families."

"Jesus, he is a sick prick," Frank said.

Emily nodded. "I might use different terms, but you are fundamentally correct. His concept of care was distorted years ago. While he knows what he was doing was criminal, evidenced by his efforts to avoid detection, he does not view his behavior as abnormal.

"It is learned behavior.

"He is, to use your words, a sick prick but nevertheless will respond to the situation in the way I anticipate. Even psychopaths and sociopaths can act in predictable ways under certain conditions."

"Yikes, I take it your husband knows better than to lie to you?" Frank said.

"I'm not married," Emily answered, and everyone caught the glance toward Josh. "Well, not anymore."

"Wow, that was smooth Frank," Tommy said. "I must be having a good influence on you."

Both Frank and Emily blushed.

"I didn't mean...I wasn't..."

"Just let it go, Frank," Josh said. "Just let it go."

XLIX   Nostalgia Can Be Dangerous

The next morning Josh drove to the office early, not expecting anyone to be there. As he pulled into the front of the station, he saw Emily Thompson walking up the front stairs.

Swinging the car around, he pulled up in front, putting the front passenger window down, and leaning over.

"Hey, Emily. Jump in. You can come in the back door,"

There was slight hesitation, then she came back down the stairs.

Silence can be the most troubling of experiences.

"So how have you *really* been, Josh?"

Josh shrugged. "I've been good. Since we last spoke, things have been great here."

"Spoke?"

Josh felt his face redden. "Well, ah, I mean."

Emily reached over and patted his hand. "Calm down, I'm just messing with you. It's a shrink thing, what happened, happened. Nothing we can say or do will alter that. How about we just lock it away in a memory and leave it alone?"

"Works for me."

"And the other thing?"

Josh parked in the rear lot and turned in his seat. "Good, in full remission since the last visit. They think they got it all. And no one here knows. I want to keep it that way."

"No one? How'd you explain the time off?"

"Well, Brennan knows. He told people he sent me to some specialized training, and I got hurt."

"Guy takes care of you, doesn't he?"

"He does. He's a good guy. Gonna miss him."

"Can I ask you something else?"

Josh seemed lost in thought, ignoring the question.

"Josh, are you in there?"

"What? Oh sorry. Drifted off there for a while."

Emily furrowed her brow. "Does this happen often?"

Catching the look on her face, Josh shook his head. "Nothing here to worry about, Dr. Thompson. I'm fine. I need to call the prison. Today is Jenkins's field trip day." Opening the door, Josh got out of the car.

Hesitating a moment, Emily got out and followed Josh into the office, but in the back of her mind she wondered.

Josh long ago put the cancer out of his mind. So far, it remained in remission, but the specter of reemerging haunted the edges of his life.

L Confronting Evil

Driving through the crowd of reporters trying to make their way to the back of the station, Fred blared the horn. "Who tipped off these bastards?".

Josh pointed to the black Crown Vic parked in front of the station bearing RI Official License Plate 4. "Take one guess."

Fred shook his head. "What the fuck is it with these guys? Don't they ever worry about anything else besides promoting themselves?"

"Nope," Josh glanced in the rearview mirror. "Here's how full of himself this AG is. The last three AGs have gone without the plate. This one insisted on it. Like a black SUV with two retired cops with high and tight haircuts and suits as bodyguards isn't enough to tell people how important he is. Another one using the office as a steppingstone to bigger things."

"I hate politics," Fred said.

"Me too. Let Brennan handle the clown show; we have more important things to worry about. The marshals are right behind us. Let's go inside before Jenkins comes in. I don't want him to see you until we're ready. Keep him guessing where you came from."

Ten minutes later, there was a knock on the door.

Tommy Moore looked at Josh. "Ready?"

"Go for it."

Opening the door revealed a now subdued and humbled man in the usual attire of a prisoner in the state's custody.

The ill-fitting, light tan elastic band jumpsuit three sizes too big, with a faded Adult Correctional Institution logo above the pocket, draped his body. He resembled an unmade bed. Shackled hands to feet, he shuffled into the office. A moving pile of dirty laundry.

Towering over him were two young State Marshals. One held out a clipboard with a release form.

"I need someone to sign and accept custody of the inmate."

Tommy glared at Jenkins. "I'll sign it. Gimme it." He scribbled his name and handed the clipboard back. The other marshal put Jenkins against the wall and took his picture.

"What's that for?" Tommy asked.

"My Lieutenant wanted a picture of what he looked like when we turned him over."

"Tell your Lieutenant for me he can go fuck himself. Nothing's gonna happen to this prick." Tommy leaned in toward Jenkins. "That is as long as he isn't wasting our time."

Jenkins's head snapped back and forth between the marshals and the detective, his face a mix of fear and the wild look of a trapped animal in a leg hold.

For Jenkins, there was no exit.

"Okay, paperwork done. You guys can go. He's ours now. I'll take you back to the sallyport."

Tommy opened the door, and the marshals followed him out. At the sallyport, while the garage door opened, Tommy smiled at the marshals.

"That was awesome. Did you see the look on that asshole's face? I wouldn't be surprised if he shit himself when you left."

"Yeah, just don't mention it to my Lieutenant. He'd shit himself as well."

"All good, thanks." Tommy watched them back out, closed the door, then ran back up to the office, two steps at a time. He didn't want to miss the show.

When Tommy walked back in, Josh had Jenkins sitting in a chair facing the wall with images of the victims and the body parts. The trapped animal look was now replaced by pure fear. He was now face to face with the reality of his situation.

As planned, Jennifer came into the office dressed like she was arguing a case before the Supreme Court. She walked right over to Jenkins.

"Mr. Jenkins, my name is Special Agent Jennifer Holmes. I will be conducting the interview along with Lieutenant Josh Williams." She pointed toward Josh who smiled and waved.

"Let me remind you again you are here freely, correct?"

Jenkins hesitated then nodded.

"Mr. Jenkins, in the interview room, we will be recording your statement. I will need you to clearly answer any questions. You must say the answer, you cannot nod or shake your head. That is not acceptable. I ask you again, are you here with no expectation of any promises by the government, the FBI, or the East Providence Police Department?"

Jenkins started to nod, then caught himself. "Yes," he said, his voice barely above a whisper.

Jennifer stared at him for a long moment. "You will also need to speak clearly, understood?"

"Yes," his voice squeaked. He cleared his throat. "Yes," he repeated louder this time.

"And English is your primary language, correct? You can both read and write in English?"

Jenkins's face noticeably reddened. This time his answer was more forceful. "Yeah, I can."

"Fine, let's start. Lieutenant Williams, will you escort Mr. Jenkins to the interview area? I have some other matters to address. Please do not begin until I get there. I will only be a minute or so." She didn't wait for a response, just marched out of the room.

Josh took Jenkins by the right arm, leading him out of the office and into the chief's conference room. They had duplicated all the evidence photos and placed a large whiteboard in the room.

When they entered, Josh made a production of turning the board so Jenkins couldn't read the contents, but not before he glimpsed a highlighted item. In bold black characters across the top of the board Fred had written, **18 US Code § 359 - Sentence of Death.** The federal death sentence statute.

There was no doubt Jenkins saw it, and the psychological war against the evil committed by this man, and others, began.

Jenkins sat facing the outside window. Fall was here, but some late season flowers were still in bloom The trees still green with a hint of color change surrendering to Fall. A cloudless day, the sun was just out of sight, but the light cast an aura of warmth around the room.

This was foreshadowing the coming dark, cold, grays of winter. They hoped the scenes of nature would spark a desire in Jenkins to go beyond trying to save his own life but to make sure anyone who'd played any part in the horror was caught.

If that meant letting Jenkins put all the blame on others while he cried poor, poor me, so be it. He was a small, but important, part of these crimes and held the information they desperately needed.

Emily Thompson had said something that chilled them all and underscored the critical nature of this interview. Whoever was capturing and killing these victims would not stop just because Jenkins was caught.

It is likely they expected this. Anticipated it. Maybe even tipped off the police because it gave them an added sense of power. They could kill at will, control others, manipulate the cops by bending them to their whims, and still get away with it.

It also explained why they kept some body parts and discarded others. They were trophies, reminders, keepsakes helping them relive the thrill of their ultimate power—the powers of life or death—over the victims.

They were, in their own minds, gods. Jenkins was a tool, a useful idiot, to be discarded when he no longer served their purpose.

Knowing that while they were investigating these past murders other victims were being taken, coupled with the medical examiner's contention that some of the dismemberment was antemortem—before the victim's death—nightmare doesn't even come close to describing it.

The urgency to stop these guys was overwhelming.

That's what sat before Josh in the interview room—a human monster who likely took part in the gruesome torture and killing of many victims. Perhaps watched or even helped removing limbs from live victims. It was hard to deal with the incongruities of Jenkins's appearance and the crimes he committed.

Josh sat staring at Jenkins. The man would try to hold his stare but kept glancing away, unable to keep his eyes off the images of the victims with the occasional glimpse out the window.

FBI profilers are a spooky bunch, Josh thought. He could almost hear Jenkins trying to figure out how he could connive himself out from under this mess. Hope, even a false sense of it, can be addictive.

In Jenkins's case, it was a bogus sense. He'd believe it for a while, maybe enough to provide useful information, but eventually hope would fade, and, like the setting of the sun, the dark reality would come.

He was going to prison for a long time. His only hope was limiting the number of years he spent in a cell.

LI Theater of the Macabre

Jennifer Holmes opened the door to the conference room and strode in. Talking on the cell phone, she ignored both Josh and Jenkins.

"Yes, of course, as soon as I am through with him. Yes, ma'am I will." Putting the phone on the table, she glared at Jenkins.

"Lieutenant Williams," she said without taking her eyes off Jenkins, "would you start the video recording, please?"

Josh flipped a switch on the camera, recording the scene.

"Now Mr. Jenkins. Can you read the English language?"

Jenkins was confused by the question at first, then became angered by it.

"Of course I can read. I'm not an idiot. And you already asked me that."

"I meant nothing by it, just wanted to insure you can follow along with the form for the recording. I am going to hand you a rights form and advise you of your rights. Please follow along and pay attention. Do you understand me?"

Jenkins nodded once then said, "Yeah, I do."

"Okay, you have the right to remain silent. Anything you say can and will be used against you in a court of law. You have the right to an attorney and to have an attorney present during questioning. If you cannot afford an attorney, one will be appointed for you.

"Do you understand these rights?"

"Yes."

"Please initial each line and sign the form at the bottom."

When Jenkins was done, Jennifer snatched the form away, slid it to Josh to sign as witness, then put it in the folder on the desk.

"Now, Mr. Jenkins, you are here voluntarily. No one with the FBI or the East Providence Police Department has made promises regarding the matter under investigation, correct?"

"Yeah, I fired my public defender. I don't want a lawyer. I just want to help you understand how I got involved in this."

"Okay, then, how did you come into possession of the head the police recovered from the bag you were carrying?"

"Gideon gave it to me."

"And who is this Gideon? What is his full name?"

"No one ever said, he only goes by Gideon."

"And he gave you the bag?"

"Yeah, told me where he wanted me to leave it. Just like he did with the other stuff."

"You mean body parts, Mr. Jenkins?" Jennifer asked.

"Yeah, body parts. He or the other guy would have me meet them, tell me what to do, and I would do what they said."

"I see. And what is this person's name?"

Jenkins eyed Josh, seeking sympathy. "I don't know his name, he's one of the guys grabbing these women. I just, I just...One calls himself Gideon, I never heard the other guy's name."

"Look at me, Mr. Jenkins. I'm the one asking questions here. Lieutenant Williams is just here to observe."

Jenkins glanced at Josh then back at Jennifer.

"They're the guys you want. I just dumped stuff for them. That's all I did. I never knew anything about what was in the bags. They just paid me to dump them."

"Stuff?" Jennifer said, her voice rising. "That stuff was once living women who you killed and dismembered. You expect us to believe you didn't know you were dumping body parts? I doubt there is anyone else involved. You did this all on your own."

The transition, Josh later said, was like a movie scene. A once timid, frightened little man morphed into a monster.

Jenkins's head tilted down, and he glared at Jennifer through the top of his eyes. He gritted his teeth. His fists began to clench and flex, and he slid his chair back away from the table.

Josh shifted in his seat, ready to block what he thought was an imminent lunge at Jennifer.

Even the voice was different. Slower, deeper, and malevolent.

"Listen, bitch, I told you I didn't know what was in the bags. Gerry just gave me money to drop them wherever Max took me. I don't care if you believe me or not. That's all I did."

At the sound of the names, Josh and Jen exchanged glances.

"Mr. Jenkins, there's no need to call me names. Just answer the questions."

Jenkins held her stare for a long minute, then rose to his feet. Josh moved in front to block him; Jennifer never flinched.

"Sit down, Mr. Jenkins...NOW!"

Rocking back and forth on his feet, Jenkins couldn't decide his next move. Josh came around the table and put his hand on Jenkins.

"Sit down, Israel. And calm down."

Jenkins was screaming now. "Get this bitch away from me. I ain't talking to her anymore. Either she leaves, or you can take me back to the ACI."

"You're not running things here, Jenkins." Jennifer said, her voice still edged with disgust.

"Jennifer, I think it best you leave," Josh said.

Jennifer kept her focus on Jenkins but answered Josh. "You're not running this interview, Lieutenant, the FBI is. I'll leave when I decide to leave."

"Agent Holmes, we are in the East Providence Police headquarters. We arranged for Israel to be brought here, and he is in my custody. You are here at my invitation.

"I am asking you to extend me the courtesy of complying with my request to leave this interview now. If you choose not to do so, I will take Israel back to my office and continue this interview there. You will not be allowed in. Do you understand me?"

Jennifer stood, then broke her lock on Jenkins. "Fine, Lieutenant, I'm leaving." And with that, she snatched the folder off the desk and left, slamming the door on the way out.

Josh took his hand off Jenkins. "Sit down, Israel. I'm gonna bring someone else in here with us."

"Fine, just not another bitch like her. One word and Gerry will gut her if I ask."

Josh smiled. Damn psychobabble shit works he thought. He opened the door and peered out. Beyond Jenkins's view, Fred and Jennifer stood smiling in the Chief's reception area.

"That was an Academy Award-winning performance, Jen," Josh whispered. "He'd chop you up if he had the chance."

"Thanks, I think. Now go finish him off."

Josh tilted his head for Fred to follow him back into the interview area. They paused at the door for a moment.

Fred, feigning trying to keep out of earshot of Jenkins said, "I told them not to let that dyke bitch near him, but they wouldn't listen."

The message got through. Jenkins face showed a return to the complacent, scared little man.

"Israel, this is Fred Robertson; he's an FBI agent but nothing like the last one. You good with that?" Giving Jenkins a little sense of control.

"Yeah, anyone but that last bitch."

Fred put out his hand, "Nice to meet you, Israel. I just want the truth to catch the real bad guys."

Jenkins hesitated for a moment, then shook his hand. "That's why I agreed to come here. To tell the truth."

"Okay," Josh said, "let's start with what was in the bag you were carrying. Did you know the victim?"

Jenkins shook his head. "Like I said, I just did what Gideon or Max told me."

Josh and Fred exchanged glances at the mention of the second name.

"You didn't know what was in the bag?"

"Nope."

"You didn't look?"

"Nope, did that once and almost puked. I didn't want to know."

Something in Jenkins's body language caught Josh's eye. He leaned in, resting his arms on the table.

"Who is Tatiana Vaca?" The micro reactions told Josh he'd hit a nerve. "How is she involved?"

Jenkins shook his head. "She's not... She's...She's, my girlfriend."

Another glance between Josh and Fred. He didn't know she was dead.

Josh changed tact.

"Who is this Gideon guy?"

"He's some kind of prophet. Some religious stuff. I'm not into religious shit, I just play along, but he's in charge. I just do what he tells me to do. They pay me and I buy dope. That's all I care about."

"And Gideon is which one, Gerry or Max?"

The look at Jenkins's face said it all. He didn't even realize he'd said the names.

"When was the last time you saw Gideon?"

"An hour before you arrested me. We met. Me, him, and Max. Gideon, ah Gerry, told me where to put the bag and left. This was over near USA Skates."

"What kind of car did he drive?'

Jenkins shook his head, "He didn't, they walked."

Time to drive the stake into the heart.

"So, when did he kill Tatiana?"

Jenkins's body jerked in reaction, wrapping his arms around himself. "She's not dead. She was with Max at the house."

Time to finish this.

"Then how do you explain her head in the bag you were carrying?"

The reaction on Jenkins's face said it all. His rage at Jennifer had clouded him so much he never realized he'd already given up the real names of the others. Now, he knew he played a part in killing the one person who'd ever cared for him.

Once the interview was over, Fred and Josh had the names of those involved and the potential existence of another house of horror.

Now, they had only to find it.

LII   Keeps Getting Better and Better

Fred and Josh waited for the sallyport door to close as the marshals took Jenkins back to the ACI. Making their way back to the office, the entire team gathered to hear the results.

As they walked in, Jennifer stepped in front of Fred.

"Dyke bitch? Really?"

Fred put his hands up in surrender. "It was Josh's idea. We wanted to win him over. It worked." He couldn't contain his smile.

Jen shook her head and sat down. "It's a good thing I like you, Josh."

"Hey, it was all Fred. I never said a thing about you being a dyke bitch."

"Real comedians, aren't you?"

"Tell the dyke bitch to quiet down," Tommy said, "I want to hear what Jenkins said," bringing the room to laughter. Even Jen laughed along.

"Okay," Josh said, "here's what he gave us. Two names, Gerry, with a G, Tavares about 50-55 years-old, goes by the nickname Gideon, and Max Baader, a little younger, 45 to 50. And he says they have another location where they stay. Knows it's somewhere in the city, but not sure where.

"Says he never went there, just heard them talking about it."

"You believe him?" Frank asked.

Josh couldn't help himself. "Oh yeah, once the dyke bitch left, he wanted to tell us everything."

Jen flipped him off but laughed along. "Enjoy yourselves, boys. I will have my turn."

"Okay, time to be serious. For now, let's hold off on more victim inquiries. If these guys are still active, and Jenkins says they are, we go after them first.

"Jen, you, Frank, Danny, and Jerry focus on Baader. The rest of us will take Tavares. I want to find out everything we can about these guys and find the other place they're using.

"Jerry, can you create a statewide list of any recent missing person reports, especially any matching our victim profile? "

"On it. I'll take a ride to headquarters and work with the tech guys there to extract the data."

"Good. Fred, can you reach out to DC and get a similar list? Let's focus on New England first; we can expand it later if need be."

"Already sent a request," Fred said, "Should have it in the morning."

"Okay, does anybody have anything else?"

"How about using the media?" Jen said. "If the missing people are adults, they may not have been reported. We could ask the public for help. Might be faster, although we'll have to screen the usual nutcases."

"Good idea," Josh said.

"Remember what Emily said about the perps trying to inject themselves into the case. They think they're smarter than us and might just offer up some information about things to stay involved.

"Might I suggest using a nutcase to screen the other nutcases?" she added, tilting her head toward Tommy.

"Hey, I resemble that remark," Tommy said. "But I will handle it. I can't wait to see the look on the Chief's face when he finds out I held a press conference."

"Yeah, well, keep it simple. Police asking for help about any recent missing persons, particularly twenty-something females. Nothing more, okay?

"Yes sir, Lieutenant." Tommy started toward the door.

"Where are you going?" Josh asked.

"Makeup, I'm gonna get ready for my fifteen minutes of fame."

Josh shook his head. "You sure this is a good idea, Jen?"

Jen shrugged, "Let's hope so."

LIII   **Clarion Call**

Early the next morning, Josh was the first in. Jen came in a few minutes later.

"I thought I was the only early riser here," she said.

"Force of habit. My wife goes to the gym at 4:30 every day, so I come in. The quiet helps me think before the chaos ensues."

Jen sat at one of the desks. "If you don't mind me asking, how are you handling all this?"

Josh took a long sip of coffee and tossed the cup into the trash. "I'll admit it's been a bit of a struggle. My wife keeps telling me nothing's changed, but it sure doesn't feel that way."

"Well, she's right. You haven't changed. From what you've told me, you grew up in a normal household with two loving parents. I'm a big believer that nurture plays a much bigger role than nature in how people turn out. Just keep reminding yourself about that."

"Thanks, I will."

"And I am around if you need to talk to someone other than the knuckleheads you work with. I'd like to meet your wife. Maybe, when this is over, I'll have the chance."

Josh nodded. "She'd like that. She thinks I only work *with* knuckleheads. Be pleasant for her to see there are some normal people as well."

"I can see why."

"So, what'd you find about Baader?" Josh asked.

"Not much. He's a big guy, 6'4", 300 lb. Bunch of prison tattoos and an impressive scar running from just over his right eye down to his cheek. Odd character, though. His prison time was related to embezzlement with computers. Bit of a computer geek. Not your typical skinny guy with thick glasses. Must have been one of the early adopters of computer crime.

"Overall, a less than handsome dude who could scare the dead and steal their identity."

"Spent some time in the Army in Germany, dishonorable discharge. Worked in intelligence of all places. I sent a request to the FBI resident office in Berlin to see what else they could find. Immigration shows he overstayed his work visa twice then somehow managed to become a citizen.

"Employment records show he worked as a computer maintenance company contractor at various military facilities."

"How the hell did he pass the security background?"

"Still working on that, but he worked on various military projects for a few years."

"Really," Josh said. "That might be the link to the victims. Clearly it makes sense Baader and Tavares would link up. Probably met in the military. Let me know if you find anything else."

"I will."

The door opened, and Tommy Moore came in. "No autographs, please. I am too busy with interviews to deal with you little people. Did you see my performance? Has Hollywood called?"

Jen shook her head. "And the knucklehead parade begins with the chief buffoon."

"I hate to say this, Tommy, but you did a good job with the media. I have a feeling you'll be fielding a bunch of calls all day."

"Thanks, Lt. I may have a future in public relations." As if on cue, the phone rang. "Duty calls," Tommy said, reaching for the phone.

While Tommy busied himself with the phones, Josh, Jen, Fred, and the others headed to the conference room.

"Okay," Josh said, "Jen is handing out a copy of the Baader background. I have one for Tavares for you as well, but I want to go over the details together and see if anything pops."

"Gerald 'Gerry' Tavares, dob 11-21-56, born in Providence and grew up in Riverside. Made it to his senior year of high school, then, just before graduation, quit to enlist in the Army. Get this, the guy was on track for an appointment to West Point. He aced his ASVAB tests and tested like some sort of genius."

"ASVAB?" Frank asked.

"Armed Services Vocational Aptitude Battery. It was tests they gave high school seniors back then. Even though there was no draft after 1973, the military liked to know about those who might volunteer and, in the event of a national emergency, where to look for the guys with potential.

"Turns out his home life was a bit shaky, absent father prone to violence when he was around. Alcoholic mother with a string of boyfriends who also abused him. Either something happened with the father or mother, and he decided to enlist.

"It never occurred to the recruiter to check about West Point appointments, why would he? But his score put him in the top 1 percent of recruits. Tavares worked in Army Intelligence and had a knack for computers which were just starting to make it out into the field. We assume this is how he and Baader met up. He didn't last long, though, three years. He got jammed up on some assault beef on a female soldier and was dishonorably discharged.

"This happened in Germany. He was arrested for stalking and Assault with a Deadly Weapon after threatening a female lawyer with a firearm. She turned out to be the former JAG officer who prosecuted him for the assault.

"The military sent him back to the US. He did four years on the ADW and several assault charges while in prison. Not your model prisoner. In 1983, he was charged with cruelty to animals. He cut the legs off a puppy and then tossed it in the trash. Someone saw the incident and called the cops."

"He what?" Tommy said. "A puppy? When we go grab this guy, I get him first. And I hope he puts up a fight. Fuck that, I *know* he'll put up a fight, and I'll cut his legs off."

"Ah, Tommy, you remember the FBI investigates civil rights violations, don't you?" Josh said, pointing his finger at Fred. "And why aren't you answering phones?"

"Didn't hear a thing," Fred said.

"Just what I need, you encouraging him."

Fred raised his hands in surrender. "Hey, my hearing is bad."

Josh rolled his eyes. "As I was saying, pretty much under the radar since then. Right after he got out of the can, he got involved with one of those apocalyptic religious groups that portray themselves as good Samaritans. They call themselves the Martyrs of the Seven Mountains.

"He's used this connection to try to expunge the criminal cases he's faced. He had a parade of religious nuts with law licenses trying to convince the court that he had seen the light. Hasn't been very successful getting the cases sealed, but he hasn't had any other contact with the police."

"How about I have the white-collar crime guys check out the Martyrs of the Seven Mountains?" Jerry said. "They have a database of these various scams."

"Great idea, Jerry. Do you need the Grand High Exalted Poohbah's blessing?"

Jerry smiled. "I shall call the detective lieutenant, who will notify the Detective Captain, who will notify the major, who will notify the colonel, who will nod solemnly and have the major call the captain to tell the lieutenant to order me to give the white-collar guys a call...which I have already done, of course."

"Do we have any idea where these guys are?" Jen asked.

"We have a Martyrs of the Seven Mountains listing from the RI Department of Business Regulation. They run a non-profit thrift shop and food pantry in Riverside Square. Fred and I are headed there next.

"Just in case, I want everyone else to be in the area. I don't want our visit to spook them with a show of force, but I would like to follow them if they leave. Jenkins says there's another location, and I want to find it as quickly as possible."

"Something just occurred to me," Emily Thompson said.

All eyes turned toward the profiler.

"You mentioned he left high school in his senior year before graduation. That seems odd. We all remember that as the easiest part of high school, right? My guess is there was some precipitating incident. Nothing as extreme as a murder, but perhaps a sexual assault of some kind that he thought might cause him trouble.

"Back then, most of these things weren't criminally charged, but there were consequences. Something must have spooked him, and he decided to leave town. If we could find out what that was, it could be helpful in refining our analysis. Early behavior is one of the best indicators of future acts."

"Frank, can you handle going to the school department and see if anyone remembers him. I realize it's a long time ago, but I'm sure some of the older teachers might recall something.

Josh headed toward the door. Tommy right behind him.

"Where are you going?"

"With you, follow these fucks."

Josh shook his head. "No, Tommy, you go stay by the phone. Let's see what comes of it. We're not gonna grab these guys right now; just follow them. If we're lucky, they might lead us to the other location, I will let you know."

"Ah, Lt., come on. I'm a street guy, not an office mouse."

"Oh, don't I know it. When I need a junkyard dog, you're it. For now, I want you here. These guys might be one of the callers like Emily said."

"Okay, but if you need me, I am there."

"Oh, I know you will be, Tommy, I know."

LIV   Conning Evil

Fred leaned against the door to the office. "How do you wanna play this, Josh?" Fred asked.

"How about you identify yourself and tell them we're looking for a federal fugitive who preys on these locations? I'm sure I've never had contact with them, so I don't think they'll recognize me.

"That way, it will keep the focus away from the city if the whole group is involved."

"Works for me."

Josh parked the car on Lincoln Ave., and then they walked to the corner of Maple Ave. and Bullocks Point Ave. The shop was in an old bait and fishing tackle store. Still ramshackle and tired, it stood out from the revitalized Riverside Square one block over.

One small sign read 'Used Clothing and Food Pantry,' but otherwise, it appeared abandoned. The windows had curtains blocking the view inside. Two crumbling and cracked cement stairs led to the weather-worn door bearing remnants of colors from paint applied decades ago.

"Maybe we can pick up a few things for dinner here," Fred said.

"Yeah, and some food poisoning as dessert."

Fred reached for the handle and pushed the door in. Like a time-warp, a bell hanging from a rusted L-shaped metal bar rang as the door brushed past.

Fred looked at Josh. "My guess is they don't take Apple Pay."

Josh smiled then pushed Fred further into the room.

A woman in her mid-fifties, wearing a long, plain, full-length skirt and a vest right out of Woodstock, stood up from behind the counter.

"How can I help you, gentlemen?"

"Ma'am, my name is Fred Robertson with the FBI," holding out his ID.

The woman came around the counter to look closer, then nodded.

"We're looking for a man who escaped from federal custody. He has been known to frequent places like these, seeking handouts and then robbing them. Has anyone unfamiliar been in? Anyone suspicious?"

The woman studied Josh for a long moment, then returned to Fred.

"First, no one would have to rob us; we'd happily give to anyone in need, thanks to God's grace. But I couldn't answer your question if you are going to lie to me about why you are here."

"Ma'am?"

She stepped toward Josh. "Sergeant Williams is it? At least that's what you were a few years ago. You don't remember me, but I was on the jury in the case where you shot that young man. A terrible thing, but I know you did what was necessary."

Josh took a deep breath, then exhaled. "It's lieutenant, now. And I'm sorry, what is your name?"

"Marie, Marie Tavares."

Josh tried to hide his reaction to the name. "Ah, Marie. That was a difficult time in my life. I didn't really know the names of the jurors. But thank you for what you did for me. I never wanted to shoot that young man."

"We all knew that. Just remember, Lieutenant, God only gives us the burdens he knows we can bear."

Josh nodded.

"Now, since this story about the fugitive is nonsense, why don't you tell me the real reason for this visit? And before you try to concoct another fable, I know it has something to do with my brother, Gerry."

Fred looked at Josh and shrugged.

"Okay, Marie. We believe your brother has been involved with another man named Max Baader and may have committed several crimes. We need to find him as soon as possible."

Marie's head bobbed in a slow nod. "I knew this day would come. I just knew it." She walked back to the counter, leaning her back against it.

"I can't tell you where they are because I don't know. When he got out of prison, I convinced him to come to meetings with my prayer group. But Gerry went way past just praying. He got us involved with the Martyrs of the Seven Mountains but then went off on his own. Way off.

"He brought that Max character into the group, and they started down very dark roads. They took the book of Revelation and built a philosophy out of some doomsday scenarios.

"Many of the original members left the group, but a few bought into it. We had always planned to set up this place to help the poor, so I agreed to run it, but I wouldn't go along with the other stuff."

Josh and Fred exchanged glances.

"What other stuff?"

Marie held Josh's gaze for a moment. "They said some sinners needed to be taken and forced to accept the truth. They started talking about the government as Satan. Their plans went very dark, it scared me. Especially Max. He terrified me.

"I decided to keep working here because we help those in need. I have nothing to do with anything else. I don't even go to prayer meetings anymore; I stay to myself."

"Where are these meetings?" Fred asked.

Marie shrugged. "I don't know. We used to meet here, but they stopped that a few years ago."

"Can you contact your brother?"

Marie shook her head again. "He does come in here, but not very often. Sometimes, he brings food or clothing, but he hasn't been here for a while. I have no way of contacting him."

"How about the others? Names?"

"We always just used first names. That's all I ever knew anyone by."

Josh handed her a notebook. "Can you write them down for me, and their ages even if it's a guess."

"Sure."

While Marie wrote down the names, Josh wandered around the place. Most of the clothing was kids' stuff with some adult things scattered around. The food area was the usual collection of canned goods, soups and pastas, and not much in quantity.

"Here, Lieutenant, I'm done. I hope it helps."

As Josh reached for the notebook, he brushed against a pile of clothing, knocking it to the floor. Bending down to pick it up, he spotted a camouflaged military shirt on the bottom of the pile.

Pulling it out, he felt his heart jump. He placed the rest of the clothing back on the table, then held up the shirt for Fred.

"Holy shit," Fred said, as he read the name Lopes above the right front pocket. "Holy shit."

"Marie, who brought this in?"

Marie's face blanched, a telling reveal. "Ah, I'm not sure. We get a bunch of stuff just left in bags at the door. Most people don't ask for a donation receipt."

Josh took a quick step toward her, and she involuntarily stepped back.

"Marie, up to this point, we've treated you with respect. And I appreciate what you did when you sat on that jury. So, let's not play any games here. Did your brother bring this in?"

Marie's head started to shake before she even realized it. "No, no. It wasn't him. It was that other guy with a weird first name. Gave me the creeps. He came in with a woman. They thought it was a consignment shop and wanted money. Once they found out what we did, they just left it with some other stuff."

"Israel? Is that the name?" Josh said, laying the shirt on the counter in front of her.

She nodded.

"Do you have these other things?"

Marie nodded again. "Some, they're in back; I can go get them. And Gerry's not my real brother. We have the same mother, but I was adopted. We tell everybody we're brother and sister."

"I'll go with you. Just point them out and don't touch them."

This caused her eyes to widen. "Why? Are they poisoned or something?"

"No, just evidence. Show me."

* * * * *

The BCI Evidence van parked in front of the second-hand store. Two detectives spoke with Josh, then began cataloging the evidence. Three of the items, two Cammie uniform shirts and a field jacket had the name Lopes. A pair of Army jump boots had a serial number stamped inside next to the name,

Braga. There were a few other military clothing items seized as well.

"I want them processed for DNA ASAP. If you need OT to cover it, I'll sign the slips and explain to your Captain. Send one set of samples to the State Crime lab and bring me the others. I'll have them sent to the FBI at Quantico."

"You got it, Lt.," Detective Evoski said. "I won't leave until it's all processed."

"Thanks, man," Josh said, then banged the back of the van once the door closed.

Marie stood on the top step, one foot outside, one inside.

"Lieutenant, I can't help you with where my brother is or what he may have done but if I find out anything I will call you." She waved his business card at him, then started back inside. Pausing at the door, she turned back to face Josh.

"There is one other thing, Lieutenant."

What's that, Marie?"

"He wants to be called Gideon. He says he's not Gerry anymore but Gideon, a warrior of God."

Josh nodded, then caught Fred's eye. "Oh, great," he whispered, "let's mix in the religious lunatic fringe."

Walking outside the shop, Fred glanced back. Marie caught his eye as she looked out the window, then closed the blind.

"Whaddya think, Josh? She gonna call him and tip him off?"

"Who knows?. I'll call the AG's office and see if we can grab her call records. If she does, we can track his phone."

Walking back to the car in silence, keeping an eye out to see if they were being watched, Josh called the others and gave them a quick update. He had them play the area for a while in case they spotted Baader or Tavares.

As he opened the door, Fred asked, "What about her being on a jury?"

"Long story."

Fred climbed in the car.

"I love long stories unless you'd rather not share."

Josh took a deep breath.

"Back in 2006 I was involved in a shooting. I killed a kid involved in a robbery. The US Attorney at the time, piece of shit named Collucci, turned it into a racial thing. The kid was black.

"Took it to trial, and I was found not guilty."

"Collucci? As in the dead Senator who was involved with the Russians?"

"Yup"

"How the hell do you find yourself in the middle of these things in this small city?"

Josh chuckled. "That's exactly what Brennan asks me every time something like this happens."

"You live that Chinese curse about living an interesting life, don't you?"

"It would seem so, Fred, it would seem so. Let's play the neighborhood a bit, then head back. I'm gonna have Jenkins brought back again. Boy was less than forthright with us, and we need to enlighten him about the error of his ways."

LV   **Hide and Seek**

Max flipped open a knife, feeling the sharpness of the blade. "I told you that bitch sister of yours would rat us out," Max Baader said. "She's gonna give us up, you watch. Should've let me get rid of her when they grabbed that fuckin' punk Jenkins.

"I shoulda done him, too."

"Shut up, Max. She doesn't know anything. What's she gonna tell them without putting herself in a trick box? Besides, where else we gonna get money right now? She's got the perfect cover. But, if need be, you can take her out, okay?"

Max smiled. "Okay, man, okay."

From their hidey hole in the old tire warehouse across the street, they had the perfect view of the second-hand shop.

"Jenkins never went to our spot in Rumford, so there's no way they know about it. We'll just lay low for a bit."

A moment later, his burner phone rang.

"Hey, Marie. What's up?" He put the phone on speaker.

"Gerry, the cops were just here. That Sergeant Williams guy. The one I was on the jury for. He's a Lieutenant now. They're looking for you and Max."

"What you tell 'em?"

"That I don't know where you are or how to reach you."

"Good girl, Marie."

"But they found some stuff here that Jenkins brought in."

Gerry and Max exchanged glances. Gerry's eyes narrowed.

"What stuff?"

"Some military uniforms with name tags on them. Jenkins and that girl brought them in. He thought we paid for this stuff, then just left it when I told him we didn't."

"I told you," Max whispered, "I told you to let me off him when we did the bitch."

"Okay, that's fine, Marie. They can't tie it to me. No problem. You make the other delivery yet?"

"Yeah, this morning, but we better not do anything for a while with the cops watching me."

"Nothing to worry about, Marie. They're not after you, they want me, but I'm too smart for them. Max will meet you at the usual spot tonight; bring all the money with you, okay?"

"Okay, Gerry. If you're sure."

"It's cool, Marie. There's another shipment coming on Friday. Be ready."

"I will, bye."

"Sounds like she's getting hinky, Gideon."

"Nah, she's cool. Cops spooked her a bit is all. That fuck Williams is an asshole. Shot some spook a few years ago and got away with it. I don't know the other guy, probably state police. Maybe we need to make this a bit more personal."

"How's that?" Max asked.

"Find someone Williams cares about and take them away from him?"

"How we gonna do that?"

"Don't worry," Gideon smiled. "I'll find a way."

LVI   Paranoia Pays

Kiera Williams was a creature of habit. Gym at 4:30, done by 5:15. Home to shower, out the door by 7:15, and at her downtown office by 7:45. Large coffee with extra cream and sugar from the coffee shop in the lobby and at her desk by 8:00.

Her law partners always tried to convince her she could come and go as she pleased as a senior partner, but she'd just smile. They said it was a benefit of her hard work, but she knew her long hours made them look bad.

Her dedication to routine and organization got her through college, law school, and the bar exam. Hell, it got her through grammar school. Why change now?

"Kiera," her paralegal Michele said, poking her head in the office. "You've got a call on line 1. Some creepy guy named Josh says he has naked pictures of you for sale." She laughed and walked off.

Kiera reached for the phone. "What do you want now, Mr. Williams?"

"How much for the pictures?"

"You remember I sleep next to you and have ready access to weapons, right?"

"Okay, okay, I'll just keep them for now. How about dinner tonight?"

"Wow, a dinner invitation. What did you do?"

"Nothing, just we've been so busy I thought we could meet at your office and find some place in the city."

"Well, I wanted to try a new place on South Main. Let's meet there, it's called Olivia's on Main. Think you can find it?"

"I'll do my best. I am a detective, you know."

"I'll text the address and a link to Google maps."

"Smart ass. Does 6:30 work?"

"Can't wait, see ya," she ended the call.

Reaching for her laptop, she flipped it open, waiting for it to come alive. The phone rang again.

"Kiera Williams."

The voice was gravelly, staccato, like a salesperson trying to hurry the words out before the other person hung up.

"Yes, good morning, Ms. Williams. My name is George Hopkins. I was in the service with a guy named Josh Williams, and I've been trying to get in touch with him. You wouldn't happen to be related, would you?"

Being married to a cop brings with it a certain inherited paranoia. While lawyers sometimes make enemies as part of their job, cops make them daily. The learned distrust of the unfamiliar kicked in.

"I'm sorry; what did you say your name was?"

"George, George Hopkins."

"Give me your number, and I will call you back," Kiera said. The line went dead.

Kiera glanced at the caller ID. It wasn't the local area code for Rhode Island, but that meant little in this age of mobile phones. She shrugged it off. The joys of being married to a high-profile cop and being easy to find online with her own burgeoning law practice.

Michele popped back in, "Wow, two calls before 8:15, bad sign."

"Last one was just a nutcase. But then again without them we'd have nothing to do."

* * * * *

6:00 p.m. seemed to take forever on this perfect Fall day. Around noon, she'd got up to close the curtain on the window. From the eighth floor all she saw was blue sky. She couldn't bear being inside when it was this nice outside.

When it finally rolled around Kiera stretched at her desk, closed her laptop, and then headed for her date with Josh.

As she left the building, something was gnawing at her. She couldn't put her finger on it. It is probably just all the nonsense of a day spent negotiating divorce settlements with people who want to ignore the decades they spent together. It never stopped amazing her how rational, successful people become raging lunatics over what amounts to the dust of life.

The dog is mine!

I found her!

She wants to stay in this house!

We're selling the house!

No, we are not!

Sometimes, it seemed her job was wrestling with adult-sized two-year-olds arguing over a broken plastic shovel.

Nothing that a nice martini wouldn't fix.

As she started crossing the Providence River overpass toward South Main Street, she stopped to watch the boats loading the stanchions for Waterfire, one of Providence's few claims to international prominence. Although the mob's legacy was often most associated with the city, its halcyon days were long past.

She thought she could talk Josh into going for a walk along the river after dinner. Waterfire was always an experience. He hated the crowds, but a smile might persuade him to come along. The implied promise of a future reward.

She caught the movement out of the corner of her eye. Two men taking turns watching her. They avoided catching her eye, but she knew something was off. One started to cross to the other side of the bridge as the other one made his way toward her.

Josh's favorite saying popped into her head. Just because you are paranoid doesn't mean they aren't after you. These guys were clearly trying to box her in.

Josh always said to do the unexpected when facing a problem out of one's control. As one of the boats carrying the firewood came close to the bridge, she yelled down at them.

"Hey, looks like you're leaking gas; you might want to check that."

The crew leaned over at the edge of the boat, waved thanks. then motored up to the ramp near Kiera.

This attention from potential witnesses had its desired effect. The man closest to her turned away. The second man turned back, rejoining his compatriot. They hesitated for a moment, then hurried back toward downtown.

She debated about following them and trying to get a plate but decided against it. Probably a couple of junkies trying for an easy score. Which would have been a mistake.

She didn't carry a gun, although Josh wanted her to. But she carried nasty pepper spray and a painful electric stunner in her pocket, her concession to Josh when she was on the streets outside the office.

With the men now out of sight, she continued toward South Main Street. Spotting Josh waiting outside the restaurant, she waved as she made her way through the rush hour traffic.

"I see you found it," she said, kissing him and pulling him close.

"I followed the map."

"Good boy. Can I ask you something?"

"Do I need a lawyer?"

"If you did, it would already be too late," she said, hanging onto his hand.

"Okay," he said, glancing at his watch, "ask away. I put our name in, but there's a thirty-minute wait for a table."

She smiled. "Wait? For you, perhaps. Follow me." Taking Josh by the hand, she led him into the restaurant. Bypassing the host station, she looked around the restaurant, then waved to a tall, gray-haired man in a sports coat and open-collar shirt.

"Kiera, you finally made it. Olivia will be pleased; she's on chef duty tonight. I will tell her you are here."

"Thanks, John. This is my husband, Josh."

John put out his hand. "Pleasure to meet you. Your wife helped us with the business plan and financing for this place. She's a marvel."

"Nice to meet you. And she certainly is a marvel."

"Are you here for dinner?" John asked, looking back at Kiera.

"We are, Josh put our name in for a table."

"Kiera," John drew out her name. "You don't need to wait for a table here, ever. I told you that."

"I know, John, but we hate to impose."

"Nonsense, come with me." He led them to the bar, calling the bartender over. "Whatever they want, Michael, on me." Turning back to Kiera, he smiled. "I'll be right back. Enjoy your drink."

The bartender smiled and put two napkins on the bar.

Five minutes later, they were seated in a corner near the window. Kiera loved the view of the city lights coming on and the traffic passing by. She knew Josh liked the corner view of the door. It was a cop thing.

As they sipped their drinks, a woman in a chef's apron and hat, wiping her hands on a towel, came to the table.

"Kiera, so glad you finally made it." Tossing the towel over her shoulder, she bent down and hugged her. "And this must be Josh."

Josh smiled.

"I'm Olivia, nice to meet you," and sailed in for another hug.

"Olivia hugs everybody," Kiera says. "She even hugged the bank executive when we signed the loan papers."

Olivia laughed. "What can I say? I love people."

"The place looks great, Olivia."

"Thanks, and I'm glad you finally made it. Let me make something extraordinary for you, if you're okay with it. Sound good?"

Josh pushed the menu away. "Works for me."

"Me, too," Kiera said, gathering the menus together.

"Any allergies?"

"Not for me," Josh said.

"The only allergy he has," Kieara said, tilting her head toward Josh, "is hunger."

"Oh, I guarantee you will not leave here hungry." Olivia hurried off, leaving them to enjoy their drinks.

"So, what did you want to ask me?" Josh said.

"What?"

"Before we came in, you said you wanted to ask me something; then we got distracted by you throwing your weight around like an east side princess demanding to be recognized."

She kicked him under the table.

"Hey!"

"Be nice, or I'll have the owner remove you. I know him personally."

Josh rubbed his leg. "If I get a bruise, I'm gonna..."

"Gonna what?"

"Gonna have to put ice on it."

Kiera smiled. "That's a good boy."

"So?"

"Were you in the Air Force with someone named George Hopkins?"

"Is that the question?"

"Yup."

"Hopkins, nah, I don't think so. Why?"

Kiera explained the phone call but omitted the part about the two men on the bridge. She knew she had to take this slowly, or Josh would have her surrounded by armed guards twenty-four hours a day.

"Do you have the number?"

Kiera took out a piece of paper and handed it to Josh. The look on his face frightened her. Josh was one of the most laid-back people she ever knew. Little rattled him, but he went full ballistic when it did.

This look was different. A quiet terror more intimidating than anything she had ever seen.

"Kiera, we might have a problem. Is there anything else?"

His look told her it was not the time to hold anything back. When she'd finished the story about the men on the bridge, his quiet demeanor terrified her.

"So, who is this Hopkins character, or the guy using the name Hopkins?"

"It might be connected to a case we're working on. I'm sure you can guess which one."

"I was hoping it would be nothing."

"Yeah, well, it ain't," Josh glanced around to make sure no one could hear him, then leaned closer. "We rattled a suspect's stepsister today. My guess is they want to make this personal."

"Okay, so I'll be more cautious."

Josh shook his head "No. These guys are seriously warped. They cut people up and freeze the parts after they've had their fun with them. Then they take delight in dropping them around the city. The FBI profilers say they're psychosexual sadists. We're not playing games with this."

"Josh, I'm not gonna be put in a cage. I have a law practice. I have a life. I'm not getting interrupted because of these bastards. If it makes you feel better, I'll carry a gun. But you're not locking me away somewhere."

Josh reached out and took her hand. "I'm not gonna try to lock you away, wouldn't even consider it. But I am also not taking chances with you. I happen to like keeping all your parts for myself and attached in all the right places." He smiled.

"Why, Mr. Williams, are you trying to seduce me?"

"This appetizer will help with that," Olivia smiled, standing over them with a dozen chilled oysters.

Kiera's face turned crimson. Josh put his head down, hand to his forehead elbow on the table.

"Enjoy, but wait until you're home before anything else happens, okay?" Olivia chuckled and walked away.

"I have a suggestion," Kiera said, as she handed Josh an oyster.

"I'm listening."

"I'll hire Chris Hamlin as an investigator, and she can stay with me until this is over."

Josh sat back in his chair for a moment. "I don't know, Kiera. I trust Chris and all, but she isn't a kid anymore."

Kiera took out her mobile phone.

"Who are you calling?"

"Chris. I'll tell her you think she is too old to help. I want to see how long it takes for her to show up and toss you around the restaurant. Bet it's before the first course comes out."

"Funny, very funny. Put the phone away. I'll call Chris and fill her in. She won't let you pay her, though. I know her."

"If she is doing investigative work for me, she will. Look, you talk to her about what she needs to know, then she can meet me at the office tomorrow morning, okay?"

"Okay, deal. But I am gonna let Providence PD know about this as well, have them be a bit more visible around the office."

Across the street, two men lurked in the shadows of the World War II memorial. One took pictures of Josh and Kiera through the restaurant's window.

"Gideon, we gonna snatch the bitch when she leaves?" Max said.

"Nah, he won't let her walk back alone. She'll become a bit harder to grab now," he paused for a moment, rubbing his crotch. "This just makes it a bit more fun. We'll snatch that bitch and make her scream. Then I'll send Williams the video of us gutting her."

"Why these pictures, then? We know what she looks like."

Gideon smiled. "We're gonna play a little game of fuck with the cop's family. Make his life miserable. He's a sinner, they all are. And we're gonna rid the world of them."

LVII   Cavalry to Calvary

The station intercom broke the morning silence. "Lieutenant Williams," the receptionist said, "Chris Hamlin is here to see you."

"Thanks, I'll be right out." Josh hung up and headed toward the door. "Come on, Fred. I want you to meet Chris."

The two made their way down the hall to the lobby side door.

"Hey, Chris, come on in."

"I bring presents in the form of donuts. I thought it might help keep Moore and the others at bay as you tell me what the hell is going on. I am retired after all."

"As I well know. I still celebrate the day you left as Emancipation Day."

"Smart ass."

"Chris, this is Fred Robertson from the FBI. Fred, Chris Hamlin, retired Lt. and my first boss on the job."

"Nice to meet you, Chris. You have my sympathies. Working with these guys couldn't have been much fun."

Chris smiled. "I like this guy," pointing at Fred. "Nice to meet you. Now is somebody gonna tell me what..."

"Oh my God," Chief Brennan said, interrupting the conversation. "Please tell me you're here collecting money for your elderly bowling team or something equally harmless."

Chris spun around to face Brennan. "You're still alive? Must be some kind of record. Didn't you become chief right after they invented electricity?"

Brennan smiled, then hugged her. "Okay, let's all go back to my office and find out why Lieutenant Williams here is calling in the gray-haired reserves."

Twenty minutes later, they had their answer.

"Who is with her now?" Brennan asked.

"Jerry Paulsen and Frank Lachance. They volunteered."

"And you think having Chris take over is enough?" Brennan put up his hands as Chris opened her mouth to argue. "I know what you're capable of, Chris, and your many, ah, skills, but there are at least two suspects."

"Here's what Kiera has agreed to do. Chris will be with her whenever I can't. She'll take her to the office and go with her wherever she needs to go. At the end of the day, she'll stay with her until I come home, then stay in our spare room until we grab these guys."

"What do you think, Fred?" Brennan asked.

"Well, it's not witness protection level, but I think it will work. These guys thrive on control. Taking on two people lends itself to problems. If they're both armed and cautious, avoiding situations where they'd be isolated, I think they'll be okay."

"Chris," Brennan said facing her. "You okay with this?"

Chris nodded. "Yup, I've got some backup as well with a few of my guys. We will take care of Kiera. Of course, none of us have a clue why she married this nitwit, but it is what it is."

She stood, looking all three in the eye. "Whatever happens, I guarantee when it's over Kiera will be fine. As to anybody who tries to change that...I make no such assurances."

Brennan groaned. "Please try not to kill anybody if you can avoid it. I wanted to just enjoy my last few months on the job, not spend it explaining body counts to the media."

Chris smiled. "No worries, Chief. There's only two of them. Hardly amounts to a body count."

Brennan shook his head and left the room.

"Do you need anything else, Chris?" Josh asked.

"Nope, got it covered. I'll head down to Kiera's office. I took the liberty of having our retired friend Joe Sarrasin from the state police install surveillance equipment at your house—camera, motion sensors, etc. That okay?"

"Wow, thanks. I was gonna call him after I spoke with you. Tell him to send me the bill."

Chris shook her head. "No bill. When Hawk heard about it, he offered, and you know how arguing with him goes."

"I do, tell him I said thanks."

After Chris left, Josh and Fred headed back to the office.

"Who's this Hawk character?" Fred asked.

Josh chuckled. "Harrison 'Hawk' Bennett, extraordinary defense lawyer, former Green Beret with four tours in Vietnam, and a thorn in the side of the Justice Department, the

Attorney General's office, and pretty much anyone who pisses him off. I guarantee you've never met anyone like him."

Fred's eyes opened wide. "And he's paying for your surveillance equipment?"

"He represented me in my criminal case. Loves Kiera. It's more for her than me."

"That makes sense," Fred chuckled. "You have some unusual friends."

LVIII   All's Fair...

A uniform cruise pulled up to Josh in the back lot. "Good morning, Lt." Officer George Fredericks said

"What's up?".

"I found this on the front steps this morning," handing him a large yellow envelope marked, *Lieutenant Williams. Personal and confident.*

Josh turned it over, flipping it around. "Obviously from some genius. When was this?"

"About 4:30, the shift commander sent me out to grab some food for the station. It was there when I got back."

"Ya see anybody around?"

"Nah, dead night. There was a van at Waterman and Pawtucket that turned toward the station as I was leaving, probably just someone headed to work. Nothing unusual."

"Did you see the driver or catch a plate?"

"Nah, I couldn't see a thing with the headlights and tinted windows. Didn't really think much of it. And I was in a hurry. You know how you Lieutenants are when you aren't fed."

"I do," Josh laughed. "Okay, thanks." Taking the envelope, he headed inside.

In the office, he tossed the envelope on his desk. "Tommy, call BCI have one of them come up here."

"You need help opening an envelope?"

"Yeah, smartass. Call!"

Five minutes later, Detective Skefton walked in.

"What's up, Lt.?"

"I want this processed before we open it. Can you check it for prints?"

"I can try. We might have a better shot with DNA depending on if it is a moistening glue sealant or the pull-off tape type. Won't know until we open it,"

"Okay, once the outside is processed, call me, then we'll open it."

Forty-five minutes later, Josh's phone rang. "Hey, nothing. Okay, I'll be right down."

Josh and Tommy made their way to BCI on the ground floor. Skefton had the envelope on an examination desk in the photo area.

"So, no prints, couple of smudges but nothing usable. I matched the envelope type to the manufacturer, and it is a moisten and seal type, so there may be DNA.

"It will take me time to extract it, and the state lab is months behind on processing, so your FBI friends might be a better choice."

"Yeah, we can do that, but I want to open it."

"No problem. We'll open it from the manufacturer-sealed end and leave the DNA processing to Quantico."

"Go for it." Josh said.

Skefton changed out his gloves for a new set, then ran a razor down the bottom of the envelope. Holding it by the sides he gently shook out the contents. A smaller, unsealed white envelope slid out.

Inside this envelope, they could make out printed pictures. Using a small set of tweezers, Skefton slid the images out and turned them face up.

"Wow," Moore said.

"Motherfuckers," Josh said, taking the tweezers and turning the pictures to have a better look.

One of the images was of Josh and Kiera sitting at the restaurant. That was bad enough, but the second one was more troubling. It was the back side of a naked woman, hands bound behind her back. A hand gripped her hair tightly as a second person stood in front of her, forcing her to lick the seal on a yellow envelope.

"Motherfuckers, they have another one. And she's alive." Josh growled, slamming the wall.

"Hey, Lt., there's something else," Skefton shook the larger envelope and a note came out.

The words inflamed Josh's rage beyond measure.

Can't wait to play with Kyerra. Don't worry. We ll send her back one peace at a tiem.

Moore looked at Skefton, both at a loss for words. Josh broke the silence.

"Lars," Josh said, his voice preternaturally calm. "Package this shit up for the FBI today and send it overnight. Or drive it there yourself. But I want it there tomorrow, understand?" Taking out his cell, Josh snapped pictures of the pictures and note.

"Make sure this is done by the numbers. Don't fuck it up, understand?"

"Yes, sir, Lieutenant."

Josh turned and stormed out of the room.

"Lars," Moore said. "If I were you, I'd charge up the cameras and fuel your evidence van. Before long, you will be processing a scene with at least two bodies. I have a feeling we are not taking prisoners on this one."

LIX   Cooler Heads

Fred walked into the FBI office in Quantico and headed to Deputy Director Jones's office. The receptionist nodded when he said his name and told him to take a seat.

"The director is on a call now. He'll be with you shortly."

As Fred took a seat, the arguments he was about to deal with reverberated in his head.

We need to assume responsibility. They're a small agency unequipped to deal with the complexities. Williams's connection to the case is problematic. Once this case crosses into another city, and it will, the local politics will compromise any prosecution.

Fred's background as a patrol officer in Philadelphia before joining the FBI gave him credibility with the locals. He differed from the FBI Academy graduates who went from college or the military right to the FBI. Having a fundamental understanding of what the average local cop did daily made his interactions with them more effective.

He'd stopped cars alone on a dark street, not knowing who or what was in the car. Most straight-to-the-FBI guys couldn't even imagine what working alone in a marked unit was like.

Despite all the TV and movies portraying the FBI as the premier law enforcement agency in the county, the reality was different. Every case began as a local case, and the FBI could never do its job without the help, experience, and dedication of local police departments.

"The director will see you now." The receptionist's voice brought Fred out of his thoughts.

"Thank you," Fred said, then made his way to the door, knocking first—force of habit from his time in the Marine Corps—then entering.

"Fred." Assistant Director Wilfred Jones said, "Come in. Have you met Deputy Attorney General Anthony Alonso?"

"Of course. Nice to see you, Deputy."

"Tony, please. No need for rank here," Alonso said, smiling. "Have we met? I don't recall."

"A lot of people think I am forgettable, Tony. We have. The case in upstate New York. Militia Group. I was in Hostage Rescue. You led the briefing."

Alonso put his hand over his mouth, studying Fred. "Ah yes, now I recall. Weren't you wounded in that operation?"

"I was, still have the round on a plaque on my wall in my home office."

"That was a great case, except, of course, for your injury."

"It's part of the deal," Fred said, turning to face Director Jones. "So, why am I here, sir?"

Jones glanced at Alonso, then came around, leaning on the front of the desk.

"This case in Providence. It has me concerned. I, ah, we wanted to..."

"East Providence," Fred interrupted.

"What?" Jones said, confusion clouding his face.

"The case is in East Providence, not Providence. Different city."

"Ah, okay, East Providence. The deputy and I are concerned about the investigation's course and whether it is being properly managed."

"Oh, well, let me assure you, both of you," Fred nodded toward Alonso, "not only is the case being managed properly, but Lieutenant Williams and his team have one suspect in custody, identified the other two primary suspects, and are focused on locating what they believe is another live victim being held by the suspects. Given the circumstances and the progress made so far, I would say their efforts have been extraordinarily effective. I would suggest it is in the bureau's best interest to continue offering our full support.

"I have the utmost confidence that Lieutenant Williams and the East Providence Police Department are fully capable of bringing this case to closure."

Fred studied their reaction. He knew what they wanted was full control to claim credit for the case. But they would go for credit without risk even more. Fred hated politics but knew that's what he needed to offer.

"Deputy, Lieutenant Williams and I have worked cases together in the past. He trusts me, and I trust him. Nothing goes on without our participation. The link between Williams and the historical case is tangential to the current case.

"Special Agents Thompson, Holmes, and I are melded into their teams. We're in the middle of this. We need to keep the focus on the goal here. When this is over, the media will be all over it and it will reflect well on the bureau.

"These guys have likely kidnapped, raped, murdered, and dismembered at a minimum of seventeen victims. They have at least one still alive, as of yesterday that is. If we try to take over, we'll delay our ability to catch these guys.

"Let's let Josh and his guys do what they do with our assistance and participation. It is an East Providence case and should remain that way."

"Fred," Alonso said, "my, our, only concern is the integrity of the case. We will respect your decision if you're comfortable letting Lieutenant Williams run the show.

"For now, the status quo stays," he said, rising from his seat and closing his briefcase. "But let me be clear. If the case crosses jurisdictional lines, introducing federal issues in any potential prosecution, I want you to assume overall responsibility for it.

"From what you've told me, this Lieutenant Williams is an officer of integrity. However, he is not a federal agent. A case like this demands the highest caliber of investigative effort. Do we understand each other?"

Fred stood and went eye to eye with Alonso. "Deputy, when this is over, you and I are gonna take Josh Williams out for a drink."

"We are?" Alonso said.

"Yes, we are. And you are going to pay for those drinks because Williams will have handed you the case of a lifetime."

Alonso smiled, then put out his hand. "I will hold you to that assurance, Fred."

"Deal," Fred said, shaking his hand. "And I know these guys, Tony. Bring a lot of money."

As Fred left the office, Alonso said, "What do you think?"

"Robertson might be too close with this Williams guy, but Holmes will keep us informed behind the scenes."

"It's not a great career move for Holmes, don't you think? I know the way rumors permeate the bureau. If agents find out she was spying on her fellow agents, nobody will want to work with her again."

Jones shrugged. "I'll find her some innocuous liaison slot in an embassy somewhere. No one there will care. They all spy on each other, trying to crush everyone on their way to the next level."

"You are a hard man, Wilfred."

"How do you think I got here?"

LX   She Who Hesitates

Chris Hamlin looked up from her newspaper. "Where are you going?"

"Coffee. Is that okay, mom?" Kiera answered. "Stay here with your newspaper. You know you're one of the five people that still read papers, right?"

"And thus the problems in this world. But you're going nowhere, not without me."

"Oh, come on, Chris. It's in the lobby. There are people all over the place. Nothing's gonna happen there."

"You got that right," Chris said, folding the newspaper and laying it on the chair. "Not while I'm there."

"Fine, come on then. I have a conference call in twenty minutes.

As they made their way down in the elevator, Chris checked her weapon.

"How 'bout I just pay for the coffee, no need to take it at gunpoint?"

Chris smirked. "Why don't you have coffee in the office? Wouldn't that be simpler?"

"Maybe, but I like the excuse to go out of the office. I usually take the stairs, but I thought..." She stopped when she saw Chris's look.

"You thought *what?*"

"Sorry, we can walk back up if you prefer."

As the door opened, Chris put out her hand to hold Kiera back, then poked her head out, surveying the crowd. Dropping her arm, she led the way out.

"Do you really have to act like you're the Secret Service protecting the President?"

"Yup, I do. And I'll take a large, extra cream and sugar."

While Kiera ordered the coffees, Chris checked over the lobby, measuring how she might try to snatch someone here. The layout didn't lend itself to any quick movements, too many obstructions masquerading as design elements.

Kiera was right, nothing would happen here.

"Here you go," said Kiera, handing Chris a coffee. "But I am a bit surprised that Ms. Healthy indulges in sugar and cream."

Chris shrugged. "It's one of my few remaining vices, that, and wine, of course. I'm not giving that up. And martinis. I'm old but not quite dead yet."

"I think you've got a lot of living left in you, Chris." She noticed her friend was not listening.

"What?" she asked.

Chris reached for her phone. "Stay here. I'll be right back." Putting her coffee on a nearby table, she moved away as she spoke on the phone.

Kiera watched as Chris made her way to the side door, slipped out into the street, and made her way to the front of the building. A moment later, Chris came back in through the front door.

"What was that all about?"

"I'm not sure. A car caught my eye. Two guys were just sitting there. I took a picture of the plate. Give me a minute while I call Providence PD and then Josh."

Five minutes later, a marked Providence PD unit drove past the building, stopping across the street from the entrance. Two uniformed officers got out and approached the car from behind.

One officer remained back a few feet from the trunk on the passenger side. The other started up toward the driver. As the officer reached the back seat door, the car lurched backward, striking the officer standing in back. Then pulled away from the curb, striking the second officer, knocking him to the ground.

Speeding away, the car disappeared in traffic.

"Go back to your office," Chris yelled, then ran to help the officers." As she ran to them, she was on the phone with 911, giving them the plate, car description, and last direction of travel.

Sirens approached as Chris reached the officer. One was bleeding from the head where he had hit the curb. He was conscious but dazed. The other struggled to his feet, then collapsed, his ankle broken. He tried to reach his radio which had fallen from his belt and was smashed by the car.

"I already called it in," Chris said, trying to calm the officer with the broken ankle. She glanced toward the other cop and saw Kiera putting a cloth on the man's head.

"I thought I told you to go to your office?" she yelled over the commotion.

"I don't take directions well."

Chris shook her head. "How's he doing?"

"Nasty cut, gonna need stitches but I got the bleeding under control."

"Who are you?" the cop with Chris said.

"Chris Hamlin, retired Lt. from East Providence. I'm the one that called in the suspicious car."

The officer grimaced. "Remind me to thank you later."

Chris smiled. "Hey, looks like I got you the summer off. You're welcome."

The cop chuckled, then winced again.

Within minutes the area was flooded with cops and rescue personnel. One of the Providence PD supervisors came over to Chris.

"Chris?"

"Hey, Jerry, wow, you're a captain now?"

"Yeah, imagine that. Been a long time since we worked the task force."

"Yeah, hell, I've been retired for a few years already."

"So, what the hell happened here?" Jerry asked.

Chris nodded toward Kiera, who was talking to the rescue guys as they washed blood off her hands. "See that woman? She's Josh Williams's wife, Kiera. You know Josh, right?"

"Oh yeah, great guy."

"Hear about the case they're working with the body parts? Couple of the suspects made threats against her. I'm babysitting. That's why I called the car in. Sorry about your guys getting banged up."

"Goes with the job," Jerry said. "Looks like they're just minor stuff." His radio went off, and he reached for it. Hang on, Chris."

"Go for D1 Captain."

"Captain, D3 detectives have the car. Stolen from East Providence yesterday. Nobody in custody. They're searching the area."

"10-4, thanks." He turned back to Chris. "Well, maybe we'll get lucky and snatch these bastards. I'll need a statement from you and Kiera for detectives."

"Okay, she and I will go to headquarters as soon as things settle down here."

"Thanks, Chris. Nice seeing you. Let's hope next time it doesn't involve injured cops, okay?"

Chris smiled, shook his hand, then walked over to Kiera.

"It would make my job easier if you would just listen to me. This could have been a nightmare if they had guns."

"Look," Kiera said, "I saw that officer go down and saw the blood. Instinct kicked in. There was no way I was gonna run away. Besides," she pulled back her suit jacket revealing a compact Glock in a holster. "I shoot back."

Chris smiled. "That's my girl. But it would be nice if I had known about that."

"Now you do, let's go replace those coffees and then we can head down to give statements." She reached for her phone. "Samantha? Kiera. I'll be out of the office for a bit. Back later. Have Linda handle the conference call on the Webster matter."

"What is it with you and coffee?"

"Fuels my waking moments."

"I see that. You grab the coffee; I better call Josh back before he has the entire department descend on your office."

Five minutes later, Kiera came back carrying two cups. Chris signaled to her to hang on a minute.

"Josh, listen to me. She's fine, and thanks for asking about me by the way. The two cops are gonna be okay. Just seemed weird. I'm not even sure it was them, so calm down. Yeah, she's here."

Kiera waved her off, mouthing the word, "No, no."

Chris pulled the phone back, making eyes at Kiera.

"She's just grabbing coffee and then we're going to Providence PD detectives for statements. I will have her call you when we are back in the office. Go do your job for once and let me do mine.

"What's that? Huh, right back at ya. Bye." She ended the call.

"The man is a lunatic sometimes."

"Sometimes?" Kiera said, handing her the coffee. "The only time he's not is when he's sleeping."

LXI   If At First...

atching from the window of the local bar while Providence officers swarmed all over the car, Max said, "Now what?".

"We grab another car, that's what."

"Hey, look. One of the detectives is walking this way." Max glanced at the bartender. "If he asks about us, we're fucked."

Gideon smiled. "Already took care of that. The bartender is a believer."

A moment later, the front door opened. The sun lit up the dark interior, and then, as the door slammed closed, it faded back to the dim, shadowy faux-nighttime ambiance the day patrons preferred.

It took a moment for the detective to adjust to the dark. He glanced around, taking an inventory of the clientele. Then the back door opened, and another detective came in.

Smart, Gideon thought, tried to flush us out the back in a panic. Not today...not today.

The first detective, young, military haircut, and well-built, went to the bar and motioned the bartender over. The other detective, older, a bit of a paunch but with fists like a boxer, kept an eye on the customers for any reaction.

"Detective Morris, Providence PD. You see anybody around that car out there?"

"Nope, didn't even see the car," came the answer.

Glancing back at the eight patrons, the detective said, "anybody just come in within the last few minutes or so."

"Nah," he tilted his head toward the men. "They're all regulars. Been here since I opened two hours ago."

The detective ignored the answer, walking toward Max. Gideon stood and started toward the men's room.

"Where you goin'?" the second detective asked, stepping to block his way.

"Take a leak, I got a kidney infection and can't stop pissin'."

The detective eyed him a bit more, then stepped aside. Once inside the men's room, Gideon took out his phone and dialed 911.

"911, what is your emergency, Police, Fire, Medical?"

He whispered into the phone.

"Police, you guys are looking for two men who ran from a stolen car. They just walked into a place down the road from where the cops are. A bakery. They're in there now. One has a gun."

"What bakery? What address?"

"Fox Point near the bridge." ending the call. As he made his way back to the bar, Detective Morris took a call on the radio.

"Come on. Perry. Somebody spotted them down near Point Street Bakery." The two detectives ran out the door.

Gideon waited for them to leave, then smiled. "Told ya, no problem. Now," turning to the bartender, "let's get a round for everybody on me."

"But we still don't have a car," Max said, leaning in, his voice now a whisper. "And we gotta dump that other bitch."

"Not to worry, my friend," then opened his hand, showing a set of keys.

"Where'd you get those?"

"This dump's owner keeps them behind the bar. He has a car out back for errands. I snatched them on the way back from the shithouse while everyone was watching the cops.

"Finish your drink, let's go make room for our new guest."

"What new guest? We're not gonna try for that cop's wife again, are we? Too much heat."

"Yeah, we are, they'll think we're lying low. They'd never expect us to try anything. So, we are gonna do just the opposite. Maybe grab that other bitch, too. The one who's been with her."

Max smiled. "I like 'em older bitches, they scream more when ya' cut 'em."

"Sinners, Max. They are sinners, and we are doing the Lord's work."

"Yeah, the Lord's work," his smile unveiling his nicotine-stained teeth, "cuttin' bitches who corrupt the world."

"The Lord never said we couldn't enjoy our work, Max. Come on, finish your drink. We gotta go meet Marie for our money."

Downing the last of the beer, Gideon slammed the glass on the bar. "See ya next time, pal."

Just the Two of Us

The bartender never moved, just grunted, his eyes glued to the latest episode of Price is Right.

LXII   **Pushing Luck**

Josh shook his head, eyes locked on Kiera, "Absolutely not. No way. Not gonna happen," he said, arms folded across his chest, foot tapping out a running cadence.

"You don't decide what I do, Josh. I can take care of myself. I am going to the office whether you like it or not."

"Kiera, what if they shoot Chris? You think you can handle two guys who are sociopaths? What happens to you then? I don't want to lose you."

"Hey, hey," Chris interrupted. "What about me?"

"Acceptable losses," Josh said, his focus staying on Kiera.

"Acceptable losses? I'll give you acceptable losses. Look, Josh, I've got this." She pointed to Kiera, "We've got this. They ain't gonna get close to her."

Josh turned, and the anger surprised Chris. "Oh, and you can guarantee that? Really? Look, you've been out of this game for a while. These guys are stone psychos," the pitch of his voice rising. "They kidnap, rape, torture, and dismember women for fun.

"You need me to bring a leg or two up here and show you? This isn't some two-bit wiseguy wannabe or gangbanger. These guys are dead fucking serious."

"Can I say something here?" Chief Brennan said, trying to bring the tension down.

"Not if you're going to tell me to let her act like this is nothing," Josh snapped, then added, "Sir."

"Josh, listen to me. We've been down this road before with these lunatics you have a way of attracting to your family. Kiera is a big girl. Chris is more than capable of protecting her," holding his hand up when Josh tried to speak.

"Let me finish. I spoke to the Superintendent. He is gonna assign two troopers full-time to this protection detail. They'll be in the lobby or following Kiera and Chris wherever they go. Flashing red lights, big giant-sized troopers. Between them and Chris, nothing will happen to her.

"Josh, you've said it yourself, never let these guys run your life. It should apply to Kiera as well."

Josh wanted to argue, but realized it was hopeless. "Okay, okay, it's just..."

"Yeah, yeah, you don't want to lose her," Chris mocked. "Calm down ya big baby."

Josh tried but couldn't fight the grin. "Why do I even try?"

It was Kiera's turn to laugh. "I've been trying to pound that into your thick head since the day we met."

"Okay, I surrender. But if you get yourself killed, I will remarry."

"Yeah, if there is someone dumb enough to do that," Chris said.

"Hey," Kiera said.

"I've said it before, Kiera. You must have suffered momentary insanity when you married the guy."

"I did, but I do love him."

"And on that sickeningly sweet note, I take my leave," Brennan said and fled the office.

Kiera hugged Josh then headed toward the door. Chris hung back.

"I'll be right there," she said when Kiera stopped to wait for her.

Once the door closed, Chris locked her eyes on Josh.

"Listen to me. You work the case, and I'll keep her safe. Those guys may be psychos but so am I. She pulled back the light jacket she had on, revealing a compact machine gun.

"What the fuck is that?"

"It's a compact Uzi. Hawk got it for me from a friend of his in the Mossad."

"And that's legal?"

"It's effective, that's what matters."

"I'm not visiting you in prison."

Chris winked, "I'm not going; remember who my lawyer is."

"Who needs a lawyer?" Fred said, hand on her back as he slid past Chris.

"Nobody," Chris said, pulling the jacket over the weapon. "But I have a nasty one on speed dial."

Fred stopped and turned to face Chris; a smile grew across his face.

"I would think someone with your reputation would know better than to underestimate me."

Chris scrunched up her face.

"The compact Uzi on the shooting harness under your jacket leaves a distinctive pattern in back," he enjoyed the look of shock on both their faces.

"I spent time in Tel Aviv with the Counterterrorism Task Force. Spent a lot of time behind guys and gals wearing those things.

"And before you turn all defensive or make a fool of yourselves trying to deny it, I will save you some angst.

"First, I was gonna suggest we get you some heavy armament under the circumstances. Second, with a quick call to my good friend, the Deputy Director of ATF, I can get you the necessary permit to carry it legally.

"Unless you want to take your chances."

"Ah, thanks," Chris said, finding herself at a rare loss for words. "You really are different from most feds I've met."

"I'll take that as a compliment."

LXIII **The Nightmare Persists**

Jennifer walked over to Jos's desk. "Josh, can I speak with you a moment...in private." This last part of Jennifer's question caused a few heads to rise in the office, then quickly turn away.

"Sure, let's go to the conference room."

Two minutes later, after chasing Tommy and others out, Jennifer sat down facing Josh.

"Ah, it can't be that bad, I haven't done anything the FBI might investigate for a long time."

Jennifer smiled. "Yeah, I'm sure, but that's not the problem."

"Just tell me, we can deal with it."

"I'm a spy."

"A spy? For who? The Russians? The Chinese?" Josh said, leaning forward, trying to keep it light but now concerned.

"Worse, the Department of Justice."

"Oh, them. We all know that."

"You do?"

"Yeah, natural paranoia around you FBI types."

"No, I'm serious, Josh. They sent me here to keep them informed by back-channel communications so they can find a way to take the case out of your hands."

"Did you talk to Fred?"

"I can't. He'd tell me to tell them to go fuck themselves, and I'd end up in Podunk, Iowa doing background checks in some basement office.

"Fred's got the drag to pull it off, I don't."

"So, spy for them, tell them what we're doing. We aren't gonna give them a reason to yank the case."

"And if they push me to do something to derail it?"

"Tell 'em to go fuck themselves," Josh smiled. "I hear Podunk is lovely in the summer."

"Thanks, you've been a lot of help."

"Look, I can't stop them, and neither can you. I'm glad you told me, now we can string them along for a while. But eventually, they will push you. Just tell me when that happens, and we'll deal with it."

'Okay, thanks, Josh." Putting her hands on the table, she pushed her chair back and walked out.

Fred came in a moment later.

"What was that about?"

Josh shrugged. "Nothin', she's just worried about fitting in."

"You mean as a spy?" Fred said, then smiled at Josh's inability to control his reaction.

"You knew?"

"I suspected. It's something HQ always does with high-profile cases. There is always a mole."

"She said she couldn't tell you because you'd tell her to tell 'em to go fuck themselves, and she'd be banished to Siberia."

Fred plopped into a chair. "She's right. It's what happened to me once. Part of growing up."

"You think it's a problem?"

"Nah, now that we are certain we can deal with it. I'll talk to her. Tell her I figured it out, so she keeps trusting you. She may still be uncomfortable running things by me.

"Okay," Josh said, taking a deep breath. "I really hate the politics of this job."

"Tell me about it. What say we take a ride to the prison and surprise our friend? Having a few prisoners see him talking to cops might persuade him to be more cooperative. Especially if he needs to be placed in permanent protective custody."

"You are a hard one, Mr. Robertson."

"That's what all the ladies say," he said, then paused, 'Well, maybe that was a few years ago.'

LXIV **Roadblocks**

Josh stood at the reception window at the Intake Center in the prison. "Lawyer? What lawyer? He doesn't have a lawyer," Josh said. "He fired the public defender."

The captain in charge of the afternoon shift in the awaiting trial unit checked the log again, then turned it so Josh and Fred could see the entry. He tapped his fingers on Israel's name. "Right here. Represented by."

Josh blinked when he read the name. "Are you fucking kidding me?"

"Nope," the captain shook his head. "So, unless he says you can talk to him, you can't." slamming the logbook closed.

"I don't believe this," Josh said.

"I couldn't read the name," Fred said, "who's the attorney?"

"Harrison 'Hawk' Bennett, that son-of-a-bitch."

Fred thought for a moment. "Isn't that the guy who represented *you* in your trial?"

"One and the same. The bastard couldn't resist."

"But this guy doesn't have any money; who's paying for Bennett?"

"Hawk has an ego the size of a planet. He does these things because he can; money is not his motivation. Disrupting the system is what this guy lives for. Come on, let's go visit my friend Mr. Bennett and see what he wants."

Twenty minutes later, Josh and Fred were in downtown Providence outside the Turk's Head building.

Fred looked up at the building facade, a large turban wearing, mustachioed face looking out over the plaza. "Always thought this seemed more an entrance to an amusement park than an office building."

Walking in the front door, they headed for the elevator.

As Josh went to push the button, the doors opened and there stood Hawk Bennett. Looking up, a smile crossed his face.

"Why Lieutenant Williams and, wait, let me guess, a representative of the FBI, here, I assume, because you are aware of my pro bono representation of Israel David Jenkins." He stepped off the elevator.

"Hawk, what the fuck. This guy is part of a crew who kidnaps, rapes, and dismembers women. Why would..."

"Allegedly," Hawk interrupted.

Josh hung his head and took a deep breath. "Allegedly. But we need his cooperation. Why would you want to represent him?"

Hawk's smile grew wider. "I do not judge the people I represent, as you well know. Everyone gets their due with me. He is entitled to a presumption of innocence and representation by counsel. That's what I do."

"Damn it, Hawk. He fired his public defender and agreed to talk with us."

"Ah yes, that age old claim by the government that there was an intelligent waiver of right to counsel and a surrender of the right to remain silent. I've long contended there is no such thing. But what happened before I took on this case will be fodder for my motions to suppress, other than that there isn't much I can do about it."

"Fine, just let us continue talking to him; you can work your magic later."

Hawk's eyebrows arched. "Are you trying to have me disbarred? Trying to make me commit professional malpractice? I will need to review the case first, then determine the conditions, if any, under which I will allow my client to cooperate."

"Hawk, these guys have a live one right now. Jenkins can help us find them. Come on, man, a woman's life is at stake for Christ's sake."

Josh caught the brief hesitation in the response. Jenkins hadn't told him about the live one, or maybe he didn't know about her.

"There is no need to invoke religious myths here. I was going to discuss the case with the US Attorney, anyway. Let's all go."

"They don't have the case; the AG's office is handling it," Josh said.

Hawk smiled once again. "Not after they find out what I have to say."

That stopped Josh dead in his tracks. "What do you mean?"

Hawk leaned closer to the two men, glancing around to ensure no one was within earshot. He glanced at Fred for a moment, then back to Josh.

"Since I trust your judgment, Lieutenant, I will assume, contrary to my normal opinion, that your FBI friend here is trustworthy as well," he nodded at Fred. "And at the risk of the very professional malpractice you were trying to compel me to commit, I will let you in on something.

"Mr. Jenkins is but a small cog on a very big wheel. This matter goes way beyond the little hamlet of Riverside or even our beloved smallest state in the Union. Once I secure a reasonable plea agreement for my client, under which I am certain his continued cooperation will be a major consideration, we can talk with him at length.

"Until then, he will remain safely ensconced under the protection of the Fifth Amendment."

Fred hesitated a moment, then said, "Going to the US Attorney at this point is a mistake."

Hawk's head snapped back. "What's this, an FBI agent who mistrusts the Justice Department?"

Fred shook his head. "Not mistrust, familiarity. They won't take this case for its prosecutorial value; they'll see it as a steppingstone for political gain. Not the local US Attorney but the inflated egos in DC.

"Your client won't have any value to them beyond that. And when it no longer suits them, they'll cut losses. We can trust the local US Attorney, Crisha Michelson, but she answers to them.

"Why not work with the AG for now? We can always move the case later. You'll have more leverage for Jenkins if you have an agreement in place with local prosecutors, and it will get us the answers we need quicker."

Hawk studied Fred for a long moment.

"I believe I have excellent reason to trust your judgment, Josh. I may not be ready to fully put my faith in this agent, and likely never will with his agency, but it seems he has potential."

"Thanks," Fred said. "I'll take that as a compliment."

"As well you should, if you ask anyone who knows me," Hawk said. "So, shall we jaunt on down to South Main Street and negotiate a deal?"

On the way to the Attorney General's office, the three walked past the World War II memorial across from Superior Court. As they made their way across the street, a car with two men stopped at the crosswalk to let them pass.

Josh locked eyes with the driver, who seemed more intent on watching him than the traffic. As they left the crosswalk, the car remained in place, and the driver leaned over the steering wheel to watch him. Josh slowed his pace, falling behind the others.

As the car pulled away. Josh made a mental note of the license plate.

Hawk and Fred stopped to let Josh catch up.

"See something?" Fred asked.

"Don't know. The driver was eyeing me as we went by. I didn't recognize him, but who knows? I'll run it later."

"Likely some former victim of your heavy-handed police tactics," Hawk offered, with a smile.

"Probably," Josh said. "Another satisfied customer. Just out of prison after you represented them."

Hawk acted like he was pulling a knife from his back. "This from a guy who would be rotting in protective custody were it not for my brilliant legal mind."

* * * * *

"Well, that went about as well as could be expected." Josh said as they left the AGs office.

"Yup, love the dance with people afraid of their own shadow." Fred said. "So now what?"

Both turned to look at Hawk.

"Now I will consult with my client, explain the offer from the AG, and see if he is willing to accept it."

"Accept it?" Josh said, grabbing Hawk at the elbow, then releasing it after Hawk glanced at his arm then locked him in a stare.

"Sorry," raising his hands in surrender, "but it is a goddamn sweetheart deal. Guy gets a walk on all but one murder, and we have at least seventeen victims. What's not to accept?"

"Perhaps he is not involved," Hawk said, walking on.

"Not involved?" Josh yelled. "He had a goddamn head in a bag. How is he not involved?"

"Allegedly," Hawk said over his shoulder and continued walking as he disappeared around the corner of the building.

"Man, that guy is a piece of work." Fred said. "I'm surprised nobody has taken him out."

Josh chuckled. "Oh, they have tried. Guy was a Green Beret in Vietnam. He's probably seventy-four, seventy-five years old and I wouldn't want to mess with him. Couple of years ago he took out someone who tried to kill his wife. He used a remote detonation Claymore mine."

"Never arrested?"

"No evidence, solid alibi. But everyone knew."

"Who'd he take out?"

"A real slime ball, he did everyone a favor. Guy was a junkyard dog for the local mob, tough kid, but Irish and disposable."

"Huh, so now what?"

Josh shrugged. "Let's go back to the office, I want to run that plate and see what else they may have found. Hawk won't waste our time. Much as the guy is a pain in the ass sometimes, he is a great lawyer and knows the difference between the law and justice."

LXV   A Nagging Suspicion

The phone on Tommy's desk rang.

"Josh," Tommy said, "dispatch has that plate info for you."

"Okay, tell her I will stop by, I want to talk to the OIC about tonight."

"Yup," Tommy said into the phone, "his majesty himself will grace you with his presence. Be prepared, shine your shoes."

Josh flipped him off as he left the office. "Why do they always give me the fucking comedians?"

Josh made his way down the hall and into the dispatch office. Dispatcher Gina Fratus was assigned to the police info desk.

"Hey Gina, what's up?"

"Hi Josh, RI Reg AB97X54 comes back registered to a John Carpenter, 11/21/1984 on a 2010 Chevy Impala gray. 210 Point Street, Providence, RI. I ran Carpenter as well. No record, valid license, no contact with us. I called Providence PD and they have him listed as a licensee on a bar at the same address, Village Café." She handed him a printout of the information including the license photo.

"Thanks, you are the best."

"Of course, I am. You guys still finding body parts?"

"Not yet, and hopefully never again. Thanks."

"If you come across a smaller ass, save it for me, will ya? Mine is growing by the minute."

Josh stared.

"What?"

"You and Moore belong in the same looney bin."

As Josh made his way back to the office, something about the information nagged at him. He was pretty sure he didn't recognize the guy. He was definitely not one of the guys in the car. Maybe it was the address. He worked with the DEA Task Force a few years ago and they'd spent a lot of time on Point Street back then.

Walking into the office, he stopped at Tommy's desk, handing him the paper.

"Tommy, you know this guy or place?"

Tommy read it over, then sat back in his chair. "Nah, not the dude, but the address is familiar. Hang on."

Tommy clicked a few keys on his computer and read the results. "Damn it, I knew it was familiar," he turned the screen so Josh could see it. "The day of the incident at Kiera's office, Providence PD recovered the stolen car just across the street from that bar. Can't be a coincidence."

"No shit, where's Fred?" Josh said, looking around.

Tommy shrugged.

"Find him, now."

Tommy headed over to the conference room while Josh grabbed his cell phone.

"Jerry, Josh Williams. Can you meet me over on India Point? We need to go talk to a bar owner on Point Street who may be involved with that body parts case." There was a pause on the line. "Great, fifteen minutes. See ya."

Tommy and Fred came back into the office.

"Tommy filled me in. You think it was the guys we're looking for in the car?"

Jos shrugged. "But the car wasn't stolen so he must have given it to them. I called Providence PD detectives; they'll meet us there."

"I'll drive," Tommy said, "We can take the four by four."

Josh shook his head. "You know that is not *yours,* right?"

"Of course."

Josh glanced at the board where they kept the seized vehicle keys. "Then why are there no keys for it on the board?"

Tommy smiled. "I am protecting a valuable asset from the inferior drivers in this unit."

Josh put out his hand. "Hand 'em over. I'm driving."

"But..."

Josh put up his hand. "No buts, give 'em up, or you'll ride in the truck bed, and it looks like rain out there."

Tommy tossed him the keys, sulking.

"And the copies you had made," Josh said, holding his hand out.

"There aren't..." Tommy said.

"Don't even try," Josh said, shaking his head.

Tommy reached into his top drawer, lifted up a stack of file folders, and handed them over.

Fred chuckled. "I'm not sure if this is a special investigations unit or child day care."

"Neither am I, sometimes," Josh said, "Neither am I."

* * * * *

On the way to meet Providence detectives, Josh kept looking in the rearview mirror.

"Is there somebody following us?" Fred asked, looking over his shoulder.

"I don't know," Josh said. "Seems awful coincidental I saw those guys on South Main Street, and I don't believe in coincidences."

"Noted," Fred said, "they may be trying to track us. Keep an eye on where we go. Let me call the AUSA here and see if we can request a tracking order for the car if we find it."

As Fred called, Josh pulled up to the unmarked Providence unit.

"Hey, Jerry, Phil, what's happening?"

"You tell me," Jerry said. "We're not gonna find more body parts, are we? My partner here has a delicate stomach. I can make him puke just by faking it."

Josh laughed. "Nah, at least I don't think so." He filled them in on the car. "I'd like to take a ride by and see if the car is there. If not, we'll go have a talk with the owner. But if it's there, Fred here is trying to get a tracking order from the US

Attorney's Office. Then we'll sit on it until the equipment gets here."

"Sounds good," Jerry said. "You drive by there; this thing might as well have lights on it."

Ten minutes later, Josh was back. "Okay, car's not there. Let's go have a chat."

Both vehicles rolled up in front of the bar. Fred and Tommy went to the back door while Josh and the Providence detective went in the front. Nobody bolted for the door, but they all knew who had walked in.

"Twice in one month, a visit by Providence PD and," said the bartender, glancing around at the rear door, "guests from, what? FBI? DEA?"

"Let's just say you've hit the jackpot, John," the Providence detective said. "We need to talk."

John put down the glass he was wiping and came around the bar. "Whatever it is, I didn't do it. And if I did, I ain't got nothing to say."

The speed of the somewhat rotund gray-haired detective caught everyone by surprise. He'd grabbed the bartender, spun him around, and placed him prone on the bar before anyone realized it. Most customers didn't even take their eyes off the Red Sox game on TV. Those who did it glanced over quickly and then found something of great interest in their drink glasses.

"Look, smartass, we ain't got time for your bullshit. Who's driving your car and where can we find them? And all I want to hear are answers or you'll find yourself very fucking sick of me camped outside your front door sending your clientele to another shit hole to drink at."

"All right, all right, Jesus, I was just kidding. Waddya mean, who has my car? Nobody does. It's out back." He stood slowly when the detective released his grip on his wrist.

"No, it ain't, John. Why else would we be here?"

"Can I go back to the back room? The keys are there."

"Go," the detective pushed him toward the rear of the bar.

A moment later, he came back. "Shit, they're gone. I have no idea who took them. I have two cars and only use that one when my other one is in the shop."

"Anybody new been around?" the detective asked. "New faces?"

"Nah, not that I can..." he stopped mid-sentence.

"Yeah, what?"

When you guys were here last time about the stolen car across the street, there were two guys here. I saw 'em when I came in to talk to the day bartender. I thought I'd seen one in here a few times, but I didn't know the other one. The regulars know I keep the car out back and I have let people use it on occasion. I bet one of them grabbed the keys."

The detective scanned the inside. "I suppose it would be too much to expect there are security cameras here?"

John chuckled. "We ain't that kind of place. At least I didn't think so."

He turned his attention to the quiet, but attentive patrons. "Any of you guys know who those mutts were? Anybody?"

No one said a word.

"No, not surprised." Motioning to the others, he said. "Come on, Josh. No luck here." He turned to the bartender. "If they come back, you call the station right away, got it?"

"Don't worry. If they come back, I will have them bagged and tagged for you."

The detective chuckled. "Don't kill 'em. We need to talk to them first. You can have 'em when we're done."

"Do I report it stolen?"

Fred stepped between them. "I'll take care of that. No need for you to do anything."

"Okay, thanks. But when you find it, don't tow it, just call me and I'll come there. I hate paying for them leeches with tow trucks.

* * * * *

The group stood outside the bar watching traffic pass by.

"So now what? You gonna put it in the system as stolen?" the Providence detective asked.

"Now we go look for the car," Josh said. "Fred here is gonna put a silent hit on the plate so if somebody runs it, we'll get a heads up and a shot at tracking them."

"Okay, I'll brief the Detective Commander about it and have him put it out to the squads. Talk to you later, Josh. And keep those body parts on your side of the bridge, okay?"

"Thanks Jerry."

As the Providence detectives drove away, Josh led the others back to the truck.

"How about we take a loop around the city? Maybe we'll get lucky."

"I have an idea," Tommy said.

"Now there's something I never thought I'd ever hear," Josh said. "What is it?"

"Before we head back, take a ride down South Main Street. We can look for any cameras that might have caught a shot of the car and passengers."

Josh turned to look over the seat. "Sometimes, Tommy, you actually have a worthwhile idea. Not often, but sometimes."

LXVI   **Every Once in A While...**

Making their way slowly along South Main, they eyed the buildings for any cameras. On a parking garage directly across the street from the AG's office Tommy spotted one.

"There," Tommy said, "over the entrance, pull over."

Jumping out of the back seat, he made his way through traffic to the automated entry control. He took out his cellphone and called the number. After a minute, he came back to the truck.

"Okay, the cameras do store recordings for thirty days and they do catch the street. The security company is pulling the recording for that day and will have it for us. They're on Waterman Street near Wayland Square."

"Tommy, if this pans out, I may have to keep you," Josh said.

"If this pans out, I want this truck assigned to me permanently."

"Done," Josh said, "unless I need it for something."

"Deal."

Fifteen minutes later, they were at the security company. The receptionist took them to the manager's office.

"Josh Williams? As I live and breathe," the manager said. "I can't believe it."

"Gabe? You're still alive? What are you, a hundred and fifty?"

"Feels like it. And who are these two gentlemen?"

"Ah one gentleman, Fred Robertson, FBI, and one lunatic, Tommy Moore, from our job. Boys, this is Gabe Armstrong, legendary midnight to eight sergeant who kept me out of trouble when I was a boot patrol officer.

"I thought you'd be off in Florida withering away in the sun."

"We did for a while," Abe said, "then the grandkids started popping out and we wanted to be close. My son-in-law owns this company, and I act like I'm the manager. Keeps me out of doing chores and changing diapers."

He reached into a drawer and brought out a USB memory stick. Here you go. I put the day before through the day after the date you gave me. Just in case they were around then."

"Thanks, Gabe. Tell Marie I said hi."

"I will. Just let me know if there is anything else."

Back in the car, Fred said, "Does everybody in Rhode Island know everybody else?"

"It does seem like it. We have one degree of separation here in the Ocean State."

LXVII A Picture's Worth...

Josh pushed the laptop away "Frank, we need your digital mastery here," Josh said, pointing at the laptop.

It had taken the better part of a day to spot the car as it went by the camera. The image of the driver was clear enough to see it was male, but that's about all.

"Can you clear this up?" Josh asked.

"Let me see," Frank said, as they all crowded around him.

It took several attempts to isolate the clearest frame, but they now had a face to work with.

"Is it enough for facial recognition?" Josh asked, looking at Fred.

Fred shrugged. "You're asking a guy who doesn't even own a computer. But the geeks down in Quantico might be able to work with it."

He took out his phone and placed a call. "Yeah, Fred Robertson, Providence Field office. I am emailing an image. I need you to clear it up and run it through the facial recognition database, and I need it yesterday. Yeah, yeah, everybody says that, but we have the blessing of Deputy Director Jones. Isn't he your boss?" Fred smiled at Josh and Tommy as they listened.

"Yup, that will be great, thanks," he ended the call. "They'll work on it first thing in the morning, they're in the middle of preparing a discovery package for a case out of the NY office."

"Hey," Tommy said. "I watch that FBI show on TV, and they have facial recognition, DNA, fingerprints, and the exact location of the bad guy's cell phone in about two minutes. What's up with you guys? You the second string? They send us the rejects from the FBI Academy?"

Fred shook his head. "It figures you learn all your investigative skills from TV. The reality is not as efficient, but these guys are miracle workers. If he's in a database, they'll find him. And if you want real police work on TV, watch Barney Miller."

"Who?" Tommy asked, a confused look on his face.

"Never mind."

"You're showing your age, Fred," Josh said.

"Tell me about it."

LXVIII Between Smart and Lucky

Fred walked past Tommy's desk carrying a file folder. "Hey Fred, have the wonder boys down there in Quantico managed to do anything for us?" Tommy asked, a smirk crossing his face.

Fred stopped dead in his tracks and turned to face the wiseass detective. "As a matter of fact, they have...but I have to discuss this with the only other adult in the room before any of his charges hear about it. This may be a bit over your limited ability to comprehend. As a matter of fact, most things are."

Tommy chuckled. "Touché` sir, well played."

Fred bowed, then walked over to Josh. "Good news, bad news."

"Of course it is," Josh said, looking up from his computer. "Go with the bad first."

"There is no DNA or prints on file for Jenkins."

"What's the good news?"

Fred handed him a printout.

Josh read it over. "Hmm, Gerry Tavares, dob 1956 dishonorable discharge US Army did time for assault of the JAG officer who prosecuted his AWOL case." Josh dropped the paper on his desk. "We know all this."

"True, but there's more. In 1979, before he got arrested, he lived with a guy named Maximillian Baader, the cousin of

Andreas Baader, one of the principal members of Baader-Meinhoff and the Red Army Faction.

In 1980, after Tavares was arrested by German authorities, Max was a suspect in the bombing of a German Courthouse where the trial of Tavares was scheduled. Later, the military recalled Tavares to duty and tried him in military court."

"No shit?" Josh said, he glanced back at the printout. "You didn't happen to..."

"Hey, we're the FBI, of course I ran Maximillian Baader. He came to the US on a work visa and then, I know this might be hard to believe, disappeared once the visa expired. Wanna take a guess who sponsored his work visa?"

"Tavares!" Tommy yelled.

"Wow, you figured that out all by yourself, did you?" Fred said.

"Yup, I should transfer to the FBI."

"Great idea!" Josh said.

"I think not," Fred said. "You're much better suited for this department."

"Okay," Tommy said, "your loss."

"Can we get back to this case, please," Josh said. "How'd Baader get into the US?"

"An excellent question to which I have no answer. But I would suspect Baader-Meinhoff had supporters in the US and may have either bribed or threatened an immigration officer. Somehow this Max guy managed to become a citizen. Besides, the international exchange of information wasn't very efficient then.

"Was there any connection to Israel?"

"Not that we could find."

"I bet these guys recruit some younger guys for the heavy lifting. That might explain the two male vics, Cary and Truell. Maybe we should focus on them. With Israel under wraps, they're probably looking for someone new."

"Or they already have one and that's who grabbed the latest victim."

Josh nodded. "Tommy, have you been looking at the missing persons lists?"

"I checked it yesterday, nothing new. I'll look again."

Jennifer Holmes and Dan Lynch came into the office.

"Hey, what's happening?" Jen asked.

"We've confirmed the identity on the two bad guys. I'm gonna need you two to take a closer look at the two male vics. I want to see if there is a connection between them other than being diced, sliced, and dead."

Jen and Dan came over to read the report.

"You guys find anything we should know about?"

"I just had a call from the lab at Quantico," Jen said. "They have a familial match on one of the unknown vics. I was just going to login and read the report."

Josh nodded. "Okay, do that first then get on the other stuff."

"Holy shit!" Tommy said, "Holy Fucking shit!"

The whole room turned to look at him.

"Are you gonna share?" Josh asked.

"I just checked the updated missing person database. There's a thirty-year old female reported missing by her husband in Providence. Last evening around 7:00 p.m."

"And?" Josh said, standing to walk toward the detective.

"And she was last seen leaving her office. Witnesses said they saw a car, a gray Chevy Impala, slow down and follow her. They got a partial plate, AB9."

"Holy shit, indeed," Josh said, "that's the plate I spotted!"

"Yup, and here's the worst part. The building where the victim works? It's Kiera's office. She's a paralegal there."

Josh's blood ran cold. He instinctively reached for his cell, but then knew if there was a problem Hamlin would have called.

"They're sending a message; we can grab anyone we want, and you can't stop us."

"Think this is another vic?" Fred asked, "or the live one we already knew about?"

"My guess is a new one," Jen said. "They're escalating since we're putting pressure on them. Doesn't bode well for the other one. They've been running under the radar for so long. This is only gonna get worse."

Det. Dan Lynch walked in. He saw the worry in their eyes. "What's up?"

"Got another missing woman from the same office building," Josh said.

Lynch's cell rang and he glanced at the caller ID. "What the hell does he want?" ignoring the call.

"Who is it?"

"My idiot brother. Been in and out of rehab. We don't talk much." The phone rang again. "Sorry, Lt., I gotta take this or the next call will be my mother."

"Go ahead," Josh said.

Lynch turned away but in an office this size there were no private conversations. "Yeh, Billy what now? You locked up...what? When? Jesus Christ why didn't you call me earlier? I'll get back to you."

Lynch ended the call then turned to face the others, his face ashen. "Lt., the latest victim is my sister-in-law. Jesus Christ I am gonna kill these motherfuckers..."

"Jesus, Dan," Josh said. "Okay we need to focus on finding these guys before it gets any worse. She may still be alive since it's been less than twenty-four hours."

"I think it's time we pulled out the stops on this," Fred said. "I'm sure Hamlin is competent but why take a chance? I am gonna put agents all over that area. Maybe they'll stick with that as their hunting ground. Tell her wherever she goes she'll have an army with her. Until these guys are in custody, we're not risking it. If Kiera doesn't like it, too bad."

"Ha! You tell her that," Josh said. "But I appreciate it. I'll call Hamlin before she spots the surveillance and kills your agents. And I want a full -court press on the two male victims. Find the link between them and these guys.

"That might give us an idea who's working with them now and where they're operating."

The phone rang and Tommy answered it. "Okay, be right there," he hung up. "Lt., there's a package out front for you."

As the words came out, the whole room went silent.

"Oh, shit..." Josh said, "Call BCI and have them meet us in the lobby. Tommy, run out and stop the delivery driver if he's still there, if not, find him and the truck."

To the civilians loitering in the lobby for sundry reasons, the sudden activity broke their boredom while they waited. Tommy had the driver taken to the office to be interviewed. The rest of the team stood looking at the package, about the size of a carryon suitcase, wrapped in brown paper. There was a printed label from the delivery company but off to the side was a handwritten address.

Lewtenant Josh Williams c/o EPPD 750 Wataman Avee, E Prov, RI

Fred looked around at the curious onlookers and the gathering of cops. "Ah, not to be overly dramatic, but you're assuming this is some body parts. What if it's a bomb? The guy was in the Army remember."

Josh's eyes grew wide. "Damn, okay, everybody out. Move these people out of here." He turned to the OIC standing next to him. "Get the dispatchers and civilians out of there. Forward the calls to the FD HQ and have them handle them from there."

The Lieutenant reached for his portable. Before he could key the mic, Josh grabbed his hand. "No transmissions, nothing. Go in there and tell them to shut communications down," Josh ordered, pushing him toward the dispatch office. "Use the landline to call the FD and tell them what's going on. Have them send an engine and rescue to stand by down the road. Frank, go outside and call the State Fire Marshal for the Bomb Squad.

"Fred, grab some cops and check the area. If it is a bomb, they might've rigged it with a remote detonator. They'll be somewhere nearby."

"What are you gonna do?" Fred asked.

"I'll stay here with the package. If it's not a bomb I want to make sure we preserve it for evidence. I hope the bomb squad has a portable x-ray or something."

"Hey Lt.," Officer George Watkins said, dressed in civilian clothes and standing at the entrance with his K-9 Banjo. "My dog here is explosive trained. Want me to run him by?"

"How'd you know?" Josh asked.

"Gina from dispatch called me. I just headed out. I live around the corner."

Sirens echoed in the distance as the fire department responded. Those evacuated from the building were all herded across the street to the old Meeting Street School campus. Waterman Ave was shut down and the sounds of horns from angry drivers competed with the sirens.

Chief Brennan poked his head into the lobby. "Nothing better to do with your time, Lieutenant Williams?"

Josh shrugged, watching as the K-9 examined the package.

"What will he do?" Josh asked.

"If he detects something, he'll sit down." Watkins answered.

"Then what?"

"Then we run."

The dog made several circles around the package but remained standing. Watkins tossed him a ball and the dog was ecstatic.

"Safe?" Josh asked.

"Banjo was top dog in his class. I'd say it's safe," he put the leash back on the dog. "But just in case, I'll head home now and hope for the best."

"Thanks, George. Thanks, Banjo," giving the dog a pat on the head.

Twenty minutes later, the Army National Guard Emergency Ordinance Disposal (EOD) team arrived. They x-rayed the package, ran tests for explosive chemicals, and confirmed Banjo's opinion.

"Lieutenant Williams?" the captain in charge of EOD said. "Can I show you something?"

Josh walked over to the laptop the captain laid out on the counter. "I'm not sure what to make of this, but this looks like a head to me. Can't be, right?"

Josh shook his head. "Sorry, Cap. But that is exactly what this is."

The captain glanced at the screen, then back at Josh. "No shit?"

"Sadly no. And Captain, this stays between us. Can you email that image to me and make sure it doesn't leak out to the public?"

"Will do, sir."

"Thanks for the quick response," Josh said, then went back to stand next to the package.

"Should we open it here, Lt.," Tommy said, "scare the dispatchers?"

"No, we take it to BCI and do this step by step. But since you're so interested, you can carry it."

"What?" Tommy said, stepping back. "I'm handling the driver."

"You were handling the driver; someone else can do that. Go on, pick it up." Josh ordered.

Tommy hesitated for a moment, then reached down to grab the package.

"Did I mention that explosive detection dogs have a 97% success rate?" Josh said, trying to hide the smile.

"Thanks, Lt." As he turned to make his way toward the door, he saw a bunch of cops standing with their fingers in their ears.

"Funny, fucking hysterical. Bunch of comedians."

LXIX No Longer Missing

Josh picked up his beeping cell. "Is it her?" he asked, "Okay, see if we can get a statement from him if he's able. Find out if anything strange happened before she disappeared." He ended the call, tossing the phone onto his desk.

"Our missing paralegal?" Fred said.

"Yup, positive ID. I gotta find Dan, he's gonna go ape shit."

"Jesus, they are sick pricks."

"Ya think? Providence PD wants to know if we need them to help or, since it's now a kidnapping if the FBI will take it."

"Yeah, we'll handle it. I think it's time we arranged a discussion with your friend Hawk and the US Attorney. FBI HQ will want to make this a formal case, might as well get out in front of it. I'll head to the US Attorney's Office and get it started."

Josh reached for his cell, scrolling until he came to Dan Lynch's number. He hesitated, index finger hovering over the call button, then made the call. He saw Fred watching him. Nobody likes to make these notifications.

A moment later, Lynch answered. "Yeah, Lt., I know. My brother called me."

"You want a few days off?" Josh asked.

"No way. I want to be there when we catch these pricks. Look, I don't like bringing my personal life into the job, but I haven't seen my brother in months. He and his wife have nothing to do with the rest of the family. It's just the way it is.

"I don't need time off. If I know my brother, he's already planning on how to spend the insurance money. I am not wasting any more time on someone who's not interested. I'm on the way back. Do you need me to do anything?"

"How about your parents, you want to tell them?"

"My dad has no use for either of them and mom is lost in the fog of dementia. I'll call him to make sure he knows but I can tell you there won't be any tears over it."

"Well, if you're sure. Just come back. I'll have someone else take a statement from your brother. If anything changes, and you need some time, just ask."

"Thanks, Lt., I'm good."

"How'd it go?" Fred asked, as Josh ended the call.

"Families," Josh answered, shaking his head. "Families."

Fred nodded. "Yeah, we all got 'em. Ok, I'm off."

Once Fred left, Josh slumped back in his chair. While he liked to pretend otherwise, the case was weighing him down.

"Josh, you up for some more, ah, news?" Jen asked.

"Why not, how much worse can it be?"

The look in Jen's eyes said it all.

"I read the latest DNA finding from Quantico when all the excitement took place in the lobby."

"And?" Josh said, sitting up in his chair.

"And the familial match is to you. DNA from what we assume is another victim, recovered from some bloody clothing found in a closet, has the same mitochondrial characteristics. The same mother."

Josh seemed lost in the fog.

"Hey, you okay?" Jen asked.

"I keep waiting for something worse to happen. I mean, first the whole dead twin sister thing. Now this familial match from Quantico. How is it I can be related to anyone who'd do this?"

Jen came over to sit on the edge of the desk. "This is nothing on you, Josh. Propensity toward such acts is a combination of genetics and upbringing. We all have a little sociopathy within. Your sister was a victim, nothing else. All we can tell from this sample is there is a genetic link. We cannot be certain of the sex of the individual or what their involvement was in the case. There are too many variables in such a minute sample. Any other links to these guys are meaningless. Focus on stopping them. Once we grab them, you'll see there is nothing closely resembling you in them."

Josh listened but the voice inside kept nagging, what if I am like them?

* * * * *

"Hey, Lt.," Tommy said, "the ME has finished the autopsy report. Just got the email. She says there were signs of brain trauma and cerebral bleeding likely from a severe beating. The skull was fractured but they may not have been the cause of death.

"She suspects strangulation. There are some bruises on the area of the neck where they severed the head which shows ligature marks, but she cannot be certain. There also was bruising to the face, a broken jaw and fractured right eye socket.

"Bottom line, they beat the shit out of her, strangled her, they cut off her head. And it gets worse, she was alive when they did it. Remind me again why I took this job."

"I wonder about that myself, Tommy. Print it out and add it to the murder book."

"I saved the best part for last," Tommy said.

Josh sighed, "I'm not in the mood, Tommy. What else?"

"They left a note."

Josh perked up. "A note? Where?"

"Jammed down her throat. The ME sent a picture."

Josh's cell rang, he saw the number for Chris Hamlin. "Hey, is Kiera okay? What's wrong?"

"I'm fine, thanks for asking. So is Kiera but she wants to know about the paralegal missing from her office. If I don't tell her something, she's coming there to beat it out of you."

"Yeah, sounds like her. The paralegal is not missing, not anymore. I have an autopsy report backing me up."

"Shit, bad?"

"Very, all we have is the head."

"Christ, she's gonna lose it."

"I know. Maybe I should come there and tell her myself?"

"If you're up to it. She's gonna blame herself, then the job, and then you."

"I know, I know. Give me twenty minutes and I'll come to her office."

There was a pause on the line, a muffled argument, then Kiera came on.

"Josh, what happened to her? Just tell me."

Josh took a deep breath. "Kiera, I'm so sorry. She's dead. We recovered, ah, her a little while ago."

The sobs came through the phone then, a deep breath. "Does her husband know?"

"Yeah, we had to notify him to identify the, ah, remains."

Another pause. "What aren't you telling me, Josh?"

It was Josh's turn to breathe deeply. "Let me come down there and explain it all."

"Damn it, stop treating me like a child. I know the case, Josh, they're sick bastards. Tell me what happened."

By the time Josh finished the story, they were both crying. "I'm so sorry, Kiera. So sorry."

The long pause scared him; the calmness of the voice terrified him.

"Find them, Josh. Find them before I do, because I will kill every last one of them if you don't." The call went dead.

A moment later, a text popped up from Chris. "Let her rant, I won't let her out of my sight."

LXX   A Message from God

The group of investigators stood around the conference room. On the large screen TV, an image of the note left in the victim's throat had their full attention.

No one said a word as they read and reread the scrawled, almost indecipherable message.

I am who am i bere the power of the Lord Godmy name is Iakobov and I am of his line we are the messengers sent to rid the world of sinners and unbelievers.

Do not stand b four us, YOU WILL NOT WHIN. You will die!

All who oppose us wil dies and b caste unto the devil.

If we live, we live for the Lord; and if we die, we die for the Lord. So, whether we live or die, we belong to the Lord.

Fight us and die! Joins us an liv

I am he that liveth, and was dead; and, behold, I am alive for evermore, Amen; and have the keys of hell and of death.

Gideon

The reddish-black stains from the victim's blood gave the note an even more ominous appearance, amplifying the horror.

"What da fuck kind of freaky shit is this?" Tommy asked.

"Biblical," Fred answered. "Some of the text comes from Bible quotes. The 'If we live' quote is Romans 14:8 and the 'I am he that liveth' quote is Revelation 6:12. They are apocalyptic visions of the return of Jesus to this world."

The whole room turned, staring at Fred.

He shrugged. "My mother wanted me to be a priest. I took Comparative Religion in college and did a whole thesis on Revelation and apocalyptic doctrines."

"And what about the name, Iakobov?" Josh asked. "Does that mean anything?"

Fred nodded. "As a matter of fact, it does. Without going into a long explanation, I am sure some of you have heard of James, the brother of Jesus."

"Wait, Jesus had a brother? I thought Mary was a Virgin or something." Tommy said.

Fred ignored him. "James is not a name with Jewish roots. It is more modern. Many biblical scholars believe the original translation of the Greek should have been Iakobov or Jacob. But James was used in translations of St. Paul and the others, so it stuck."

"Jesus," Tommy said, "I should have paid more attention when I was in catechism."

"Yeah, that would've helped," Josh said. "So, these guys are what, religious fanatics, zealots, what?"

"It fits with the doctrine around the Seven Mountains from the book of Revelation. Babylon, Rome, Pergamum, Thyatira, Sardis, Philadelphia, and Laodicea. It's the final confrontation between good and evil. Each of the mountains plays a role in the apocalyptic battle.

"My guess is Tavares has messianic delusions and Baader is an acolyte. He sees Tavares as an actual representative of God. Because of that, he'll do anything asked of him. To recruit others, they look for vulnerable, probably drug or alcohol addicted individuals with little hope and fill them with a purpose in living, a mission from God.

"Alcoholics and Narcotics Anonymous meetings are ripe hunting grounds. Parole offices and halfway houses are as well with the lack of substance abuse and mental health services. They get ready-made damaged and malleable individuals looking for meaning in their lives.

"This sense of family or belonging, as warped as that may sound, masks violence and horror. The victims are someone they feel superior to in a long life of inferiority."

"Hey, Fred," Tommy asked. "How come you aren't with the whack-a-ding-hoy profiler squad in Quantico? Sounds like you know what you're talking about."

"I'll take that as a compliment from you, Tommy. I was with them for several years, but the demons and nightmares wouldn't go away. I needed to find a different career path before they were profiling me."

"Bet you're sorry you answered my call," Josh said.

"Nah, not really. To be honest I missed the work. This way here I stay on the periphery of the case and keep my head on straight."

"So now what?" Josh asked. "Is this helpful or just something nice to know?"

"Well, anything we find on these guys is helpful. Despite my time in the unit, I am a bit out of touch with the latest techniques. Let's get Emily Thompson back here to give us her take. That might give us an idea of what to do next.

"Call Hawk and arrange a meeting with just us. No attorneys and not at the office. I think under the circumstances we can appeal to the better angels of his nature."

Josh smiled. "You don't know him like I do. That expression where angels fear to tread applies directly to Hawk. But he is always good for buying the drinks, so we have nothing to lose."

LXXI The Art of the Deal

Of all the legendary bars in Providence, Rhode Island, at least as far as those frequented by cops, lawyers, and judges, Christopher's on Pine Street was the standard by which others were measured.

More criminal cases got resolved there over drinks than were ever settled in court. Dropping the formality of court rules, ignoring the inappropriateness of ex-parte discussions, and simplifying the complications of trial and appellate issues lubricated the criminal justice system.

No one would ever admit it. No one would even acknowledge the process. But this reality stood the test of time.

There were occasional disagreements. More often than not, these occurred within cloistered groups—cops vs. cops, lawyers vs. lawyers, judges vs. judges—and, on the rare instance they turned physical, were settled without either fanfare or long-lasting animosity.

Cops, lawyers, and judges by day, referees, combatants, or both by night, on occasion.

Hawk Bennett attributed the overwhelming success of his legal career to his ability to navigate these complicated, quasi-judicial conversations. He could placate the most adamant cops, outraged prosecutors, offended co-counsels, and prickly judges.

Hawk almost always resolved a case long before he ever made a trial appearance on the client's behalf. The courtroom was just theatrics. Yet, where compromise was impossible, his considerable legal skills, supplemented by fearlessness earned as a Green Beret in Vietnam, made him a prodigious opponent.

Those naive souls with brand new law degrees or those young zealous prosecutors looking to make a name for themselves soon learned the advantages of a Christopher's sidebar.

Justice may be blind, but wine or scotch can get her to peek under the blindfold.

Fred and Josh walked into Christopher's late that afternoon. The bar was already crowded with court clerks, cops, and lawyers. Josh said hi to the ones he knew, nodded at the familiar faces, and scanned the crowd for Hawk.

Pat, the head bartender and unofficial presiding justice, nodded at Josh then pointed.

Hawk occupying his seat, a spot most considered permanently reserved at the end of the bar, watched them walk in. Two vacant seats, a shock considering the crowd, remained available next to him.

Making their way through the mixed throng of the thirsty and the well-lubricated, they arrived just as Pat put an ice-cold Becks at one seat and then turned to Fred.

"And what will my friend from the FBI be having?"

Fred smiled. "The same, thanks."

Pat nodded, reached under the counter, and put another Beck's on the bar. He winked, "I had it open already. And they are on Hawk, of course."

Both Josh and Fred held up their beers and took a long drink.

"Okay, Josh, I don't have a lot of time this evening. My wife is dragging me to some new art exhibit at RISD and if I am even a moment late, I shall suffer untold torments. So just tell me what you want, I'll say no, and we can finish our drinks."

"Did you talk to your client? Did he agree? There is something else we think you should know."

Hawk threw up his hands in mock surrender, drained his scotch, and put it on the bar. Before he said another word, a fresh drink appeared.

Fred raised his eyebrows, and his eyes widened.

"I figure I have paid the mortgage on this place several times over," Hawk said. "It's the least I deserve."

"I guess so," Fred said.

"Okay," Josh glanced at Fred, "you heard about the paralegal kidnapped from Kiera's office, right?"

Hawk nodded.

"Well, the FBI are taking jurisdiction, or at least they will soon. Before DC starts sticking their noses in this, we'd like to have the cooperation agreement in place with your client. We believe the bad guys have another live one and won't stop there. If your client can help us find these guys, and save any more victims, it would be more ammunition for you to ensure the best deal."

"Immunity from prosecution?"

"He's already got a sweetheart offer. How about accessory after the fact for one murder, minimum sentence."

"Ah well, it looks like I will be early for my date. I thought you guys were serious."

"Come on, Hawk. We caught the guy with a head. A human head."

A few people nearby turned to look, then turned quickly away. Regulars knew better than getting involved no matter how intriguing the discussion. No one wanted to end up testifying before a grand jury.

"Let me correct you on that. For the sake of argument, I will leave out the various and sundry avenues available for me to suppress this seizure and arrest. You took my client into custody for having a bag in his possession. In and of itself, there is no probable cause to show he had committed, or was about to commit, a crime.

"There is no evidence I have seen to show, beyond a reasonable doubt, that he had any knowledge of the contents. Let alone any connection with disconnecting it from a body."

"Hawk, he has no license. The bike was not registered. They got a search warrant to open the bag. I know your reputation, but I think we will win on this one."

"Okay, if you want to take your chances. But I know the judge you used for the warrant. He's never read an affidavit in his life. He just signs away hoping, if he is ever stopped after one of his four or five martini nights, someone will recognize the name and save his ass.

"But I digress. We are here having a friendly preliminary discussion in the furtherance of justice. I might consider this, Unlawful Disposal of a Corpse. Suspended sentence and he is released on bail immediately."

Fred glanced at Josh. Josh nodded.

"If I may suggest something,"

"Go right ahead, Fred," Hawk said.

"We put him under house arrest in FBI custody. He gives us a full debriefing on his association with these guys. Full immunity on any crimes he admits to except murder. If he took part in a murder all bets are off.

"If his cooperation leads to the arrest of these guys, we charge him with one count of conspiracy to obstruct justice. He agrees to spend six months in a federal psychiatric facility and, pending the results of their evaluation and if he is found not to be a danger to the public, he walks.

"I can have this in writing from the US Attorney herself to you by tomorrow morning."

Hawk thought for a moment. "And if I say no?"

It was Fred's turn to smile. "Then *we* charge him with kidnapping and murder, since the head he had used to be attached to a victim living in Massachusetts. That puts the federal death penalty back on the table.

"Now I've heard all about your reputation. You aren't the least bit intimidated by me, the FBI, or the legal challenge, but the reality is your client is just a small cog in this machine. Why let him pay the price for these animals still out there?

"Doesn't keeping this simple, a gentlemen's agreement between us, make more sense for your client?"

Hawk's eyes met Fred's, and he held the gaze. He took a long sip of his drink then put the glass down. Pat appeared, but Hawk put his hand over the glass, all without breaking his stare.

"Josh, I have to tell you something. You've managed to do something I thought nearly impossible until this very moment."

"What's that?" Josh asked.

"Find an FBI agent with brains and balls enough to win my grudging respect. You bring that offer in writing and I will talk to my client. I have no doubt, once he understands the options, that he'll see this is in his best interest."

He rose from the bar and called Pat back. "These guys are on my tab for the night." He threw a couple of hundred-dollar bills on the bar. "But keep them in check, every drink shrinks your tip."

Pat laughed, grabbed the money, then put two more beers on the bar. "You guys are now shut off," he said, and walked away smiling.

LXXII Selling Ice to Inuits

Fred, Josh, and Emily Thompson walked into the US Attorney's Office in Kennedy Plaza. Ignoring the alarms from the security screening portal, they made their way to Crisha Michelson's office. The receptionist told them to have a seat, offered coffee or water, then left them alone.

"So, what do you think she'll say?"

"Dunno," Fred said. "I'm hoping Emily here can persuade her that it was necessary to save more victims. I don't like giving Israel a walk, but sometimes you gotta deal with the devil."

They hadn't heard the door to Michelson's office open.

"I deal with devils every day, Fred," Michelson said, standing in the doorway. "Come on in and share the demon story with me."

The three glanced at each other, then made their way inside the office.

Michelson pointed to several chairs around a small conference table. As they sat, Emily noticed the oversized Rhode Island State Police emblem on the wall. Josh spotted her reaction.

"Yup, believe it or not," Josh said, "Crisha here was actually a trooper. Then they found out she could read and made her leave."

Michelson chuckled. "The truth is Josh here is just jealous since he couldn't pass the height requirement to be on the state police, but East Providence hires on a sliding scale."

"Wow," Emily said, "this is such a strange state. but I do miss it."

That made the whole room laugh.

Michelson put out her hand, "Shame on me for not introducing myself. Crisha Michelson. I, unfortunately, know these two, but I haven't had the pleasure."

"Emily Thompson, Special Agent, FBI Behavioral Analysis Unit, Quantico," she replied, shaking the US Attorney's hand.

"Weren't you with the AGs office a few years ago?"

Emily nodded. "I was. My college roommate at Georgetown was from here. Her father was a Deputy and talked me into taking a job here. I was only there for a couple of years. My apologies, but I don't recall a case with you."

"Oh, I was just new in detectives then. I sat in on a few meetings. Never said a word. Anyway, let me guess, you need a court order to take Josh to Quantico and study him. I can have that for you in minutes. I have one in my desk on standby."

Emily smiled. "No, I don't think even we're prepared for that level of crazy."

"Ouch," Josh said.

"Okay, enough with the pleasantries. Go ahead, ruin my morning."

Fred and Josh took Michelson through the investigation up to the package delivery at EPPD HQ. They could see the recent kidnapping and horrific murder bothered even the veteran prosecutor and former detective. She did not like these things happening in her state. She seemed even less inclined toward the possible cooperation agreement.

"Wow, that is quite the deal," Christa said. "I'm not sure I can sell that to the Justice Department, considering the publicity around this case."

"Well," Fred said, "Emily here can offer some insight into the psychology of these guys that might make it more palatable. Okay?"

Michelson nodded. "But first, let me get my Criminal Division head in here. He's only been here for a couple of months, but I want him in on any decision. He'll be the one to own this thing." She went to her desk, made a quick call, and then came back. Two minutes later, a tall, athletic, thirtyish gentleman walked in.

"Emily, Tony Delgudice, from the criminal division. Tony, this is Special Agent Emily Thompson, FBI Behavioral Analysis Unit. I'm sure you know Fred and Josh."

Emily and he shook hands, then Delgudice took a seat.

"Okay Tony, I'm sure you've guessed this is about the body parts case in East Providence. They've identified one victim—kidnapped, murdered, and taken over state lines—which puts it within our jurisdiction. They have a proposal for a deal with the one in custody, the guy who was carrying the victim's head, that is, to say the least, distasteful but perhaps necessary. I want you to hear the reasoning behind it."

"Oh, great. Sounds like major headache material. But that's why I love this job so much. Okay, Emily, tell me why I need to sell my soul to this devil."

Emily opened her notebook and took out several printed sheets. She handed copies around the table. "I prepared this summary which highlights the major points I want to discuss. As I explain each one, you can better follow along, ah, if that's okay?"

Michelson nodded. "Have at it, I cleared my morning for this."

"Let me start with an overview of this particular phenomenon, Messianic Hyper-religiosity.

"This already has a name?" Crisha asked.

"Sort of an unofficial designation within BAU" Emily replied. "After Jonestown, Waco, and the Heaven's Gate incidents, the BAU decided to classify any such groups with religious overtones as a separate phenomenon instead of putting them into just cult or gang-type organizational compartments.

"While there are many dissimilarities among these three examples, making them difficult to put under one classification, there are enough similarities to make identifying and analyzing evolving groups easier based on our research into the others.

"The most common similarity is the primary individual controlling the group. The "Messiah" if you will. They are almost always male, white, middle aged—although David Koresh of the Branch Davidians was an outlier at thirty-four— generally have some post high school education and were early social outcasts with few friends. Their family background was often littered with problems, uncaring mother, distant or domineering father."

She paused a moment to shuffle her notes. "If you'll bear with me, I am still trying to focus on the high-level analysis so as not to take up too much time."

Crisha reached over and put her hand on Emily's arm. "You take your time, the more you give me the easier it will be for me to make a decision. Take all the time you need."

"Thank you. Ah, if you look at the first three bullet points, you'll see I focused on a well-established concept of Delusions with Religious Content. This is something often encountered with patients suffering from mania, schizophrenia, and other psychosis.

"These patients exhibit a high propensity for dangerousness. The delusion, fueled by biblical texts taken out of context and accepted as the sacrosanct word of God, masks the violence and brutality of the behavior.

"Because they believe they are acting under the direct word of God, and those recruited to assist them see the leader as a Messiah figure, any action they take is justified. The victims are not seen as human but demons in disguise. Their death is a benefit to society, and they believe they are saving the victim for their eternal life.

"In this case, the segmentation of the bodies and the subsequent placement all over the state acts, in their minds, as a warning to other demons that this is a protected realm."

"And you believe this Tavares character is the messiah of the group?" Tony asked.

"Exactly, unless there is someone we have yet to identify. But it would seem from what we have about him—his background, difficulty with authority, sexual violence toward women—all point to a Messiah complex."

"What about this partner, Maximillian Baader?" Crisha asked. "What's his story?"

"He is the heir to the crown. Messiah personalities almost always identify a successor, someone they can rely on to manage all the other individuals with ruthless devotion. Keep in mind, these guys really believe Tavares has the ear of God. He controls their destiny. He can send them to Paradise or Hell. By manipulating these malleable individuals and giving them an oversized sense of importance, he totally controls them.

"Tavares spent time in Germany. The name Baader would have been well known from the Baader-Meinhoff/Red Army events around the same time. It would give them a bit of a sense of destiny to carry the mantle, albeit with the political motivation replaced by sociopathic behavior."

"And this Israel David Jenkins?"

"A follower. A true believer, but not at the level of Baader. He is, to borrow a phrase, a useful idiot to be disposed of and replaced when necessary. I firmly believe, had he not been caught, he would have found himself a victim whenever it was convenient for Tavares to get rid of him. Tavares would accuse him of being possessed by one of the demons he seized and ordered him killed.

"And there would be a long line of volunteers to take on the task and assume that mantle."

"Here's the big question," Crisha said, leaning forward and folding her hands. "Is cutting a deal with Jenkins worth it? Is there any other way to stop these guys? Can we find them without his cooperation?"

Emily glanced at Fred. He nodded for her to answer.

"I would say no. My biggest fear is they will move on, try a new approach by hiding the body parts instead of displaying them. We'd lose sight of them. They could move cross-country, and we'd not know of it for months or years until the bodies, or body parts, started piling up.

"From what we learned at the initial scene, these guys are changing, becoming bolder. They are not stupid or careless, but they are increasingly engaged in riskier actions. Snatching the paralegal was a major escalation.

"In the past, they operated under our radar. My guess is Tavares and Baader are psychosexual sociopaths. They enjoy the hunt, but only so much as it is necessary to acquire new victims. Their real pleasure is domination and absolute control of the victims. They play with them using a combination of sadistic sexual torture and, to encourage the victim to "play" along with the fantasy, offering the victim false hope of release. Once they grow tired of them, they are disposable. Somewhere along the line—prison, drug counseling, halfway houses—they hit upon the religious angle, and it took over their thoughts.

"This religious overtone gave them several advantages. One, they could recruit the "faithful" to help snatch victims and reduce their own risk of arrest. Two, these acolytes are a continuity of their control fetish, live versions of their victims if you will. They can command them to kidnap, torture, and kill as they like. And, three, in the event they find themselves without a new victim, they turn on one of the acolytes as a traitor. This increases their hold on any others through fear and satisfies any momentary lack of victims.

"Tavares is, by all indications, inept and ineffective in normal social settings. So is Baader. This hyper-religiosity gave them power and purpose. One thing I haven't mentioned is funding. How do they afford to do this? My guess would be narcotics trafficking and burglaries.

"This is where Jenkins can be the most useful. By now, they have moved somewhere else. Somewhere Jenkins won't know. They may have always had another location kept secret from any of the others.

"But Jenkins would have been involved in narcotics trafficking. He knows their distribution channels, locations, meeting places. He may be able to point us to dealers we can put under surveillance. This may lead us to Tavares and Baader."

Emily, taking a deep breath, put her notes down, sitting back in her chair. "If there are any questions, I'd be happy to answer them."

Crisha looked around the room. "Tony, it is your call. What do you think?"

Tony rubbed his hand over his mouth then placed both palms flat on the table. "I think stopping these guys mandates we use extraordinary measures. As much as I detest cutting this guy a deal, I don't want to have to live with losing any more victims if we can stop them.

"These guys are dangerous, we need to take them into custody as soon as possible. I think we should go for it, Crisha."

"I agree." the US Attorney said, "Do what you need to do to make it happen."

"Okay. Fred," Tony said, "why don't we go to my office and work on the agreement. Emily, that was an enlightening yet horrifying presentation. Excellent work. You may have insights into the language we need to use to ensure full disclosure by Jenkins. Why don't you come along as well?

"Josh, if you want to call Hawk, since you seem to be one of the few people he actually likes, and arrange for him to meet here as soon as he can, that would be great." He stood and walked to the door, Fred and Emily right behind him.

"Thanks for making my day, Crisha. I knew working with you was going to be a joy."

Crisha smiled. "Anytime Tony, keep me in the loop."

"Oh, don't worry. I will. I plan to share every gory moment of this."

As they filed out of the room, Crisha shook Emily's hand. "I'd like to say thanks for coming in, but I may withhold my judgment until this thing is over."

Emily smiled. "I don't blame you. See ya, Crisha."

* * * * *

"How 'bout her?" Baader said, as they watched from inside the stolen van as Fred and Emily left the US Attorney's Office. The early evening shadows a perfect cover.

"Nah, she's a cop," Tavares said. "She'll have a gun and put up a fight. This is just to understand who the devil is sending against us."

"What do we do now?"

"Nothing, with them. We need to take another demon from the office where Williams's wife works. Show them we have the power of God with us." He turned in his seat to face the young, unkempt, bleary-eyed man lying on the floor in the back.

"You think you can drive this thing?"

"Wha? Yeah, yeah, I can drive anything."

"God has commanded me to seize another devil like the last one. You will answer his call."

The man bowed his head. "I am your servant, Gideon. I serve the Lord and his Messiah."

"Excellent," Tavares smiled. "Tonight, when it gets dark, drive the van to the same parking garage. I will send an angel with you and point out the demon. Be quick and silent. Do her no harm, or she will take possession of your soul. Just control her and bring her to me. The angel will show you the way."

"As you say, I will do." The man bowed again, then lay back on the floor, a serene smile on his face as he stared at the van's ceiling.

Tavares started the van and headed toward the highway.

"You think he's up to it?" Max whispered, glancing back at the still prone figure.

"He's just a pawn doing the Lord's work. God will guide him. Pick someone else to go with him. There'll be no problems."

Baader shook his head. "Okay, Gideon. You know best."

LXXIII One More Time...

Josh rolled over, putting his arm around Kiera. She nestled closer, warming both on this cool night. His hand found her breast, and he felt her stir, turning to face him. He knew her eyes were open - even in the dark he knew the look - and began kissing her on the neck.

For a moment, the only sound was her breathing growing more rhythmic, then he felt her hands reaching for him.

"Why Mr. Williams, I do believe you're quite aroused."

Lost within each other, the entire world disappeared, even for the briefest of moments, and they were one in their own little part of the planet.

Her head on his chest, she listened to his breathing as he fell back asleep. She followed soon after, and all seemed right.

The sound of Josh's phone buzzing interrupted their comfortable moment. Shaking his head to clear his mind he fumbled to find the phone.

"Leave it," she whispered, and rolled over on top of him, kissing her way around his body. With her right hand she tossed the phone under the bed.

* * * * *

The sun peeking through the curtains, and an impatient bouncing yellow lab, finally woke them.

"Well, good morning, my love," Kiera said. "Sleep well?"

"I always sleep well with you, babe," Josh said, stretching. "What time is it?"

"Ah, it's Saturday. Who cares? How about I put on the coffee and let Tripod out while you warm up the shower? I'll be right there to join you."

Josh jumped from the bed like a five-year-old on Christmas morning. "Deal, and hurry."

Even with the shower running full force, they could hear the phone buzzing and chirping. After ten minutes of trying to ignore it, she gave up.

"Go, answer the damn thing and get back here."

Josh stepped out of the shower, wrapped a towel around himself, and went to the bedroom.

He took a moment to find it under the bed. He grabbed it, hit the answer key, and snapped, "Yeah, what is it?"

"Josh, Fred, sorry to bother you, but I knew you would want to know. They snatched another one last night, in the parking garage. A twenty-five-year-old woman. Same MO."

"Oh, what the fuck," Josh said. "You sure it's them? Not a copycat with all the media coverage?"

"They left a message for you."

"What? What's the message?"

"You're not on speaker, are you?"

Josh glanced toward the bathroom and could still hear the shower running. "No, it's okay."

"They wrote it in blood on a wall near the woman's car. I'll text the image."

A moment later, the phone beeped with a text notification. Josh opened the image, and his mind exploded with rage.

Nex time, Kyerra gets to be oure guest.

"The writing and grammar are consistent," Fred said. "And they spelled Kiera's name the same way."

"Jesus Christ, I'm gonna kill these motherfuckers."

"I'll pretend I didn't hear that, just in case."

"Yeah, thanks. I'll be right in."

"Take your time," Fred said. "I've already got people out looking for cameras and canvassing. We can handle it for now."

"No, I need to come in. But I'll have to tell Kiera first. See ya."

"Tell Kiera what?" she said.

Josh turned to see Kiera standing there with two cups of coffee. He hadn't heard the shower go off or her walk into the room.

"Ah, that was Fred. He had to tell me about a new development."

Kiera's eyes narrowed. "Bullshit, why would you need to tell me any of that? Give it up, Mr. Williams, or no coffee for you," she paused for a moment, letting the towel drop. "Or anything else."

Josh sighed. "The assholes grabbed another woman from your building. A twenty-five-year-old secretary."

Had she yelled and screamed about hunting these guys down and decapitating them, Josh would not be worried. Her absolute silence scared the shit out of him.

He took the coffee cups and placed them on the dresser. Pulling her into his arms, he held her tight. "We'll find them, Kiera. I promise we will."

The silence continued.

"Listen, whatever you are thinking of doing, don't. Forget it. You don't like it when I try to interject myself in your work. Let me do mine."

She pulled him closer, whispering in his ear. "Back to bed, Mr. Williams..." she took his hand and led him to the edge. She pushed him down, climbing on top and taking him inside her. "Then go nail these motherfuckers before I forget what you just said..."

* * * * *

It was close to 6:30 when Kiera watched Josh's car pull out of the driveway, then pushed the send button on her phone.

"I heard," Chris Hamlin said, with no greeting.

"Come pick me up. Time we flushed these sons-a-bitches out into the open."

LXXIV Sometimes We Get Lucky

His one day off plans ruined, the sun struggled to warm the day as Josh pulled into the back lot. He saw Fred, Jerry, Frank, and Tommy running for their cars. Pulling up, he yelled out the window. "What's happened?"

"She escaped," Frank said, "We think this latest victim escaped. She's with one of the Rumford cars in the Narragansett shopping center. Rescue is on the way."

"Jump in," Josh said, and Frank ran to the passenger side.

Flying out of the lot, an angry truck driver flipped him off as he was forced to jam on his brakes, barely missing the unmarked unit. Frank looked out the back window.

'Oh, oh, he's pulling into the station. Another complaint, Lt."

"Good, I haven't had one yet this week," Josh said turning north on Pawtucket Ave. "How'd she get away?"

"Don't know yet. Station got a call of a naked woman screaming and running on New Road. Post five officer found her in the shopping center. She claimed to have been kidnapped in a parking garage in Providence."

"Sometimes we get lucky, Frank, sometimes. Maybe this is one of those times."

Pulling into the lot, Josh rolled up on the uniform officer. The woman sat wrapped in a blanket in the front seat.

Josh walked over, crouching down to talk to her. "Are you hurt anywhere?"

The woman tried to slow her breathing, but the sobs kept coming.

"It's okay, nobody can hurt you now. We've got rescue coming. They'll take you to the hospital. Is there anyone I can call to be with you?"

"My, my, my...my fiancé. He, he, he's a doc, a doctor at Mir, Mir, Miriam. Doc, doc, doc, Doctor Ponti. He might be working now."

"Okay, I will call the hospital myself." A siren interrupted the conversation as a rescue truck pulled into the lot.

"Can you tell me where you were, or how far you ran?"

"I, I, I don't know. Whe, whe, when I got the rope off, I just jumped out the window right through the screen and ran. I don't know, ah, know how, how long. Seemed like forever."

"That's okay, take a deep breath. You're safe. Do you remember anything about the house? Color, shape, anything?"

She shook her head. "Sor, sorry, sorry I don't. I just, I just ran. I thought they would kill me."

"Do you remember anything about the people that did this?"

"At least two guys, maybe three, then, ah. I'm sorry, my head is throbbing," slumping back in the seat.

"It's okay," Josh patted her shoulder. "We'll have you looked at first and when you're ready we'll talk again."

Two rescue firefighters came over and started to examine her. Josh tapped one on the shoulder, pulling him aside.

"Do me a favor. Do what you need to treat her, but we need to preserve her like she's a crime scene, okay?'

The firefighter nodded, "Got it."

"And when you're ready to transport, we're going to Miriam."

"Miriam's closed to rescues. Rhode Island's the only open ER."

"Trust me," reaching for his phone, "they'll open for her. I want an officer in the rescue, and we'll be following you there. I'll call ahead so you'll have priority, got it?"

"Got it, Lieutenant."

Josh took a step back as Fred and the rest came over, asking them to wait a moment.

"This is Detective Lieutenant Josh Williams, I need to speak to whoever is in charge of security right away. Thanks," Josh tilted the phone away.

"Tommy, let's do a grid search off Roger Williams. Hard to say how far she ran, but they are all single-family houses in the area. It may be one of those. Tell everyone if they see anything, anything at all, to call me first before they approach. Tell them to pay special attention to any vans.

"If these guys are still in the area, they may try to lay low and avoid the chance of being stopped, but you never know."

He moved the phone back to his ear. "Yeah, listen we have a kidnap victim we are bringing to the hospital. She's engaged to a doctor there, Dr. Ponti. Yeah. Can you have him meet us in the ER? Great. Thanks."

Ending the call, he reached for his radio, keying the mic.

"701."

"Go, 701"

"Move some more units up here. I want to seal off the area between the Pawtucket line and Center Street. Notify Pawtucket what we have."

"10-4 701, the OIC said detectives are sending everyone as well."

"Okay, have Lt. Ford meet the unmarked units to assign areas. Put a marked unit on North Broadway at Center and one at Pawtucket and Newport. Have the other marked units flood the area. I want to panic these guys into making a mistake."

Over the next few hours, Rumford looked like it was under invasion. Pawtucket units, state police, Providence officers along with every on-duty East Providence officer and several off-duty who'd heard about the situation brought the area to a standstill.

Not a car moved that wasn't checked. Not a pedestrian made it any distance without an officer speaking to them. Every business, bar, and restaurant had a visit from a cop from some agency.

By midnight it was clear it had all been for naught.

Josh leaned on the hood of his car in the parking lot near the Rumford Motel. The lot would normally be jammed packed with the rooms-by-the-hour, Me-and-Mrs. Jones lust affairs, but most had fled the unwanted attention.

Tommy and Frank pulled up and got out of their cars, soon joined by Fred.

"They must have gone to ground," Josh said. "This other location must be nearby, and they just hunkered down."

A few moments later, Det. Lieutenant Ford pulled into the lot.

"Hey, Lt.," Tommy said, "ain't this way past your bedtime?"

Ford smiled, went to his trunk and opened it.

"Hey, Tommy," Frank said. "Don't detectives keep shotguns in the trunk? Maybe he's gone 'round the bend and is looking to take you out."

Tommy smiled, then started to back-pedal.

"Moore, if I wanted to kill you, I'd throw a donut off the Washington Bridge," Ford said, hefting out two six packs of Beck's Beer. "You guys earned this, even if it didn't work out."

Passing out the beers, Ford did what he did best, turning what seemed like defeat into a triumph.

"Look, you guys have a live victim. That's major. All the pressure you've been putting on them probably pushed them out of their routine, giving her a chance. That's a fucking big deal."

As the beer also worked its magic, Josh smiled.

"What's so funny?" Ford said.

"You remember when you were the OIC on midnights?"

"Yeah, I hated midnights."

"But do you remember what you used to do in this lot?" Josh looked around and he had everybody's attention now.

Ford looked around and then a smile crossed his face. "Eh, eh. Can't do that anymore, nobody has matchbooks."

"What the fuck are you guys talking about?" Tommy asked.

Josh smiled. "When old Lt. Ford here spent that year back in the bag, he was the OIC in my group. Every Friday he would grab coffees and donuts and meet with the guys working the various areas. In Rumford, we met here.

"Ford would go in the motel and grab matchbooks. The clerks didn't care, they liked the extra protection. Then, he'd walk through the lot and look for unlocked cars or open windows and toss the matchbooks in the car."

"Oh, man, that's cold," Tommy said.

"Yeah, it was. Lt. why don't you tell 'em the best part?"

The smile on Ford's face was as wide as it could be. "There was this low-rent defense lawyer who somehow became a District Court judge. One Monday I was in court having a warrant signed. This judge calls me to the bench and asks me to meet him in chambers,

"I'm thinking, ah man, he wants me to squash some nitwit relative's possession case or some such nonsense. But no, it was much better than that." Ford took a big swig of beer, then put the bottle back in the holder.

"So, I'm in his chambers and he asks his clerk to leave us alone. When she leaves, he starts complaining about car break-ins at the Rumford Motel. Says his wife found a matchbook in the car and wants to divorce him."

"Holy shit!" Tommy said. "What'd you do?"

"I told him these fuckin' young guys just don't care about the job anymore and that shit never happened when I was on the road."

"You are a prick, Lt., but a funny one," Moore said.

LXXV **Spit in Their Eye**

The next morning, Josh sat in the office alone. Fred came in a short time later.

"Josh, did you know about this?" handing him his phone.

"What is it?" Josh took the phone and restarted the video. It took only a second for him to realize the nightmare now unleashed.

In the video, Kiera and Chris are standing in front of the law office announcing a $100,000 reward for any information leading to the arrest and conviction of Tavares and crew. Josh raised the volume.

"...these animals are cowards who hunt innocent women, and they deserve to be behind bars. It's time to do something to stop these weak and sick individuals from taking any more victims." Kiera looked directly into the camera. "If you think you've intimidated us with your actions, you are mistaken. I dare you to try and come after me. It will be a fatal mistake."

"Jesus Christ, I told her not to get involved. Now every nut in the world will call us. Goddamn it, Kiera."

Fred grabbed his phone. "Maybe this isn't all bad."

"How?"

"While these guys won't fall for the implied challenge and make a rushed attempt, they also won't let it go. When you think about it, this may work to our benefit. In these serial cases, sometimes we hold press conferences to put information out there that may spur the subjects to react.

"I wouldn't have done it this way," wagging the phone in his hand, "but I bet it will spawn a reaction."

A moment later, Brennan walked in.

Josh put up his hands in surrender. "I know, I know, Chief. I saw the video."

"I'd ask you to control her," Brennan said, "but I realize *that's* not happening. If Chris were still working here, I'd bury her on midnights for the rest of her career. I suppose we're gonna have to deal with the lunatic tsunami unleashed by the lure of money. If I could, I'd make the two of them answer all the calls."

Brennan turned and marched out of the office.

Josh looked at Fred who seemed lost in thought.

"What?"

"The Chief may have hit on something. These guys are fixated on Kiera. It goes against the depersonalization of the victims, which is more common in these matters. This is personal with them. This may be the weakness that brings them down.

"Maybe, if we make it known that Kiera will be answering the phones, we can get them to speak to her. This obsession might make them less cautious and give us the chance to trace the calls. It's a long shot, but at this point we have nothing to lose, right? She already lit the fuse.

"And—now hear me out before you say no—we have her hold another press conference to update the case status. We can let it slip that she is answering the phones. The draw to somehow be at the event will be strong. These guys believe they are smarter than us, almost omnipotent if you would. Their arrogance might draw them out."

"It won't work, Fred. They'd never come to the PD for anything." Josh said.

"We don't have it at the PD. She has it at her law office. We, making the air quote sign, have nothing to do with it, officially."

Josh shook his head, pursing his lips. "I don't like it, too uncontrolled."

"I'll bring in a bunch of agents from Boston and Hartford. All new faces posing as reporters. We'll be in the building but out of sight. These guys probably found your picture online, we can't take the chance. Hell, they may have found *every* EP cop's picture they could."

"I don't know, Fred." Josh shook his head. "Too many aspects we can't control. No metal detectors. We'd be leaving them too exposed."

"We can cover it with video as well. Nobody will get near them. Listen to me, Josh, they're coming after Kiera one way or the other. At least here we have a measure of control. Not perfect, but better than winging it. The variables are out there, but here we can have some control.

"Look, we might get lucky. They will want to provoke us, to let us know they were there. We just might spot them and grab 'em."

Josh's cell started blowing up with calls and texts. He ignored them, just glancing at the screen, then pushed it away. Then the song "You" by Jane Olivor started playing. It was Kiera calling.

"It's Kiera; let me find out where she is," holding up his hand. "Well, if it isn't Miss I-promise-not-to-get-involved. Jesus, Kiera, what were you thinking?"

"I wanted to flush them out. You in trouble with Brennan?"

"No, but Chris may have to go into witness protection."

"She'll handle it. So now what?"

"Where are you?"

"We're at the bagel shop on Waterman."

"Stay there, and I mean stay! Fred and I have an idea."

* * * * *

Five minutes later, Josh and Fred sat with Chris and Kiera over coffee.

"So, what's this idea?" Chris asked.

LXXVI **Rising to the Bait**

As everyone expected, reporters, the curious, the newshounds, and assorted lunatics mobbed the lobby. Sprinkled within were FBI and ATF agents trying to look inconspicuous.

In the security office, just off the lobby, Josh, Fred, and Tommy gathered around a wall of computer monitors each displaying camera views of every entrance and exit. A master screen focused on the crowd. Tommy zoomed in and out on any face catching his eye.

Kiera and Chris paced back and forth just behind them.

"What's this, Chris Hamlin nervous?" Josh joked.

Chris smirked. "Nah, just rehearsing in my mind the best angle for a kill shot without risking any innocent lives."

"Ah, we'd prefer to take these guys alive," Fred said. "And I had to sign for all these agents. I need to have them back in one piece. No holes."

"Tell 'em to duck," Chris said. "If I spot the son-of-a-bitch I can't guarantee what I may do."

Fred took two steps toward the former officer. Chris's eyes gave a micro-indication of surprise.

"Hand it over," putting out his hand.

Chris shook her head. "Not on your life." Then locked her eyes on him.

Fred stared, matching her look. "Now, or I have a couple of these agents wrestle you out of here." He pushed his hand closer. "Your choice."

Chris glanced at the two young agents. Short hair, muscles straining the buttons on their pressed white shirts, she knew she'd lose the struggle.

Reaching slowly, she unhooked the Uzi from the holster, removed the magazine and the chambered round, locking the bolt back, and handed the weapon to Fred.

Fred, without taking his eyes off Chris, reached back and handed the weapon to one of the agents. "Both of them," keeping his hand out.

Chris smiled, reached into the small of her back and pulled out the Sig Sauer. Repeating the process to make the weapon safe, she handed it over.

"Is that it?" Fred said.

"I have no more weapons, sir. Nothing. You're welcome to search me," raising her arms.

"No, I will trust you on this." He turned to face Kiera. "Ready?"

"Yup."

"Tommy, anything?"

Tommy scanned through the monitors one more time. "Nothing I can see. Couple of nuts near the front door carrying signs about the end of the world, but no one jumps out at me."

"Okay, you're on. Remember, if anything happens you just duck. Let us handle it. There are two agents right near the podium who will move to cover you and Chris." He looked at Chris. "Let them do their job, okay?"

Chris nodded.

"We'll be here unless something happens. After you finish, just head to your office. You'll be covered all the way."

Kiera reached out and held Josh's hand. "See ya in a bit, okay?"

Josh pulled her in for a hug, then let her go. One the way out, Kiera turned back to look one last time, then left the room.

As they walked down the hallway, both looked straight ahead.

"Still got it?" Chris asked.

"Of course," Kiera smiled, reaching into her waist and pulling out the compact Glock. As she passed by Chris, she slipped the weapon to her.

"That's my girl, The FBI is so predictable."

When the first of the reporters spotted Kiera and Chris, they began shouting questions.

"Have you heard from the killers?"

"Have you been threatened by these guys?"

"Why aren't the police doing more in this case? Have they identified anyone?"

Kiera raised her hands to silence the crowds. She stepped toward the podium, gathering her thoughts.

"Thank you all for coming. For those of you who may not know me, my name is Kiera Williams. I have a brief statement then will take some questions." Glancing at the podium, she shuffled her notes.

"As you are aware, one of my paralegals was kidnapped and murdered by these brutal animals. They have been preying on women in the most horrific ways. These inhuman beasts are cowards and need to be stopped.

"While the police are doing all they can to capture these men, we believe some of you out there may have information that can be helpful. Even the slightest bit of info can make the difference. That is why we funded this reward and have set up a tip hotline.

"Please, I am begging you. If you have any information, call the tip line or the police. We need to make sure there are no more victims. Just imagine how you would feel if this were your wife, daughter, mother, or friend.

"Help us stop this before anyone else suffers. Thank you."

The crowd began shouting questions, Kiera pointed at one young reporter.

"Kiera, have you received any useful information on the tip line?"

"We have, I've taken several calls myself that offered promising leads."

"That was slick," Fred said, as he looked at the monitors. "She put it out there without making it obvious."

"Who's that?" Tommy said, pointing toward a rear door monitor, then zooming in with the camera.

A stocky man dressed in an OD green military shirt and blue jeans made his way along the wall, watching the press conference but staying in the shadows.

Josh started for the door.

Fred grabbed his arm. "Wait, let me move my guys. Let's not overreact."

LXXVII   A Most Personal Message

Josh and Tommy watched as the agents in the crowd slowly approached the man. They had to admit these agents were pros. If you didn't know who they were, it looked like they were trying to find a better position to ask a question.

"I'm going out there, "Josh said, heading toward the door.

"Wait, Josh," Fred said, grabbing his arm and pointing at the monitor. "Look, there's three agents right at the podium. They're between this guy and Kiera. Two others have him surrounded. If he makes a move he's done. We got this."

"Come on, Lt.," Tommy said. "How many times do you get to watch the FBI smoke somebody as it happens?"

Every fiber of Josh wanted to rush out there, but he knew he'd make little difference. Those agents weren't gonna let anyone near Kiera. He needed to let someone else handle this.

While most in the crowd remained oblivious to the movements of the agents, it was not lost on Chris.

Glancing toward the direction of the movement, she spotted the guy in the green shirt. Her first instinct was to shoot him, but something nagged at her. Something Hawk had told her about surviving in Vietnam.

Hawk's words echoed in her mind. "It's never the threat you see, the real threat is the one you can't see."

What would you do? How would you go after Kiera? The thoughts raged in her mind. The threat you can't see. The threat you can't see...and then she knew. Scanning the crowd, one reporter stood out. While she appeared like all the others, she had a notebook in her hand.

No one used a paper notebook anymore when a phone was the perfect note taking accessory. She slipped behind Kiera and whispered, "Be ready to duck." Keeping her movements slow and steady, she moved closer to the woman.

Kiera glanced at Chris but kept answering questions.

Chris could tell this woman was neither a reporter nor a professional. The woman focused on Kiera and ignored everything around her. A pro would be looking for problems, all this woman was looking for was the right moment.

"Gun! Gun! Gun!" as the man in green drew a weapon.

The shouts of the agents followed by multiple gunshots sent the crowd into a panic, all except this woman who kept staring at Kiera.

And Chris knew. The man in green was the diversion.

Drawing the Glock from her waist, she leaped and brought the gun down full force on the woman's skull, sending her crashing to the ground in a heap.

As most of the crowd made for the exits, Josh and Fred came running from the hallway.

"Kiera," Josh yelled, "you okay?"

"Yeah, I'm fine. Go check on Chris."

"Chris?" Josh said, "Why Chr...? As he turned, he saw Chris standing over a woman on the ground. The woman was bleeding from the head.

"Chris, what the hell?"

Fred came over with several other agents. "What's this?"

"The threat you don't see," Chris said, reaching down and pulling a.45 caliber handgun from the woman's purse.

"I thought you said you didn't have any other weapons?" Fred said.

"She didn't," Kiera said, still surrounded by three agents. "I had it. I gave it to her to hold."

Fred looked between the two women, then put his hand on Josh's shoulder. "Josh, I almost feel sorry for you."

The other agents hustled the man out the door while Fred and Chris waited for the EMTs to treat the woman.

"Think she'll cooperate?" Fred asked, looking between the prone woman and Josh.

Josh shrugged. "I'm wondering if she'll be able to cooperate with that dent in her skull."

It was Chris's turn to shrug. "Hey, we neutralize threats, remember? She'll heal."

LXXVIII   Take the Win

Josh paced outside the emergency room waiting for the doctor.

"So, is he gonna live, Doc?"

"Hard to say, Lieutenant. One of the rounds nicked his aorta and he lost a lot of blood. It'll be touch and go for the next few days. And, with that level of blood loss, there is the possibility of brain damage. Frankly, his chances of full recovery are slim. If he lives, he'll likely be incommunicative, perhaps in a persistent vegetative state."

"Thanks, Doc. Please call me if anything changes."

"I will, Lieutenant," then glanced around. "Can I ask you something?"

"Sure."

"Is this one of the suspects in the body parts case?" his morbid curiosity overwhelming his professional demeanor.

Josh hesitated for a moment.

"I was on the night they brought in Dr. Ponti's fiancé, one of the attending physicians."

"Yeah, he's one of them. Not the guys we really wanted but involved."

The doctor looked over his shoulder, then leaned in. "Maybe it would be better if he just died." Not waiting for a reaction, he left the waiting area and returned to intensive care.

Josh raised his eyebrows at Fred. "Yikes."

"Yikes, indeed. Let's hope he doesn't hasten the process. Not that the guy could tell us anything, he's just a pawn."

"So now what?" Josh said.

"Let's go see if we can talk to the female. Other than the dent in her head from Chris, she's fine. Take the win, Josh, maybe she can help us." Fred reached for his phone.

"Who you calling?"

"The AUSA, I want to have a plea agreement in place in case she lawyers up. So far, that hasn't happened, but these cases attract the righteous knights who think all cops are evil and the suspects victims of our trampling their rights.

"Yeah, hi, it's Fred Robertson." Fred put his hand up for Josh to wait.

Josh only heard bits and pieces.

"Yeah, exactly. Thanks,"

"So?"

"Delguidice already has something ready. Soon as he heard what happened, he knew we'd be asking. Okay, let's go. What room is she in?"

"We put her in one of the rooms used by the prison for inmate treatments. Top floor, 610."

As they made their way to the elevator, Chris Hamlin stepped off.

"Do I even want to ask why you're here?"

"Now, Josh, I was just paying my respects to that lovely woman who suffered that unfortunate injury."

"Chris, if you..."

"If I what, Fred? If I made it crystal clear to the poor young thing that cooperation was not only in her best interest as far as the case is concerned but also as far as her continued improvement health-wise, so what?"

All Josh and Fred could do was watch as Chris walked toward the lobby, turned the corner, and disappeared.

"She's like a drug-resistant infection, isn't she?" Fred said.

"One thing you have to learn about Chris, she is never, ever dissuaded by logic, threats, or promises once she's made up her mind about something."

Fred pushed the button for the sixth floor.

"Trust me, if she didn't think the woman could be helpful, we never would have seen her, and there'd be a dead body in the room. Obviously, there is something she can do for us."

LXXIX New Level of Devotion

The young trooper stationed outside room 610 didn't look old enough to drive.

"Damn, I am aging faster and faster every minute," Fred said.

When the trooper spotted the two investigators, instinct kicked in, and he rose to attention.

"Good morning, sirs. Trooper Morrison."

"Relax, Trooper," Fred said, waving the kid to sit. "Last time anyone saluted me was before they invented electricity.

"Sir?"

"Never mind, relax. Just kidding."

Josh put out his hand. "Lieutenant Josh Williams. Nice to meet you. This is Fred Robertson from the FBI."

The trooper's first reaction leaned toward resuming attention and saluting but the smile on Josh's face relaxed him.

"Nice to meet you, sir," taking Josh's hand.

"Josh will do."

"Ah, Ken, sir, Ken Morrison."

"So, Ken. Who else has been in?"

"Ah, Agent Hamlin from the FBI was here a few minutes ago. I'm surprised you didn't run into her. She left just before you arrived."

"She was, was she," Fred glanced at Josh. "And did she say why she needed to speak to the prisoner?"

"No, sir, just asked me to keep any of the medical personnel away while she spoke to her. Said you'd be in shortly and she needed to verify some information for you. Said the woman was an informant of the bureau but wanted to keep that confidential from hospital staff."

Fred rubbed the back of his head.

"Something wrong, sir?"

"No, no. I'm just sorry I missed Agent Hamlin. I guess I'll just have to catch up with her later."

"We might be in here for a while if you want to go grab coffee or something." Josh offered.

"Ah, my lieutenant might show up, and he will not approve."

"Tell you what, you go grab a coffee and if your lieutenant shows up, I'll tell him I insisted. I'm sure it will be fine."

"Thank you, sir. I'll be right back." The trooper double-timed down the hallway, choosing the stairs instead of the elevator.

"Man, if I could just find a way to bottle that enthusiasm."

"You and me both, Fred, now let's see what we can find out."

As they entered the room, the soft rhythmic beeping of the monitors was the only sound. The woman, head wrapped like a mummy to a point just above her two very black and swollen eyes, turned to look at them.

"Are you, Josh?"

"Yes, I am. This is Fred Roberston from the FBI."

"Chris said I should just tell you everything. And I want to do that, but I don't know if it will help."

"Well, Karen, right? Your name is Karen?" Josh asked, getting a surprised reaction.

"Yeah, that's my real name. Karen Whitmore. But Gideon called me Gabriella. He said I was part of God's plan."

"Where did you meet Gideon?"

"At the shelter downtown. He and Max came there and offered us a place to stay. They were nice, brought us food and helped us pray."

"Where did you go?"

"First, we stayed at a place near the water, Riverside, I think. I'm not from here, I'm from Brockton, Mass., but I heard people mention it when we drove there."

"Do you know the address?" Fred asked.

She shook her head. "To be honest, I was usually high. Gideon said the drugs were from God and would help me. He said it wasn't heroin or anything like that."

Fred nodded.

"Could you find the place if we took you in our car?" Josh asked.

"Maybe, I don't know. I could try."

"Did they take you anywhere else?"

"We went to places where I brought packages in for Gideon. Lots of places. I knew they were drugs, but I didn't care. I had a place to live, food to eat, and got high whenever I wanted."

"So, tell me what happened the day you were arrested? What were you supposed to do?"

"Shoot the she-devil."

"Who was the she-devil?"

"The woman talking at the podium. She was trying to steal our souls by telling lies about Gideon and the mission God gave us."

"What was that mission?"

"Destroy all the demons."

"Who gave you the gun?"

"Max, he carried all the weapons."

"Did he show you how to shoot?"

Karen shook her head. "Didn't have to. I was Army, six years, combat firearms instructor until I got hurt when some idiot captain decided to show off his quick-draw skills. Put a round through my kneecap.

"Then I got hooked on pain meds. Army separated me with a medical discharge. I tried to fight it but lost."

"Did you ever go anywhere else with them? Maybe after the Riverside house was raided?"

"It's all a fog. There was a place with some kind of tire ads and then a place with car filters. An old building, abandoned, I think. It's all kinda messed up in my head."

Josh noticed the blood pressure and respiration indicators rising so decided to cut it short.

"Karen, I'm gonna talk to the doctor. If she says it's okay, will you take a ride with us when she says you're well enough and point out the places you remember?"

"Yeah, anything to get out of here. Gideon said he'd never leave me alone but here I am and he ain't coming for me. Demons must have taken him."

"Okay, you rest for now and we'll be back."

Josh and Fred headed toward the door.

"Josh?"

"Yeah, Karen."

"I'm sorry for what I tried to do. I didn't know it was your wife. Gideon lied about her. Chris told me he's the devil. I'm sorry he fooled me."

"That's okay, Karen, she's fine and you're safe here."

Outside the room, Trooper Morrison stood as they exited the room. A sheepish grin crossed his face.

"Sorry, force of habit. They beat it into us in the academy."

Josh smiled, "No worries, take care Ken. I will be sure to mention how squared away you were to the bosses."

"Thank you, sir! Ah. Lieutenant, ah Josh," the smile wide across his face.

As they got to the elevator, Fred turned to wave at the trooper, then snapped a perfect salute that had the trooper on his feet returning it.

"We Marines know how to salute," he said as he waited for Josh in the elevator.

"Troopers and Marines are one of a kind, jar heads to the end." Josh said, chuckling. "Let's go find the doctor handling her and see when she can travel.

LXXX Wait a Minute

The nurse pushed the wheelchair out the revolving doors as Josh and Fred waited outside. Standing near the front passenger door, Fred helped Karen to her feet and into the seat. The head wrap was gone and the swelling around her eyes barely noticeable.

"Aren't you sitting up front?" she asked.

"No, no," Fred said, holding the door. "We want you to be comfortable. Ready?"

Karen nodded and smiled as the door shut.

"First stop, Dunkin' Donuts or McDonald's or whatever you want, Karen." Josh said, pulling from the curb and onto Summit Ave. "What'll it be?"

"I'd love a coffee and donut."

"Why one? I'll grab a dozen and a large coffee. How's that?"

"Thanks, wow. This is almost fun."

Settling back in her seat, she took a deep breath and watched the world go by.

* * * * *

Twenty minutes later, after finishing two donuts and working on her third, Karen looked out as they passed the sewage treatment plant on Bullocks Point Ave.

"Take the next right, Josh. I think that's where the house was."

Turning onto Washington Street, Josh slowed the car as Karen looked from side to side.

"There! There! That's it!" pointing with the half-eaten donut.

"Great, Karen. Who was at this house with you?"

"Gideon, Max, and some older chick, I think she was Gideon's sister."

Josh glanced at Fred. "And this older woman, what did she do there?"

"Brought money for the drugs. She was selling for Gideon."

"Okay, anybody else?"

"There was this little mousy guy, he kept trying to get in my pants, but I wouldn't let him until..."

"Until what?" Fred asked.

"Until Gideon told me to let him. Said it was my duty as a woman to please men."

"Do you know this guy's name?"

"Yeah, it was a weird name, Ishmael or Israel, or something like that. He would come into my room whenever he wanted, and I just went along."

"Did you see any other women there?"

"No, well, just the demons disguised as women. Gideon and Max would catch them and keep them in the basement.

They told me God wanted them to save these women but sometimes the demons wouldn't surrender, and they couldn't."

Karen turned away as a tear fell from her eye. "Sometimes they had to die to be set free."

"How did they do that?" Josh asked.

"Gideon would bring the women up into the living room. He'd tie them up, put a gag over their mouth, and lay them on the floor. They would always be naked. He liked to watch as Max and the other guy would take turns fucking them.

"Gideon never did, though. He said he had to be pure to drive out the demon.

"Then, Gideon would pray over them, yelling for the demon to leave. After a while, he and the others would start beating the women, screaming 'Be gone, demon, be gone.' There was blood everywhere.

"After the women stopped screaming, Max and Israel dragged them back downstairs to the basement. I never saw them again."

"How many women?" Fred asked.

"I don't know," shaking her head, sobbing. "Five or six while I was there."

"Did you worry it might happen to you?" Josh asked.

"No, Gideon said I was sent from God. He explained the name he gave me, Gabriella, means God is my strength. He said I was put here on earth for this moment, and that God had a purpose for me before Jesus returned."

She turned to look right at Josh, her eyes now filling with tears.

"He said all my suffering up to now would be rewarded for my devotion to God's will. He promised me I'd be happy in heaven." She turned back to stare at the house. "But all of that was bullshit, wasn't it? He expected me to die when he sent me to kill your wife, didn't he?"

"I'm sorry, Karen. Gideon, that's not his real name, is a killer who preys on women. Why he treated you differently than the others we may never understand. But we gotta find him and stop him. Is there anything else? Anywhere else he took you?"

Karen reached up and wiped her eyes, taking a sip of coffee.

"Isn't that cold? You want another one?" Josh asked.

"If I could."

"Of course, there's a Dunkin Donuts every five feet here in Rhode Island." Josh drove back up Washington turning right onto Bullocks Pt. Ave. They caught the light at Lincoln Ave.

Karen leaned forward looking down the road.

"See something?" Josh asked.

"I, I'm not sure but go slow here, there's a place we went to delivering some drugs right around here. I remember because Max and I walked; it was close to the house."

Josh pulled forward, slowing as they passed through the square.

"There," Karen said, pointing and bouncing in her seat. "I remember now. That older chick runs the place. We brought a bunch of packages to her. She gave me some clothes to wear. She was kind to me, I guess. But she was dealing for Gideon."

Josh glanced at the consignment shop where they'd found some of the victims' uniforms.

"Thanks, Karen. Ah, remember at the hospital, you mentioned something about tires and air filters? An abandoned building?"

Karen nodded.

"Do you think you could find it?"

"Maybe, I only went to the tire place a couple of times and the other place only once."

"Did you drive there, or walk?" Fred asked.

Karen perked up at the question. "Wait, we walked there once. I remember now because Max told me to wait outside. It was near the consignment shop, but it was at night and..."

"And what, Karen?" Josh said.

"And I was high. Plus, I knew if I went inside Max would try something. He kept grabbing my ass while we walked. I tried not to pay much attention."

"Do you remember how long it took to walk back to the house?"

"Yeah, it was quick, not much farther than the consignment shop. We walked on the bike path for a little bit."

"Good," Josh said, smiling. "You're doing fine. How about the other place? You said something about filters?"

"Yeah, I used to work with my dad on his car and he let me change the air filter. I recognized the boxes in the warehouse."

"Can you describe it?"

She thought for a moment, finishing the last of the coffee. "It was dark, brick, I think. There were a bunch of buildings. Some of the windows were broken out. But one way in the back had a lock on it. Gideon had the key.

"We kept some demons there for a while, tried to save a few but they died. There were no houses around, so it was a secluded place to hide them from the others."

"Others?" Fred asked. "What do ya mean?"

"The other demons. Gideon said we had to keep moving them so the others wouldn't try to take them from us."

"How long ago was this?" Josh asked.

"A month, maybe two. We moved there after the cops caught that guy Israel, or whatever his name was, and he betrayed us. Told you where our house was."

"When was the last time you were there?"

"The day of the press conference. Gideon, me, and Max were there and one of the helpers brought in another demon. She might still be there."

Josh glanced back at Fred.

"Anything else you can remember? Did you drive there? Anything?"

She shook her head. "I was in the back of the van. I wasn't watching where we went."

Josh nodded.

"Oh, but I remember one thing."

"What's that?"

"Letters"

"Letters? What letters?"

"U S A. and they were rainbow colored. I laughed 'cuz it reminded me of the Army, right? USA, United States Army. But I don't think it was."

Josh tried to put a place to the letters, but nothing came to him. Karen kept bouncing the empty coffee cup on her knee beating a rhythm only she could hear.

"Let's go buy you another coffee, then take you back to the hospital."

They drove in silence most of the way, Karen happily sipping her coffee, feet up on the dash like she was out for a leisurely drive. Fred and Josh lost in thoughts on how best to deal with that lying bitch at the consignment shop.

Karen broke the quiet.

"Am I going to jail?"

It took a moment for Josh to form his answer. "Well, Karen, I'm gonna speak to the prosecutor and explain how helpful you've been. But once you're released from the hospital, yeah, you might have to go there for a while."

It was Karen's turn to consider her response.

"That's okay, maybe this is what God had planned for me all along. Help the cops catch these guys. That's a good thing right, Josh?"

"Yeah, it is, Karen. Yeah, it is."

LXXXI A Nagging Thought

As soon as Josh and Fred got back to the office, the team peppered them with questions.

"What'd she say?"

"Anything we can use?"

"Where are these guys?"

"Whoa, whoa," Josh said. "Let me at least sit down and I'll tell you all about it."

It didn't take long for Josh to fill them in. Most of what she'd said, they already knew. But the letters U S A kept nagging at him.

"U S A, huh?" Frank said. "U SA? U S A? Where would she see..." The abrupt end to his repeated question caught everyone's attention.

"What? You got something?" Tommy asked.

Frank smiled. "U S A, United Skates of America. On New Rd. I worked details there when I was in uniform. There's a big sign with the name on it and U S A is highlighted."

"Holy shit," Tommy said. "Holy shit. Look," he walked to a map of the city hanging over his desk. "Here's Skates," he said, pointing to New Road at Pawtucket Ave. Then he slid his finger across the street to an area just off Campbell Ave.

"What's that?" Fred asked.

"The old Fram Corporation. Been abandoned for years but some of the buildings are still standing," he said, looking around the room. "And they made car filters. There are old boxes of them in storage sheds there. It makes sense. Not many houses near there and it's a straight shot to where the victim who escaped was seen."

"No shit," Josh said, "I knew there was something familiar. We assumed it was a house. Makes sense it would be this place."

"Let's go," Tommy said, grabbing for his favorite set of keys.

"Whoa, big fella," Josh said. "We need to think this out. These guys plan for eventualities. They may have already abandoned the place after the vic escaped. This isn't gonna be a charge in the front door event.

"Lt., they may have another one there. If we wait, it might be too late."

Josh eyed anxious faces; Cops always want to do something, to rush toward a problem. Sometimes that works, sometimes it creates bigger ones.

Glancing at his watch, he reached for the phone. "Let me request the SRT guys here. It will be dark soon and we can use their skills. Until they set up, why don't you and brother jarhead here use some of your creepy crawly skills and see what you can see up there.

"But don't do *anything* without telling me. If they are still there, I want to overwhelm them with force. I don't want to spook them. Think you can handle it?"

Both nodded, then made for the door.

"We'll go in through the sewer treatment plant," Tommy said. "Lots of cover back there. No way they'd expect us."

"Sewer treatment plant?" Fred said.

"Yup, hope you have a change of clothes 'cuz you'll never get the smell out." A huge smile broke out all over his face.

"He loves this shit, doesn't he?" Jennifer said.

"Oh yeah," replied Josh. "No doubt he'll have Fred all camouflaged up with face paint and night vision equipment. You guys just hang tight, let me go brief Brennan on the latest before he sees all the troops showing up."

* * * * *

"You think they're still there?" Brennan asked, feet propped up on his desk.

Josh shrugged. "My bet would be no. They're smart. When the vic escaped they probably beat feet, but then again since nothing's happened, they might just think it's clear. They have done a pretty slick job of keeping the place off the radar so far. I think it's worth a shot."

Brennan slid his legs off the desk, leaning forward in the chair. "You got eyes on the place?"

"Tommy and Fred are on their way. Going in through the woods from the sewer treatment plant."

Brennan nodded. "You think you can keep that maniac from storming the place?"

"Yeah, he'll do what I said, or Fred will shoot him."

"Hmm," Brennan smiled. "Might be a win-win."

Josh laughed.

"Okay, I'm gonna stick around until this plays out. Keep me in the loop."

"You got it, Chief."

Back in the office, Frank and the others were gathered around one of the portable radios. Frank looked up when Josh came in.

"Hey, Lt., they've got movement up there. Somebody is there. They can see lights from inside one of the buildings and shadows of somebody walking around."

Josh reached for the radio. Keying the mic, the digital identifier chirped as the radio connected. "Tommy, what've you got?"

Tommy's voice was a muffled whisper. "At least two people. Can't see in the windows because they're covered but we can see light and movement."

"Any vehicles?"

"Not that we can see, but there is a garage."

Josh saw the SRT team commander come in, listening to the conversation.

"Ask him how many doors there are."

"Tommy, SRT wants to know how many doors."

"Hang on, Fred was making his way around to check that."

The silence, lasting just a few moments, seemed interminable.

"Two doors, one facing the road and one on the east side. The garage is on the west side, also facing the road. No windows in back. Two sets of double windows to the right of the door as you're facing the building. A small window on the east side next to the door. And, the screen is pushed out. This has to be where they had the one that escaped."

The door to the office opened and Brennan came in with the on-duty Deputy Fire Chief.

"Josh, Deputy here has detailed plans for the place. They're a couple of years old but not much has changed as far as the layout is concerned."

The Deputy handed Josh a printout of the building footprint.

"Thanks Dep. Can you pre-position a rescue close to the scene? Just in case."

"I already moved Rescue Two into the area. Barrington sent us a rescue to cover Riverside. I'll move the Special Hazards truck up as well. Never know in these old buildings."

"Okay," Josh turned to SRT. "Okay, Captain, your show. Put together an entry plan and let's go grab these guys."

LXXXII   **Consolation Prize**

The SRT Operations vehicle made its way down the driveway toward the target. Using the infrared illuminator allowed the night vision equipped operator to drive in complete darkness. The rest of the team huddled in the back.

150 yards from the target, the sniper teams deployed and set up positions covering the front and side doors. At the last corner in the road before the building, the vehicle stopped, and the rest of the team took up assault positions.

"Tommy, any update?" the SRT commander asked.

"Nope, all the movement seems to be in that front room. Fred's got the back covered. Nothing moving back there."

"Okay, I've got two of my guys making their way to help cover the back. We're gonna approach and take out both doors simultaneously. I'll give you a heads up when we're in position."

"Got it, Captain."

It took just three minutes for the SRT members to move into position. The team leader for each group gave the commander the thumbs up, ready to go signal.

"Tommy, on my count we hit them. Stand by." Raising his hand, he pointed at the teams and counted down on the radio. " ...five, four, three, two, one. Go! Go! Go!"

Both doors crumbled under the assault by the rams. The entry teams flooded the rooms. Flash bangs disoriented those inside while shouted commands, "Down, everybody down!" mixed with the smoke from the grenades echoed off the walls. The speed of the entry teams ended any possible resistance.

It took all of three minutes for the two men inside to be handcuffed and placed prone on the floor. Switching their illumination to regular lighting, it took just seconds for the horror before them to register with the cops.

"Jesus Christ,' the SRT commander said, taking in the scene. He reached for his radio. "Josh, get in here."

Josh ran from the SRT vehicle and stepped over the splintered front door. The SRT members stood frozen in place, the only movement was their heads looking from side to side.

"Oh, my fucking word," Josh said, "Okay, everybody out. Take those guys to the station, in separate cells and I want a cop with them. Do not leave them alone." He keyed his mic. "701."

"Go, 701," the dispatcher answered.

"Send BCI here and notify the Chief, two in custody but not the primary targets. No injuries."

Josh turned to face the wall. Among the images of bloodied, tortured, dying women were two that captured his attention and sent him into a rage.

Yanking the photos from the wall, he made a sound like a wounded animal in agony. The entire room turned to look.

"Josh, what is it?" Fred asked.

Josh looked up, his face red, veins pulsing in his neck. Handing Fred the pictures, he stayed quiet for a moment.

Fred stayed focused on Josh.

"These motherfuckers are dead. I will pull them slowly apart limb from limb while they're alive," then stormed out of the building.

Fred glanced around the room, then down at the pictures. The two pictures of Kiera shocked him. One walking her dog in Colt State Park and one of her working out at the gym. Scrawled across one picture in the now familiar scratch of Gideon was one short line.

"I'm going to enjoy every moment with her."

Fred knew there was more to the images than the immediate horror. These guys had been after Kiera for a long time. They were playing with Josh to make it more painful.

LXXXIII **This Has to End**

It took BCI detectives two full days to process the scene with help from the FBI crime lab, Rhode Island State Police detectives, and the Rhode Island Medical Examiner's office. The horrors inside that building gave them all nightmares.

"How many, Josh?" Brennan asked.

Josh looked at his notes. "As best we can determine, forty-three victims. But right now, all we have are images in over a hundred videos showing various torture sessions. All of our known vics are in the images and the rest we're working on."

"And there were more body parts?"

"Forty-three right hand middle fingers, one from each victim, we assume. They had them nailed to the wall."

"Jesus Christ this has gotta end. Maybe we are in over our heads." Brennan massaged his forehead.

"It's not just our case. Never really was from the beginning. Between the FBI agents, state police, the AG's investigators, and the local US Attorney it's a task force case with an ad hoc task force."

At the sound of the words, task force, Brennan perked up.

"You may have hit on a solution there, Lieutenant."

"A solution to what?" Josh asked.

"Have you seen the latest headlines? They're saying we're Mayberry homicide investigating Jack the Ripper."

"Fuck 'em, who cares what a bunch of political hacks say?"

"I do if I want to leave on my own terms. If they force us to give up the lead on the case, and it goes south, they'll blame us. If they make an arrest, it will be because they took over. I don't want that after all that's happened, especially to you."

Josh looked at the floor. "It doesn't matter."

"It does matter, Josh. Look, I can't imagine what you've experienced. But I know this, if I were in your place I'd want to be the one that got to the truth. I believe you're more than capable and you deserve the opportunity."

"Thanks, Chief. So, what do we do?"

"The task force is a sexy concept. If we propose it to the other agencies as a joint task force everybody can take credit or shift the blame no matter how it turns out."

"Thanks for the vote of confidence, Chief."

"Look, I'm sure between you and your guys, the Feebs, and the troopers we can handle this, but this will take heat off the politicians to do something that will complicate matters.

"I'll call the Colonel and the local SAC to bring them up to speed and then we can do a dog and pony show for the AG and US Attorney."

"You know, this job would be fun if not for all the politics." Josh said.

"Tell me about it. So, what's next?"

"We're gonna talk about that now. It will be weeks if not months before all the DNA is processed. Just trying to figure out our next plan."

"Okay, you worry about catching these assholes, I'll deal with the politics."

"Thanks, Chief."

Josh headed toward the door.

"And Josh," Brennan said.

"Sir?"

"If you do kill them, make sure it's done right. I don't give a shit what happens to them, but I want you still standing when this is over."

LXXXIV   Planting a Seed

The team gathered in the conference room.

"Can I suggest something?" Frank said.

"Have at it," Josh said.

"Why don't we use a decoy? I know we shot it down before, but things have changed. Since they're fixated on Kiera, we have someone who looks like Kiera drive to the office. We set up surveillance and snatch them if they try to grab her when she leaves."

"We had considered that, Frank," Fred said. "But since they seem to have gone to ground, it's probably a waste of time. Wouldn't they expect her to be well covered?"

"Not if we give them a reason to come out."

"And how do we do that?" Josh asked.

"Hold a press conference. The stunt Kiera and Chris pulled didn't pan out, but it did provoke a reaction. They did talk to her. They're paying attention to us. Suppose we announce something that will piss them off. I bet the mind readers," he glanced at Emily Thompson, "I mean, ah, the Behavioral Sciences Unit agents could come up with something."

Emily smiled. "As much as we like to think we can read minds, it's not quite that simple. But Frank here may be on to something. I've been thinking about why they suddenly went silent after the calls to Kiera. There are a couple of reasons.

"First, they may have been arrested and the agency hasn't processed the DNA yet. Second, they got spooked by the last woman escaping and left the area. Or," she glanced at Josh, "they have decided to make one last big play. Something cataclysmic since their attempt on killing Kiera failed.

"Their religious overtones lend themselves to an apocalyptic act designed to shock the world. In their minds they want to do something to prove they are God's avenging angels. I think they'll go after a high-profile target and taking the wife of the cop trying to catch them would demonstrate, at least to their followers, their omnipotence."

"You think they still want to go after Kiera?"

Emily nodded. "I think of the three scenarios that one makes the most sense. I doubt they've been arrested elsewhere. They are unlikely to leave this area as they are comfortable here and have managed to avoid us so far.

"They're still here and planning something."

"You think Frank's idea might work?" Josh asked.

Emily thought for a moment. "I think we could script a press conference that might provoke them. Announce the two in custody are the main guys and have been stopped.

"My worry is they may decide Kiera is too risky and go after someone more vulnerable. If we assume they are somehow keeping tabs on Kiera, we need to make it appear she is not fully protected. They must see gaps in the coverage."

"Josh, Kiera would have to agree to this," Fred said. "You think she'll go along?"

"If it means catching these guys, yeah, she'll go along. But she won't like the idea of someone else taking the risk. Who we gonna use?"

Jennifer Holmes walked into the conference room. Until that moment, it hadn't occurred to anyone the similarity between Jennifer and Kiera. The entire room stared at her.

"What?" she said, looking at the smirking faces.

"How'd you like to be Josh's wife?" Fred asked.

"Wife? He's got a wife, no thanks. Not my thing."

"Not really his wife, just play one on TV as they say." Fred explained the idea.

"Hmm, now that sounds like I finally get to do some real work. I'm in. What's first?"

Josh stood up. "First, you and I will go see Kiera. She'll want to know who is taking the risk. You'll have to convince her you can handle it."

"Okay, let's go."

"While you two are off talking Kiera into this, Emily and I will craft the press release," Fred said. "Assuming we can have something by the end of the day, we can start setting the stage in the morning. Sound good?"

Josh nodded and headed out. The rest of the team scattered to their other duties while Emily and Fred started brainstorming.

LXXXV Truth is Fluid

Jennifer walked into the office, the transformation into Kiera remarkable.

"Wow. You ready for your debut?" Josh asked.

"As I'll ever be."

"Let's just go over it once more. We've put cameras at every entrance door and floor entrance. There is total coverage of the fourth floor. We'll time your entry so when you hit the third floor of the parking garage, one of us will pull out of a spot near the exit for you.

"If we see anything before you get there, we'll give you a heads up. If that happens you stay in the car like you're on the phone. Make them come to you. If something happens after you're out of the car, there'll be at least three of us there to take them out.

"You okay with this?"

Jennifer nodded, but the tension was palpable.

Josh smiled. "Look, undercover ain't for everyone, if you want out just say so."

"Nah, I'm good. I want to do this. I want to nail these pricks."

"Pricks?" Josh chuckled. "You been around Tommy way too much."

"Hey," Tommy said. "I've been training her to be a real cop."

Jennifer shook her head, checked her weapon once more, then grabbed the keys to the car. "Come on, let's go catch these guys."

"Go," Josh said, pushing Tommy out the door.

* * * * *

They spent the next several days in the same routine. Jennifer would drive in, and a different car would leave the fourth floor, opening a parking spot surrounded by cameras. Jen would park and then go into the office.

On the fifth day, Chief Brennan called Josh into the office.

"So, how long are you planning to do this? Seems to me these guys have left the area."

Josh shook his head. "The FBI profilers said to expect this. They may have found new territory to hunt, but they are comfortable here and think they can outsmart us. There've been no reports on body parts. Let's give it a few more days."

Brennan nodded. "Okay, but if nothing happens by the end of the week, we call it off. Understand me?"

"Yes, sir, Chief. Thanks." Josh left the office.

"He getting antsy?" Fred asked.

"Yeah," Josh said, "gave us to the end of the week."

"Oh boy."

"I have an idea," Tommy said.

The room went silent.

"You have an idea?" Josh said, breaking the spell. "I can't wait to hear this."

"I have ideas all the time," Tommy said, "I usually keep them to myself."

"Thank Christ for that. But, by all means, let's hear this one."

"Declare victory and go home," Tommy said.

The silence resumed.

"Tommy, what the fuck does that mean?" Josh asked.

"I think he's onto something," Emily Thompson said.

Everyone in the room turned to look at the FBI profiler.

"You do?" Tommy said, smiling.

"I do, Tommy. These guys have been laying low. The pressure to act will be enormous. They can't go much longer, but there is no telling how long that will be. If I understand what you're suggesting, we force their hand by making them irrelevant.

"We announce the investigation has identified the suspects, and we believe they have committed suicide. We don't say specifically that we've recovered their bodies but merely imply it."

Tommy nodded. "Yeah. This will piss them off and force their hand. I ain't very religious, but I remember something about some religions say suicide prevents you from going to heaven. They'd have to save face in front of the others to keep control."

"But the announcement of the two already in custody didn't work," Josh said. "Why will this be any different."

"I'm not certain it will, but the point Tommy had about suicide makes sense. It just might be the trigger we need.

"I'm genuinely worried they may look elsewhere for victims. My read on Tavares and Baader is they are not inclined to martyrdom," Emily said. "But it is still our only option other than waiting for them to make a move. I believe they will want to prove how they can operate right under our noses. Tommy's right."

Josh glanced at Tommy smiling like he just won the lottery. "Tommy is right is not something we hear very often here, but if you think it's a good idea let's go for it."

"And I think you should be the one to make the statement to the media. You'll have the most effect on them," Emily paused momentarily. "There is a risk here, though."

"What's that?" Josh asked.

"This will put your wife right on their radar. She'll be their only focus. While that may be our intent, we cannot control how or when they will target her. And while I don't know her well, I have the impression she will not be kept away from her office much longer.

"These guys will need to act, but they have demonstrated remarkable patience. They may grab a victim to satisfy their immediate need, they may already have one, and take their time targeting Kiera.

"Or, and this is a common pattern with these groups, they may go full on apocalyptic. Try to take her and you out, and as many others as they can. Die in a spectacular and very public manner to bring on, in their minds, the return of the messiah.

We might be igniting something that we cannot know how or when it will detonate."

Josh looked around the room. Most chose not to meet his eyes, unwilling to be part of the decision, except Tommy.

"Lt., what's it gonna be?"

Josh hesitated, then said, "Let's go for it. I'll call Kiera and Chris. Frank, line up the media for the press conference." He turned to Emily. "Can you craft something that will piss them off?"

"I believe I can. There are some precedents from other cases I could rely on. Give me a couple of hours. Fred, can you work with me?"

"Of course. Let's go to my office downtown. Be easier to access the files in Quantico."

* * * * *

Three hours later, the team gathered in the SIU office. Josh and Emily reviewed the press release while the others searched for any sign of activity by the bad guys in other states.

"Hey, I've got something here," Frank said. "There's a missing person report from Brockton, MA. A thirty-two-year-old female missing from a lawyer's office where she was a paralegal. Been missing for three days.

"I'll give Brockton PD detectives a call, see what I can find out."

"What do you think?" Fred asked.

Josh shrugged.

"If these are the same guys, this whole idea might be a waste of time or force their hand on this other victim. I'm not sure we should move ahead."

Josh looked at his cell phone. "We've got twenty minutes before the media starts gathering; let's see what Frank can find out."

LXXXVI   No Easy Choices

Frank hung up the phone and gathered his notes.

"Okay, here's what they have. The woman went missing right after lunch the day she disappeared. They found her car parked in a Drive 'n Fly lot near the airport in Hartford, CT. The Brockton detective in charge of the case said the woman was recently divorced and depressed.

"She pulled this disappearing act once before but let her boss know she'd be back at some point. There was some blood in the car, but they didn't think it came from a struggle or serious injury."

"I bet she found some hot new piece online and decided to go for it," Tommy said, smiling. "You know, get a little mud on the turtle. Bang away the blues. Horizontal mambo."

Fred shook his head. "As crude as that analysis is, I gotta admit he's probably right. It doesn't fit the pattern. Daytime snatch, taking the victim's car, long-distance travel, a different M. O. I don't think it's our guys."

"There is one thing," Josh said.

"What's that?" Fred asked.

"Remember when we took Karen on her field trip. She said she was from Brockton. She never said where she met these guys, just that they found her at a shelter.

"Suppose it was a shelter in Brockton? I told you I don't like coincidences."

"Good point, and maybe some of the latest batch of evidence from the Fram site might also tie back to other states. Brockton ain't that far away. Let's not discount the incident yet."

"Okay, then," Josh said, " Keep that in the nice to know category for now. We need to deal with things here. Let's do it."

"I hope those words aren't prophetic," Fred said.

Josh looked at him with a furrowed brow.

"Gary Gilmore said the same thing."

"Gary Gilmore?" Tommy said.

"He killed two people in Utah and was sentenced to death. He demanded a firing squad. The day of the execution, a Catholic priest gave him last rites and escorted him to the execution area. When asked if he had any last words, Gilmore said, 'Let's do it."

Josh said, "Thanks for sharing."

Fred chuckled. "Just doing my part, Josh."

Josh and Emily went down the corridor to the rollcall room. Inside, the room was jammed with media. Chief Brennan stood chatting with several of the local reporters, regaling them with colorful war stories of his soon-to-be-ended career with East Providence PD.

One of the reporters, a recent addition to the Channel 12 team, asked Brennan if she could interview him about his career before he left the department.

"Sure, Katie, call my office and arrange a time. But nothing about this case, agreed?"

The reporter nodded.

Yeah, right, Brennan thought, then looked toward the door.

As Josh entered the room, the reporters began bombarding him with questions.

"Has there been an arrest?"

"Have you found more body parts?"

"What are you doing to catch these guys?"

Chief Brennan, now standing at the sergeant's podium in front of the room, rose to his full height, towering over everyone, and boomed, "Quiet, please, there'll be no more questions. Lieutenant Williams has a prepared statement for you. Copies will be made available. Please take your seats so we can start."

Josh took over standing at the podium, laying the statement down, and looked over the crowd.

"Good afternoon, for those of you who don't know me, I am Lieutenant Josh Williams, and I am in command of the Special Investigations Unit." He turned to Emily. "This is FBI Special Agent Emily Thompson who works with the Behavioral Sciences Unit in Quantico. The FBI, along with the

Rhode Island State Police, have been assisting us in this investigation.

"I want to share with you the latest information on the status of this case. Due to the sensitive nature of the matter, I will read the prepared statement but will not take any questions at this time.

"With that, if you bear with me, I'll start."

The statement took them through the history of the case up to a point. Josh was deliberate in his presentation and built the moment up to the conclusion, as Emily recommended. They hoped it would be these last words, broadcast over TV, radio, print, and social media that would have the greatest effect on the suspects.

"We have identified two suspects, Gerry Tavares and Maximillian Baader. The FBI profile classifies them as ineffectual and disorganized personalities with significant psychopathological deficiencies. We believe, as part of their apocalyptic belief, they have most likely committed suicide. We base this on the fact no more victims have been found, and no other activity linked to the suspects has been reported.

"We believe there is no risk to the public, and it is only a matter of time before fully closing this matter. Thank you for your time."

Brennan positioned three uniformed officers to create an alleyway through the crowd, allowing Josh and Emily to exit while ignoring the shouted questions. Brennan's massive size was so intimidating that reporters avoided trying to impede his exit. He needed no such escort.

As the TV cameras set up for their news feed to the studio, one of the uniform officers handed out copies of Josh's statement. The other reporters called in their stories, eager to be the first to break the news.

Josh sat down at his desk in the office.

"What do you think?" he said.

"I think it went about as well as we hoped," Fred said. "Some of the savvier reporters might figure it out, but they'll run with it anyway, just in case. We on for sending Jen back in the morning?"

"Yup, and let's hope the bad guys watch TV."

"Oh, you can bet on it.," Emily said. "The only thing better than the act of committing the crime is being able to relive it and hear about the fear and panic they cause."

LXXXVII   A Little Too Well

Max stood next to Gerry, trying to read over Gerry's shoulder. "What did they call us?" Max leaned in, his eyes darting to the screen of Gerry's cellphone.

"In simpler terms, they called us stupid and weak."

"What are we gonna do about it?"

"Let me think, here. This doesn't make any sense. Why guess what happened to us and tell the media? They're trying to make us do something stupid. Go after his wife so they can catch us."

"Are we? Gonna grab the wife, Gerry?"

"Oh, we're gonna grab her, but not before we make them look like idiots. First, let's find a few more devils to capture. Use them to send a message to this Williams guy that we can't be stopped."

"We gonna grab another one from the office?"

"Nope, something even better."

"Who?" Max asked.

"That reporter, Katie Gonzalves. She's the devil's messenger, and we'll send Williams a few pieces of her tortured soul to remind him we have God on our side."

Max smiled. "I like having the young ones to play with; their demon fights back."

* * * * *

"What the fuck?" Josh said, looking at the package on his desk. "Where'd this come from?"

Tommy shrugged. "One of the records clerks brought it over. Said it was delivered by UPS for you."

Josh could see the light go on in Tommy's head. "Oh fuck, you don't think...?"

"I don't know what to think but call BCI up here. Now!"

Gently moving the package down to the BCI processing area, the whole team gathered around. It took ten minutes to process and remove the wrapping. Just as they were ready to open the box, Chief Brennan walked in.

"What's in it?" the Chief said.

"Just about to find out, Chief," Detective Evoski said, using Kelly forceps to pull back the tape. With the tape removed, the cover opened slightly, and they could see a green trash bag surrounded by icepacks. He paused every few seconds to let the other BCI detective take pictures.

"Oh shit," Tommy said "Shit, shit, shit." Then he backed away.

Each ice pack was removed and set aside for processing. Then, Evoski slid the package out of the box and onto the table.

Slowly removing the twist tie securing the bag, he spread it open. There was a collective gasp as the woman's face stared back at them out of the bag. Then they saw the two breasts tucked in on either side.

"Jesus Christ," Fred said.

A folded piece of paper was stuck in the mouth. Evoski slipped it out and laid it on the table. Unfolding it, he turned it toward Josh.

As a group, they all leaned over to read it.

Williams. You can't stop us. We have the power of God behind us. We have his chrisas for our work. We will kil all the demons and noting you can do to stop it. We shall prevale in are sacred duty. Soon you will know our power

Ze hu guphi

Ze hu dami

Maranatha!

Deus nobis verbum dedit et nos instrumentum vindictae suae contra omnia daemonia fecit

Gideon

Josh turned to Fred. "You understand any of it?"

"Yeah, the terms *Ze hu guphi* and *Ze hu dami* is Aramaic or Hebrew. It comes from the consecration of the host and wine in the Mass. They literally mean, 'This is my body; This is my blood.' These guys are equating what they do to their victims as consecrating them by killing them to rid them of a demon."

"And *maranatha?*"

"It's a blend of two Aramaic words 'marana' and 'tha' and translated various ways. One is 'Our Lord, come.' Some divide the word as 'maran' and 'atha' meaning 'Our Lord has come!'

"Early Christians used it as a code word of sorts. Since they faced serious persecution at the hands of Romans and their collaborators, they needed a way to identify themselves with each other. Greeting with the word 'Maranatha!' would be a way of saying 'I am Christian' without being obvious to the uninitiated.

"These guys are deep into this stuff. They probably use the code word as a way to communicate everything is okay."

"What the fuck is that last part?" Tommy asked, "German?"

"Latin," Fred said. "I'm a bit rusty, but I think it reads, 'God gave us the word and made us the instrument of his vengeance against all demons.'"

"Wow, guy can't spell yet writes Latin like a college professor and quotes Aramaic," Frank said. "Go figure."

"The misspellings and bad grammar are intentional; They're trying to point to someone uneducated. Put us off their trail."

"Fred's right," Emily added. "Their pre- and post-crime actions show planning, thought, and organization. They may have dictated the notes to one of their 'acolytes,' as he calls them, and made them figure out the spelling.

"These guys are anything but unintelligent, which makes them even more dangerous."

"What's that word?" Josh asked, pointing to the letter. "Chrisas."

"It's Greek, appears a lot in the Bible. Roughly translated as 'anointed.' These guys believe they are anointed by God. Combine that with their psychosexual pathology, and you have a dangerous combination."

Tommy stared at Fred. "Is there anything you don't know?"

"Yeah, Tommy, a lot. Like where these assholes are, which would be a lot more helpful than Latin or Greek."

Brennan pushed his way to the front to take a better look inside the box, his face blanched.

"Christ!" he said, drawing everyone's attention. "She's the Channel 12 reporter who was at the press conference. She asked me for an interview before I left the department. Christ, she's just a kid."

The silence engulfed the room. No one spoke, but they all held the same thought: Did they cause this?

"Call Channel 12, get her next of kin info," Brennan said to Frank. "Find out when she went missing and why they didn't report it." He turned to Josh. "You take your team and get these sons-a-bitches. I don't care how you do it or how long it takes. I want these bastards in my cell block, or dead, and off the street now!" He glanced at Fred, who nodded.

Brennan barged from the room. Josh thought he'd seen a tear in the Chief's eye. The idea worried him.

"Alright let's go. Jen, you'll be going back in the morning. Fred, take John Harris and trace the package. It came UPS, so someone had to drop it off. It might be something we can use."

Josh turned his attention back to the BCI detectives. "You guys do what you have to do to preserve this for the ME. Call them now. I want them here ASAP. If you find anything else call me or text me right away.

* * * * *

"Think they have it by now?" Max asked, wiping the blood from his hands as he finished dismembering the rest of the body.

"I'm sure they do," Gerry said, a smile crossing his face. "And if Williams has even a little skill as a cop, they'll trace where we shipped it from and see our second message."

"So, what do we do now, Gideon?"

"We take another demon. God commands, we obey. Use the same two who took the reporter. Instruct them in the same way. They are not to harm the demon; just seize it and bring it to us."

"What about William's wife and the she-demon?"

"Oh, you and I will handle them," Gerry pointed at his laptop. "We have his address. While they are trying to stop the others, we will visit his home and leave him a message he will never forget."

"But if Williams and the other cops are watching the office lot, won't they get caught?"

Gerry shrugged. "Part of God's plan. A sacrifice for the cause that is necessary. They shall be rewarded on Judgment Day. No one will dare come after us once we demonstrate our power to seize even the most protected demon. The power of God will make them quiver in fear."

* * * * *

The next day, Jen drove into the office building and took on the role of Kiera. Her arrival at the office was uneventful. The surveillance team settled in and waited. They'd been on the stakeout for eight hours when Josh's cellphone rang.

"Josh, Fred. I'm gonna send you an image you need to see."

"Where are you?" Josh said.

"We just got back here; I'm two blocks over on Benefit Street. The AUSA just got the information from UPS security. These guys are getting bolder."

A moment later, the phone began to beep. Josh clicked the link, and the image filled the screen. Gerry Tavares and Max Baader stood smiling at the surveillance camera, holding the package with the reporter's head.

They made no effort to hide themselves. On closer look, Josh saw something in Tavares's hand. It was a middle finger. A goddamn finger. They were holding up the middle finger of the victim.

"Jesus Christ."

"No shit," Fred said. "Anything here?"

"Not yet, but I still think..." The radio beeped and Tommy's voice rang out. "702 to 701, a ratty old van just pulled in. It went right to the fourth floor."

"You got eyes on them?" Josh asked.

"Yup, Frank and John are in the 4x4 two rows over."

"701 to 703."

"703, go Lt.."

"Anything?"

"Yeah, a slimy-looking dude with long hair just got out, walked by Jen's car, then got back in the van. They parked two slots over closer to the door. We got a perfect view of them."

"Okay," Josh said over the radio. "Sit tight, everybody. Let's give them a few minutes to make sure they're not just looking to break into some cars."

Time seemed to stop as the team waited for these guys to show themselves. After ten minutes, Josh grabbed the radio again. "701 to all cars, I'm gonna text Jen to head out. Soon as she leaves the door, I want cars blocking both exits one floor down.

"Frank and John, you guys wait for them to move, then cover Jen. I'll be on foot making my way along the wall near her car. I want these guys alive, okay. So, let's make it a quick grab."

Josh reached for his phone.

"Stand by, I just sent the text, and she is on the way."

A minute later, Jen emerged from the door. As they planned, she stayed near the wall so they couldn't pull her into the vehicle.

"They're out of the van, moving toward her. One is near the wall the other is in the open lane trying to flank her."

Josh positioned himself behind the car four vehicles over from Jen's. He had one guy in sight. He keyed his mic and whispered. "I got the guy near the wall, you guys grab the other one. On my signal."

The guy closest to Josh looked around then took a quick step toward Jen.

"Excuse me, Ma'am. Where's the exit? I can't seem to find it." As he talked, he edged closer, reaching into his pocket.

"Now!" Josh yelled and ran full force into the guy, bouncing him off the car and slamming him to the ground. The guy moaned, struggling to regain his breath.

Frank and John, who'd moved to put the other guy between them, tackled and cuffed him.

Jen ran over and helped Josh cuff his guy. A quick search found a stun gun and zip ties in the guy's pocket. Dragging him to his feet, they did a more thorough search of both. The rest of the team arrived and searched the van.

Inside, they saw clear evidence of blood and some blond hairs.

"Any id's yet?" Fred asked.

"Nope, but it's not Tavares or Baader," Josh said. "They must have decided to send these mutts just in case."

"Lt.," Tommy yelled. "Get over here, now."

Josh shoved the guy back over the hood of Jen's car and jogged to the van.

The look on the detectives' faces told him this was not good news.

"Is there another body?"

"No, there's this." Tommy handed him a paper.

Josh grabbed it, and his blood ran cold. Written on the paper was his address and the words "bring the demon here."

Without saying a word, Josh ran to his car and screamed out of the garage. Fred told Frank and John to stay with the van and prisoners, then ran to his car. Josh's words came flooding back, "I'm gonna kill these motherfuckers."

The normal drive from Providence to Rehoboth is twenty-five minutes. Josh made it in ten. He'd radioed to have the station tell Seekonk and Rehoboth to clear the way, but he needed luck several times to avoid killing himself.

Fred did his best to stay with him, trying to convince him to wait so they could think it through. Josh ignored him at first, then reconsidered. These guys *wanted* him to react. He needed to play this smart.

"Fred, Josh, I'm at the bottom of the hill just before the house. Meet me here."

"Two minutes, and I've got the cavalry on the way."

LXXXVIII Avenging Demons

Shadows from the lights painted a mix of shadows and glare as Gerry and Max made their way closer.

"You sure this is the place?" Max asked, crouching in the woods behind the house.

"Oh yeah, I'm sure. Stay here. I'm gonna move closer and see if I can find where the wife is in the house."

"What about the cameras?" Max said, pointing.

"Watch this," Gerry said, reaching into his pocket. A moment later, an intense green beam of laser light hit the lens of the cameras at the corners of the house.

Gerry smiled. "Now they're blind, just the way I like 'em." He handed the laser to Max. If anyone comes out, hit 'em in the eyes with this.

Crouching low, he half-crawled and half-frog-walked to the stairs at the bottom of the red deck. Glancing toward one of the windows, he saw the curtains open and then close again as if someone peeked out for a moment.

Someone is watching, he thought. Or noticed the cameras going dark. Then he smiled. But it wouldn't matter.

A spotlight came on next to the sliding glass door, casting more shadows under the deck. Waiting to ensure the door didn't open, he returned to Max.

"They're in the kitchen. At least one is. We need to drive them upstairs." Gerry reached for his cellphone.

"911 what is your emergency? Police, Fire, or EMS?"

"There's a man with a gun. He just shot two people in the parking lot of the high school. He's chasing more people. Please help us."

"Please stay on the line..."

"What was that all about?"

"Rehoboth is a small department. Probably only one or two cops on the road. This will pull them far away from here and give us time to snatch the demon."

Movement caught their eyes, silencing them. The sliders opened, and a dog sauntered out onto the deck. At first, it stayed staring back into the house, then turned back sniffing the air.

"He senses we're here," Max said. "What do we do?"

"Nothing," Gerry said, screwing the silencer onto the barrel of the semi-automatic handgun. "I planned for this."

The dog took a few cautious steps down, sniffing the whole time. Gerry grabbed a rock and tossed it a few yards in front of them.

At the sound, the dog barked and charged toward them. As he got to the rock, Gerry fired, and the dog collapsed. The muffled sound was barely audible even in the quiet of the woods.

"Now to draw them upstairs."

Grabbing another rock, Gerry stood and tossed it, bouncing it off the wall on the second floor. As he expected, the lights went out and he knew they were considering what to do next. One would go upstairs, one would remain to cover the entrances. People are so predictable.

"Max, go around the front. When you hear me throw another rock, bang loudly on the front door. Then come back here."

Two minutes later, Gerry launched the second rock. At the sound of it striking the wall, Max did as he was told.

As he ran around back, he spotted Gerry making his way up the stairs. He followed. At the top, Gerry put slight pressure on the slider. It opened as he expected. They had left it unlocked for the dog's return. Human habits are hard to change.

Glancing back to make sure Max was behind him, he slid the door open and rushed in. A shadow emerged from the living room. Gerry fired and the threat fell to the ground, soft moans and shallow breathing signs of a serious wound.

Max made his way to the body and snatched her weapon.

"Should I finish her?" he asked.

"Nah, let the demon die a slow painful death."

From upstairs came a voice.

"Chris, Chris! You okay?"

"Now, now Kiera. Your friend is alive, but not for long. If you don't come down here, unarmed, we will have to make sure she dies right here. It doesn't matter to me. There's no need for her to pay the price for protecting you."

The silence showed indecision. She wasn't sure what to do.

Gerry kicked Chris, causing her to moan in agony. A little psychological persuasion to hasten the decision.

"I'm coming down," Kiera said. "Leave Chris out of this."

"There you go. Come on down now, but no tricks or your friend's brain will be all over this house."

As Kiera stepped down, Chris struggled to rise, yelling, "Fuck him, Kiera. Stay there and shoot the prick when they try to get to you."

Max brought the butt of his gun onto Chris's head, and she went silent.

"Now, if you want to save your friend you better get down here quick. She doesn't have much time," Gerry said, then turned to whisper to Max.

"Go get the car. Her conscience won't let her stay up there. She'll come down soon enough."

* * * * *

"Fred, see the light on the second story? I told Kiera if there was a problem to turn it on; we never use that room. They're in the house."

The front door opened, and Max came out.

Josh started for him, but Fred held him back. "Wait, he's alone. Let's see what he does."

They watched as he made his way to a dead-end street. A moment later, the car pulled into the driveway.

Josh pushed Fred away and made for the passenger side. As Max got out, Josh came from behind and was on him, bringing the butt of his weapon onto the top of his head. Max went down, out cold. Fred came over, put cuffs on Max, then used a second pair to cuff him to the fence. Looking around he spotted a rag in the back of the car.

Waving it at Fred, he smiled. "He's exercising his right to remain silent," then jammed the rag into his mouth. But by the look of the dent in his skull, regaining consciousness would not be anytime soon.

"Now what?" Fred asked.

"You go around back so he can't escape out that way. I'm going in."

"Wait, the SWAT team will be here any minute. That's a better choice."

"Fuck it, my wife is in there with that lunatic. I'm not waiting." And with that, he ran toward the front door, pausing to listen to the voices inside.

"Come on now, Kiera. Time to end this. Your friend here is breathing rather shallowly. I have some experience with death. She doesn't have long. Come on down now while there's still time."

Josh peeked around the door but couldn't tell where Gerry was. Unsure where Kiera or Chris might be, he decided not to risk firing into the dark.

"Gerry, it's Josh Williams. Let them go, it's me you really want."

A shadow off to the side of the door moved and Josh made a dash for it. Missing the man by a foot or so, he tumbled to the ground as his gun slid away. Gerry fired, striking Josh in the left shoulder.

"Well, well isn't this pleasant. Nice of you to join us, Williams."

"Oh, Kiera, if you don't come down here right now the next sound you hear will be the bullet entering your husband's brain. Now you wouldn't want that to be the last moment of your marriage, would you?"

"I'm coming down," Kiera said. "I'm coming down."

As she appeared from the darkness of the stairway, Gerry backed up a bit, keeping his gun on both.

"Now, that's much better. What shall I do with you? I assume you've killed Max, so I can only handle one of you. Choices, choices."

Kiera moved in front of Josh.

"Isn't that heroic, protecting your wounded husband? How noble."

As she faced Gerry, Josh saw the Glock concealed in her waistband. She stepped back and the gun was now in reach.

"So, what's it gonna be, you sick bastard? Do you really think you can handle me alone?"

"Oh, I'm certain I can. You and I are going to have a lot of fun before I seek my reward in heaven."

"Now, Kiera," Josh said, snatching the weapon, raising it, and firing as Kiera dove out of the line of fire.

Gerry spun around and fell to a knee. Grabbing his wounded shoulder, then rubbing his hands together, he smiled.

Rising slowly, holding his arms outstretched as if on a cross, he said, "I bear the sign of my savior."

He staggered, then leaned back against the wall.

"So, this is how it ends, eh? No worries. I will continue my ministry from prison. My acolytes are everywhere. This won't stop anything."

"You know what I learned from my husband?" Kiera said.

"What's that?" Gerry asked.

"Come here and I'll tell you."

Gerry started forward.

Kiera pulled another gun from her waist.

Gerry's eyes grew wide, shock coupled with an unfamiliar fear, but his momentum carried him toward her.

"I learned about bullet trajectories and always having a backup," firing one round dead center into Gerry's forehead.

As the round punched its way into Tavares's brain, Fred came in from the kitchen area. Quickly assessing that Josh was okay and Kiera uninjured, he went to Chris.

"Hang in there, old girl. Rescue is on the way."

"Old girl? When I get out of the hospital, I'm gonna kick your FBI ass all the way back to Quantico."

Fred had to laugh, all while keeping pressure on her wound. "Of that, I have no doubt."

LXXXIX   Loose Ends...

Jerry Paulsen pulled up to the front of 321 Meshanticut Avenue and sat for a moment looking at the ocean. Taking a deep breath, he stepped from the car and walked to the door.

John Daniels stood just inside looking out the storm door, eyes red and watery.

"Det. Paulsen, right?"

"Yeah, John. Call me Jerry. Can I come in? Unless you don't want me to upset your wife."

Daniels looked at the floor, then took a long, shaky breath. "No need, my wife passed away yesterday afternoon. I was about to head to the funeral home to finish making the arrangements."

"I'm so sorry, John. I can't imagine what you've experienced."

"Thank you. So, what brings you here?"

"Well, I promised I would come back and tell you what we found out about your daughter. It's not much, but I did promise."

John backed into the kitchen, leaning against the stove. Jerry stood next to the small table covered with photo albums.

"I was going through the pictures for the wake, hard to believe it's all over..." his voice broke, and more tears came. It took a moment, then he regained his composure.

"Sorry, we were married forty-eight years. It's the only life I ever wanted."

"I understand. I won't take up much of your time, but I thought you'd want to know."

John nodded, folding his arms and tilting his head back to stem the flow.

"Based on evidence we recovered from the investigation and interviews with some witnesses, we think Solange was trying to protect her friend, Vanessa. I can't be certain, but I think she tried to get her away from some bad people and ended up getting herself in a situation that overwhelmed her.

"I realize it's not much, but I hope it helps a little."

John reached out to shake Jerry's hand. "It does, Jerry, it does. I just wish my wife had lived long enough to hear that as well. The last thing she said to me was 'John, please find Sol and bring her home.' Maybe they're together now and Sol can keep her company until it's my time."

Jerry patted John on the shoulder then made his way out of the house. It took a few minutes for the tears to clear before he could drive. Sometimes, he thought, I wonder if there is any joy in the world at all.

XC　　**Tight Ends...**

Fred stood leaning against he office door.

"It looks like the Medical Examiner report and forensics are consistent. Tavares was moving toward you," Fred said. "But you already knew that didn't you?"

"Yes, I did, Fred," Josh said. "Yes, I did."

Fred put out his hand. "Been a real experience, Josh. Lose my number. Are you coming, Emily?"

"I'll catch a ride later. I've got something I need to do."

"Okay," Fred shrugged and walked out of the office.

When the door closed, Emily stared at Josh, a long uncomfortable silence between them.

"Look, Josh, We've all made choices in the past we might want to undo. But we both know that isn't possible. I'm glad I got to work with you on this and I hope you'll let whatever negative feelings you have about the things you learned fade with time.

"I was a different woman back then. I think you were a different person as well. When I walk out of here, let's leave it at that, okay?"

Josh leaned against the desk for a moment, unsure of his next words. "Okay, Emily, we'll leave it in the past." He started to rise from the desk as Emily came forward and hugged him.

"Maybe, in a different life, Josh. Maybe it would be a different story." She kissed him on the cheek, then let him go.

Turning away, she walked out the door.

Josh hesitated a moment, started toward the door, then caught himself. You can't undo the past, he remembered, but you can let it go.

XCI   **Finality**

Heading home, Josh had time to consider the last few months. It was a nightmare no one could ever imagine. But somehow, they survived it.

Pulling into his driveway, he saw Chris and Kiera standing on the front stairs. Chris's head still had a turban bandage, and one arm hung in a sling, but she was on this side of the dirt.

Kiera smiled and waved.

Josh got out of the car and adjusted the sling on his left arm. The wound was healing but sore, but it was still better than the alternative.

"What's up?"

"You're the detective," Kiera said. "You figure it out."

"He never was much of a detective," Chris said. "I carried him the whole time."

"Yeah, right. Seriously, why are you two standing here?"

As the words left his mouth, a partly shaved, partly furry, three-legged dog hobbled down the steps.

"Tripod?" Josh said, and the tears came down.

Josh ran to the dog and hugged him.

"I told you he'd be more excited about the dog than me," Chris said.

"I like the dog," Josh joked. "You, I just tolerate. I thought he had to stay in the hospital."

"Mercy Hospital worked wonders," Kiera said, coming to hug Josh. "He still only has three legs, but they managed to get the bullet out. And Josh..."

Josh looked up from petting the dog. Chris had this goofy smile on her face.

"What?" he said. "She's not moving in here to recover is she?"

"No," Kiera smiled, "she's not, but someone else is coming to live with us."

Josh stood up, glancing between the two. "I do not like being the only one who doesn't know what everybody else does."

Josh tilteded his head, then glanced at the paper in Kiera's hand.

"What's that?"

"Confirmation," Kiera said.

"About what?"

"God, you are so dense sometimes."

"Sometimes?" Chris said. "I've never known him not to be."

"Will somebody just tell me what's going on?"

"Josh," Kiera said, reaching for his hand, "you're going to be a dad."

"Fate help the child with you for a dad," Chris said, then a smile broke out on her face. "Congrats, Josh. You guys are going to be great parents."

Josh didn't hear a thing, his head buried in Kiera's shoulder, hiding his tears.

Maybe, just maybe, there are angels standing between us and the demons...

About the Author

Joe Broadmeadow was born in Pawtucket and grew up in Cumberland, Rhode Island. He lives wherever his wanderings take him with his wife, Susan.

After twenty years with the East Providence, Rhode Island Police Department, he retired with the rank of Captain. He served in various divisions within the department, including the Commander of Investigative Services. He also worked in the Organized Crime Drug Enforcement Task Force and was on special assignment to the FBI Drug Task Force.

Pieces of the Past is the latest in the ***Detective Lieutenant Josh Williams*** series of novels. The two previous novels featuring Lieutenant Williams from the East Providence (RI) Police Department, ***Collision Course*** and ***Silenced Justice,*** continue to garner rave reviews and are available on Amazon.com

A Change of Hate is the first of the Attorney Hawk Bennett series. It is a spin-off of the earlier novels and is also available on Amazon and wherever books are sold.

When Joe is not writing, he is hiking, taking pictures of the stars and planets, or fishing (and thinking about writing).

Joe completed a 2,185-mile thru-hike of the Appalachian Trail in September 2014. After completing the trail, Joe published a short story, *Spirit of the Trail,* available on Amazon.